INCARNATE

INCARNATE

A NOVEL

JOSH STOLBERG

EMILY BESTLER BOOKS
—
ATRIA
New York   London   Toronto   Sydney   New Delhi

ATRIA

An Imprint of Simon & Schuster, Inc.
1230 Avenue of the Americas
New York, NY 10020

First Emily Bestler Books/Atria Paperback edition July 2017

EMILY BESTLER BOOKS / ATRIA PAPERBACKS and colophon are trademarks
of Simon & Schuster, Inc.

For information about special discounts for bulk purchases, please
contact Simon & Schuster Special Sales at 1-866-506-1949 or
business@simonandschuster.com.

The Simon & Schuster Speakers Bureau can bring authors to your live event. For
more information or to book an event, contact the Simon & Schuster Speakers Bureau
at 1-866-248-3049 or visit our website at www.simonspeakers.com.

Design by Bryden Spevak

Manufactured in the United States of America

10 9 8 7 6 5 4 3 2 1

Library of Congress Cataloging-in-Publication Data

Names: Stolberg, Josh, 1971– author.
Title: Incarnate : a novel / Josh Stolberg.
Description: First Emily Bestler Books/Atria Paperback edition. | New York :
   Emily Bestler Books/Atria Paperback, 2017.
Identifiers: LCCN 2017000038 (print) | LCCN 2017006941 (ebook)
Subjects: LCSH: Serial murder investigation—Fiction. | Women psychiatrists—Fiction. |
Women detectives—Fiction. | Multiple personality—Fiction. | BISAC: FICTION / General. |
GSAFD: Suspense fiction. | Mystery fiction.
Classification: LCC PS3619.T652 I53 2017 (print) | LCC PS3619.T652 (ebook) |
   DDC 813/.6—dc23
LC record available at https://lccn.loc.gov/2017000038

ISBN 978-1-5011-3657-3
ISBN 978-1-5011-3658-0 (ebook)

For Leila, Asher, and Xander

PROLOGUE

Isabel Wilcox had run track in high school. She had taken gold in regionals for the hundred-yard dash. Still, she had never run faster than she was running right now. It should have been cause for celebration, if not for the fact that she was running for her life.

Isabel should have stayed home that night. She should have been happy with her score for the day. She had cleared five grand since breakfast, but she was unable to resist the easy money. Then things went south. She was grabbed from behind, a bag thrown over her head, and she was stuffed into the backseat of a car.

But now she was free. And she was fast. And she was sprinting through the woods.

Tears rolled down her face, leaving tracks of mascara on her cheeks. Her neck was marred with her own blood. "Oh my God, help me!"

The response that rang back was the report of a rifle. She felt its slug graze her open jaw before its sound reached her ears. The searing pain sent her careening into the trunk of a cedar. The skin of her forehead ripped off like a piece of bark on the centuries-old tree.

The head wound opened a faucet over her right eye, pouring

blood. She lay back into the cushion of fallen leaves, applying pressure to the gash and wiping the red that pooled around her eyes. Her ears rang from the gunshot and her out-of-breath sobs were muffled now, sounding as though she were crying underwater.

Isabel tried to compose herself. Catch her breath. Control the bleeding. But there was so much blood. She remembered when she was fourteen, babysitting for Michael Squitteiri, and the time he fell off the monkey bars, splitting open his eyebrow. She had been surprised that so much blood could spill from such a small body. She remembered the paramedic soothing her, explaining that the face has more capillaries than any other part of the body. Like a spiderweb of blood vessels just under the skin. It's why we turn red when we blush.

She looked up at the tops of the trees, swaying in the breeze. Serene. Lovely. She thought about closing her eyes. Allowing the flow of blood to carry her peacefully to sleep.

But then she heard footsteps in the distance. She was not ready to die. Not now. Not like this. She caught her breath, ready to run again.

Isabel stood and sprinted off. She couldn't be sure that she was running toward help, just that she was running away from the sound of her attacker.

A few yards later, Isabel's foot came down hard on a fallen branch and her ankle twisted painfully in her high-heeled suede ankle boot. *Shit*. She took a few hobbling steps before regaining her balance and forging ahead. Each lungful of air scraped painfully, her heart pounded like it was going to explode, and her muscles screamed in protest. How long had she been running since escaping the car? Five minutes? Ten? Something shrieked in the branches above her; something else rustled in a nearby thicket.

She'd give anything for Brad to be here now. She'd never brush him off again. She'd return his calls, and cut him in his full share. Or, no, forget Brad. If someone, *anyone*, would show up and rescue her, she'd give up *all* of it. No more drugs, no more fake IDs, no more—

There was a loud clang, and her foot fell into a hole, pitching her forward, face-first onto the ground. Her palms skidded over scratchy foliage and her jaw bounced off a log, but even worse was the excruciating pain that suddenly shot up her leg, like it was being crushed by a huge boulder. She tried to jerk it free, but it was held fast. Blinking dirt out of her eyes, she twisted her body and was horrified to see that her foot was caught in what looked like giant metal teeth. They'd sliced the suede of her boot, piercing through the delicate skin of her feet.

Isabel's voice was hoarse from screaming. She could feel her energy slipping away, along with what looked like a gallon of blood soaking her jeans and the ground below. She wrapped her hands around the trap but it was no use—she could barely reach the heavy springs, much less release them, and trying made the pain even worse.

More blood drained from her body, saturating the ground around her. She was getting dizzy. Her brain tried to reckon with the agonizing pain . . . tried to latch on to a happy memory. Her first kiss with Jeffrey Lampman in seventh grade after show choir. Pledging Theta Pi and doing tequila shots, licking the salt off Lauren Swick's neck. But nothing worked; she couldn't trick away the burn. *And there was so much blood.*

A branch snapped behind her. She whipped her head around.

A man dressed all in camo came jogging into the clearing and stopped short. His face was covered by an orange knit mask with holes for the eyes and mouth. Was he here to help? Or was he the one who had taken her? He stared down at her for a full beat before dropping his rifle on the ground and kneeling in the brush next to her, pulling off his gloves and reaching for her wrist, feeling for a pulse.

He thinks I'm dead, Isabel realized, and though she tried with all her might to convince him otherwise, she could barely move her lips.

"Help me," she moaned, although it came out more like "Hemmie," so soft she wasn't sure he'd heard her.

The man leaned into the spring, grunting with the effort of prying it open. Her leg still hurt, but thankfully it was beginning to go numb. It was almost as though Isabel was watching from a distance as the trap finally sprang open, revealing the bloody mess of severed skin and muscle and tendon showing through the torn suede and denim.

Her liberator sat her up, ready to lift her onto his shoulders when—

Pfft. Something zinged past her ear. And, suddenly, the hunter's hold on her relaxed. A moment later, he crumpled down beside her. Isabel screamed again, but all that came out was a hoarse shriek. She felt something at her back—a boot?—and for a moment it rested there, lightly, almost gently, and then it gave her an enormous shove and she tumbled forward. There was no time to throw her hands up to protect her face as it slammed down hard in the center of the reopened trap. In the split second it took to fall, she saw the jaws of the reopened trap rushing up to meet her.

The last sound she heard was the screech of metal on metal as the teeth clamped through her neck.

And then the pain was gone.

ONE

"Hey," a voice murmured, so close to her ear that Dr. Kimberly Patterson could feel warm breath tickle the hairs on the back of her neck. "Upsy-daisy. I think you're going to want to see this one for yourself."

"Don't wanna," Kim mumbled into the drool-dampened spot on the cheap mattress. She was curled up on the lower bunk in the darkened residents' sleep room of the Jarvis Regional Hospital. "Make the other resident do it."

"She's not on call tonight. You are. And I already let you sleep an extra eleven minutes."

"Just one more minute." Kim rolled away from the voice so that she was facing the wall that was painted a shade reminiscent of the lunch trays at St. Katherine's School for Girls, where years ago she had graduated forty-ninth out of a class of fifty.

"Come on, Kim," the voice said, more firmly this time. It belonged to her boss, Dr. Kyle Berman. "You're on at three, which is in four minutes. Get up."

"Eat me."

"God, I wish. But between your schedule and mine, our next day off together isn't until— Hey. Hey, seriously, didn't we talk about this?"

Kim had managed to sit up in the bed, the thin, scratchy sheets sliding off her bare shoulders. "About what?"

"About having consideration for others in the common sleeping space."

"But it gets so damn hot in here."

"And yet, somehow, every other resident manages to keep their clothes on."

"My clothes *are* on. My pants, anyway." Kim blinked the sleep from her eyes as she dug through the sheets and came up with a scrub shirt. The shirt was a much-laundered, faded green one that she had inherited from Ethan Kuhn, along with the apartment he no longer needed when he quit his residency to weave seagrass baskets in Ketchikan. "Besides, I read the whole welcome packet when I started here, and there wasn't anything in there about sleeping room regulations."

"Yeah, because most people don't need it spelled out for them, that you need to keep more on than just your . . ." Kyle pushed his glasses higher on his nose with one hand and gestured at her while looking the other way.

"Bra. You can say 'bra,' Kyle. It's not a dirty word, I promise."

"Come on, Kim, you know the review board is looking for any reason to come down hard on you. Do you *have* to bend every single rule in the place?"

"Mmm, you know how I love it when you get all bossy," Kim said, but the mention of the review board was enough to propel her out of bed. At twenty-nine, she was eager to finish her residency and open her own practice. She yawned as she stepped into her rubber clogs. "Do I have sleep breath? Do you have a mint?"

"Could we hurry, please? Graver called us down to the ER. They have a patient who came in missing a finger. He's telling them he ate it."

"You should have opened with that. Now *that* is interesting,"

Kim said, running her fingers through her long, tangled hair and following him to the door. "Thanks for cutting me in on this."

"My pleasure," Kyle muttered sarcastically.

———

"NICE OF YOU TWO to take time out of your busy day to visit us." Dr. Miranda Graver, the Jarvis Regional Hospital's chief of staff, was waiting for Kim and Kyle in the hall outside the nurses' station, the only place in the ER that afforded even a little privacy. "And I see you took note that the invitation specified 'creative formal,' Dr. Patterson. Rest assured that your effort is not lost on me."

Kim looked down at her shirt and winced. Before decamping downcountry, Ethan had washed some of his clothes along with rags he'd dipped in paint thinner, and the result looked like a cat had thrown up on it. "I'll try to do better," she promised.

"I seem to have heard that before." Dr. Graver's stare could freeze water. "Okay, here's what we're working with: severed fifth digit, clean bilateral cut right below the distal phalanx on both hands. Left side's an old injury, healed up pretty well. Right side's infected with significant discharge, swelling, and tissue deterioration. The patient keeps changing his story when asked what happened, but he told Jennings that he cut it off on purpose . . . and ate it."

"That's a new one for me," Kyle admitted.

"Let me talk to him," Kim suggested. The fact that Graver had been called downstairs for this case made it a perfect opportunity to score some much-needed points with the woman who had the power to make or break Kim's medical career.

"As far as I'm concerned, he's all yours," Graver said, and after a brief hesitation, Berman nodded. "But, please, Dr. Patterson, do keep our little hospital's policies in mind this time."

Kim kept her expression neutral as the chief of staff stalked back toward the elevators in her perfectly tailored and pressed navy suit. Graver sidestepped a patient whose two front teeth were missing—his mouth bleeding profusely. At first, because of his clattering footsteps, Kim thought he was wearing high heels, but then she realized the clicking sound came from the ice skates he wore. Alaskan emergency rooms treated even more hockey-related injuries than you might expect.

But patients who ate their own fingers . . . not so much.

"I'll come in with you," Kyle offered when the chief was out of earshot.

"No, let me go in alone," Kim said. "Teaming up on this kid isn't going to help."

"Kim, the review board specifically recommended supervisory oversight for all your patient interactions," Kyle said. "And since I'm your supervisor—"

"Technically, it was only a recommendation," Kim pointed out. "Plus, nothing was put in writing."

She ducked around a passing cart and into the examination room before he could answer, praying he wouldn't follow. As fragile as her situation with the review board was, she couldn't give her patients the attention they deserved with Kyle breathing down her neck. He was only thirty-three, but sometimes Kyle's seriousness made him feel much older. She needed to be able to bond with this kid.

Sitting on the side of the bed staring at his phone was a lean, scraggly-haired teenager. Sure enough, he was missing the tip of the pinkie finger on his left hand. Kim could see that the stub had healed well, the skin shiny and pink at the end. His other hand, the fifth digit freshly bandaged, rested beside him on the bed, and an IV line trailed from that arm. A quick glance at the boy's chart showed that the wound had been drained and cleaned and a course of intravenous antibiotics had been started.

Kim dropped into the chair next to the bed and put her feet up on the bed rail. "Good decision, going for the pinkie finger," she observed. "You can do without it for like ninety-five percent of everyday tasks. Plus, there's a whole theory that the human fifth digit is evolving into a vestigial appendage. You know, like a dew claw on a dog?"

The boy looked up from his phone long enough to give her a withering glare. "Fuck off."

"Ah. Uh-huh. Right. You think I'm patronizing you."

A shrug.

"Look, Wallace—" Kim said, glancing at the chart for the boy's name. "You go by Wally? Wall-man? Wall Dog? Okay, Wally, I know it's not like you dreamed you'd grow up and become a cannibal when you were a little kid. I know you don't wake up every day and go, like, *Hey, what's it going to be today? Maybe an earlobe? A nice chunk of thigh filet?*"

No reaction from the kid. Kim plowed on.

"What you're dealing with is a compulsion. It feels like you literally can't stop yourself, right? I get that, I really do. We've all got compulsions. Believe me, you do *not* want to know what I do when I think no one's watching. And Dr. Berman out there? He's got both his testicles pierced like twelve times—one of 'em got infected a while back and swelled up like a watermelon, and he had to borrow a knee cart from orthopedics to get around." She leaned forward and lowered her voice. "I mean, maybe don't let him know I told you that. All I'm saying is, everybody does weird shit. We just wanna help you figure out how to tone it down a little so you can still type on that thing."

Wally glared at his phone bleakly. "Whatever."

"What did you use, anyway?" She made a sawing motion with her hands.

"You know." He peeked up from under a fringe of long lashes, suddenly looking much younger than his seventeen years.

"Actually, I don't. And I'm genuinely curious. This is off the record. It's just me and you chatting here."

He sighed and let his gaze drift back down to the floor. "Table saw, the first time. But my stepdad freaked and locked up his tools, so I had to use a knife."

"Ah," Kim said. "Probably took one out of the kitchen drawer? Same one your mom uses to cut up chicken? That could explain the infection. I'd say first disinfect the knife next time with plain old rubbing alcohol, except I'm kind of hoping there won't be a next time. Maybe we could try to get you to cut back to just your hangnails or something. What do you think, are you okay with talking to someone about this?"

He shook his head. "I'm not going to that fat Nazi counselor again."

"School counselor?" Kim asked sympathetically. Judging from his cheap sneakers and the fact that his phone was at least three versions out of date, Wally's family likely couldn't afford a private psychiatrist.

"Yeah." Wally hung his head lower.

Autophagia was an extreme example of an impulse-control disorder. Some people experienced excitement or even arousal at the prospect of consuming their own flesh, and the practice was sometimes associated with psychosis or schizophrenia, but Kim was guessing that for the young man huddled on the bed, looking like he wanted to disappear into the floor, the act offered temporary relief from the stress and anxiety that hounded him. What Wally needed, once the infection was under control, was a complete psychiatric evaluation and treatment for what was almost certainly underlying depression and severe anxiety.

"Tell you what. You let me work out the logistics," she said. "I'm going to put a special 'no Nazi' clause in your paperwork. I've got someone in mind. I think you'd like him. Works in a clinic so far across town that you won't have time to get back to class after—and it's guaranteed one hundred percent confidential, so you can tell that school counselor to go suck ass and he won't be able to do a damn thing about it. The clinic will also help your family figure out all the paperwork so insurance will cover it. What do you say?"

Before Wally could respond, a muffled crash and a series of screams sounded through the exam room doors. "I think that's for me," Kim said, smiling wryly. "Gotta run. Listen, I'm going to hook you up with my friend, and I'll keep tabs on you. Deal?"

Wallace gave a desultory shrug.

"Okay, I'm going to take that as a yes. So, ta-ta for now." Kim backed out of the exam area, flipping him the bird through the curtain at the last moment. "Just giving you a reason to hold on."

A ghost of a smile flashed across Wally's face as he returned the one-finger salute with both hands.

In the hall, Kim pushed past Kyle, who been eavesdropping along with Dr. Jennings, the emergency room physician who'd admitted Wallace. The screaming grew more distinct closer to the doors separating the exam rooms from the waiting area, and Kim could make out occasional phrases—all of them variations on a theme involving *bitch*, *crazy*, and *psycho*.

"Really, Kim?" Kyle chided, coming up behind her. "My *testicles*?"

"What's up with that one?" she asked, ignoring the question and pointing toward the waiting room. "Sounds like fun."

"I think we can handle it on our own," Jennings said. "Guy came in with facial burns. Not really your area of expertise, is it?"

"I don't know, Arthur, I'm very good at a surprising range of things," Kim shot back. Like her, Jennings was still a resident, but he was privy to the same hospital gossip as everyone else—and enough of a dick to taunt her with it.

"Yeah, I bet." Jennings leered, letting his gaze wander down to her cleavage, which Kim had failed to notice was on display in Ethan's oversize shirt.

"God, Arthur, grow up. Come on, I'm already here. Let me sit in, okay?"

"I don't know—not sure we can afford the liability."

"I heard Gyno kicked you out of their poker game," Kim retorted. "Caught you drawing a full bush on the STD poster."

"Enough," Kyle said, covering his ears. "Jennings, don't make me pull rank here. If you aren't man enough to handle Kim for twenty minutes, just say so, and I'll tell Graver you clocked out early to go home and have a good cry."

"That's—that's just great," Jennings sputtered as Kyle headed back down the hall. "Does he always let you push him around like that?"

"He's delicate." Kim shrugged. "Probably stemming from psychogenic sexual dysfunction. Tell you what, let's you and me be friends, okay? I feel like our love deserves a second chance."

Jennings ignored her as she followed him out into the waiting room, where one of the intake clerks was trying to coax the screaming man into a chair, with the help of a girl of around eighteen or nineteen. The girl was murmuring softly and trying to tug at his sleeves, but he kept flinging her hands away. His face was grotesquely burned on one side, a crisscross pattern of seared flesh bubbling and peeling, blackened bits stuck to red, weeping tissue.

"It's about time, Dr. Jennings," the clerk snapped. "I've called for security, but they're tied up with a fender bender in the garage."

"Thank you, Brenda. Sir, I understand that you are in pain, but we need to get some information before we can—"

"Get her away from me!" the man hollered, shrinking away from the girl while trying ineffectually to kick her as she nimbly dodged out of the way. "Crazy bitch tried to kill me!"

"He doesn't mean it," the girl said apologetically. "I think he's just confused from the pain. Come on, Darren, they're trying to help."

"They should lock you up!"

The girl gave Kim an imploring look, holding back tears. "It's just that there was an accident at the restaurant earlier. I don't remember how it happened, but the— *Ow!*"

One of the man's boots had connected with the girl's shin. "Okay, sir, listen," Kim said. "We'll keep her out here, okay? Those doors are locked. If you go inside with Brenda here and finish up your paperwork, there's no way the crazy bitch will be able to follow you. Sound all right?"

"Tie her up!" the man screamed. "Burn *her* face off; see how she likes that!"

"Okay, yeah, sure, that sounds like a plan," Kim said. "I'll just run upstairs and fetch a few bungee cords and my ethylene torch. But in the meantime, I'd feel a lot better if you'd go in with them. You look like you're in a lot of pain."

The man wavered, looking from the girl to Kim to the clerk. His burns were at full thickness and would require painful debridement followed by grafting. Eventually, reconstructive surgery might be an option, but even with the best possible outcome, he was going to end up with some very distinctive scars.

"Don't let her in there," he implored.

"We won't," Jennings said reassuringly. "Now go on ahead with Brenda, and I'll meet you in the exam room in a few minutes."

After the doors shut behind them, Jennings turned to Kim. "Score another one for your famous bedside manner. I don't know how you do it, Kim. Got the crazies eating out of your hand."

"Aw, you make me blush," Kim retorted, already making her way to the sign-in desk to get the intake paperwork for the girl.

"Okay, you had your fun, but now you can leave the real medicine to the real doctors," Jennings said coldly, never one to miss a chance to share his disdain for the practice of psychiatric medicine.

"Knock yourself out." Kim thanked the attending nurse when she retrieved the clipboard for the girl. The somber teenager looked up from where she hunched on the edge of one of the waiting room chairs. Her hair had been obscuring her face and a dog-eared copy of *Better Homes and Gardens* lay upside down in her lap. "I'm going to shoot the shit with this menacing criminal over here." She smiled at the girl but got only a blank look in return.

Jennings huffed through the doors into the examining area to treat the burn patient, leaving Kim with the much more interesting mystery to solve: who this girl was and why she couldn't remember what must have been an exceptional act of violence.

TWO

Once Kim started asking questions, the eerie blankness retreated from the girl's face and she returned to fervent declarations of her own innocence. It took only a few minutes of gentle probing before the girl broke down in huge sobs that, at least to Kim's discriminating eye, seemed absolutely genuine. The intake paperwork lay forgotten at the girl's side, but Kim had managed to coax a few details from her: her name was Scarlett Hascall, she was nineteen, she lived at home, and she had been working at the Burger Barn since graduating from high school last year.

Also, she couldn't remember a single thing about the incident that had landed Darren Fenstrom in the emergency room. She swore that the last thing she remembered was clocking in for her shift and putting on her grease-stained white apron.

"Tell you what," Kim said, thinking the girl might be able to relax away from the chaotic waiting room. "How about we go up to my office, where we can have a little privacy. It's nothing fancy, but I've got some soda in the mini fridge . . . and a whole box of Kleenex with your name on it, if you want it."

Catching sight of a police officer entering the ER waiting room, the girl nodded meekly and followed Kim up to the third floor.

Unfortunately, Kyle was standing outside Kim's office, reviewing a chart. Jennings must have tipped him off that she had gone AWOL. Kim resolved to devise a suitable revenge later.

"Hi, Dr. Berman!" she chirped brightly, flashing him a fake grin. "Wish I had time to chat, but I need to take Ms. Hascall's history now."

"Is that right?" Kyle said stonily. "Tell you what, I've got a few minutes—I'll observe. Maybe I can help out."

Kim refused to give him the satisfaction of seeing her dismay. "That's great. I'm sure I'll learn something super important from you, like I always do."

Holding the door open for Scarlett, she saw the girl glance uneasily at Kyle and wondered if he'd missed her obvious discomfort, or if he simply didn't care.

If Scarlett minded wedging into Kim's closet-size office, she was too polite—or distracted—to say so. Instead, she folded her slender frame into the threadbare chair while Kyle took up a position in the corner, flattened against the emergency-evacuation poster.

"Something I'm a little confused about," Kim said cautiously, scooting her own chair close so that she was knee to knee with Scarlett. "You don't seem too surprised by Darren's accusations. Most people, they get accused of something like that, they're likely to fly off the handle. Or at least make it clear that they weren't involved."

Scarlett shrugged and averted her eyes. "I mean, I don't remember doing anything. I don't think I *would* do anything like that. But I guess if he said I did it . . . maybe I did."

"Don't mind me," Kim said, shining a light in Scarlett's eyes to check her pupils. "So you really don't remember anything?"

Scarlett blinked, ducking her chin nervously. "It happens. She . . . loses time."

She? Kim glanced at Kyle. He cleared his throat. "I've read her chart. She's had some similar episodes in the past. Scarlett, I think we might need to adjust your medications."

He started flipping through the pages of the chart he'd been carrying.

"It's okay," Kim murmured gently as she checked the other eye. "Just keep looking at me." She wished Kyle would leave them alone for a few minutes so she could establish a rapport with the girl.

Scarlett nodded unconvincingly. When Kim put down the light, the girl rubbed her eyes and looked around the room. Her gaze fell on the mirror above the small scrub sink. As Kim watched, her expression seemed to waver and shift, almost as though she was startled by her own appearance. She frowned and narrowed her eyes, staring intently. After a long moment, she turned back to Kim. "Did I really mess him up like that?" she asked.

"Yeah, 'fraid it looks that way," Kim said. "But he's going to be fine. And, hey, I get it—we've all had an evil boss at some point, right?"

She inclined her head subtly at Kyle, earning a faint smile from Scarlett. She seemed to relax fractionally, pushing her hair out of her face. The motion caused her sleeve to slide back on her wrist. Thin, pale scars crisscrossed the skin on the inside of her arm.

"You know," Kyle said, setting the chart down, "it's a positive sign that you're worried about the guy."

"'Cause it shows I'm not a psychopath?"

"Hang on, we haven't completely ruled that out yet," Kim said with mock concern. This time Scarlett's smile seemed genuine, to Kim's relief. Without the girl's trust, it was going to be a lot harder to dig more deeply into what was going on, and there were a number of red flags in Scarlett's case. The scars, for one thing—and the fact that her high-tops had words scribbled on them in pen: *Aneurysm. Dumb. Lithium.* Then again . . . "So, Scarlett, did I ever tell you about the time I partied with Dave Grohl?"

"I just *met* you," Scarlett pointed out, as if Kim were an idiot. After a moment, she added, "But did you really? Party with him, I mean?"

"Yeah. And he told me something I'll never forget. He said . . . 'The best way *out* is always *through*.'"

As Scarlett seemed to consider her words, Kyle scowled. "That was Robert Frost, actually."

Kim winked at Scarlett. "Buzzkill," she stage-whispered, standing up and moving toward the door. "But you get the point."

Kyle pointed at the clipboard where it sat next to Scarlett. "If you could update your personal information, please. Dr. Patterson and I are going to step out for a moment."

Kim paused at the door and turned around. "Hey."

Scarlett looked up, pen in her hand.

"I mean it, though. We're going to help you get *through*."

Scarlett nodded unconvincingly and bent over the clipboard.

Kim closed the door gently behind her and caught up with Kyle, who was waiting for her with his arms folded. "So what's your take?" he asked.

"Actually, I'd like to hear what *you* think. Being a resident and all, I'm eager to learn from my superiors."

Kyle glowered at her but let the sarcasm pass. "You want to know what I think? I think we need to step very carefully here, given that girl's record." He passed Kim some files, which she tucked under her arm to read later. "Police Chief Plunkett paged so he could share his concerns. Scarlett Hascall has been in and out of treatment since she was six. Different doctors, different diagnoses. She was sent here eighteen months ago after she sucker-punched a classmate at school. I was supposed to get her in a six-month course of therapy, but she bailed after our second session. From what I've seen, I'd say she's got a serious mood disorder, possibly bipolar. This latest assault—that's type one mania. She's a cutter . . . self-mutilation . . . probably depressed."

Kim took the chart from him and scanned the history.

"Lithium, Klonopin, Zyprexa . . . Jeez, I mean, there must be, what, a dozen different meds on here? Let me ask you something— was she ever tested for DID?"

"Dissociative identity disorder? Are you serious?" Kyle shook his head, keeping his voice down as if afraid passing hospital staff might hear Kim's theory. "Split personality's a bit of a stretch, don't you think? There's no history of abuse. No childhood trauma."

"That you know of," Kim pointed out. "She displays some signs. She was surprised when she saw her own reflection, like she didn't even *recognize* herself, and she referred to herself in the third person. And did you smell her?"

Kyle's lip curled in distaste. "I try not to sniff my patients."

"Aftershave. *Men's* aftershave. The mirror, the smell, both suggesting a confusion of self. Add to that the blackouts . . . the lost time . . ."

Kyle raised his eyebrows. "You're being pretty selective about the details. How about what she wrote on her shoe? *Lithium*? A bipolar drug. How does that fit into your little theory?"

"*Lithium, aneurysm, dumb*. I saw them. My theory is that she likes Nirvana songs."

Kyle reddened as he realized she was right.

"Kyle . . . let me take a crack at her. In treatment, one-on-one. I mean, what have we got to lose here?"

Kyle sighed and considered her for a long moment. "Did you really party with Dave Grohl?"

"Nah." Kim grinned, knowing she'd won this round. "Too busy reading Robert Frost."

"Okay, fine. She's your patient. But keep me updated and try not to break any more rules. This can't be like San Diego. Not again."

Kim shot him a look. "Hey, I'm not all terrible. If I didn't break the rules now and then, I wouldn't be having sex with you."

She blew him a kiss and turned back toward her office . . .

. . . where the door stood wide open.

The room was empty. The half-filled-out paperwork was sitting on the counter, the pen next to it, the plastic gnawed.

She glanced frantically around the tiny office, as though Scarlett could be hiding in the file cabinet or the minuscule bookcase. The faint scent of aftershave was still detectable in the air—but the girl was gone.

Kim cursed under her breath. Losing a patient would not do her any favors with Kyle, or the board.

She raced back into the hallway and saw Scarlett moving quickly toward the staff elevators at the end of the hall, her feet making no noise in their rubber-soled tennis shoes.

"Hey, Scarlett!" Kim called, waving. But Scarlett didn't give any sign that she had heard. The doors opened and she stepped inside.

Kim ran down the hall, but by the time she arrived, the doors were closed. The display above showed it descending: 2 . . . 1 . . . B.

Kim stabbed at the DOWN button, debating whether to take the stairs, when the second set of doors opened. The elevator crept agonizingly slowly, and by the time she reached the basement and stepped out, the corridors were empty. Scarlett was nowhere in sight.

The basement was home to the hospital's mechanicals and a few storage areas and unused offices, as well as the morgue. An overhead light flickered and buzzed, casting the hall in gloom. A faint smell of engine oil and formaldehyde and other unidentifiable, unpleasant notes permeated her sinuses.

"Scarlett?" Kim called, cautiously moving down the hall. "Scarlett, you're not allowed down here. Please, talk to me."

There was a fleeting, small sound—like a footfall on the linoleum floor—and Kim followed it down the west corridor. As she drew closer to the doors at the end, she thought she saw a flash of movement and heard the click of a door closing. She raced toward the door and found herself face-to-face with an old sign stenciled in flaking paint: HOSPITAL MORGUE.

Kim pushed the door open, heart racing. Nearly everyone used the new entrance, accessible from the other set of elevators and staffed by a clerk; she'd never taken this back entrance before. She let her eyes adjust to the interior of the storeroom: the exposed, dripping pipes; the crumpled body bags mounded on a table; the bone saws and fluid extractors and other equipment lining the shelves. Naked bulbs cast inadequate light and long shadows on the cracked and peeling linoleum floors.

A shadow passed by the pane of frosted glass set into the door to the refrigeration room. "Scarlett? Is that you?"

Kim put her hand on the doorknob and hesitated: if it wasn't Scarlett on the other side of the door, she was going to have a heck of a time explaining what she was doing in the morgue. Kyle's earlier warning played in her mind, though she hadn't needed him to remind her that this job was her last chance to salvage her career.

Then she thought of Scarlett, of the eerie, blank expression that had repeatedly replaced her bewilderment and fear, and pushed the door open.

Inside the chilly room, lit by the fluorescent bulb overhead, Scarlett was pulling back the sheet covering a body. Her auburn hair fell in unruly waves around her shoulders as she bent closer, studying the face; then she moved to the next steel table and began to examine a second body.

Kim opened her mouth and then closed it again, fascinated. Scarlett didn't appear to notice her, frowning in concentration as she continued examining the bodies one by one. Her expression was inscrutable, sharpened by curiosity and purpose, with none of her earlier hesitation or resignation. Kim took a step backward, deciding it was more important to try to understand what the girl was doing than to interrupt her just yet.

After all, the people on the tables weren't going anywhere.

As she backed up, Kim bumped against an instrument cart behind her. A tray slid off it and clattered to the ground, spilling metal tools everywhere. Startled, Scarlett snatched a scalpel off one of the nearby tables and spun around to face Kim.

"Who are you?" she demanded, her eyes flashing as she wielded the wicked-sharp blade.

Kim slowly raised her hands to show Scarlett that she meant no harm. "I'm Dr. Patterson. Kim. We just met, upstairs. Don't you remember?"

Scarlett shook her head, clearly confused. Without letting go of the scalpel, she backed away from Kim, toward the final covered corpse, and pulled off the sheet, letting it fall to the floor. Apparently satisfied that Kim wasn't trying to stop her, she looked down at the body of a middle-aged woman, her eyes open and milky, staring at nothing. Scarlett's shoulders sagged.

"Scarlett, what are you doing?" Kim demanded.

The girl slowly raised her gaze to meet Kim's, her expression one of defeat. Tears welled in her eyes.

"I'm seeing if I died."

THREE

Detective Zack Trainor drained the last of his coffee as he pulled in toward the docks along the western edge of town and jammed his lidded commuter mug in the cruiser's cup holder. Ordinarily he liked to finish his coffee at home, while catching up on the news on his iPad, but he'd received a call from the print shop that the new batch of flyers he'd asked for were ready. Posting them would give him a chance to pop in on his only current suspect in a missing-persons case that was quickly going cold.

Zack didn't have much hope that the flyers would lead to new information, but he was running out of ideas. If Isabel Wilcox's boyfriend was responsible for her disappearance, maybe posting the flyers near his place of work would trigger someone's memory. And if not, at least it would irritate the bastard.

Brad Chaplin's official job was overseeing maintenance of the town docks, which looked like a postcard this morning under the brilliant blue skies. Legend had it that a Scandinavian fisherman named Jarvi Lssila had been the first person to stake his claim in Jarvis, a tiny town in the crook of a bay along the Alaska shore, in short order sending for a bride and siring seven sturdy sons to help him build a cannery, sawmill, and dock—but Zack would bet it was a

Chaplin who came along and bilked Lssila out of everything he had. Chaplins had a long history of small-time crime in town, and Brad seemed to be following in his father's shiftless footsteps.

Then again, the missing girl in question, Isabel Wilcox, was something of a wild child herself. Zack had arrested her once for selling a fake ID to a minor, but the charges had been dropped when a combination of an expensive attorney and her mother's tearful promises to get her daughter help had convinced the judge to give her another chance.

It was nearly eight thirty when Zack pulled the cruiser up to the marina offices and got out of the car, shielding his eyes from the sun. Already, several of the commercial fishing boats were back in, having offloaded their haul of mackerel and cod to the larger tender boats anchored farther out. Their sails had been secured, their decks swabbed until they sparkled in the sun, and their crews had peeled off their blood- and scale- and salt-soaked gear and rinsed out their thermoses. Some were already headed home to the square little timber houses dotting the hill; others took rooms at the boardinghouse during the season and worked their asses off, then passed the winter in warmer climes, spending their savings on other pursuits.

Zack walked along the docks until he spotted Brad Chaplin talking to the captain of the *Sweet Lola* while the crew hosed down the decks and packed away the nets.

The captain must have spotted Zack when he was still a few dozen yards away and alerted Brad, because his posture went rigid and the captain hightailed it down into the bowels of the ship. Being one of the few black guys in a mostly white town, Zack could rarely go anywhere incognito. But he wasn't here to give the captain trouble, even though he'd bet a year's salary that this guy had been scoring the heroin that Brad brought in from Anchorage, keeping a tidy middleman's profit for himself.

By the time Brad turned around, he'd composed himself. His good-looking face was only slightly scarred from taking a puck in the cheek during a high school match, and he kept himself in shape. He wore his dark hair cut short, and had even, white teeth. He might have had a career as a model if not for the scar—and the tattoo that crept up his neck, which Zack was pretty sure was meant to be a foreboding sea serpent, but in the hands of an unskilled tattoo artist it resembled a cross between a startled Pekingese and the Miami Dolphins logo.

"Detective Trainor," Brad said in a faintly mocking voice. "What brings you down to see us working stiffs on such a beautiful morning?"

Zack raised an eyebrow. "I can tell what *they're* doing," Zack said, pointing at the crew hosing blood and fish guts out of the hold. "But how exactly are *you* working?"

"Hey, I'm an account manager," Brad said evenly. "Dock's got two hundred and forty mooring contracts in the inner marina and it's my job to ensure that every one of those represents a satisfied customer."

"Yeah, I'll bet," Zack said. "My guess is that *this* customer is going to be pretty satisfied about an hour from now when he's back home dipping into that little plastic bag you just sold him."

Brad's eyes went wide with indignation. "I have no idea what you're talking about."

"Save it," Zack snapped. "Let's talk about your girlfriend instead. You hear from Isabel yet?"

"No, but I've been thinking," Brad said, settling back onto his heels and adopting his characteristic slouch. Zack knew he'd already lost his advantage. Like every con man, Brad was most comfortable when he was spinning lies. The deepening of the voice, the faintly bored tone, the smirking suggestion of intimacy—Brad was a master of the game. "You asked if I had an alibi, and lucky for me,

I remembered that I do. I was with two people who will be happy to tell you that they were with me the night Isabel disappeared."

"Well, that's interesting, considering we don't know exactly which night it was," Zack pointed out. "She was last seen two weeks ago Tuesday, and her mother called it in early Thursday morning, so that's at least two nights we haven't accounted for."

Brad blinked, slowly and lazily, like a lizard. His oily smile didn't flag. "Good thing I was with them both nights, then. Starlatta La-Bonne and Cherise Lassiter. They go to school over at Jarvis Community College."

"And I suppose you were, what, *tutoring* them?"

Brad was unfazed. "Strictly social, man. We listened to music, had a few laughs—you know how it goes."

"Not really."

Brad punched Zack playfully on the shoulder. "Tell you what, I'll text you their deets. Look 'em up—just between us, Starlatta's always ready to party."

Zack narrowed his eyes. "I trust you still have my card?" he said.

"Yes, indeed."

"And you'll let me know if you hear anything from Isabel."

Brad's face underwent another transformation, his elastic features knitting themselves into a look of concern. "Yeah, anything to help, but I doubt I will, man. Hear from her, I mean. I've got to face the fact that she's dumping me. I just wish she'd had the courage to do it to my face."

"If that's true, then she's got a lot more sense than I've given her credit for," Zack said.

Brad nodded curtly, clearly wanting the conversation to end. But Zack wasn't done with him. "You know, only problem with your theory is that we haven't had a single sighting of Isabel in over two weeks. You don't need me to tell you that doesn't look good."

After logging a frantic call from Jen Wilcox, whose daughter,

Isabel, hadn't returned any of her texts for two days, Zack and Chief Holt Plunkett had conducted a thorough search of Jarvis and the surrounding area. They'd talked to the other residents of the apartment complex where Isabel lived, her classmates at the community college, even friends from high school who she no longer kept in touch with. Her family members were little help—Isabel kept her distance, and they couldn't say how she spent her time, or whom she spent it with.

Zack had reviewed the passenger lists on every commercial vessel leaving the harbor, and every plane, commercial or private, taking off from the tiny municipal airport. There was one highway that came through town, and while there was no way to track all the traffic going in and out, Isabel hadn't been on any bus that stopped in Jarvis, or rented a car; hers had still been parked in her space at the apartment building.

"I guess you might as well haul me in, then," Brad said, shaking his head. "Do what you got to do. Give me a lie detector test."

"I'm considering it," Zack said.

"Do that."

After a long stare-down, Brad smiled. "We should hang out, Zack. Tell you what—next time I've got too much pussy to know what to do with, I'm calling you. I bet you know how to party." Zack just stared. "Hey, speaking of hotties, how's your sister? Brielle?"

From Zack's expression, Brad knew he was on thin ice. But he couldn't help himself. "She's your twin, right?"

Zack nodded, barely perceptible.

"Can I ask you something? About having a hot twin sister?"

Brad knew a punch was coming. Soon.

"Now, I heard about this thing called twin sense, where twins have a psychic connection. One gets burned, the other feels it. You heard about this shit?"

Zack nodded again, still barely perceptible.

"Okay, so let me ask you something, if she's getting rammed, like a once-in-a-lifetime fuck, do you sometimes feel like you're getting the D, too?"

Brad saw that Zack's fists were balled up tight. But he knew the pain was going to be worth the expression on Zack's face.

But then . . . Zack's radio buzzed on his belt, the urgent staccato blasts signaling a call for immediate backup. "Don't fucking move."

He turned away from Brad, pulling the radio from his belt to call the station. "Trainor here."

"Chief wants you at the hospital," Janice Sudermeyer said. "Might want to get there fast. A Burger Barn manager apparently just about got his face burned off, from the sound of it, and he's saying it was one of his own employees who attacked him."

"Copy that. On my way."

Disappointed that he wouldn't be able to lay Brad out on his back right now, he holstered his radio and turned to the ex-jock. "Don't go anywhere without notifying us. We'll finish this conversation later."

He walked away, a little relieved that he managed to avoid a disciplinary write-up for now. Though it was petty, he was glad he'd had the last word.

———

JARVIS HAD ITS SHARE of fast-food restaurants, but the Burger Barn was a local favorite, with a menu that offered old-school fare: ground chuck, fries cut from spuds on-site, and not a single item on the menu that could be described as free-range, organic, or gluten-free. Though Zack tried to steer clear of meat on vaguely ethical grounds, he still dropped in to the Barn every couple of months for a double bacon cheeseburger.

Chief Holt Plunkett had beat him to the ER. When Zack walked in, Holt was talking to a nurse in a pink scrub shirt that featured kittens chasing balls of yarn.

"Felicity here has been kind enough to give us a little background, but I've held off on talking to Mr. Fenstrom until you got here."

"The Burger Barn manager?" Zack recognized the name; Fenstrom had been a few years ahead of him at Jarvis High, an obnoxious stoner with truancy issues. Time had not improved him much: the department had received a few complaints from women, from his sending unsolicited dick pics to female customers, to the most recent grievance filed by a former girlfriend who accused him of sleeping with her sister—the outraged woman threw a brick through her own windshield when the officer, taking her report, had explained that wasn't a crime.

"That's the one. Felicity says he's got third-degree burns on thirty percent of his face."

The nurse nodded, gazing respectfully at Holt's badge. Women always loved Holt Plunkett—he was like a grizzled teddy bear with a gun. He hadn't dated since being widowed fifteen years ago, which naturally only increased his appeal. "We'll be keeping him here for a spell."

"Mr. Fenstrom wants to press charges against a Ms. Scarlett Hascall, an employee of the restaurant," Holt continued. "He says Ms. Hascall attacked him with a fry basket."

"A fry basket," Zack repeated. "That's a new one."

Holt turned back to the nurse. "Do you mind bringing us back to see Mr. Fenstrom now, dear?"

"Righto," Felicity said brightly, and waved the pair of detectives inside. Holt and Zack followed her through the emergency room doors and into a curtained-off cubicle. Sitting on the paper-lined table was a man in a greasy T-shirt emblazoned with the Burger Barn logo. A filthy apron was still tied around the man's skinny hips, and his face was largely obscured by a giant bandage that covered half his face.

Seeing Zack and Holt, Fenstrom lifted up his bandage dramatically.

"I want to press charges!" he yelled. "Look what she did to me!"

"Damn." Zack whistled. "We could play a game of checkers on your cheek."

"'Fraid there's not a whole lot we can do without someone to back your story up," Holt added. "The young lady in question told the nurses she didn't do it. And she did drive you to the hospital, which hardly seems like something a person who wanted to harm you would do."

"What? She attacked me! She almost killed me!"

"And what did you do to deserve it?" Zack demanded.

Fenstrom glared at him furiously, spittle collecting at the corners of his mouth as he sputtered. "Just 'cause you put on a badge, Trainor, don't mean your past gets erased."

Zack laughed. "Hey, I've paid for all my mistakes. Learned from them, too. I can't say the same for you."

Holt stepped between the two men, holding up a hand with an easy smile. "We'll just give your boss a call, Mr. Fenstrom, and let him know what's happened. Maybe we'll follow up with a couple of your other female coworkers and see if *they* have any idea what might have precipitated this attack."

Fenstrom bobbed his head between the two police officers, trying to come up with a suitable retort. The effort seemed beyond him, however, and he gave up and sagged against the wall, muttering.

"Tell you what, when the face heals up, and you're back to your modeling career, why don't you stop by the station so you can give us a full report. You have a good day now, okay?"

"You really shouldn't provoke him, son," Holt said when they were out of earshot, tucking his notebook back in the pocket of his uniform shirt, which was stretched taut over his sloping gut. "Take a walk with me, okay? I could go for a little something from the vending machines."

On the way, Holt filled Zack in on the rest of the details.

"Wait a minute," Zack interrupted, when Holt mentioned the girl's name again. "Scarlett Hascall. Didn't Evelyn pick her up at the high school a while back?"

"Yep. She got in a fistfight in a girls' restroom. Gave some gal a heck of a shiner before a teacher managed to pull her off."

"She sounds a little crackers. Maybe she *did* do what he said, attack him for no reason."

"So you feel bad for giving him a hard time now?"

"Fenstrom?" Zack shook his head. "Guy called my sister a slut in tenth grade. If I knew for sure this girl wouldn't hurt anyone else, I'd bake her cookies."

"Yeah, well, I talked to her psych doc, Berman. Pretty good guy, seems to know his stuff. He says they're evaluating her and they'll let us know what they come up with. My take? There's a good kid inside there somewhere. But these episodes are escalating, and they need to stop."

"They don't have any idea what's motivating her?"

"Don't think so, not yet, anyway," Holt said. He poked a stubby finger at the vending machine buttons and a package of cupcakes with lurid red frosting slid off the hook.

A piece of paper posted on the message board next to the vending machines caught Zack's eye, and he moved closer to examine it, pulling off layers of notices and flyers. It was one of his department's missing-persons posters from when Isabel first disappeared. He studied the image of a pretty, blond young woman beaming at the camera, a view of mountains behind her. *Isabel Wilcox, age 22.* Thoughtfully, Zack replaced the other papers, pinning them farther away so that the flyer could be seen.

Holt had peeled off the plastic and managed to devour half a cupcake already. "One more stop here at the hospital," he said, through a mouthful of cake. "Berman was going to arrange a meet and greet with the resident who's treating Scarlett. Want to come with me to follow up?"

"Sure," Zack said, wondering if he should tell the chief about the smudge of frosting on his cheek, but he decided to let it go.

That was one of the things about working for the man who raised you—you never really forgot that he was the one who taught you to tie a tie, or took you for haircuts on Saturday afternoons, or made you write an apology to the jerk who owned the convenience store where you shoplifted a bag of Skittles. There were those who made the mistake of thinking Holt's easygoing charm was a sign of weakness—but Zack knew better. Behind the drawl and the ruddy, freckled skin lay courage, conviction, and an unwavering moral compass.

They took the stairs up to the top floor—Holt had been trying to lose thirty pounds for as long as Zack had known him—and Zack showed his badge to get past the locked entrance to the psych unit. A receptionist pointed out Dr. Berman, who was talking to a brunette with a messy ponytail and stained, poorly fitting scrubs.

"This is Dr. Patterson," Berman said after Holt introduced Zack. "She's the one who spoke to Scarlett today."

"Hello, Detectives," the woman said coolly. Zack started when she turned around—he hadn't expected her to be attractive. Her eyes were a flinty, depthless green. A stray lock of wavy chestnut hair curved over one cheek, down past her chin, coming to rest on an expanse of skin near her shoulder that her ill-fitting scrubs left exposed.

"He's actually the chief," Zack replied, matching her tone.

"Ah. My mistake. But chief or no, I still can't discuss Scarlett with you. Doctor-patient privilege, and all that." She crossed her arms. "Besides, I'm sure you guys have more important things to do with your time—she's hardly a threat."

"Is that a professional opinion?" Zack asked. "Because she just assaulted a guy with a fry bin."

"Zack," Holt murmured warningly. To Kim, he added, "Please forgive my partner. He gets a little nervous around strong, intelligent women."

"Flattered," Kim said, sounding anything but, her gaze not leaving Zack. "But I still can't talk to you about Scarlett's case. My hands are tied, I'm afraid."

"Understood," Holt said. "Wouldn't want my shrink telling secrets about me, either. We all have our jobs to do. We protect the peace, you protect the peace of mind."

That, at last, got a real smile out of her. "I suppose you could say that. Now if you'll excuse me, I've got a full schedule this morning." She turned and walked down the hall.

Holt chuckled as they both watched her walk away. "What do you know, son, there's one woman in Jarvis who *can* resist those famous Trainor dimples."

FOUR

A day later, Scarlett was back at the hospital for her first official appointment following the incident in the morgue—an incident that Kim had conveniently forgotten to tell Kyle about.

Shortly after Kim found Scarlett examining the bodies, Scarlett emerged from her trancelike state with no idea where she was or how she'd gotten there. The only bright side to the troubling turn of events was that Scarlett had been frightened enough to agree to treatment.

Kyle had, thankfully, offered his office for the occasion. Kim and the other resident, Andrea Kaston, shared their miniature counseling office with several interns, and it was frequently double-booked.

"Make yourself comfortable," Kim said when Scarlett arrived, taking Kyle's messenger bag off the spare chair and motioning for Scarlett to sit down. She grabbed Kyle's chair and scooted it around to the other side of the desk, so she and Scarlett were sitting knee to knee again.

"I like Dr. Berman's . . . what are those, exactly?" Scarlett was pointing to the clay worry stones that Kyle had brought back with him from Thailand. He claimed that they had been made by novitiates in a Buddhist monastery, and that when he held them, he was able to focus his mind and achieve serenity even on the most hectic day.

"Oh, those," Kim said. "Fossilized mastodon turds. They date back to the Pliocene age. He's a bit of an archaeology buff."

Scarlett blinked. "Oh. Cool."

"Scarlett, I understand that Darren isn't pressing charges. So even if you did . . . you know"—she mimed beating herself over the head with a stainless-steel basket—"my guess is that he provoked you somehow and he knows it. You still don't remember what happened?"

"No. I mean, I know I probably did it," Scarlett said. "But I'm glad that, you know, I'm not getting arrested."

"Do you remember anything leading up to the incident?"

Scarlett shook her head, her eyes downcast. The skin of her eyelids was thin and luminous, showing a fine network of tiny blue veins. She had beautiful bone structure, and her hair would probably be lovely if it hadn't been hacked off at her shoulder in what appeared to be a home haircut. Also, she could stand to eat something—like a dozen cheeseburgers with a milk shake chaser, for a start, and even then, she'd barely fill out her jeans.

Kim felt a pang of sympathy for the girl, which was completely unprofessional but all too familiar. She took a breath and vowed to push past it. "All right. No problem. Tell you what—let's start somewhere else. Tell me a little bit about yourself. About growing up. Things you remember from your childhood, good or bad."

"Do I have to?" Scarlett sighed. "I've done this, like, four hundred times." She picked up one of the worry stones and closed her fingers over it.

"But not with me, right?" Kim said.

A sharp cry, muffled by the closed door, could be heard down the hall. Scarlett looked alarmed.

"I'm sorry," Kim said, dropping her bright tone. "I know that can be distracting, but I can assure you that our patients receive excellent care and we certainly don't take their distress lightly."

"I know," Scarlett said dully. "I've been here before. It's, like, nothing new."

Kim said gently, "I'm sorry. I know this is— This probably sucks for you. But indulge me a little, okay? I want very much to help you, and—"

"—to *help* me you have to *understand* me," Scarlett cut in with a wave of her hand. "I know, I know."

"Scarlett . . . mental illness isn't anything to be ashamed of. If we can figure out if an underlying disorder is causing your episodes, then we're that much closer to figuring out how to help you live with it."

"Do you want to know how many *disorders* I've been diagnosed with?" Scarlett demanded, her nostrils flaring and a spark of defiance in her eyes. "OCD, ADHD, psychotic episodes, schizophrenia— that's always a favorite—"

Kim held up her hand. "I understand. It's really frustrating that despite all the advances we've made in medicine, the brain remains a mystery in many ways." She tried to keep her breathing even, calm. She couldn't let Scarlett know how much this brought back memories of her own teen years; things had to stay professional if Kim would possibly be able to give her any help.

Scarlett shrugged. "Yeah. And when I fail to match up with whatever diagnosis they've given me, my shrinks always start trying to figure out what fucked-up thing from my past made me this way. But the thing is, there isn't anything. No one ever believes me, but our family is totally normal. I mean, okay. Kenny Latham showed me his penis when I was six, but I wasn't abused or molested. There were no skeevy uncles or online predators. My mom left when I was fourteen and, yeah, that blows, but my crazy stuff started way before then. I've smoked pot three times, but the only other drugs I take are the ones *you guys* prescribe." Scarlett rolled her eyes. "And there've been a *lot* of drugs, if you want to pursue that angle. But this started first, obviously, or else no one would have given me drugs to begin with. Hmm, what else? I'm not sexually active 'cause who'd want to get freaky with a freak. Anyway . . ." Her rant petered out in another shrug. "Whatever."

Kim set down her notepad and regarded Scarlett thoughtfully. "I hated therapy, too," she said quietly. "Answer the same stupid questions over and over again, but no one ever really gets it."

Scarlett's head snapped up, and she finally met Kim's eyes. "You were in therapy?"

"After my parents died, I lived in a psych ward for three years," Kim said carefully. In general, she tried to keep the focus entirely on the patient, but in this case, her gut told her that revealing their common experience might help her gain Scarlett's trust. "Look, I *know*, therapy sucks. But . . . if you're willing to do the work, it can help. It helped me."

Scarlett looked a little taken aback. Kim picked up the personal information form that Scarlett had partially filled out the day before, finally asking the question that had been weighing on her mind.

"Last time you were here, you started to fill out this questionnaire. It says your address is 653 Madigan Lane, and your age is twenty-two . . . ?"

"That's not my address," Scarlett said, startled. "And I'm nineteen. I wouldn't have written that. Are you sure it's mine?"

Kim nodded. "You also wrote that your name is 'Izzi.'"

Scarlett stared at her blankly.

"Listen," Kim pushed on, "have you ever heard of DID? Dissociative identity disorder?"

Scarlett shook her head, mystified.

"They used to call it multiple personality, or split personality, though those aren't very accurate terms," Kim said, keeping her tone light. "It's nothing to be ashamed of or afraid of. Scarlett, you have a few of the . . . signs. Like this." She held up the paper. "Maybe you thought you *were* twenty-two when you wrote it."

Scarlett looked like she was about to ask question, but then another panicked cry sounded, closer to Kyle's office, followed by someone speaking in low, soothing tones. Abruptly the first voice started yelling. "No, no, *no*! You're hurting me, stop it!"

"Don't worry," Kim said, cursing the interruption that came just as they were making progress. "I promise you, no one is being hurt. Sometimes patients suffering from delusions—"

She broke off at the sound of a strangled yelp. "Help me!" the voice came, sounding ever more desperate. "Oh my God, help me!"

Kim was about to reassure Scarlett again when she noticed a change come over the girl's face. Another episode. Kim sat completely still, torn between wanting to help and needing to observe in order to know better what was going on. Scarlett was blinking rapidly, and then her features tensed up, her mouth contorting in a rictus of a grin before going slack, the muscles of her face twitching. Her eyes fluttered and her arms and fingers went rigid, gripping the arms of the chair so hard her knuckles turned white.

"Help me!" she echoed, in a voice eerily similar to the one outside the door. "Oh my God, help me! Help . . . help . . ."

She looked wildly around the room, but Kim had the feeling that what she was seeing wasn't the bland decor of Kyle's office. She pushed away from Kim, backing her chair into the far end of the room, panting shallowly and shaking. Her terror seemed absolutely genuine.

Kim jumped up from her chair, then stopped herself from going to Scarlett, which might only further disorient her. But if the girl truly did suffer from DID, it wasn't Scarlett at all, but an alternate identity who was cowering in the corner. Moving very slowly, Kim lowered herself to the floor, kneeling in front of Scarlett. "You're safe here," she whispered soothingly. "It's okay."

Scarlett whimpered and looked around frantically. "No, he's— he's—"

Continuing to reassure her softly that she was safe and that everything was okay, Kim maneuvered herself so she was directly in front of Scarlett, forcing her to make eye contact.

"Hi," she said, more calmly than she felt. "I'm Kim. What's your name?"

"I know you," Scarlett mumbled in a voice unlike her own, both higher-pitched and with a more nasal accent. "I *saw* you."

"You saw me? When?"

"*You* know. In the morgue. When I was trying to find . . . my body. When I was trying to find out if I was dead."

"Why did you think that—that you died?" Kim said, willing herself to act as though the conversation was completely routine, as though they were discussing nothing more important than the weather.

"I . . . don't know. I'm here, right? With you?"

"Your name is Izzi?"

Scarlett's features relaxed slightly and she gave a sigh of relief. She ran her fingers through her hair and then flipped it over her shoulder. "*Yes.* My mom still calls me Isabel but everyone else calls me Izzi."

"Isabel is a pretty name," Kim said.

The girl nodded. "Isabel Wilcox."

Kim suddenly felt like the oxygen had been sucked out of the room. "Wilcox . . . ? Really?"

"I know, right?" Scarlett scowled, twisting the ends of her hair around her fingers. "Boys had a field day with that one. Izzi Will-Suck-C—"

"No, wait, I think you've made a mistake," Kim said, her heart hammering. "I think you may have borrowed that name. Did you maybe see it on a missing-persons flyer?"

Scarlett's eyes narrowed, and she looked at Kim with a mixture of suspicion and fear, her fingers stilling in her hair. "Missing persons?"

Kim grabbed her phone and did a quick Google search, bringing up the Jarvis Police Department's website. She clicked on *Bulletins* and there, right at the top, was an image of the flyer. She held out her phone for Scarlett to read. The girl stared in shock for a moment, then started shaking her head. "No. No, that's not, it isn't— Where am I? Please, you've got to tell me, *where*?"

She tried to get to her feet and push past Kim, but she was trapped in the corner of the room between Kim and the wall. Her trembling intensified as she fell to her knees and tried to crawl around Kim, her hands scrabbling ineffectively on the carpet.

"Izzi. Isabel," Kim said, putting her hands on the girl's shoulders. "Please, you've got to stop. It's time for you to—for you to take a step back and—"

Scarlett gave her a tremendous shove, and Kim fell back against the coffee table, shattering the glass. She felt a shard slice through the heel of her hand as she tried to push Scarlett back, away from the glass, but Scarlett continued to struggle. She scrambled to her knees, trying to crawl again, cutting her knees and hands. Kim got shakily to her feet, blood pouring from her hand.

"Isabel, I need to talk to Scarlett," Kim shouted, trying to shield the girl from the worst of the glass. But Scarlett seized a large shard and brandished it in front of her, wielding it like a knife.

"Leave me alone! Get the hell away from me, you fucking slag!"

Kim raised her hands defensively. "I'm—all right, Izzi, I'm not going to hurt you, I swear. Please, tell Scarlett to come back. *Scarlett. Now*."

Scarlett went still, her face slack, her nose twitching slightly. "Scarlett . . . isn't here. *I* am. *Izzi*. You have to talk to *me*."

"I'm afraid I can't do that right now," Kim said more firmly, try-ing to keep the fear out of her voice. "I promise not to let anything bad happen to you, Izzi, but I really need to talk to Scarlett now. We can talk again another time."

"You're just saying that," Scarlett mumbled. "You're lying. You're a lying bitch."

"No, Izzi," Kim said, slowly reaching for the hand holding the glass. She closed her fingers gently around Izzi's blood-soaked wrist, and the girl's fingers flexed, the glass falling to the floor. Kim bit back a jagged sigh of relief, but she didn't let go. "It's all right, Izzi. You can go now."

Her pupils seemed to dilate, then return to normal. The trem-bling slowly subsided as she sank back on the floor, her knees pulled up under her chin. She suddenly looked very young.

Scarlett was back. Kim was sure of it. "Dr. . . . Dr. Patterson? Oh my God, what happened? You're bleeding!" Scarlett looked down at her own hands, turning them over so she could examine her palms. "*I'm* bleeding. Oh no, please, please, tell me what I did this time!"

FIVE

im didn't see Scarlett again that day after escorting her downstairs for stitches. The staff insisted she let them attend to her own injuries, and as she endured the sting of the antiseptic and the application of several butterfly bandages, she thought about what had just happened upstairs.

An alternative identity—the identity of a missing young woman—had taken over Scarlett Hascall's mind and body. Kim was absolutely sure of it. She'd dealt with a lot of delusional and dishonest patients in the past, and was confident that Scarlett was neither; her body language, both when under the influence of an alter, and when back to herself, was too authentic to be faked. It was like two different people had been in that room with Kim, though they shared the same body.

On the other hand, true incidents of dissociative identity were so rare that Kim's exposure to patients suffering from the disorder had until that moment been purely anecdotal. Could she really trust her own diagnosis, based on so little clinical experience?

When the attending physician was finished, Kim went to the desk to ask if she could see Scarlett but was told that her father had already come to take her home.

Kim left the hospital as the sun was beginning its descent over the distant snow-topped mountains. Waiting at one of Jarvis's three stoplights with the windows down, a rare enough pleasure in a town whose average temperature was only thirty-five degrees, Kim inhaled a big lungful of cool, pine-scented Alaskan air . . . with top notes of deep fryer and singed cheese.

The Burger Barn loomed just ahead. Struck by both inspiration and hunger, Kim pulled a semilegal U-turn, earning the ire of a man in a jacked-up Tundra with a set of moose antlers mounted on the front grille. Giving a sheepish wave and a shrug, Kim squeezed her '98 Civic into a narrow space between a couple of hulking Chevy Silverados, which seemed to be the most popular vehicle in town. There were advantages to driving a car like hers, at least during the few months a year that snow was unlikely.

Kim had arrived in Jarvis four months before, during an unseasonably pleasant May. She had enjoyed her first mild summer and had easily adapted to daylight lasting until midnight. Now it was September, and winter loomed terrifyingly near. In a month or so, Kim hoped to have banked enough overtime to upgrade to, say, the rusted-out F-150 that her neighbor currently kept up on blocks in his front yard.

Inside the Barn, desultorily cleaning up a mess of food wrappers, cups, and smeared ketchup littering one of the booths, was just the man she wanted to see.

"Hi, Darren!" she said brightly. "Check it out—samesies!" She held up her bandaged hand, which paled in comparison to the huge, puffy white bandage that was taped from Darren Fenstrom's purpled, swollen jaw to his partially shaved head.

He glared at her balefully. "She go after you, too?"

Kim winked. "If she had, I would've had the sense to duck."

"I narrowly missed having skin grafts taken from my ass, so forgive me if I'm not laughing along with you. Fucking kids." He

picked up a burger wrapper on which someone had drawn an an-
atomically disproportionate penis and testicles in Sharpie. "Their
parents ought to lock them in cages when they're not in school."

"Or send them to the Lower Forty-eight," Kim suggested, hoping to get on his good side. Adopting the locals' contempt for trans-
plants to the state was a cheap move, but Kim wasn't above it. "Hey,
how about I buy us both a couple of Barn Bacon Doubles and we
can have a nice little chat."

"I'd rather plunge my face in a bucket of steaming pig shit, thank
you," Darren said. "I've been working here since I was sixteen years
old. When I arrive in hell they will be serving Barn Bacon Doubles."
He paused, and looked her up and down. "But you can buy me a
drink next door if you want."

"Sounds like a plan!" Kim's face hurt from holding the fake grin,
but after the scene in the hospital earlier, she'd do whatever it took
to get some answers.

Darren whipped off his greasy apron and flung it on the seat
of the booth. "Candace!" he yelled, and an acne-speckled teen
peered out over the cash register. "Finish cleaning up this booth
and you can take your break when I get back. I've got to do an interview."

Kim raced to keep up with him as he headed out the door. "It's
not exactly an interview—"

"Yeah, I know, I just have to say that. Corporate's up my ass right
now. I have to justify every fucking piss break, so we'll just pretend
you came in to apply for a job, okay?"

Kim pretended to mull it over. "You know, I'm almost tempted. I
mean, no more eighteen-hour shifts, free food—"

"Plus, you get me as your boss," Darren said, smiling at her so
wide that she could see a missing molar in the back of his mouth.
They walked through the parking lot to the shack next door. A
flickering neon sign proclaimed OLD BEE ON TAP, along with an

outline of a go-go dancer whose glowing purple breasts appeared to shimmy as her nipples blinked off and on. "Or are you as crazy as the rest of the girls I meet? I sure do seem to be able to pick 'em."

Kim declined to answer, as her eyes adjusted to the dark, dank interior of the bar. A couple of guys in leather vests and flannel shirts sized her up over their beers. One of them had what looked like lunch stuck in his beard, and the other had gathered what little remained of his hair into a greasy ponytail.

Darren hoisted his thin frame up onto a barstool with practiced ease and patted the one next to him in invitation. Even here, Kim could smell the faint scent of grease wafting from him. She pulled a twenty from her purse and laid it on the bar.

"Keep 'em coming," she said to the bartender, a woman in her hard-miles fifties wearing a tight T-shirt emblazoned with the phrase *Eatin' Ain't Cheatin'*. Her hair was dyed an unnatural yellow and braided like the girl on the Swiss Miss box. "Wine cooler for me and whatever the gentleman is having."

"Wine cooler?" the woman asked, clearly affronted. "You fuckin' with me?"

"Well . . ." Kim hesitated. She was technically off the clock, but seeing as she was investigating her patient's case, she had thought it prudent to remain as sober as possible. "What else do you have that is low in alcohol?"

The woman gave her a look, then fished under the counter, coming up with a couple of bottles that she slammed on the bar: 7Up and something called a Blue Hawaiian malt beverage. "We don't keep much on hand for lightweights," she snapped. "You can mix it yourself." She wiped her hands on her jeans and disappeared behind the swinging doors.

"Now you've offended her," Darren observed, sliding off the stool and around to the other side of the bar, where he drew himself an enormous beer with a respectable head and then poured the

7Up and malt into a large mug, where they bubbled like a science experiment. "Are you a recovering alcoholic?"

"No, and I'm pretty sure the 'recovering' thing means you don't drink *any* alcohol, not even the shitty kind." She glanced around. "Are you part owner of this place or something?"

He waggled an eyebrow at her. "Just a friend of the bartender . . . with benefits."

Kim tried to wrap her mind around that thought—then attempted to mentally backpedal from the horrifying image of those pigtails bouncing with carnal abandon. Darren made himself comfortable on the stool again and took a deep, long drink, his Adam's apple bobbing. He let out a low burp and wiped his mouth on his sleeve. "So, I guess you want to hear about Scarlett."

"Well, I'd like to hear your side of what happened, yes."

He shrugged. "Not much to tell. I'm minding my own business, prepping the cheese for the night shift—you have to peel every damn slice off its little wax paper square, it's a real pain in the ass—when all of a sudden, *bam*, my face is on fuckin' *fire*."

"Could you be a little more specific?" Kim interjected. "This will go better if we dispense with the hyperbole."

"Dis-what with the who?" He blinked. "I'm telling you the God's honest truth here, Doc. She picked up that fry basket and hauled off on me for no reason at all. I mean, check out the security tape, it'll totally prove it. I gave it to the police and everything—can't imagine why she hasn't been arrested by now. I ought to sue her after all. Or her old man."

"She's nineteen," Scarlett pointed out. "An adult. So I don't think you can go after him, and I'm guessing she hasn't exactly amassed a fortune working for you."

"Whatever," Darren muttered. "I've still got to live with scars on my face, man. My face was, like, an *asset*, and what she did, I mean . . . somebody ought to pay."

"Listen, Darren, is there any chance that you were making, shall we say, unwelcome advances?"

"Unwelcome?" he echoed. "I mean, you said it yourself, she's nineteen. Legal in all fifty states."

"Hmm," Kim said, the picture clarifying in her mind. "So you might have made comments or suggestions of a sexual nature . . . ?"

Darren raised his eyebrows and smiled, but before he could expound, the bartender came back through the swinging doors, wiping some white residue off the tip of her nose. She glared at Kim, who made the quick assumption that the woman wasn't eating powdered doughnuts in the back room.

"Okay, well, I got to scoot," Kim said before the woman could suggest a duel for Darren's affections. "Real nice talking to you."

The woman snatched up the twenty and stuffed it in her jeans pocket. "Don't let the door hit you in the ass, honey."

As Kim started up her car, she reflected on what she'd learned. It sounded like Scarlett had good reason for defending herself from Darren, given his insinuations. But if Scarlett herself didn't remember, did that mean it was a protective alternate personality, trying to keep Scarlett safe? Could that be Isabel—or were there more alters hiding inside Scarlett, ones that Kim hadn't met yet?

KIM WAS STANDING IN her tiny kitchen surveying the contents of a take-out container doubtfully, trying to remember exactly when she'd stashed the remains of the pad thai in the fridge, when there was a knock on the door. She hastily ran a hand through her hair and pulled her tank top down to cover the slice of midriff above her ancient, sagging flannel pants before opening the door.

"Oh," she said in relief, seeing it was only her boss.

"*Oh?*" Kyle echoed, pushing past her into the living room. "Not

'How was your day, honey?' That's okay, I'll go ahead and tell you anyway. My day was just great until Graver called me upstairs to chew me out for opening a case on a patient who didn't even admit herself first."

"You mean Scarlett Hascall."

"Bingo! You nailed it—oh, shit, that looks bad," he said, his tone suddenly changing when he saw the bandage around her hand. It was spotted with blood from when Kim had unwisely used that hand to wrestle with her car door, thereby reopening the cuts. "Nelson told me you cut yourself, but she made it sound like a scratch."

"It was. Seriously, it's nothing," she said, warding him off.

"I wouldn't call it 'nothing' when a patient attacks you in my office," he said. "When I got up there, the coffee table was gone, the place smelled like a cheap car air freshener, and one of the nurses said something about Scarlett Hascall being taken out in restraints."

"That's not true," Kim said, rolling her eyes for show as she tried to figure out how to spin this one. "It was a minor accident. Tripped over the coffee table, needed a Band-Aid. Which, sorry, I'll replace your table—but hey, at least they got the stains out of the carpet, right?" She felt a little bad about lying to Kyle, but then, she didn't want his concern for her to get in the way of what was best for Scarlett.

"Forget the table, maintenance is bringing me a new one. And let me guess, you were only trying to 'help,'" Kyle said sarcastically. Then he sighed. "Never mind. Just let me take a look, okay?"

Kim allowed him to peel back the bandage, feeling the tension drain out of her at his familiar, gentle touch. As he checked the wound, his free hand squeezed her shoulder, kneading the muscles.

"Mmmm. You missed your calling, seriously," she said, relaxing further. "You ought to work in one of those reflexology spas, you know, with the foot diagram in the window? It's only thirty bucks an hour, but I bet you'd make hella tips."

"Right," Kyle said stonily, letting go of her arm after peeling the bandage all the way off. "You need a new bandage. Tell you what, how about you get me your med kit and then you can explain exactly what you and Ms. Hascall discussed in my office while I fix you up."

Kim wasn't surprised that Kyle saw right through her lies from earlier—his own ethical switch was permanently set to overdrive. She fetched supplies from the bathroom and submitted to his ministrations while she outlined her theory in the broadest strokes possible. It felt good to have someone caring for her, something she allowed only very rarely. Kim tried to ignore the psychologist voice in her head, the one that was concerned that Kim could essentially count on one hand the number of people she'd ever allowed to get this close to her.

When Kim mentioned DID, Kyle paused in the middle of tearing open an antiseptic wipe. "Come on, Kim. Please tell me you're not still pushing that."

"Just hear me out," she said, tearing herself out of her introspection. "Typically, alternate personalities are created to help dissociate from the real world. But what about an alter who claims to be another *real, living person*?"

"That's—"

"Sure, some sufferers say they're Joan of Arc, Jesus, Elvis, whatever—but why would Scarlett claim to be a missing girl? Why Isabel Wilcox? That tickles," she added, as Kyle dabbed gently at the edges of her cuts.

"Whoever cleaned this needs to get their eyes checked," Kyle scowled. "There's a sliver—"

"Ow!"

Kim plowed on as Kyle teased out the glass fragment, determined to make him at least consider her hypothesis. "Isabel's missing-person pictures are plastered on every street corner, so I'm not surprised she imprinted that name—"

"Hold still, damn it."

"Or maybe it's not Scarlett. Maybe it's a mischievous alter—
pretending to be Isabel."

"Or maybe you need to consider your new patient isn't really
split. Maybe she's faking it. Munchausen syndrome." He showed
her his fingertip triumphantly, the tiny sliver sparkling on the tip.
"Factitious disorder."

"Okay. But for what purpose?"

"To get attention. You said her mom left the family when she
was still an adolescent, right?"

"No. Her symptoms started years before that. There's something
else . . . something I'm missing."

Kyle applied the fresh bandage with the same expert efficiency
and took the other to the kitchen to throw it out. As he returned,
he paused in front of a frame leaning against the wall, one of several Kim hadn't yet decided where to hang. It held a photo taken in
her first year of medical school. Kim was clearly drunk, and clearly
partying with the Foo Fighters.

"Seriously, Kim? I thought you said you made that up about
Dave Grohl. You were too busy reading Robert Frost, remember?"

"I'm just full of surprises," she said lightly, though he couldn't
possibly know how very true that was. As his scowl deepened, she
added, "What? You don't have a past?"

Kyle shrugged. He picked up her hand again and ran his fingers
along the edge of the bandage, pressing it securely to her skin—and
igniting all kinds of sensations in the process. "You really should
have had stitches, you know."

Kim just wished he'd stop talking and simply keep doing more
of what he was doing. "I'll heal."

Kyle gave her a probing look, his fingers lightly touching the
faint lines on her inner arms. "Maybe, maybe not. But then, what's
one more scar—"

"I *said* I was fine." Kim tried to pull away, but his grip on her arms was too firm. *This*, she thought wryly. *This is why I avoid closeness*.

Kyle was still studying her. "Kim," he said finally, his voice heavy, lacing her fingers through his, "I think I should assign the Hascall case to someone else."

"Do I submit my resignation letter to you or the board?" She tried her best to look serious, but Kyle wasn't biting. She doubled down. "I've always wanted to try my hand as a pastry chef."

Kyle shook his head. "Nice try. But I'm reassigning the girl."

"What? Why?" Kim swallowed, trying to keep her voice steady.

"You've had one session with her, and you already need stitches? Come on, I'm concerned."

"Don't—don't make this about us. Please." The words were out before she could stop herself.

Kyle's expression hardened and he released her hand. "It's not about *us*. You're my resident. I'm responsible for what happens to you. And you know you're under a microscope right now. We *both* are."

Kim spun away, walking over to the kitchen where she fiddled with a wineglass, wishing she had something other than old beer in the fridge. "It was an *accident*, like I told you. Trust me, I can handle her. Whether you agree with me or not, I can help this girl. Don't take that away from her." She rubbed her hands together, missing the warmth of his touch in spite of herself. "And don't take it away from *me*."

She glanced up and saw him watching her intently.

"Kim . . ."

"Come on, Kyle, please. *Please*. I know . . . I know I haven't made your life easy."

"You can say that again." He dropped his eyes, and Kim walked back over to him, wanting to make things right the only way she knew how.

"But I've made it . . . interesting, right? At least a little?" She hesitantly lifted her uninjured hand to his cheek, combed her fingers through his hair.

The corner of his mouth twitched. Kim knew he was trying to resist—and that he wouldn't be able to, not for much longer.

"I do appreciate you," she murmured softly, dropping her hand to trace circles on his chest. "And if you'll just take a break from giving me the third degree, I think I can prove it."

"I know I'm going to regret this," Kyle sighed as he pulled her in for a kiss.

Not if I can help it, Kim thought. Because what they both needed—what *she* needed, anyway—was to simply lose herself for a while, to give in to the sensations of his touch and forget, if only for a moment, the darkness that stalked her patients during the day and colored her dreams at night.

SIX

"So, Starla," Zack said, relaxing as much as possible into the uncomfortable plastic chair. They were crowded into Interview Room 1, which was actually the only interview room that the Jarvis Police Department could lay claim to, and which also served as the photocopy room and the staff lounge. Currently it was redolent with the aromas of leftover curry that Phil Taktuq had had for lunch.

Zack was focusing intently on the young woman's nostrils so as to avoid staring at her twin lip piercings, studded with what looked like tiny silver fangs. "You say you left the club at—"

"It's Star*latt*a, actually," she interrupted him. She had a distracting lisp, perhaps the result of the fangs. Zack realized then that the elaborate script tattoo scrolling across her collarbones spelled out her name, giving him, in effect, a cheat sheet.

"Starlatta. Right, sorry," Zack said. "You and Cherise left the club at approximately two fifteen in the morning, and you say Brad was still there?"

"Yup," Cherise said, bobbing her head, which made her magenta bangs flop over her eyes. She shifted in her chair, and then uncrossed her legs and recrossed them, managing to make the everyday action look lurid. "He was definitely still there."

"Doing what, exactly?" Zack always had trouble at this kind of interview—girls like Starlatta and Cherise made him uncomfortable, despite his training. Distracted by his discomfort, he always struggled to break through, to get anything real out of them. Holt, of course, thought it was funny. Damn him.

"Dancing," Cherise said, at the very same time Starlatta said, "Talking." Starlatta was the more assertive of the two, and she gave Cherise a withering glare.

"Talking while he was dancing?" Cherise said meekly. "To, like, this blond girl. I think."

Zack pressed his thumbs to his temples, a hopeless attempt to stave off the headache that was threatening to overtake him. He couldn't tell what was making it worse, the completely unhelpful interview, or the cheap perfume they both were wearing.

"See, here's the thing," he said, willing himself to remain patient. "I've reviewed the video feed from that night. I've got you two there from eleven until around two thirty, just like you said, give or take a few bathroom breaks." Six of them, to be precise, ranging from seven minutes—when they might actually have been using the bathroom for its intended purpose—to a highly suspect thirty-four, when they'd disappeared down the staff corridor with a waiter. "But Brad just simply wasn't there. I ran it forward, backward, slo-mo—zeroed in on every male in the place. And unless he was wearing a cloak of invisibility, I'm afraid you're not going to convince me he was ever there."

The girls stared at him like twin sphinxes, making Zack realize that even the most accessible literary allusions were probably beyond these two. Hopefully he hadn't just lost them. "So," he said, switching tactics, "let's chalk that one up to getting our dates crossed, and focus on your relationship with Isabel Wilcox instead."

"Oh," Cherise said dolefully. "Well, she was, like, a role model for me."

"*Was?*" Zack echoed. Maybe he was finally getting somewhere.

But Cherise just wiped away a tear, clearly putting on a show, while Starlatta chewed vigorously on the tip of one of her long fingernails.

"She's not coming back, is she," Cherise said, her voice full of soap opera drama. "I mean, if you guys don't find her in the first hour, it's, like, she's statistically dead, right?"

Zack sighed. "I take it you're a fan of *CSI*," he said.

"I mean, I've seen it a few times," Cherise hedged.

Starlatta rolled her eyes in disgust. "Okay, look," she said, sitting up straighter. "We were *with* Brad that night, like I told you. And it is really terrible that Izzi's gone missing. But if you're thinking he did something to her—" She gave a shrug that managed to convey that Zack was the most dim-witted man she'd ever encountered.

"Help me out here," he said. "Why do you think Brad's innocent? I'm not going to come down on you for anything." He held up his palms and resisted adding "Scout's honor," an urge that had been hammered into him during the four years that Holt had served as his troop's scout leader. "I'm just trying to get to the bottom of what happened to Izzi. We all want to bring her home safe, okay? So now's the time to share what you know."

He leaned forward, elbows on the table, and gave the girls his best sincere, vulnerable gaze. "For all we know, she's out there alone, in trouble. The three of us, we have a chance to do some *good* here," he added, disgusted with himself while hoping this would work.

"Izzi's into some bad stuff," Cherise blurted. Before Starlatta could stop her, she added, "I mean, not that I blame her, right? She's had it tough. But I mean, the videos . . ."

"Videos . . . ?" Zack held her gaze with everything he had. He was in—as long as Starlatta didn't interfere. "Tell me what happened, Cherise. I know it's tough, if you've been . . . swept up in things that got out of hand. But I want to help."

Cherise's heavily mascaraed eyelashes trembled. "I don't think she ever meant it to go as far as it did," she allowed.

"Oh, *fuck*," Starlatta said, pulling out her vape. In seconds she was blowing bilious clouds of steamy vapor.

"Start from the beginning," Zack said, setting down his notebook, the better to focus on his potential star witness; he was, of course, recording the entire conversation anyway.

"I mean, all I wanted was a good fake, you know? I'll be twenty-one in two months, but when I met Izzi it was, like, over a year off and she set me up and didn't even charge me. Said I reminded her of her at that age. Which was kind of sweet, you know?"

Zack nodded, working hard to keep the skepticism from his eyes.

"So she got me this ID that said I was twenty-two—Oregon, you know, so they don't look too close—but then she was, like, you have something special, Cherise, you could really do well for yourself with just a few hours a week. And I mean, I was all ears. I have two roommates; one roommate doesn't even speak *English* and she puts her disgusting plates back in the cabinet without *washing* them, so yeah, I was totally interested."

Cherise was really warming to her story now. She'd dropped her affected pose and was leaning over the table, earnest. "And it wasn't like I had to do anything with a *guy* or whatever." She fluttered her fingers. "Just me and the camera. Izzi always says, just imagine it's some hot guy, but you always know it's just a *camera*, right?"

"You should shut the fuck up," Starlatta suggested. "Detective Trainor, for the record, I personally never let Izzi record me for remonsteration."

"I think you mean *remuneration*," Zack suggested. "You're saying you never videotaped yourself?"

"Never for money." Starlatta smiled.

Zack smiled back. "Look, even if you did . . . which I'm not say-

ing you did, because clearly you're a good girl, it doesn't matter, because as I said, I'm only trying to gain insight into Izzi's habits."

"Wouldn't know." Starlatta huffed. "Other than my study group
and worship on Sundays, I pretty much keep to myself." She smiled
again. "Because I'm a good girl."

Zack resisted the urge to roll his eyes. After another hour of
talking in circles, he escorted the girls out, sure he'd heard everything Cherise knew. He'd gotten what he needed—confirmation
that Izzi was in way over her head.

And confirmation that Brad hadn't been anywhere he could
prove on the night Isabel Wilcox disappeared.

<hr />

FORTY-FIVE MINUTES LATER, ZACK was attempting to relay this new
information to Holt, as he paced back and forth in the conference room in front of the Wilcox case evidence board. Pinned to
the board was everything they had managed to gather pertaining
to Isabel: selfies from her various social media accounts, many of
them taken at the community college; family photos with her parents, and several of her and Brad together. Nothing out of the ordinary for a young woman, but they didn't tell the whole story. They'd
missed something huge; Isabel had been wrapped up in Brad's business, and when drugs and girls were on the line, he could have any
number of reasons to want her gone. Now, at last, they might have
something to work with, if he could convince Holt that Brad's alibi
didn't hold water.

"These girls, Starlatta and Cherise—I think they might be pros,"
Zack began.

Holt rubbed the soft belly of the sleeping dachshund on his lap.
He'd been bringing Tubbs in to work ever since the elderly dog
started requiring medication in the middle of the day.

"Well, Chaplin wouldn't be the first guy around here to pay for sex. Maybe not even the second."

Zack nodded, point taken. "Yeah, I know, but I think Isabel Wilcox is the one who recruited them."

Holt's eyebrows shot up. "How are you suggesting she did that?"

"I think she lured them in by supplying them with fake IDs, then convinced them to make amateur porn. She had access to young girls over at the community college, and it would have been fairly easy to send them down the slippery slope, once she got their attention. Now, I'm not saying it was her idea. If Brad was the guy behind the operation, and Izzi wanted out—or was threatening to turn him in—that would give him a compelling reason to get rid of her."

"Hmm," Holt said, gently nudging the dog from his lap before standing to take a closer look at the evidence board. "Do you have any hard evidence Isabel was involved in Chaplin's drug enterprise? Maybe setting up a channel for him over at the college?"

"Well—nothing *yet*. But, in my gut I know—"

"We need more than that to build a case, son. You need to find me something real that we can go on, more than just your gut feeling."

"Brad is behind this."

Holt just stared at his protégé, a blank wall.

Zack finally relented. "Okay, I know it's just my gut."

"And you hardly got a gut to go off of." Holt shook his finger at Zack's hard waistline before patting his own belly. "But don't worry, in time . . ."

But Zack didn't give him the satisfaction of a smile, his frustration boiling over. "She's been missing two and a half weeks. When do we start doing more than tacking up flyers?"

Holt sighed. "I hear you. But what do you suggest we do? We have a lot of resources directed toward this investigation. We're going to continue to monitor Brad's whereabouts, but at some point, unless we can find more evidence . . . more *hard* evidence . . ." He shook his head. "Personally, I'm still hoping she's backpacking across Europe."

"More likely she's dead in a ditch somewhere." Zack paused, staring at a picture of Isabel sitting on Brad's lap, holding a frosty cocktail. "Brad Chaplin knows something. Kid's a lowlife."

"He also claims he's got an alibi for the night she went missing."

"Come on, Holt, he's not on the bar tapes from that night. Those girls just admitted to making amateur porn. You think they wouldn't lie for a few dollars more?"

Zack's phone rang, and he glanced at the screen: Milton. Zack glared across tops of the cubicles to the other side of the station, where he could see Conrad Milton perched on his stool. It wouldn't have killed the guy to walk a dozen yards and tell him whatever it was in person, but Milton always called instead. "Yeah, what," he answered.

"A Danielle DeWitt is here, Detective. She wants to file a missing-person report. Says her husband was due back from his hunting trip two days ago and she hasn't heard from him."

"Another one?" Zack looked back at the sea of images of Isabel Wilcox pinned to the wall. "Can't we go a single month around here without someone going missing?"

His words were met with wounded silence, and Zack regretted the outburst immediately. After all, it wasn't Milton's fault. Besides, a majority of missing-person reports ended up being closed when the disgruntled teen or errant spouse turned up, even in Jarvis, which had more than its fair share of missing-persons cases for a town its size. A casualty of living on the fringes of civilization, Holt always said, though Zack knew it needled him, too.

"I'm still working the Wilcox case. Send her on back to . . ." He cast his eyes around the station. Phil sat at his desk. An uneaten sandwich lay on his desk as he scrolled through news coverage on Isabel's disappearance, absentmindedly running his fingers through his gray hair. He didn't look busy, but then Zack was still wary of giving too much at once to Phil. He was a lifer, been on the force nearly as long as Holt, but he'd had a breakdown early last year after botching a heroin ring sting. He'd taken a six-month leave and was still getting his sea legs back. That left . . . "Evelyn."

"What was that about?" Holt asked as Zack set down the phone.

"Missing person. Husband on a hunting trip. Probably just lost track of time, or something."

They stood in the open door of the conference room, watching a middle-aged, pleasantly round blond woman in a yoga outfit make her way to Evelyn Skorczewski's desk. Her carefully applied makeup didn't disguise the fact that she had been crying. Zack felt a twinge of guilt about his callousness.

When Mrs. DeWitt reached Evelyn, she seemed to hesitate, a typical reaction when people came face-to-face with the latest officer to join the department. Nearly six feet tall, with a mound of platinum-blond curls, wide blue eyes caked with as much mascara and eyeliner as Holt would let her get away with, and curves that even a polyester uniform couldn't disguise, Evelyn was hardly a typical officer of the law. But Holt had hired her sight unseen based on her scores from the academy, as well as the recommendation of her first training officer, who promised that she'd never seen a recruit more committed to upholding the law than Evelyn.

All of which was true, though she didn't mention that Evelyn, a former beauty queen from Sitka, was a preacher's daughter, the only girl in a family of six brothers, and she could cuss like a trucker while quoting scripture in the same sentence. She was hell-bent on seeing as much action as she could, and she had chosen Jarvis because of its recent upticks in meth and heroin busts, as well as sex trafficking, porn, and illegal gambling.

"That's Danielle DeWitt," Holt said, as Evelyn invited the woman to take a seat. "I've known her husband for ages. Give you five-to-one that George is sleeping off a bender in the back of his truck in the Walmart parking lot."

"Come on, Holt, you know we aren't supposed to gamble on the citizen's time." Zack conveniently forgot that he'd just advanced a theory on the man's whereabouts not two minutes ago.

"Hmm. Okay, well, let's pick this up in ten. I've got to go see a man about a horse."

As the chief lumbered off toward the men's room, Zack decided to stretch his legs a bit, maybe eavesdrop on the new case. He patted the now-asleep Tubbs gently on the head, then ambled over until he stood a few yards away from Evelyn's desk, pretending to read the notices on the missing-persons board while Evelyn patiently offered up Kleenex to the sobbing wife.

"Was your husband in any disputes recently?" Evelyn was asking. "Anyone who might have had a beef with him?"

"Well . . . ," Mrs. DeWitt said, peering uncertainly at Evelyn's long, lacquered nails as the officer took notes. "I mean, sometimes I wonder if he's really going where he says he is. Like, he'll say he's going to the store for cigarettes, but he comes back an hour later and forgot to buy them. There've been calls to the house where, when I answer, the caller just hangs up."

As Zack listened to Evelyn interview an increasingly upset Danielle DeWitt, his gaze fell on a faded, curling notice that had been there ever since he'd first joined the force. Rose Gulliver, a leathery old crow of a woman who'd terrified him and his sister Brielle as children, chasing them down her front walk with a garden rake. After she'd disappeared, they'd found her basement crammed full of unopened merchandise from every department store in the state, most of it with the tags still on.

Zack touched the flyers, straightening a few, re-pinning one that had come loose. So many flyers . . . so many missing citizens. What was it with the town of Jarvis? There was no unifying thread, no hint of what had happened to them. Men, women, rich, poor, old, young, newcomers, and old-timers.

They were all just . . . gone.

SEVEN

I n the morning, with an entire day off ahead of her, Kim took a long look at Ethan's old scrub shirt, abandoned in a puddle on the floor, before deciding it was past saving and tossing it into the trash. Invigorated, she sorted through a couple of moving boxes she'd somehow never gotten around to opening and put together a respectable outfit. She took her time getting ready, shaving her legs and plucking her brows while she thought about her various obligations: to the hospital, to Kyle, to Scarlett. It seemed impossible to satisfy everyone.

But only Scarlett seemed defenseless against the things that were happening to her. Only Scarlett had asked Kim for nothing—except to be believed. But what possible explanation would Scarlett have for impersonating a missing girl? No, it was almost certain that Scarlett truly had alters inside of her. And one of them had latched on to this idea of Isabel, the missing girl, creating a grisly tale. To what end? Perhaps the idea of being *lost* was the connection—Scarlett seemed lost emotionally, so her alter focused on that physical reality, exploring the idea of being lost literally as well as psychically. . . .

Kim set down her hairbrush and stared at her reflection in the mirror. She'd irritated a lot of people in her life, infuriated several—

but she'd helped some, too. And she had a chance to help someone now. If no one else would believe that Scarlett's alters were real, Kim had to find a way to prove it, and help the girl reclaim her life as her own.

She'd barely convinced Kyle not to reassign Scarlett to Andrea Kaston, the other psych resident whom Kim shared an office with. He'd grudgingly agreed to let her continue talk therapy but made it clear that if there was one more incident like the one in his office, where she lost control and endangered herself or anyone else, Kim would no longer be allowed to treat the girl, even though Kim had repeated that the broken coffee table was the result of an accident. He also forbade her to prescribe any medications without consulting with him first, which was fine with Kim, because she wasn't convinced Scarlett needed to be medicated in the first place.

Kyle hadn't said anything about speaking with Scarlett outside their scheduled appointments, however; probably because he knew that *Kim* was aware that this was strictly off-limits. But at least this way she wouldn't be directly lying to him. Before she could change her mind, Kim called Scarlett and asked if she could come over. This was not something that Kim would ordinarily consider with a patient in her care, but her instincts told her that if she had any hope of helping Scarlett, she was going to need to work with her outside the confines of a clinical office.

On the drive over, Kim recorded an update to her case notes on her iPhone.

"Identity based on actual people rather than constructed from patient's own experience. Highly atypical. Strike that, make that unprecedented." She made a note to confirm that there were no other confirmed cases of an "invading" secondary identity, one based on an actual person unknown to the patient.

"If patient is manufacturing the alternates . . ." Kim forced herself to consider this angle and thought about the possibilities for a few moments before continuing. "Possible narcissistic personality disorder? Psychosis with delusions? Compensating for unknown trauma?"

A car horn blared, and a woman in an Explorer swerved and flipped her off. Kim realized she'd rolled through a stop sign. "Sorry, sorry, sorry," she mumbled, pantomiming a mea culpa at the angry driver. She needed to focus on her driving, but there was one more thought that she wanted to make note of for later, an unpleasant but necessary possibility to explore.

"Need to consider treatment bias and my own personal investment in outcome. Consider . . . reassigning the case."

It would be a blow for Kim to be removed from this case, but it could be catastrophic for Scarlett. The girl had a long history of not being believed, and though Kim considered all her colleagues competent, she knew that none of them had experience in alternate therapies of the type she was considering. And judging from the unfavorable reactions Kim had received from the review board, Jarvis Regional was not exactly eager to employ experimental treatments. All of which meant that if Scarlett were reassigned to Mackie or any of the other staff psychiatrists, she was probably going to be right back on the treadmill of misdiagnosis and ineffective and potentially harmful drugs.

She needed to do whatever she could to make sure that didn't happen. And that meant visiting Scarlett at home and getting to the bottom of what was really going on with her alters.

Kim arrived at the Hascalls' address, a nicely maintained trilevel with a big pot of geraniums out front. As she walked up the front steps, she heard shouting coming from the upstairs window.

"Stop it! Stop it!"

Kim couldn't tell if it was Scarlett's voice. She knocked on the door, but no one answered. Twisting the knob and finding it unlocked, Kim let herself into the house, heart pounding.

Inside, the voice was louder, accompanied by grunts and the sound of something thumping against a wall. Kim took the stairs two at a time, reaching the upper floor in time to see two girls struggling, through the open door of a bedroom. Scarlett was standing on a twin bed made up with a lime-green comforter, holding a doll high in the air while she tried to cut its head off with a pair of kitchen shears.

"Stop it, you crazy bitch!" the other girl yelled, making ineffective swipes at the doll. Scarlett jabbed at her with the scissors, narrowly missing stabbing her in the arm, and then returned her focus to the doll. She sliced through its neck, the head landing on the bedspread, where two other headless dolls lay, their plump stuffed bodies dressed in frilly costumes.

The other girl bent down and picked up one of the severed heads from the floor, sobbing and yelling. She was beautiful, dressed in a Jarvis High Cheer sweatshirt, with long, glossy straight hair and lovely features. Scarlett's younger sister, no doubt. Catching sight of Kim, she implored, "Please, make her stop!"

A man came running into the room, shoving Kim aside. He was wearing enormous leather gloves that came up over his forearms. He clambered onto the bed and grabbed Scarlett from behind. She let out a guttural shriek and stabbed at him, but the force of the blow was blunted by the thick leather. The man wrestled her down, grabbing the scissors as she toppled onto the floor, where she lay breathing heavily. Abruptly, Scarlett's demeanor changed. She went limp and then seemed to come to her senses, looking around the room in confusion and then dismay. Her features settled into despair, and she curled up into a fetal position.

"Oh, hell," the man said. He knelt beside Scarlett, removing the gloves and tossing them on the floor, and cautiously patted her shoulder. She pulled away from him, curling up more tightly. "Oh, Scarlett. Sweetheart."

"Daddy, she got all of them!" the younger girl wailed, and he got to his feet, obviously torn between his two daughters.

"I'm sorry, honey girl," he said, gathering Scarlett's sister into his arms. "I had to get the gloves or she could have hurt us." He surveyed the carnage of the ruined dolls, a dozen heads littering the floor. "I'll buy you new dolls, I promise. I'll replace them."

"You can't! Those were from Mom. Scarlett wrecks everything."

"Who the hell are you?" the man said, just now registering Kim's presence.

"I'm Scarlett's doctor."

He grimaced. "Dr. *Patterson*? From the hospital? Obviously you're not making much progress with my daughter."

"I'm doing my best, Mr. Hascall," Kim said, kneeling to examine Scarlett, who was lying still with her eyes closed. "What happened?"

"My sister's crazy, that's what happened," the girl said. "She's gone full-blown bunny-boiling psycho!"

"This is my younger daughter, Heather," Mr. Hascall said. "I don't know why Scarlett would . . ." His voice trailed off as he shook his head in dismay. "I mean, it's never been this bad before. I've never thought she'd actually hurt us."

"She wasn't trying to hurt me, Dad," Heather groaned. Kim's heart went out to her. Like so many siblings of mentally ill adolescents, Heather's feelings were probably deeply divided between loyalty and love for her sister and the longing for a "normal" life.

"Kim?" Scarlett mumbled, trying to sit up, blinking and running her hand through her tangled hair. "What are you doing here?"

"I believe one of your alters took over just now," Kim said as calmly as she could, trying to inject a note of clinical detachment into the situation. "What do you remember?"

"I was— I was brushing my teeth. Oh, shit. Shit." She picked up one of the doll heads, and her eyes went shiny with tears. "Did I do this? Oh, Heather, I'm so sorry, I'll—"

"Forget it!" Heather yelled, and ran out of the room. A few seconds later the front door slammed.

"She'll be all right," Mr. Hascall said heavily, helping Scarlett stand up. He gave her an awkward hug. "I'll clean this up, honey."

"I'm sorry, Dad," Scarlett said in a small voice, holding back tears. "I would never . . ."

"I know you don't mean it, honey. Why don't you two go on downstairs? There's still some coffee left, maybe you can fix a cup for Dr. Patterson."

"You can call me Kim." She looked around the room at the massacre, the headless dolls in their satin and lace. The violent episode could be explained by psychosis or another disorder, but the way that Scarlett had reacted when her father restrained her—as though a switch had been struck, instantly restoring her to normalcy—didn't line up. Unless it had been the behavior of an alter who retreated when challenged. It was the only theory that made sense, Kyle be damned. "Mr. Hascall, could I speak to you for just a moment?"

"That okay with you, honey?" Mr. Hascall asked his daughter. She shrugged morosely and headed down the stairs.

Once she was out of the room, Hascall's expression changed from anguished concern to hardened anger.

"Before you say anything, Doc, I want to make one thing perfectly clear. My daughters have been through hell. Both of them."

"I understand that. I know you want the best for Scarlett, and it must have been really frustrating not to receive a consistent diagnosis all this time."

"You have no idea," Hascall muttered. "I wouldn't wish what our family has been through on my worst enemy."

"I assure you, I'm committed to doing my best for Scarlett," Kim said.

"Yeah?" Anger flashed in the man's exhausted eyes. "How you

gonna do that? Forgive my skepticism, but you barely look old enough to have a medical degree. What makes you think you can make a difference when people with a lot more experience than you haven't been able to do a damn thing?"

Kim cast about for the words that might convince him. "I have— I really care about Scarlett," she finished lamely, earning a bark of derision.

"Well, it's just great that you care. But *caring* hasn't kept my daughter from getting suspended from school or kicked out of her extracurricular activities. It hasn't kept the neighbors from crossing the street when they see us coming. What we *don't* need is more false hope, because let me tell you, it's killing us." His voice broke with emotion, and he cleared his throat angrily. "So unless you really think you can make a difference—you can pack up your caring and concerned bullshit routine and get the hell out of my house."

Kim started to speak, then merely nodded. "I know this has to be hard on all of you," she said quietly. "But I have some ideas that are . . . that may not have been tried before. I just need you to give me a chance."

She held her breath for a long moment while Hascall seemed to deliberate with himself. Finally, he turned and stalked out of the room. "You've got one shot," he muttered over his shoulder.

Downstairs, Scarlett had set out mugs of coffee along with a pitcher of milk and a sugar bowl. They took their places around a scarred, but clean, oak table. Keenly aware of Scarlett's father's distrust, Kim launched directly into the speech she'd worked up on the way over.

"As I told you when we spoke on the phone a couple of days ago, I believe that Scarlett may have a condition called dissociative identity disorder. I didn't give you a full explanation of the condition then, and I would like to do so now."

Hascall gave her a terse nod.

"Sometimes, DID sufferers . . . they can find themselves at the mercy of one, or even several, alternate personalities, or 'alters.' You can think of these alters as fuses in a breaker box. When things in the mind get too difficult to process . . . *pop*, the mind blows a fuse to make life easier to handle. It's a protective response, really, not so different from many other things the body does when presented with a threat. We instinctively close our eyes when looking at the sun, for instance, or pull away from a burning flame. Only in this case, it's the mind that reacts to protect itself."

Scarlett dabbed at her eyes with a tissue. "I don't care what it is—I just need this crazy to stop!"

"You're not crazy, Scarlett," Kim said gently. "It's actually an extraordinarily effective response. Listen, the attack at the Burger Barn? What happened just now with the dolls? You just—blew a fuse."

"Great," Scarlett barked, dropping the wadded tissue on the table and reaching for another one. "So whenever I get stressed-out, I go ballistic? I can't live like this."

"You don't have to," Kim reassured her. "The better we understand your alters, the better you'll be able to control them."

"You don't get it!" Scarlett snapped. "I've done therapy. I've taken my meds. They don't work!"

Hascall, his face contorted with anguish, took his daughter's hand. She squeezed back hard. They shared a glance, a bit of Scarlett's defiance and fury abating, as though he was absorbing it.

Hascall turned to Kim. "I'm going to ask you again. What makes *you* better than the nine other doctors who promised to help my daughter?" he demanded.

Kim's heart broke for the gruff man in front of her who just wanted to help his daughter.

"When I was a little younger than Scarlett," she said quietly, "and . . . struggling, myself, hypnosis helped me. Although it's against hospital policy," she added quickly. She was walking a fine line, wanting to make it clear that she had to tread very, very carefully, or risk exposing the hospital to legal challenges and even lawsuits—and endangering her own career, as she had done once too often in the past. But at the same time, Kim couldn't turn away from a chance to offer Scarlett *real* help. "Which doesn't take away from the fact that it can be, in the right circumstances, very effective. That's why I'm here now to talk to you, instead of waiting for our next appointment . . ."

"Why is it against hospital policy?" Hascall asked. "I mean, is it even *real*? I don't believe in hypnosis."

"That's okay," Kim said, with all the conviction she could muster. "I do."

Scarlett looked from her father to Kim. "If it'll help, let's just do it. Please."

TWENTY MINUTES LATER, SCARLETT was lying on the sofa in the darkened living room, the drapes pulled tight. Hascall had given his grudging permission before leaving for work, but not before a terse admonition that Kim had better watch her step. "My girls mean the world to me," he'd muttered, and only the desperation in his eyes kept it from sounding like a threat. He'd wanted to stay behind, but his daughter had convinced him she'd be fine—and that he couldn't miss more work. Kim could see how close this family was to coming apart, and it only made her more determined to get to the bottom of Scarlett's condition. If the girl was faking the alters, hypnosis could expose the ruse.

Kim had guided Scarlett through some standard relaxation exercises, and now Scarlett was breathing deeply, her eyes closed, her hands folded on her stomach.

"In front of you is a dandelion," Kim said softly. "A white one, full of tiny seeds. So many seeds it looks like a perfect white circle. As you watch, the breeze lifts a seed away . . . and then another . . ."

She kept her volume soft and as steady as the flow of her words, employing a near monotone so as to lull Scarlett into ever-deeper relaxation.

"As the seeds drift away, they slowly reveal something. A single letter. Then another. And another. As the breeze carries the seeds away, a word is finally clear enough to read and . . . that . . . word . . . is . . . *sleep*."

As Kim pronounced the final word, Scarlett's head sank a little, and she gave a tiny sigh.

"Scarlett," Kim said calmly. "You find yourself in an empty room. It's a safe place. Nothing can harm you here. There are several doors on the walls, and as you slowly turn, you can see that each one is closed. They won't open without your invitation. There is no reason to be afraid. Can you nod, please, if you understand?"

After a moment, Scarlett nodded faintly.

"Good. Now, I'd like you to step away for a while so I can chat with the young lady I met before. Isabel. Izzi. When you're ready, the door will open and Izzi will come through, and you can simply rest while I talk to her."

Scarlett moaned softly and shook her head, all the while her eyes remaining closed. Then, suddenly, her face twitched violently. She lifted her head, eyes flying open and scanning the room frantically before settling on Kim. She looked terrified.

"Hi," Kim said soothingly. "I'm Scarlett's friend, Kim. Is that you, Isabel?"

Scarlett's lip trembled and she made a tiny mewling sound. It took her a couple of attempts before she could speak, her voice childlike and small.

"Isabel isn't here right now. I'm Henry."

"Nice to meet you, Henry," Kim said, keeping the surprise out of her voice. "How old are you?"

"I'm . . . five."

"*Wow*. Five years old. And you're being very brave, aren't you? Just like a grown-up."

Tears ran down "Henry's" cheeks. "Grown-ups don't get afraid," he snuffled.

"What are you afraid of, Henry?"

"I'm afraid of the dark. It's dark here. And cold." Kim could see that Scarlett's skin was breaking out in goose bumps, even though the air in the family room was warm and comfortable.

"Where are you, Henry?"

"In the spaceship. I can't get out!"

Scarlett started breathing more heavily, almost hyperventilating, rubbing her eyes with her fists. Kim cautiously reached for her, but when she touched Scarlett's knee, her face suddenly turned cold and serious, the Henry alter vanishing instantly. Scarlett slapped Kim's hand away, the contact hard and vicious.

Kim forced a reassuring smile, withdrawing her hand. "And . . . what's *your* name?"

Scarlett's face, contorting in sly anger, glared back. Kim had to resist recoiling from the sudden shift in her mien: her eyes were shadowed and suspicious, her lips curled in a scowl.

"I'm Dr. Patterson," she tried. "I'm a friend—"

"You're a liar. Like the others. Pushing scripts to keep that whiny bitch in her place."

Kim leaned in, moving slowly so as not to provoke the alter. "You seem angry . . . what is your name?"

"Julian."

"Are you the one who cut the heads off those dolls, Julian? Did you hit Scarlett's boss with the fry basket?"

Scarlett laughed mirthlessly. "Well, it sure as shit wasn't Scarlett, was it? Anyway, what are *you* going to do about it? I could kill her anytime I want—just like that." She snapped her fingers.

Kim tamped down the anger building inside her and leaned in even closer. She needed to let him know that he couldn't intimidate her. "Okay, Julian," she said coldly, "listen to me right now. You don't control Scarlett, because she's stronger than you. Because you're nothing without her. Do you understand me? So why don't you go hide and let me talk to Isabel."

"You bitch, you're *nothing*—" Julian's words came out garbled, which seemed only to incense him further. "I *am* strong—"

"Go away now," Kim cut him off decisively. "I want to speak to Isabel. *Now.*"

Scarlett's face twitched again, and her body trembled, fear etched across her face. Her hands clawed at air as she twisted back and forth.

"Isabel . . . ?" Kim tried. "Izzi?"

"I—I can't breathe." Scarlett's voice came out odd, almost as if she had liquid in her lungs.

"I'm here to help you."

"You . . . can't . . . I'm . . . dead."

Kim wanted to recoil from the burbling, wet, unnatural sound of Scarlett's voice, but she forced herself to look Izzi in Scarlett's eyes.

"You're not dead . . . Julian, is that you again? Are you trying to scare me? Because you can't. You aren't Izzi. Come on, I know you're not."

For a moment they were locked in a staring contest, Scarlett's eyes cloudy and confused. Then, without warning, she shot out her hand and grabbed Kim's cell phone off the coffee table. Startled, Kim allowed her to take it, curious to see what the alter would do.

Scarlett stabbed at the screen with shaking fingers, gulping as though she couldn't get enough air. Her fingertip brushed against the speaker icon, but instead of the sound of ringing, voice mail picked up immediately.

"Hey!" The voice was bright and flirty. "It's Izzi. Leave me a message. If you wanna buzz in my jeans."

"Julian, I know it's you," Kim said, keeping her tone firm to belie her own uncertainty. "You're not going to scare me by impersonating Isabel Wilcox. Anybody could have found that number."

Scarlett's breathing grew increasingly labored, a faint, rasping gurgle seeming to come from deep in her lungs, as she dialed a second number. It rang, once, twice, before a weary male voice answered:

"Wilcox residence."

Scarlett gripped the phone tightly with both hands, shaking violently now. "Daddy . . . help . . . me."

"What?" The man's voice roared through the phone. "Who is this? What the hell do you—"

Kim snatched the phone out of the girl's hands and hung up, then dropped the phone in horror. She stared at Scarlett, seeing her face rippling with emotion, her eyes rolling up in their sockets.

"Come get me," Scarlett moaned. "I'm in the bay . . ."

"It's—it's time to wake up, Scarlett," she finally said, voice shaking. "I'm going to count down from five. With each and every count, you will wake up a little more. Five . . . four . . ."

Scarlett began to shake violently, grabbing her head as if in terrible pain. Kim watched, stunned, as a trickle of bloody water gurgled from her mouth and trailed down her chin and neck.

"Three . . . two . . ." she managed, swallowing hard. She had to regain her composure, for Scarlett's sake. But the trickle turned to a gush, a steady flow of bloody water pouring from her mouth and splashing onto her shirt and the sofa.

". . . One."

Scarlett gave one last convulsive shudder, and went slack.

EIGHT

"Honey, you're making me a little nauseated. I don't suppose there's any chance I could get you to sit still while we talk?"

Kim plopped back in her chair and studied the screen, where her father's kind, familiar face smiled a little blurrily at her through the FaceTime session. "Sorry, Dad. It's just, I do my best thinking when I'm on my feet."

"Don't I know it," Roger Patterson chuckled. "Remember when you were fourteen, and we used to practice for the spelling bee while jogging around the block?"

Kim gave a small smile. Those had been maddening afternoons—maddening and also wonderful. Her father would offer up word after impossible word, then treat Kim to long, meandering definitions that dipped into many other disciplines, ignoring her pleas that all she had to know was how to spell the word, not every detail of its usage and etymology.

It was Roger Patterson who'd instilled intellectual curiosity in Kim, and that was one of only a thousand reasons she was missing him. But right now, she needed her father's professional counsel more than she needed one of their leisurely conversations, so she swallowed down her homesickness and focused on the subject they'd been discussing.

"Anyway, I wish you could've seen it, Dad. It was like something out of *The Exorcist*."

"Honey..."

"Sorry, I know how you feel about that movie." Roger Patterson was a theology professor with a strong disdain for what he considered the entertainment industry's grossly inaccurate portrayal of most religions. "But her voice . . . it sounded like she was underwater, and then she spit up this—this—*liquid*—"

"It may interest you to know that in *The Exorcist*, they used pea soup."

"No kidding? That's disgusting. No, this was like . . . bloody water."

Roger looked intrigued, twirling his reading glasses by the stem. He was in his book-lined office in the house where Kim had lived for much of her childhood. Behind him, Kim could see the familiar artifacts from her parents' travels sitting on the shelves between volumes.

"Was it *real* bloody water or merely 'like' bloody water?"

"Damn. Good question," Kim said. "I should've taken a sample and gotten it tested. Didn't think of it at the time."

"You were spooked. Besides, real or not, even 'testing' can't explain—"

"—*all of life's mysteries*. I know, I know. But, Dad, I called for advice, not a theology lecture. I mean, medically speaking, it could be anything. Bronchitis. Pneumonia. A pulmonary embolism. Tuberculosis. Dieulafoy's disease. Microscopic polyangiitis—"

Her dad held up a hand. "I'm sorry I asked. But listen, what's with the fancy outfit? Do you have a date tonight?"

Kim looked down ruefully at herself. "It's not a good sign if putting a shirt on that didn't come from the hospital supply catalog qualifies for a special occasion. But no, for your information, I don't have a date tonight. And don't change the subject. What I still can't explain is why one of her alters claims to be this missing girl, Isabel Wilcox. Unless . . . unless, God forbid, this Julian alternate personality actually *did* something to Isabel . . ."

"Or maybe your patient isn't split," he said pensively. "Maybe she *is* actually channeling the dead girl's thoughts."

Truthfully, this wasn't the first time that idea had occurred to Kim. But it was so discordant with the way her medical colleagues thought, she'd instantly banished the notion every time it had appeared before. There was something satisfying about her father, a highly educated man, giving voice to the crazy theory. "But Isabel isn't necessarily dead. She's just missing."

"Ah, yes. So you said." Her father swiveled around in his chair and looked up at his collection of books, pondering. "Still . . . there have been recorded examples in many cultures of superhuman behavior in response to acute emotional duress. Communication with the dead is just one example. As humans we lean too heavily on *a priori* thinking when we encounter something unfamiliar, something that exceeds the boundaries of our experience."

Hearing a knock at the door, Kim twisted away from the screen. "Hang on, Dad. I'm going to answer the door." She opened it, and there was Kyle, dressed in a sport coat and pressed shirt, gold cuff links glinting at his wrists.

She gave him what she hoped was a bright smile. "Hi! Listen, I'm talking to my dad on FaceTime—do you mind? I'll just be a few minutes."

Kyle wandered over to the sofa, picking up a magazine from the coffee table. If he was annoyed, he didn't show it. Always considerate, that was Kyle.

"I'm back, Dad."

"Hear me out. There are cases, fully documented, of people speaking to the spirit world. And not just fortune-tellers—there've been spiritual leaders, respected shamans, even Thomas Edison tried to develop a device to communicate with the dead. If you give me a day or two, I'll have more to tell you."

Kim glanced at Kyle and made a *cuckoo* gesture, twirling her index finger at her ear. "My father. Early-stage dementia. You'll have to forgive him."

"Hey, I heard that," Roger chided.

"You know I'm kidding! Listen, I got to go. I'll call you later. Love you, 'bye," Kim said.

"So that young man is the reason you're not in scrubs for once?" her dad asked.

Kim clicked the button to end the session, and her father disappeared from the screen. Kyle gave her a searching look.

"Before you say anything," Kim said hastily, "he's a professor at Harvard seminary, not some crazy quack."

Kim went to sit next to Kyle on the couch. She put her arms around him and kissed him hello, then pulled away, sensing that something was on his mind.

"Hey . . . did something happen with Scarlett today?" he asked.

"What? Um, no, why?"

Kyle frowned. "I wasn't eavesdropping, but it was pretty clear that you and your dad were talking about the case."

"Oh, come on, what you heard—"

"I'm not talking about the specifics of your conversation with your father, which are none of my business. But Scarlett Hascall *is* my business. And I know for a fact you didn't have an appointment with her today. Kim . . . if you were in contact with her outside the course of treatment, it raises all kinds of questions for me. Questions we ought to deal with now before it becomes a bigger problem."

Kim hesitated. The last person she wanted to lie to was Kyle, and not just because he was her boss. But telling him the truth now could have repercussions for both her personal *and* professional lives.

"Okay, okay, I just . . . need some time to put my thoughts together on her case. I'll come to you when I'm ready . . . okay?" Before he could respond, she kissed him again. This time, she made sure that he'd lose track of what they'd been talking about.

NINE

The building didn't look like much on the outside. A faded sign stenciled on the window still read PUPS 'N' STUFF, and the paper peeling from the windows gave a glimpse into a dusty retail space with a few grimy plastic kennels in the corner. It would have been easy for Zack to miss the separate door leading down to the building's basement, if he hadn't pried the information out of Cherise with cash from the department's discretionary fund. Two hundred dollars was only a fraction of what she'd once made for a few hours' time in that very basement, but as she confided tearfully to Zack, she was no longer sure she was cut out for that life anyway.

Cherise had explained that filming generally took place in the morning, so it was a little too early in the day for Zack to use his standard pizza-delivery-guy cover. Instead, he paid a visit to the municipal plant, where a friend from high school worked on the maintenance crew. The friend had been happy to loan him one of the town's orange vests and hats and a clipboard marked with the town logo. Zack put on the vest before returning to the old pet store and rapping on the door. As he heard footsteps approaching on the other side, he wondered if it was too much to ask that Brad Chaplin would be on the other side. But when the door opened, it was a skinny young guy with an overgrown beard and ear gauges that hung down almost to his shoulders, Zack offered a quick glimpse of the fake ID card he'd created in Photoshop.

"Sewer issue," he said. "Gotta take a quick look at the main down here. Doughnut shop up the street's got six inches of sewage on the floor—hate to have that happen to you guys."

The bearded guy looked over his shoulder nervously. "Yeah, well, it's not really a good time."

"Ha. It's never a good time for a foot of raw sewage," Zack said good-naturedly as he started to push past the guy.

"Listen. We're doing a fashion shoot. Paying these models by the hour. You know?" The man was standing firm.

"Oh, sure. I mean, it won't take long, I just need to clear you and I can be on my way. I can find the shutoff, you don't even have to come with me, Mr. . . . ?"

"Olsen," the man responded, then looked as though he wished he hadn't. "I don't know," he added hurriedly, glancing over his shoulder. "How about you talk to the building manager and come back when he can let you in. I'm paying for the space by the hour and I need to finish up this session. I really can't deal with delays today."

"Huh," Zack said, crinkling his nose as if sniffing the air. "Is that . . . oh hell, yeah, that's how it starts. I hope you don't have a lot of money invested in your equipment. You could have sewage up to your ankles so fast you won't have time to get to the electrical. And you better tell your models to get out of there unless you want to watch 'em light up like Christmas trees."

"What? I don't smell anything," the guy said, but he looked nervously down the hall.

"Tell you what: I'll check it out down there; you turn off the main."

Zack made a beeline for the stairs, taking them two at a time. Olsen followed, hot on his heels.

"Hey, I don't know where the fuse box— Hey!"

"Oh, whoops!" Zack said in mock surprise as he threw open the door and stepped into a room lit with a dozen pink-toned bulbs. Lounging on a leopard-print throw on an enormous bed in the center of the room were three girls in various states of undress, all of them engrossed in their phones. When they noticed Zack, two of them grabbed for robes and hastily covered up. The third was hampered by the rope that bound both of her legs and one wrist to the bedposts, but she managed to use her free hand to pull a sheet up over herself.

"This is off-limits," Olsen sputtered, rushing around the room picking up a variety of sexual accoutrements. Feathers, canes, clamps, candles all went flying. "And there's no sewage here!"

"Yeah, that," Zack sighed, pulling out his badge. "Unfortunately I moonlight as a cop, and I'm afraid I'm going to have to let someone know about the working conditions down here. I mean . . ." He toed an enormous fuchsia dildo that had rolled off the bed and clattered to the floor. "This looks downright unsanitary."

"Motherfucker," Olsen said in disgust, while one of the girls worked to untie her colleague and the other stuffed her belongings into an oversize handbag.

"Tell you what," Zack said to Olsen after glancing at the table behind him. "Why don't you head down to the doughnut shop for an hour or so. I was just kidding about the sewage thing. Have some coffee and give me a chance to talk to the, uh, models and I'll see if I can figure out a way to clear this whole thing up." He figured the girls might be more talkative without their "boss" present.

The guy was gone instantly, the metal stairs ringing with the sound of his retreating feet, never noticing that Zack had grabbed his wallet from where it sat on a nearby table—complete with Olsen's ID. Timothy Olsen, 14 Seaview Lane. Born in '95. Eyes: blue.

Hair: brown. Zack would be paying the young man a visit a little later, right after he got a search warrant for 14 Seaview Lane.

"What the hell is wrong with you?" one of the girls demanded. "You can't just come in here like this, it's private property."

Zack studied a display of DVD cases on a table, arranged in orderly stacks. It looked like the videos produced in this basement would only be sold on disc, never streamed, to limit their traceability. The titles on the spines seemed to follow a specific theme: *Teen Slut Lesbo Orgy*, *Pop Her Teen Cherry*, *Barely Legal Ass Parade*.

"Don't worry, I'm not here to make trouble for any of you." Zack continued down the stacks, noting variations in kink and tone, though all the DVDs featured young women until he reached the last stack, which, unlike the others, had been stored in a black plastic case. He lifted the lid and examined the DVD on top, which featured a naked, frightened-looking little girl who couldn't have been older than ten or eleven. Zack swallowed down his revulsion and turned the case over, reading the lurid description on the back.

Zack regretted letting Tim skate so quickly, but now that search warrant would be an easy get. He was going to enjoy locking the scumbag away.

"We don't have anything to do with that shit," one of the girls said forcefully. "We're all legal."

"What do you know about this?" Zack said, going down the stack, noticing the ages of the children were going down, as well. Zack worked hard to shut down his emotions; the fury the images elicited in him would only cloud his judgment and interfere with his ability to go after the source of this evil. He forced himself to keep his tone even. "Were these filmed here in Jarvis?"

The girls glanced at one another. "No," one said, at the same time one of the others said, "I don't think so."

Zack examined several more of the cases from the last stack, confirming that an entire sideline of child pornography was being offered for sale. He didn't recognize any of the young girls' faces. Many looked to be Native American Alaskans, probably residing in villages outside the reach of his law enforcement. While Alaska was one of the more beautiful places in the world, it also happened to have one of the highest incidents of sex crimes. There was one sex offender for every three-hundred-odd people, compared to almost twice that for the national average—and the child sexual assault average was six times the national average.

"Go ahead and get dressed," Zack said. "I have just a few more questions for you."

They did so quickly and silently, the atmosphere in the room charged with tension. Zack took a seat in the only chair in the room, pointedly looking the other way while they toweled off their heavy makeup and pulled on their clothes. Finally, when they were lined up on the edge of the bed in their jeans and sweatshirts and sneakers, Zack turned around to face what looked like three ordinary college girls.

"This is about Izzi, isn't it?" the redhead said.

"What makes you say that?" Zack asked.

The girl who'd been tied up, a skinny blonde with a tattoo of a heart on her wrist, blinked rapidly. "I mean, everyone has been saying that she's probably dead by now."

"Who's 'everyone'?"

This brought him nothing but silence. A knock came at the top of the stairs, three blows in quick succession, a pause, and three more.

"Let me guess," Zack said. "Secret password?"

"It's just a customer," the redhead offered. "Don't answer, he'll go away."

"Maybe he'll be more interested in having a conversation with me," Zack said, walking up the stairs and putting his ear to the door. "Yeah?"

"'A stately pleasure-dome decree,'" a muffled voice said.

Zack recognized the line from Coleridge, raising an eyebrow and adjusting his opinion of the operation's ringleader, who was apparently capable of a literary reference. If he wasn't mistaken, the work in question had been written under the influence of opium, which dovetailed nicely with Brad Chaplin's other enterprises. Zack opened the door and found himself face-to-face with a stooped old man in a greasy fishing hat and an ancient yellow Members Only jacket.

"Isn't that from 'Kubla Kahn'?"

The man looked at Zack in confusion. "Where's Tim?"

"Tim had to step out, but I'm sure I can help you," Zack said, taking the man's arm and propelling him down into the basement. The man walked slowly, with a pronounced limp, one leg dragging behind the other. "What can we do for you today?"

The man looked past him at the girls, then back to Zack, putting two and two together. "I think I made a mistake. I'm looking for the . . . rehab facility. I have a physical therapy appointment."

The redhead rolled her eyes as the man tried to sell the lie with a crooked smile that revealed one tooth that was trying to escape from his mouth, curled up and poking into his lip.

"I have to go," the old man said, edging back toward the door. Each step seemed to hurt him; his bad leg came down hard, causing him what seemed like shuddering pain.

"Hang on, what's the rush?" Zack said. He couldn't detain the man without a reason, and it looked like he was smart enough not to give Zack one.

"Physical therapy," he muttered again, letting the door slam behind him.

"Creep," the redhead called after him.

Zack stared at the door where the man had exited, wondering just how many local men frequented this basement. Then he refocused on the girls. "Was Izzi involved in these?" Zack asked, returning the cases to the black box.

"Hell no. That's Tim's side gig. Izzi hated it. She wanted him to drop it."

"She just does the recruiting," the redhead said.

"Right," Zack added. "For the . . . artistic videos that you shoot." Zack took a deep breath and went back at them. "Do any of you know who that gentleman was?"

"Albert," the third girl said. She had been silent until now, hiding under a huge fringe of green-dyed bangs, hugging herself with skinny arms. "Albert Sullivan."

"You know him?" Zack said.

"He lives in the neighborhood where I grew up," the girl mumbled. "All us kids used to be afraid of him."

"Afraid of him? Why?"

"He was mean." The girl looked like she was on the verge of tears. "He used to yell at us if we rode our bikes down the sidewalk. We called him Peg Leg . . . like a pirate?"

"Did he ever . . . ?"

"He didn't try anything with us," the girl said quickly. "It's not that. I just didn't want him to recognize me, you know?"

Zack figured he did know. These girls were young and inexperienced enough to be caught on the fine line between innocence and dangerous exploitation, but they weren't bad kids. He felt a fresh rush of anger at Isabel Wilcox for involving them in this, but he forced himself to reserve his judgment for when he got to the source, the man responsible for setting up the whole ugly enterprise.

Zack turned his attention back to the girls. "So, let me guess," he sighed. "You three used to go to JCC, right? Met Izzi there?"

"How did you know?" the blonde asked.

"Shut up, Destiny," the redhead said. "You don't have to tell him anything."

"Come on, ladies, all I'm doing today is trying to find Izzi Wilcox. I'm not arresting any of you. But anything you can tell me about her could help. Like, for instance, how did she get you down here? Did she offer you drugs? Coerce you by force? Blackmail?"

The redhead blinked slowly and regarded him as if he was stupid. "Uh, no, all she did was offer us money. Five-hundred-dollar bonus up front."

"I used to make ten dollars an hour working as a babysitter," Destiny said. "I couldn't pay my rent on that. I didn't want to ask my parents for help again."

"Izzi was nice." The girl with green bangs sighed. "She did my nails once."

"We used to talk about classes sometimes. We were both marketing majors," Destiny said.

"Sometimes she brought muffins."

Zack asked them a few more questions about the operation, Isabel, who was in charge, but the girls didn't seem to know anything else useful. Apparently Izzi had just set up schedules for them, and they showed up, did what Tim told them to do, and got paid—simple as that. He made a point of getting their names and numbers in case he needed to follow up, and gave them all his card. "Please let me know if you think of anything at all that could help us find her, okay? And I don't need to tell you that I don't want to find you back down here, right?"

Three heads bobbed in affirmation.

"And look, I'm going to be . . . following up with Tim. There's a limit to my generosity. If you're smart, you'll forget you ever came here. Do you understand?"

"Yeah," Destiny said. "Thanks." Zack caught sight of a tear silently sliding down her fresh-scrubbed face, and quickly looked away.

AFTER THE GIRLS BEAT a hasty exit, Zack called for backup to process the basement and collect the evidence they'd need to lock up Olsen, and to see whether there was anything on file about Albert Sullivan. Evelyn called back almost immediately with the unsurprising news that Sullivan had quite a few complaints on record, charges that never stuck . . . plenty of people accusing him of lewd or suspicious behavior, but never anything that would hold up. Unfortunately, there were no known personal connections between the old man and Isabel Wilcox, although she and her boyfriend, Brad, were apparently Albert's supplier for all things pornographic.

As far as solving Izzi's murder, Albert Sullivan was most likely a dead end.

The evidence techs arrived on scene, and Zack was on his way up the stairs when his phone rang. He stopped mid-flight and squinted at the screen. Holt.

"Where are you?" Holt demanded almost before Zack could get in a hello. "I need you to meet me at the Hascalls'."

"What's going on?" Zack said, instantly on alert.

"Might be nothing. Got a couple of calls from neighbors who saw Scarlett wandering around on the street this morning. One old lady said she looked like she was in a daze, like she'd been out all night."

"Old lady, huh," Zack said. The problem with some of the elderly citizens who called in was that their reports were often unreliable, details conjured from their fears and poor vision rather than reality.

"Yeah, I know. But we had another report that she walked right in front of a car, nearly got herself killed—and that caller said she was wearing a hot-pink sweatshirt. Just like the girl the witnesses saw breaking into Brad Chaplin's place."

"Hang on," Zack said. "What break-in? I've been down in a basement for the last hour."

Holt quickly filled him in. "Chaplin's apartment got broken into last night. He came in this morning to file a complaint. He says it was Scarlett Hascall."

Zack's mind raced, trying to process this new information. As far as he knew, there was no established connection between Chaplin and Scarlett. "How does he know her?"

"That's what we're trying to find out. He says she came at him. Smashed up some stuff, tried to beat the crap out of him, then just took off. I'm about three minutes away from the Hascall place—how fast can you get there?"

"Gimme ten," Zack said and hung up, sprinting up the rest of the stairs.

He made it in eight. He could see Holt's flashers going from two blocks away; he spotted the motley collection of lookie-loos in front of the house seconds later. He tapped the siren to get the crowd to move back so he could park behind Holt's SUV, but the oglers quickly closed in again.

"Step back, step back," he yelled as he jogged for the front door. Someone grabbed his arm, and he instinctively spun into a ready stance, one arm blocking any potential attack, the other on his gun, when he recognized Brad Chaplin.

"She's gonna run," Brad yelled, apparently undaunted by the fact that Zack was poised to draw his weapon. "You need to lock her up!"

The front door flew open and Scarlett came tearing out, hair flying, too-long sleeves flapping over her wrists. Zack shot out a hand and grabbed a fistful of pink sweatshirt; the girl tripped over her own feet and went down like a bag of bricks.

Holt came lumbering out of the house, his face flushed, Peter Hascall on his heels.

"I told you," Brad Chaplin said disgustedly. "Told the chief, too, but he wouldn't get off his fat ass and do anything about it."

"Watch your mouth, boy," Holt said. "One more outburst from

you and you can spend the rest of the day as a guest of the town, scrubbing out the bathrooms with a toothbrush."

Zack stifled a grin, having suffered the same threat from Holt during his own teenage years. He bent down and offered Scarlett a hand, holding tightly so she couldn't wrestle out of his grip. "Convince me you're not going to run again, or I'm putting the cuffs on you."

"Whatever," Scarlett mumbled. It looked like only her pride was injured, but Zack didn't miss the way she tried to evade the gawking neighbors by edging behind him.

"Tell you what, how about we talk inside," he suggested, doing his best to ignore his feelings of sympathy and concern for the scrawny teen, who looked more mortified than dangerous.

"Haven't you bothered us enough for one day?" Peter Hascall asked angrily. He was breathing as heavily as Holt, but from fear and anger. "If you want to pick on someone, how about that thug standing on my lawn?"

Brad cursed under his breath and kicked at the matted grass, as another cruiser rolled up to the house, and two more officers got out. Holt motioned to them to deal with the onlookers, and within moments the crowd had dispersed, leaving just Brad and the Hascalls.

"Take her inside," Holt told Peter. "We'll be in momentarily. Scarlett, we're not finished here, you understand me?"

"She isn't—" Peter began.

"Enough, Peter," Holt said firmly. "Come on, now. You know I'm right—let us do this by the books, and if everything Scarlett says checks out, she doesn't have anything to worry about."

Hascall didn't look convinced, and he gave Brad a murderous look before ushering his daughter into the house.

"I told you we'd handle this," Holt said, folding his arms over his chest. "So I'd like to know exactly what business you've got coming over here."

"That crazy bitch tried to kill me!" Brad said, his voice taking on a distinctly whiny tone.

"So you said, already. Head home, and we'll call you if we need you."

"I'm not leaving until I'm sure you're going to *arrest* her," Brad sputtered.

"I think you're under the mistaken impression that your opinion matters," Zack said, stepping between Chaplin and the chief. "If you behave, you can wait on the other side of the street like everyone else. Otherwise . . ." He let his words hang.

Brad wavered for a moment before giving up and trudging away from the house.

"Thanks," Holt said. "That one's like a gnat. Annoying, but almost impossible to smack down."

"So what's Scarlett's story?"

Holt shrugged. "She isn't exactly denying that she left the house this morning, but now she's claiming she doesn't remember any of it. Tell you what—how about you give it a try with her? Maybe you can get her to open up."

Zack led the way into the house. The scent of coffee and cinnamon wafted in from the kitchen, where Scarlett was huddled on a kitchen chair with a blanket wrapped around her shoulders, rocking rhythmically with her eyes closed as her father made a fresh pot of coffee. Zack sat down cautiously across from her while Holt retreated to lean against the kitchen counter.

"Scarlett," Zack said softly, not wanting to spook her.

Her eyes fluttered open, and she gazed up at him with eyes wide with fear. "I don't understand," she whispered.

"What don't you understand?"

"What's happening to me. I don't know what's happening to me." She buried her face in her hands, and Zack wondered if she was playing him. If so, she was a hell of an actor. Her thin frame trembled with the force of her sobs.

"What do you think is happening to you, Scarlett?"

"I don't know!" she said in a strangled voice. She looked at him through a tangle of overgrown hair. "It's like—it's like something has taken over my mind. And not just my mind, but . . . I mean, if I'm doing things I can't remember all the time, it's like it has control of my body, too, you know?"

Zack shook his head, resisting the pull of sympathy for the distraught girl. Something wasn't right here.

"She was asleep at eleven last night," Hascall said tensely. "In her bed."

Zack registered the fear and exhaustion in the man's eyes. He was clearly worried about his daughter. Worried enough to lie to give her an alibi?

"Pete, I hate to do this now, but I gotta ask you some questions." Holt clapped a meaty hand to the other man's shoulder. "Do you know why Scarlett would go over to Brad Chaplin's? She busted up his place pretty bad, plus he's saying she attacked him—though it doesn't appear she did all that much damage."

Hascall stared into his coffee cup. "No," he said after a moment. "She wouldn't do that."

Holt clucked sympathetically but left his hand where it was. "We have multiple witnesses saying they saw a girl of her description in his neighborhood in the early hours of the morning."

Hascall shook his head, his face drained of color. "She . . . I don't know. She's been getting worse. This new doctor claims she's got—" He glanced at his daughter, and stopped himself. "That she's got some sort of multiple personalities, that some of 'em could have violent tendencies. But I don't think . . . Besides, she was home all night."

He wiped a hand across his brow, shaking his head. Holt squeezed his shoulder supportively. "You let us deal with Chaplin. We just have to ask Scarlett a few questions, and then we'll have to wait to see if Chaplin presses charges. Zack, now that things are under control here, why don't you go take a crack at Chaplin. Get him talking, see if you can sort him out."

Zack looked from Holt to Hascall. Evidently the chief felt they weren't going to get anything further out of Scarlett, and Zack had to admit that Holt was doing a better job of keeping Hascall's temper under control than he could. "Got it."

Brad was nowhere to be seen among the dwindling crowd. Zack made a few inquiries, but no one seemed to know where he went. He was climbing into his car to drive to Brad's apartment when Holt came out of the house. "Hang on a sec, son," he called.

Zack rested his arm on the driver's-side window and waited for Holt to walk over and duck down to his window.

"Let me know what Chaplin has to say," he said. "If I were you, I'd encourage him to drop this."

"How long you and Pete Hascall been friends?" Zack probed, already knowing the answer. "Any chance you're letting that cloud your judgment?"

Holt laughed. "Hell, I'm friends with just about eighty percent of the folks in this town," he said. "And the rest of 'em either just moved here, or they've got good reason not to like me. But don't worry, I won't go easy on the girl because of that. It's just that Brad . . . well, some people just have it coming. Don't know many young men more in need of a beating." Holt shrugged. "Oh, and hey, I forgot to tell you . . . guess who called me this morning to let me know he was getting crank calls and what was I going to do about it?"

Zack raised his eyebrows. "No idea . . ."

"Don Wilcox. Isabel Wilcox's dad." Holt paused for a moment to let that sink in. "So I looked up the number. Guess who called over there and got him all riled up, pretending to be Izzi, begging him to come help her?"

Uneasiness spread through Zack. "Who?"

"The good doctor," Holt said, leaning down so he could look Zack square in the face. "None other than Dr. Kim Patterson herself."

Interesting. One more unexpected turn in the very twisted path that this case was taking. "Okay, I'll go talk to her about that later today. And I'll have Evelyn pull her call records," Zack said, putting the car in drive. "Right now I want to go finish up with our boy. Can't have him sulking because he got his feelings hurt."

———

CHAPLIN LIVED IN A nondescript town house with a dead potted plant on the porch. Zack peered through the screen door and found Chaplin sitting in a large leather recliner watching a daytime talk show and drinking a Red Bull.

"Nice place you have here," Zack commented, noting that the only furniture other than the recliner and a cheap pressboard media stand was a dinette set, a worn couch, and a coffee table. If Chaplin was turning a healthy profit from his various enterprises, he wasn't spending it on home decor.

"Fuck off," Chaplin muttered, long red scratches running the length of his neck. His lip was swollen and a purple bruise was blooming over his left eye.

Zack snorted and opened the door a crack. "Got beat up by a teenage girl? Come on, Chaplin, you can do better than that. Maybe we could start with people you might have come in contact with through your *business*." He put extra emphasis on the last word, to make it clear he wasn't talking about the docks.

For the next ten minutes, he came at Chaplin from every angle he could think of, trying to convince him to reveal something about his porn-distribution ring, anything that could give some leads about Isabel, but Chaplin clammed up and resorted to one-syllable responses interspersed with moaning about the pain he was in, until Zack couldn't take it anymore.

"So you're sticking to your story—you're saying this girl, who you've got at least six inches and fifty pounds on, came over here and beat the shit out of you for no reason at all."

Brad glared at him for a long moment, and Zack knew there was something he was holding back.

"She must have had a reason," he tried. "What was it, Brad? You stiff her on a drug buy? Tried to force her to join your little porn circus? Come on, what was it?"

"It wasn't anything like that," Brad muttered.

Bingo. Zack knew he was close, and shifted his tone to suggest he was more sympathetic to Brad's situation. "Look, I know she's unstable," he said. "I've seen a lot of messed-up, freaky chicks in my time, and that one . . ." He tapped his forehead.

"It was just one time," Brad said. "And I didn't realize what she was like. She came on strong, you know? It was, like, zero to sixty with her. One minute it's 'Hi, how you doing,' and the next minute she's got her hand down my pants."

Zack raised his eyebrows. "You're saying . . . you *slept* with Scarlett Hascall?"

"One time," Chaplin repeated. "And it was a long time ago."

"She's nineteen. A long time ago, like before she was legal?"

"Naw, just after that." Brad avoided eye contact, placing the Red Bull against his swollen eye.

Zack realized that he was going to lose Brad if he continued down this road. He forced a smile. "Okay, so a while back, you and Scarlett hook up. And, what, she finds out about your . . . 'relationship' with Cherise and Starlatta?"

Chaplin was already shaking his head. "It wasn't some jealous ex-girlfriend rage thing. I've never seen a girl get like this. She didn't seem . . . like *herself* at all. And the most fucked-up thing was, she went psycho when I wouldn't call her Izzi." He shook his head, a look of genuine disgust on his face. "*Isabel Wilcox.* Something is clearly not right with that girl."

"She wanted you to call her Izzi?"

"She said she *was* Izzi."

Zack took in Brad's wide, bloodshot eyes and trembling fingers. He had to admit that Brad actually seemed . . . scared. And then there was what Mr. Hascall had said about her identity disorder. Could it be . . . true? Could she really be suffering from multiple personalities, some of which were violent? Nothing in Zack's experience supported such a far-fetched theory.

Brad had little to add after that, and after a few more minutes, Zack left, calling the chief from the car to check in. "This situation is so messed up. You know how Peter said Scarlett has multiple personalities? Well, Brad says Scarlett was pretending to be Isabel Wilcox."

"Huh. What do you make of it?"

"I don't know," Zack mused. "Scarlett's smart. And there's definitely something . . . off about her. Could be she's a better actor than we've been giving her credit for. Maybe . . . maybe if you bring her in, and we get her into the interview room, away from her dad, we can shake a little more out of her."

"Yeah . . . I don't know," Holt said. Zack could picture him thinking it over, rubbing his chin the way he did when he was deep in thought. "Well, I guess it wouldn't hurt. You free now?"

"Actually, give me an hour," Zack said. "I need to make a stop first."

TEN

Kim gave herself a little extra time to finish her rounds that afternoon, feeling guilty about letting Scarlett Hascall's case take the lion's share of her focus.

"Mr. Jacobson. If you tell me I look like Greta Garbo one more time, I *will* commit you," she said, patting the arm of the elderly man she'd found in just his underwear outside his room.

Down the hall, a man got off the elevator and moved toward her with purpose: Zack Trainor. He was wearing a leather bomber jacket over his uniform that emphasized his broad shoulders. He hadn't bothered to remove his sunglasses, and the mirrored lenses obscured his expression. Kim gave Mr. Jacobson a final, distracted pat.

"Leslie, could you please escort Mr. J back to his room?" she called to a young orderly. "I think I'm about to be busy."

"No fair," Leslie sighed, eyeing Zack. "How come I can't get interrogated instead?"

"Doctor. I need a word," Zack said. He removed his sunglasses and jammed them in his pocket, never taking his eyes off her.

"Fine. We can talk right here." She made a show of looking at her wrist, which wasn't terribly effective, considering she'd forgotten her watch again. "I'll give you five minutes."

Zack pulled his phone from his pocket. "Mind if I record our conversation?"

"Sure, as long as you don't mind if I don't say anything."

Zack regarded her thoughtfully, a small smile playing at the corners of his lips, before putting his phone away. He crossed his arms over his chest and nodded. "Okay, we'll do this your way. For now. What do you know about Isabel Wilcox?"

Kim tried not to let her surprise show. She truly had no connection to Isabel—unless Zack somehow knew about Scarlett's alter. But she wasn't going to be the one to tell him. "Nothing. Absolutely nothing."

Zack drilled her with his intense gaze and let a moment go by. Finally, he sighed. "This is supposed to be where my silence coaxes you into unwittingly telling me more than you want to."

Kim rolled her eyes. "I'm a psychiatrist. It's going to take a lot more than that to get me to break patient confidentiality."

"Isabel Wilcox is your patient?"

Kim pressed her lips together, realizing she'd just implied a connection between Isabel and Scarlett. Maybe he was smarter than she'd realized. "You know I don't have to answer that."

"Relax. All I'm trying to do is establish some background information for my missing-persons case." He leaned toward her slightly. "Believe it or not, I'm one of the good guys here. I like the new duds, by the way. Huge improvement."

Kim glanced down at her plain white jacket, still creased from the package. "You've got me all figured out, don't you?"

"Okay." Zack sighed, and some of the friendliness drained from his voice. "I was trying to give you a chance to tell me yourself, which, frankly, would have eased my mind about the . . . irregularity of certain things that have come to my attention."

"I don't know what you're talking about."

"I know you called Isabel's home. You spoke to her father, pretending to be Izzi. Scared the crap out of him, understandably. What the hell are you playing at here, Doctor?"

Damn. "It . . . wasn't me," she hedged. "I mean, it was my phone. That part's true. Come on, let's talk in my office."

She set off down the hall, buying herself some time.

Zack followed, keeping pace at her elbow and ignoring the curious looks from the other staff and patients.

"Okay," he said, "that's a start. Now tell me exactly who used your phone to call Don Wilcox, and why."

"Look, Detective," Kim said when they'd arrived at her office. She fumbled with her keys. "I told you I can't discuss patients who are actively in my care."

"I'm not asking about your patient," he persisted. "I'm asking about *you*. Did you or did you not make the call?"

Kim deliberated a moment more. If she told him what happened, it was going to make him suspicious about Scarlett. But if she lied, she risked jeopardizing her own credibility, which could hurt Scarlett in the long run. "Okay, fine," she blurted, finally getting her door open and wishing she could close it in his face. "Scarlett made the call . . . but it was during a session, so I can't say anything more."

"*Scarlett* made the call?"

"Was I not clear? Or are you hoping for a different response?"

Zack shook his head. "No, that was just a stall tactic. While I was just putting some pieces together in my mind." He then went silent. She knew he could tell it was killing her.

Finally, she asked, "What pieces?" He remained silent. "What kind of pieces are you putting together?"

"Oh, so we're going to help each other now?"

"I didn't say that."

"Did you know that Scarlett was sleeping with Isabel's boyfriend?" Zack said. "Because Isabel has been missing for three weeks now, and let me tell you, jealous lover is as good a motive as any to make someone disappear."

Kim inhaled sharply. "Don't be ridiculous."

"She went after Brad. Last night. Went to his house and attacked him." Zack looked like he was going to say more, and then changed his mind. "If there's something more you know about Scarlett—if there's any way that she could be involved with the Isabel Wilcox disappearance—I hope you'll tell me."

Kim's mind raced, wondering if what the detective was telling her could be true. If an alter had taken over, could she really be sure of Scarlett's innocence? Yet her instincts told her that Scarlett had nothing to do with Isabel's disappearance; she believed in her patient. "Scarlett did not kill Isabel Wilcox, any more than I did."

"If that's so, I hope you have a good alibi."

Kim huffed, not rewarding the halfhearted threat with a dignified response.

"So you're saying Scarlett couldn't have killed Isabel? Then let me ask you . . . what about her 'violent tendencies'?" Seeing the shock on Kim's face, Zack added, "Peter Hascall told us about your diagnosis. And Brad Chaplin told us that Scarlett was *pretending* to be Isabel."

"She's not 'pretending.'" Kim hated how defensive she sounded.

Zack took a deep breath. "If some dangerous personality took the wheel while Scarlett 'blacked out' and she hurt someone . . . that doesn't make her any less guilty."

"You don't have the faintest understanding of her disorder." Kim felt her heart pounding, the tingling sensation in her extremities that signaled a rush of adrenaline. "It's true that an alter can 'take over' motor function in a very limited sense. When under the influence of an alter, a host might go places she wouldn't ordinarily go, or have conversations she wouldn't later remember. She might lash out in fear or anger or experience any number of unfamiliar emotions. But she wouldn't do something that drastically contradicted her sense of right and wrong. She wouldn't *kill* someone."

"You're sure about that, Doc?"

Zack's gaze was unwavering, his scrutiny like a spotlight bearing down on her. Kim shifted uncomfortably: *was* she sure? While Kim held strong opinions about dissociative identity disorder, the condition had an army of detractors—it was still one of the most controversial and misunderstood mental disorders in the medical community. Kim was lacking in indisputable facts to back up her theories. What if she was too personally invested in this case? Could she even trust her instincts?

"How about you let me do my job and you stick to doing yours instead of trying to diagnose my patients?" she resorted to saying, aware she was deflecting his question. Somehow it was easier, with Zack, to go on the offensive than to examine her defense too closely. "Now, if you'll excuse me, I have to go check in with my boss about a patient."

Zack raised a brow. "Your boss? I thought he was your boyfriend."

Kim glared at him. "How did you know he's my boyfriend?"

"I didn't. But I do now."

"That's—that's—" Kim could feel her face flushing, and she looked away in annoyance. It wasn't often that someone got the best of her.

"Okay, truth? After I found out you called the Wilcox residence, we ran your phone records. I saw a lot of calls to Dr. Berman's cell . . . in the middle of the night. A *lot* of calls. And hey, I've made a few of those calls myself. I mean, not to Dr. Berman, but . . ."

"Okay, I think that about does it for now," Kim snapped. She pushed past him into her office and shut the door behind her, locking it. She sank into her desk chair and pointedly turned her back to the door, staring at the blank screen of her computer monitor.

Zack had gotten a rise out of her with very little effort, and Kim was left trying to figure out why. Either his questioning of Scarlett's innocence was hitting even closer to home than she knew . . . or she had completely lost her professional remove.

ELEVEN

The whole drive back to the station, Zack replayed his conversation with Kim in his head. He smiled, thinking of how flustered Kim had gotten when he called her out on dating her boss. It was nice to know he'd gotten under her skin the same way she managed to get under his. She was just so incredibly confident and stuck on her convictions. She seemed utterly convinced that Scarlett was innocent, but for Zack, it was one coincidence too many. He felt it in his gut that some way, somehow, Scarlett was involved in Isabel's disappearance. Now it was his job to prove it.

He'd decided to stop for doughnuts, hoping to put Scarlett at ease, make it seem like they were having a friendly conversation versus a full-fledged interrogation. In the interview room, Zack leaned back in his chair casually and slid the doughnuts toward Scarlett as she shifted in her seat and examined the split ends of her hair.

At first, Scarlett insisted she wasn't hungry, but as Zack edged the plate slowly across the wooden table, she finally grabbed a jelly-filled doughnut and ate it in about three bites, licking the sugar from her fingertips.

"Thanks," she said in a voice barely louder than a whisper.

"Not much in this world that a good doughnut can't make better," Holt said, patting his belly with satisfaction. Zack had brought Holt's favorite, a couple of maple bars, and tamped down his impatience while the other two ate.

"Okay," Zack said, after Holt scooped up the crumbs and made short work of them. "Scarlett, I want to talk to you about a session you had with Dr. Patterson. You apparently, er, borrowed her phone to make a call to Isabel Wilcox's house. Do you want to tell me about that?"

Her wide, frightened eyes flicked up to his for a brief second before she resumed staring at the table, her hands twisting nervously. "No."

Zack sighed. "All right, let me put it a little differently. Unless you want this to escalate into a situation where you have no choice but to tell me, you might want to . . . open up little."

"I don't remember." Her voice was anguished. "Any of it."

"You don't remember the session with Dr. Patterson?"

"No, not that. I—I remember talking to her, and when she started the hypnosis and all that. But there's a big blank space in the middle. It's like—like if you've ever had surgery, like when I had my tonsils out, and they put the mask over your face and the next minute you're waking up in another room hours later and you can't remember how you got there?"

"I'd say that's pretty damn convenient," Zack said. He felt terrible as soon as the words came out of his mouth, but he had a job to do.

"You can give me a lie detector test. If you want," Scarlett offered.

"It may come to that," Zack said, though he knew from experience how unreliable polygraph tests could be. Anyone skilled at lying and able to remain calm under pressure could game the system. And a false-negative could sink an airtight case.

"This theory the doc's got," Holt said, breaking in. Zack knew the chief would attempt to disarm Scarlett with his folksy affability, while Zack hammered away relentlessly at her weak spots. It was their well-honed good-cop-bad-cop routine. "The, uh, multiple personality thing. What do you make of it?"

Scarlett burst into tears. *Here we go*, Zack thought darkly; now she was playing on their sympathies.

"I hate it," Scarlett snuffled, while Holt pushed a box of Kleenex her way. "How would you like it if you blacked out and had no idea what you'd done while you were out?"

"I wouldn't like that at all," Holt said kindly.

"Well, *I* might," Zack snapped, "if it meant I could get away with things and then claim I couldn't help it. Like if I had a beef with someone, I'd just wait until I was conveniently out of it and then hammer the crap out of them. Kind of like you did with Brad." He judged it the right moment to pull out his ace card. "Why'd you do *that*, Scarlett? Was it because he wouldn't give you the time of day after you slept with him? Don't tell me you thought your little one-night stand actually *meant* something to him?"

Scarlett sobbed harder, dabbing her eyes with wadded tissues. "I never slept with Brad Chaplin! Why would I—he's awful!"

"That's not what Brad says," Zack shot back. "And while it's a toss-up between the two of you as far as who's less trustworthy, I think you're the better liar."

"Was that it, honey?" Holt said sympathetically. "Was it hard to see him go to Izzi after being with you? Maybe he made promises, maybe he told you what you wanted to hear—"

"And you figured you'd just take Izzi right out of the picture," Zack concluded. "Get her out of the way so Brad would come back to you. It sounds like you fell pretty hard for him . . . and who wouldn't, right? Local hockey hero, smooth talker, and from the way he gets around with the women in town, probably pretty good in bed, too." Zack hesitated a half a second before hitting her with his closer. "The way he tells it, you were pretty wild in the sack yourself."

There was a knock on the door. Zack frowned; he'd given instructions that they weren't to be bothered unless it was important. He excused himself and stepped into the hall, where Phil Taktuq was waiting. There were dark circles under his eyes and his cuff was fraying at the hem. He gazed at Scarlett for a brief moment, frowning, before focusing on Zack.

"Evelyn just picked up El Da Fusion," he said. "Thought you'd want to know—he says he was with Brad Chaplin both nights when Izzi went missing."

"No shit," Zack said. El Da Fusion was a heroin dealer from Anchorage who the department had long suspected was the source of most of the product that made it to Jarvis, though they'd never been able to prove it. "Damn. You feel sure about this?"

Phil shrugged. "Timing works. Fusion hadn't been around for a few months, so he was probably due. I talked to his parole officer in Anchorage, and he missed an appointment that week. Plus there were those two busts the week after, remember?"

"Because the scag hit the streets," Zack said, nodding.

"Yeah. Fusion had photos on his phone of them at a party out in the abandominium. Evelyn's checking out witnesses now, but if Brad was there, it makes sense why he didn't want to tell that to us."

Zack sighed. The abandominium—an abandoned condo on the waterfront where users congregated—had been a thorn in the department's side for months. "Okay, thanks," he said.

"No problem."

Zack stood outside the door of the interview room for a few more moments, thinking. If Brad had been with Fusion, there was no way he'd been out murdering Izzi. Brad's business depended on his sources in Anchorage, and even though he was only a small-time middleman, there was no way he'd jeopardize his income by taking chances.

Which meant they were back to square one, with no suspects other than the tear-stained waif on the other side of the door. Damn. But his mood brightened considerably when he saw Tim Olsen being led into the station, hands cuffed behind his back.

"Tim!" Zack shouted out like he'd just seen an old college buddy across a crowded pub. Tim whipped his head around so fast that his long, stretched-out earlobes flapped like an old man's drooping underarms.

Tim shook his head, testing out his best innocent face. "I have no idea what this is about."

"No?" Zack smiled wide as he walked over, throwing his arm around Tim's shoulder as he escorted him toward booking. "Well, it might have to do with those DVDs you left behind at your office. You know, the ones with titles like *Underage Bangers*."

Tim's face fell, but he still pleaded innocence. "I have no idea what you're talking about."

"No?" Zack gently nudged Tim toward processing. "Then I'm sure your dirty fingerprints won't be all over those cases. Right hand, please." Tim looked down to see they were standing over a inking pad and a pristine fingerprint card.

Zack rolled Tim's index finger so hard in the ink that he almost bent the digit backward, breaking it.

Sometimes, being the bad cop had its perks.

TWELVE

On the way home from work, Kim made a snap decision to drive by the Wilcoxes' house. After Zack left, she'd finished her rounds, then spent a few minutes online reviewing Izzi's parents' tearful pleas for help from anyone who might have information on what had become of her. Their Facebook pages were full of photos of their daughter and loving messages. Though Izzi may have made some questionable life choices, it was clear that she loved her family. The many pictures on her Instagram account of her with her parents, her dog, her cousins . . . all of these spoke of a bond that might have been strained but was not broken.

It was nearly dark when Kim arrived at the two-story brick house, letting her car idle across the street. The house was well maintained, surrounded by neatly trimmed hedges and pots of flowers. In the driveway of the Wilcoxes' house, a large golden retriever was on its hind legs, trying to reach something in the garbage bin. As Kim watched, a pretty brunette woman in jeans and a pink sweater came out of the house and stood on the front porch with her hands on her hips. Kim recognized her from the online photographs as Jen Wilcox, Isabel's mother.

"Cupcake! Stop that right now!" When the dog growled at her, she added, "Don't you talk to me that way, you cheeky slag!"

Kim sat up straight. *Slag* . . . the same odd word choice that the Izzi alter had used when she raged against Kim in her office.

As she watched, Jen Wilcox pushed her hair out of her eyes and flipped it over her shoulder . . . a perfect imitation of the gesture Scarlett had made when she was under the influence of the Izzi alter.

As Mrs. Wilcox struggled to get her dog to drop the chicken carcass it had managed to snag from the bin, Kim drove away slowly, lost in thought.

Izzi was her mother's daughter, it seemed. Used the same expressions. The same gestures.

She could barely believe what she was considering. That her father's hypothesis might actually be true . . . that it might truly be *Isabel* inside Scarlett, not an alter imitating her in order to cause trouble. That Scarlett was, somehow, harboring a dead soul. But there was no way Scarlett could have perfected Izzi's speech and mannerisms unless she'd studied the girl intently *and* practiced until she could pass them off as her own. And when would she possibly have done that? There wasn't a known connection between the two girls.

Kim drove through town as darkness fell, watching lights come on in the houses, wondering whether it was possible to prove this crazy theory, or if she was doomed to ridicule if she even brought it up. Either way, one thing was for sure: She and Zack Trainor couldn't both be right about Scarlett. Scarlett was either inhabited by something—*someone*—and struggling to stay in control, or she was the most inscrutable psychopathic liar Kim had ever encountered. Whether it was Kim or Zack, *one* of them was making a terrible mistake . . . but what would it take to figure out which?

THIRTEEN

Zack was just getting to work the next morning, dawn breaking over the tall pines that rose above the town, when a call coming over the scanner caught his attention. The caller identified himself as a security guard down at the docks.

Near the end of his shift, he'd found a badly decomposed body floating next to the pier.

"Shit," Zack muttered, reaching for his jacket, as Jeannette, the overnight dispatcher, assured the caller that an officer was on his way.

Since most of Jarvis was still in bed, Zack made it to the docks in no time at all. The coroner, who served the entire county and lived half an hour outside the town, was on his way. A tripod light had been set up on the dock in the early dawn, and Zack could see two figures standing there together.

He headed onto the dock, squinting to make out the two men illuminated in beams of early morning sun.

"Mr. Kanga?" he called. "Detective Trainor."

Close up, he could see that Kanga was well suited for his job. Short but powerfully built, he would make an imposing deterrent to the kind of petty mischief that tended to plague the area.

Kanga shook hands and introduced the other man, Fred Smetts, who looked vaguely familiar. Zack soon remembered why: Smetts, who held the town docks contract, had once sponsored a Little League team that Zack had played on. His handsome, craggy face hadn't changed much in the last fifteen years.

"Nice to see you again," Zack said.

"I still remember that no-hitter you pitched against the Tornadoes," Smetts replied. "Nasty slider for a twelve-year-old."

Kanga must have called his boss right after calling the police. Together, all three men peered down into the water.

"It's, uh, right there," Smetts said almost apologetically, pointing to a patch of sodden fabric floating near the water's surface. Closer examination revealed that the fabric was actually a shirt. The dark shape underneath was the body, bobbing near the surface.

As Zack peered closer, he made out a pale line trailing from the dark shape through the water to emerge next to the dock: a rope had been looped around the body's waist, tethering it to one of the cleats.

Zack knelt down on the rough wood of the dock and dipped his hand into the cool water, reaching for the rope. He pulled gently, and as the body slowly floated closer, he saw that there was a good reason the rope hadn't been looped around its neck . . . the body was missing its head.

"Sorry about the rope," Kanga said hastily. "I meant no disrespect. I didn't want it to float away."

"We didn't want to disturb anything until you got here," Smetts added.

The older man was avoiding looking at the body. It was bloated from the water, and large patches of skin and flesh were missing where small fish had eaten away at it. The edges of the neck wound were jagged and distorted. "You did well," he told both men. Zack knew the emotional damage a sight like this could have on an innocent psyche and he always tried to help mitigate that damage. Kanga nodded his thanks; Smetts looked like he was trying not to vomit.

Now that he'd confirmed that there was indeed a body, he radioed Jeannette to call for the CSI team; soon the dock would be swarming with investigators and equipment. "How'd you notice it, anyway?" he asked Kanga.

"I check down there for kids, couple times a night," Kanga said, glancing at his boss. "Some of them like to get down there in skiffs or what have you, get up to things."

"So you were doing your routine check . . . ?"

"And I saw it. Figured right away it was a body, kind of distinctive shape, you know. Tried to pull it in, just in case it was, uh, not dead, but . . ."

"Do you mind giving me a hand with this?" Zack asked, crouching down and pulling on the line. "If you'd rather, I can wait for backup."

"Nah, I'll help," Kanga said, while Smetts stepped back.

It took both of them to wrangle the waterlogged body up onto the dock, its limbs flopping uselessly and drenching them in the process. As they pulled, it became evident that the reason the legs hadn't been visible from the surface was that one ankle had been tied to an object to weigh it down—what looked like a giant metal comb, rusted and tangled with seaweed. The other ankle was lacerated to the bone, the muscle and tendons grotesquely exposed.

Once the body was laid out on its back, the damaged ankle askew and the metal object dripping in the sun, Zack was able to estimate that it belonged to a young woman, approximately five feet four inches tall, had her head still been attached. Scavengers—likely crabs and shrimp—had nibbled away flesh in patches, and the skin was pale and swollen. But there was enough left of the body for Zack to conclude that it could belong to Isabel Wilcox.

"Now that's a damn shame," Kanga said, while Smetts stared resolutely out over the water.

"Gonna be a long morning," Zack said, feeling sorry for Smetts. The man had the decency to come out—Zack could at least do him the favor of excusing him from the worst of it. "Any chance you could brew some coffee, sir?"

Smetts scuttled gratefully off to the dock offices. For the next hour Zack pitched in, running interference with the returning fishermen and keeping bystanders off the dock, while the CSI team secured the scene. Holt arrived, followed soon after by the coroner, Marty Volp. By then the sun was fully up, the town bathed in glittering morning brilliance.

After his examination, Volp came to stand with Holt and Zack, peeling off his gloves. He pulled a wax-paper-wrapped roast beef sandwich from his pocket. "You guys mind?" he asked.

"Uh, no," Zack said. The idea of eating anything after spending the morning with a decomposing, headless body turned his stomach.

"Go right ahead," Holt said politely. "So—what do we think about her head?"

"MIA," Volp said cheerfully. "But it could have been severed with the same bear trap that weighted her down. Which, by the way, could have been responsible for the injuries to her leg."

"Wait, what bear trap?"

"You've never seen one of those?" Volp asked.

Zack squinted at the metal weight tied to the victim's leg. Sure enough, at the corners were the rusted-out remains of the bolts that had once connected the brutal teeth to the rest of the contraption. Zack had never been a hunter—Holt had always taught him that guns were tools best left to law enforcement—but he'd spotted the enormous, almost medieval-looking traps in outdoors supply stores, and it was easy to imagine the sharp teeth snapping shut on the pale, tender skin of a young girl.

Zack winced. He had a fairly strong constitution and had seen a lot during his time on the police force, but the idea of the device severing Isabel Wilcox's head from her body was a little too much, even for him.

"Body's been in the water for a couple of weeks," Volp went on, talking around a big bite of sandwich. "Small crabs ate away the fingers, and you kind of need those buggers to get prints. Got a partial tattoo on the back of her neck, but can't see all of it due to the decapitation."

Zack flipped through his notebook, finding the pages from the interviews he'd conducted with Isabel's parents. "She had a butterfly tattoo on the nape of her neck. Think that could be a butterfly . . . ?"

"Eh, I guess. Adipocere and bloating makes it tough to tell."

Zack swallowed and jammed his notebook back in his pocket. "Well," he said to Holt, "the only bright side here is now we have confirmation of foul play. We can call Scarlett back in, maybe trip her up on her story."

Holt raised his eyebrows. "You still like the Hascall girl for this, Zack?"

"I realize a decap murder and body dump don't really line up," Zack conceded. Typically, female killers were not as violent in their methods as men; there was also the matter of the considerable physical strength that would have been required to transport the body, and Scarlett was even smaller than Isabel. "But she's already proven she's violent. She had a history with Brad. A pretty twisted one, considering her age and background. So yeah, I still think she could be good for it."

"Well now, that'd be something you don't see every day. Young girl like that, doing something like this," Volp said, crumpling the wax paper and stuffing it into his pocket.

"You never know," Holt said thoughtfully. "About a dozen years back, I helped out with a case in Valdez. Teenage girl was killed, body mutilated, letters cut into the skin with a butter knife, post-mortem."

"I vaguely remember that," Zack said.

Holt snorted. "You were so green at the time, I didn't let you near it."

"Letters?" Volp asked.

"The ABC's. Girl who did it was eight. Stabbed her oldest sister in the head in her sleep. Because her sister ate the last Pudding Pop in the freezer. Used a butter knife because the little girl said that her mom and dad wouldn't let her touch a steak knife . . . too dangerous."

Volp shook his head. "No shit." He shook his head again while licking the juice from his rare roast beef sandwich off his fingers. "Some people . . ."

TWENTY MINUTES LATER, ZACK pulled up behind Holt's SUV in front of the Hascalls' house. Peter Hascall was just coming out the door, checking his watch and carrying his lunch pail. When he saw the officers, his face fell.

"What now?"

"We'd like to talk to Scarlett."

"You're serious? Again? You don't think you've dragged her through enough yet?"

"Come on, Pete," Holt said calmly. "We'll be fair. You know we will. But we have to follow procedures here, and there's some new developments we need to talk to her about."

Peter glared at them for a moment before finally dropping his gaze. His shoulders drooped in defeat. "I'll take you up," he said. "But please, remember, she's just nineteen years old. Anyway, I doubt she's even awake yet."

Zack and Holt followed Hascall into the house. It smelled of fresh coffee and laundry detergent, and the living room had been recently vacuumed and dusted. Zack scanned the house for Scarlett's presence. Now that he had a real suspect for this case, he wasn't going to let anything get in the way of a full interrogation.

"Daddy? What's going on?" Scarlett's younger sister wandered out of the kitchen, a Diet Coke in her hand. Hascall went to her, murmuring something in her ear and wrapping an arm around his daughter.

Holt nodded to Zack, and hung back with the Hascalls while Zack took the stairs to the second floor two at a time, reaching for his handcuffs. Yet door after door opened to no Scarlett. Finally, at the end of the hall, he reached Scarlett's bedroom. Slowly, he twisted the knob, and then moved quickly into the room—

But nobody was inside. Instead, all Zack could see were the rays of sunlight streaming through Scarlett's window, which was wedged wide open—wide enough for Scarlett to have disappeared through it without anyone in her family knowing she'd gone.

FOURTEEN

Kim was assembling a lunch of a peanut butter and honey sandwich, raisins, and shortbread cookies. She'd exchanged a few more e-mails with her father about Scarlett's case, and it had made her nostalgic for the lunches he used to pack for her to take to school. Besides, Kim couldn't endure another dry turkey sandwich from the cafeteria. She was just putting the sandwich in her backpack when someone knocked on the door of her apartment. She glanced at the clock and frowned. It was a quarter to ten in the morning, an unusual time for visitors, unless her elderly neighbor needed help getting her windows open again.

But when she opened the door, Kyle was standing there. "Well, this is a nice surprise," she said. "Sweet of you to visit, but I was headed your way."

"You're not scheduled until noon," Kyle said.

Kim's smile faltered. "Couldn't wait that long to see me?" she tried, hopefully.

"We need to talk."

Kim stepped aside to let him into the apartment. "You just went from a guy about to get laid to an ex-boyfriend I tell pathetic stories about."

"This is serious, Kim." Kyle took a breath and jammed his hands in the pockets of his coat. "They found Isabel Wilcox's body this morning. She was murdered."

Kim gasped. "No—"

"They pulled her out of the bay, apparently. And there's a rumor going around that she was decapitated."

"*The bay,*" Kim echoed. "Shit." She remembered the session with the Izzi alter in the Hascalls' living room when bloody water had trickled and then flowed from her mouth. *I'm in the bay*, she'd moaned, words that made no sense at the time.

Could the Izzi alter have actually been reporting on her own death? Was this the confirmation Kim was looking for? Or was it proof that Zack was right, and Scarlett was more dangerous than Kim had realized?

"Yes, she was found in the bay," Kyle said. "What are you not telling me, Kim? Do you know something about this?"

Kim scrabbled for a plausible explanation for her reaction and came up only with the story about Scarlett coughing up the water during therapy, which she grudgingly admitted to Kyle as he scowled disapprovingly.

"God *damn* it, Kim," Kyle said. "When were you going to tell me?"

Kim turned away, trying to compose herself. She went into the kitchen to get a glass of water, buying herself time. Kyle followed her. "What else haven't you told me?"

She didn't answer, trying to think of a way to explain things that wouldn't sound like she'd directly violated their agreement.

"Please, tell me you followed hospital policy," Kyle said, a dangerous edge to his voice.

"I used a treatment technique that has had some success elsewhere," she hedged.

"*Kim*—"

"Okay—I hypnotized her. But it was in a safe environment. I

used reasonable precautions." She didn't add that the "safe environment" was Scarlett's own house, which Kim had visited without Kyle's permission.

"You *hypnotized* Scarlett," he repeated in disbelief, as she ran the tap, filling a glass. "*Knowing* it was against hospital rules."

"*Stupid* hospital rules," Kim corrected. Then, she desperately tried to change the subject. "Did you know it's a rule, an actual law, in Juneau that you can't bring a pet turtle into a barbershop?" She earned an angry stare from Kyle. "Really. It's on the books. Well, it says you can't bring *any* animal . . . not just turtles . . ."

Kim's story sputtered to a stop as she finally took a drink, unable to meet his eyes. Hypnotizing Scarlett had been the right thing to do, the only thing she could think of to help her patient. But she was digging herself into a deeper and deeper hole with Kyle. After all, he'd already warned her that the case reflected on both of them.

"It's a rule for a reason. The insurance company won't—"

But Kim interrupted, "Did the insurance company go to med school? Has the insurance company seen hypnosis save people's lives? Does the insurance company care about Scarlett?"

"Well, I guess it's sweet that you have so much faith in your patient that you'd break hospital policy *again* for her, but guess what? Now she's missing."

"Missing?" *Shit.* "So police think Scarlett may be involved?" Kim asked.

But Kyle was far too incensed to focus on Scarlett. "Do you even remember why you're here in Jarvis? San Diego Psych is a money machine. They can wash a multimillion-dollar settlement when you have a meltdown and break all the rules to satisfy your manic id. We can't. If the board found out—"

"I took an *oath*," Kim blurted, unable to stop herself, even more agitated because she knew he was right. "To help people. Not kowtow to insurance companies."

"You can't help people if they take away your medical license, Kim. It's that simple."

"I came here because you *liked* my approach to psychiatry," Kim reminded him. "You said I was 'inspired.' 'Nonconformist.' 'Unconventional.' *Your* words . . . Or did you hire me because I was *easy*?"

"Oh, trust me, you're *anything* but easy," he shot back angrily.

For a moment they stared at each other. Finally, Kim set down the glass and crossed her arms over her chest. "Good one."

"Look," Kyle said, taking a breath. "I thought we were . . . I thought we were in this together."

He stepped away, turning his back on her, and Kim realized he wasn't just talking about the job. She grimaced, furious with herself for letting things go this far when she'd known he was the kind of man who couldn't tolerate this sort of ambiguity. A sensitive empath . . . the one kind of man Kim should know better than to come anywhere near. But instead of learning from her past mistakes, she'd jumped right in, as always. Ready to get hurt, and to hurt anyone else who got too close.

She followed him into the living room, putting her hand on his arm. He yanked it away. "Come on," she pleaded.

He spun around. "What?"

"Listen to me for just one minute. We both . . . need to cool down. We need to remember that we want the same thing. To help people."

"The way *I* help people, Kim, is to practice medicine the way I learned over a decade of working my ass off. To cooperate with my colleagues to get the best outcome I can for every patient. Not to run off half-cocked on my own every time I get a hunch—"

"It wasn't a *hunch*," Kim snapped. "I'm not practicing voodoo or something, the way you seem to think I am. I was using a tested therapeutic method—"

"—which has not been adopted by Jarvis Hospital, and isn't

going to be anytime soon. Kim, we can go round and round on this all day. It's not going to change the way I feel."

He glared at her, his eyes intense, and Kim was reminded of the first time she'd met him, at the medical conference at UC San Francisco. How she'd gone after him verbally in front of a crowd of health professionals during a Q&A on psychoactive medication, and how she'd gone after him physically in the back of the hotel bar later that night. A year later, he'd given her an out when her residency at San Diego had blown up. It was the power of his convictions that had initially attracted her, the same resolute energy that was now being directed against her.

Kyle Berman was a good man. A brilliant one, too. If only she could make him see . . .

"Kyle," she began, caught between her frustration and her desperate need to make him understand. "I'm not trying to *change* you. I just want . . . I want . . ."

She was standing close enough to see the angry glint in his eyes, to watch his chest rise and fall as he battled his temper. His lips were parted, his thick, dark hair slightly mussed. His monogrammed shirt cuffs, usually perfectly pressed, had been carelessly pushed up his arms.

His anger sparked dangerously between them, blending with her own, threatening to ignite. Kim reached for him, pulling his face down to hers, tasting him hungrily. For a moment he was frozen, but soon he was kissing her back, his hands in her hair. He allowed her to push him onto the couch, where she straddled him and wrapped her arms around him only for a moment before he growled and flipped her over. The delicious weight of him on top of her allowed her to forget some of the anxiety about Scarlett that had held her in its grip.

But as the kiss deepened, a faint voice inside her shrieked that she was out of her mind, that she was jeopardizing her most important patient. Before Scarlett, it didn't matter. Before Scarlett, it was only Kim who could be hurt. But she couldn't lose this job now. Sure, she realized this was her last chance to prove herself, to hang on to the career she'd worked so hard for. Sure, without it, she would lose her ability to help others—and without that, who would she even be? But now there was Scarlett.

It was all getting away from her again, as it had too often in the past. But here, now, in this moment, she had Kyle. A good man, a healer . . . but also a solid presence that she could rely on.

"This is not why I came over," Kyle said warningly, pulling away.

"I don't care." She hooked her hand around his neck and pulled him down to her again. And this time, they had no more use for words.

FIFTEEN

Kyle's visit had ended well, but as soon as he left, Kim had gone right back to worrying about Scarlett, who was now apparently a suspect in an investigation *and* a missing person. She tried calling the Hascalls' home line, but nobody was picking up.

Finally, she was desperate enough that she was willing to deal with Detective Zack Trainor. He clearly didn't want to talk to her, however; it was obvious he'd told his staff not to put her through. It took her the entire length of her drive to the hospital just to get someone at the station to connect her to Zack's line. Now she was on hold, waiting for him to pick up, as she stalked through the halls of the hospital. Reaching her office door, she was already fumbling for her keys before she realized it was unlocked—and someone was inside.

Just as Zack answered his phone, Kim pushed her door open—and saw Scarlett herself, sitting in Kim's desk chair.

"Hello? Dr. Patterson? Are you still there?" Zack's voice was openly hostile.

"Sorry, Zack, I'll have to call you back," Kim said distractedly, and stabbed at the button on her phone to end the call as she stared at the figure in front of her. "Scarlett?"

Kim closed the door behind her and was about to ask for an explanation, when a glint of metal in Scarlett's hand caught her eye.

A scalpel.

Kim froze, and then, moving very cautiously, approached Scarlett. She was sitting very still, staring into space, seemingly not even aware that Kim had entered the room.

"Scarlett, listen to me, I know you're scared, but—"

"My mom was right. She always said I was kissed by the devil. Nothing I could do about it." Her voice was monotone, emotionless. She didn't look at Kim. "If I did kill that girl, I should be punished."

Her hand closed more tightly around the scalpel. The blade sunk into the soft skin of her palm. Blood dripped onto her jeans.

"Scarlett—you didn't kill anyone," Kim said, trying to keep her voice calm.

Scarlett's eyes flashed. "How do you know? Were you there? You don't even know me."

"You're right, I don't," Kim said, thinking fast, trying to come up with a bridge to reach the troubled girl. "But I know me. And I know that for years, I punished myself for things . . . things that weren't my fault."

She was playing a dangerous game, but if she didn't get through to Scarlett here and now, it might all be over for the girl. "Do you want to compare scars?"

Finally, Scarlett's eyes flicked to attention. She looked at Kim with a mixture of mistrust and curiosity. "Is this some kind of bullshit trust exercise?"

"No. I promise. I've *lost* people. People who put their trust in me . . . a long time ago."

"Who? Who did you lose?"

Kim took a breath. She'd spent her adult life deflecting questions about her past. When she'd been in school, she made up elaborate stories, lies about her childhood that began to seem almost real the more she embellished them, until she could almost believe them herself.

"I . . . lost my parents. In a carjacking. They never found the guys who did it." The words sounded strange on her lips, words she had never said out loud before. "I was in the car."

"Oh no," Scarlett said softly, her anger draining away instantly. "I'm so sorry."

"I was just a kid." Kim closed her eyes, knowing that she couldn't let the balance between her and Scarlett be completely upended by the confession. "I was lucky; I was adopted by a great couple who are now my mom and dad." The truth. "I, uh, had a pretty normal childhood." A lie. "All things considered."

"But you did things," Scarlett said, her eyes flicking down. "I saw. On your arms."

Of course she would have noticed. It takes one to know one, and at some point Scarlett had seen the faint lines tracing the underside of Kim's forearms, so faded now as to be nearly invisible, and known the truth.

"I did," Kim agreed. "I never could shake the feeling that somehow I was responsible for my parents' deaths. That I let them down. That I failed them."

Scarlett looked at the scalpel in her hands as though she couldn't remember how it got there. After a few seconds, it went slack in her fingers.

Kim's door opened. Kyle stood at the threshold. He took in the scene with a shocked expression, the two women sitting close together, one of them with a scalpel in her hand. Before Kim could say anything, he made a quick motion to the side—the red button, installed just outside door, the one the staff was strictly forbidden from calling the "panic button" even though everyone knew that "assistance call button" meant exactly that.

"Kyle—no. You don't understand," she said, jumping up. "Call security, tell them you made a mistake—"

"You can't be serious," Kyle said. He grabbed her arm and dragged her against him.

Scarlett watched, her face changing from open to impassive.

Kim struggled to get out of his grip, but he was too strong. She had only seconds before security responded, and she knew how it would look.

"I'll help you, Scarlett," she said, keeping her voice as even and calm as she could, even as Kyle's arms wrapped more tightly around her torso. She could feel his labored breath against her neck. "I promise. We'll get through this. Together."

Scarlett blinked and opened her mouth as if to speak, but before Kim could manage to break free, the door was flung all the way open and a security guard rushed in, his gun in his hands. Kim bit back a yell as he pointed it at Scarlett.

"Drop it!" he ordered. "Hands in the air!"

"Stop it!" Kim pleaded. "Put the gun down! She's not danger- ous, I promise!" She made one final effort to twist free of Kyle, using her elbow to jab his arms free. At last, he let go, and Kim threw herself in front of Scarlett, blocking her. Kyle cursed and practically tackled her in an effort to push her out of Scarlett's reach, but Kim put all her weight into resisting him, grunting with the effort.

In the confusion, Scarlett slipped off the chair and shrank against the wall, the scalpel firmly in her grip once more. She stared at it, then raised it slowly until the sharp blade was resting against her own neck. "This . . . this is the best way," she said.

"No!" Kim screamed. The guard pointed his gun at her, at Scar- lett, and back, clearly having no idea what was going on. But if Kim didn't do something fast, Scarlett was going to try to kill herself right here in her office.

An idea flashed into her mind, as risky and unorthodox as anything she'd ever been accused of doing. But there was no choice, no other options. She raised her hand and slammed her palm flat against the wall, as hard as she could. The impact made the books jump on the shelves, getting Scarlett's attention.

"Help me! Oh my God, help me!" Kim screamed.

They were the words that had triggered Scarlett once before, when the sounds of a scuffle in the hospital corridor had interrupted her therapy session in Kyle's office. Last time, the words had triggered an altered state; Kim was desperately hoping that the same thing might happen again, at least long enough for Scarlett to let down her guard.

In the seconds after Kim's words rang in the air, the girl went stock-still. Her pupils dilated, and her hands went rigid. Her mouth twitched, and she looked around the room, her gaze falling on the guard, who was still crouched in front of her with his gun leveled directly at her.

Scarlett threw herself toward the door, sidestepping Kyle as he tried to grab her arm. A split second later she was running down the hallway. The guard cursed, shoving Kyle out of the way, but Kim nimbly stepped in front of him.

"Scarlett! Wait!" But the girl didn't turn around. She was almost to the emergency exit stairs. "Isabel!" Kim tried. "Please!"

The girl paused, her hand on the door to the stairwell. She turned around and locked gazes with Kim for a second, before pulling open the door and disappearing.

Kyle grabbed Kim's arm and spun her to face him, furious. "Do you have any idea what you—"

Kim shook her head angrily, too frustrated and scared to deal with him, even though she could almost hear the remnants of her career tearing in half.

But then something occurred to her, and she straightened,

brushing Kyle's grip off as though he were nothing more than an annoying mosquito.

"I know where she's going."

The guard holstered his gun and reached for his radio.

"Wait," Kim said. "This has all been a huge misunderstanding. And look—no harm done." She bent to the floor and picked up the scalpel, which Scarlett had dropped before running.

Kyle snatched it out of her hands. "No *harm*?" he demanded. "I don't know how you can possibly say that, Kim, you've—"

"Give me an hour," she said, "I swear I'll make this right." She turned to the security guard. "There's no need to report this," she said with as much sincerity as she could muster. "As her physician, I can confirm that Scarlett Hascall is not a danger to herself or others. The scalpel she was holding . . . it could have been a pen, or a stick of gum, for all she was aware of its purpose."

"Doc, I *saw* her put it up against her neck."

"Role-play," Kim said, backing out of the office. "Therapeutic exercise. Really nothing to worry about. I've got to run, but Dr. Berman here will back me up."

As she strode down the hall, she prayed it was true—that whatever shred of affection remained between them after this last episode would prove to be enough for Kyle to give her this last chance.

Either way, she needed to find a quiet spot to make a call. She ducked into the visiting room, which was stocked with games and puzzles and shelves of books, and curled up in the recliner facing away from the door, knowing that it would hide her from inquisitive glances.

She dialed the number she'd hung up on less than an hour ago.

"Detective Trainor, please."

SIXTEEN

Zack got there first, gunning it from the station so that he could establish the scene before Kim Patterson arrived. The Wilcox house was a stately colonial, the shrubbery neatly trimmed, the lawn manicured, the front door flanked by sculpted topiary in porcelain pots. But even from the outside the place had an air of mourning, the drapes pulled tight across the front window, the garage door lowered. Holt arrived right behind him, and Kim appeared seconds later, blocking him in with her ridiculous rust bucket of a car.

Zack strode to her window before she could get out, and leaned down.

"Stay here."

"*I* called *you*, remember?" she demanded.

Suddenly, a scream pierced the air. They both looked up, following the sound to an open bedroom window on the second floor.

Zack dashed to the front door. Holt was already in, his gun drawn. Zack followed suit and entered the house.

The foyer was thick with the cloying scent of the flower arrangements that sat on every available surface. From somewhere in the bowels of the house, a woman could be heard crying. Holt headed up the stairs, treading surprisingly lightly for a large man. Zack followed close behind.

As they reached the landing, a flash of movement caught Zack's attention. A figure came rushing at them from the darkened hall, wielding a baseball bat. Zack automatically ducked out of the way, shoving Holt into the other wall, but Holt was already aiming a short, efficient jab at the attacker's wrist.

The bat thudded on the carpet as the man emerged from the shadows. It was Isabel's father, looking worse for wear since the last time they'd been to the house, shortly after his daughter disappeared. In the space of a few weeks, he seemed to have lost ten pounds and aged twenty years, with deep circles under his eyes and gray stubble lining his face.

"We're here to help! Where is she, Mr. Wilcox?" Holt demanded, as Wilcox raised his hands in the air.

He pointed mutely down the hall to the room at the end. Now that their eyes had adjusted to the lack of light, Zack could make out a hand-painted pastel sign that read IZZI'S ROOM. Behind him, Kim came up the stairs, taking them two at a time.

"Don't hurt her," Kim implored. "She's just a kid."

Zack shoved her protectively aside, keeping his gun trained down the hall. "Step back."

He followed Holt, who tried the knob and found it locked. Silently, Zack counted off on his fingers, nodding to Holt. *One, two* . . . on three he kicked in the door, wood splintering, and the two of them entered, working quickly to secure the room.

But it was empty. Eyelet curtains fluttered against the open window. Purple and yellow pillows were mounded on a neatly made bed. Posters of rock stars popular half a dozen years ago lined the soft yellow walls. Had Scarlett escaped again? Zack felt like screaming in frustration.

Mrs. Wilcox hurried into the room, her hair pulled back in a

headband that matched her gray sweater. Kim followed close behind. "Mrs. Wilcox—"

But the woman ignored her. She didn't appear to notice Zack,
either, but focused intently on the wall beside the bed, kneeling in
front of it.

"Izzi . . . ? Baby?" she crooned softly.

Muffled sounds came from behind the wall. Mrs. Wilcox
crouched closer and ran her hands along the wainscoting. There
was a mechanical click, and then the wall seemed to split, a panel
hidden by the decorative molding sliding to the side to reveal a secret cubbyhole a few feet deep and wide. Inside, curled in a ball,
Scarlett lay clutching an old, battered doll that was missing an eye.
She looked up at Mrs. Wilcox, her face full of fear.

". . . Mom?"

SEVENTEEN

"Please, honey," Mrs. Wilcox said softly, nudging a plate of cookies closer to Kim, "call me Jen."

Kim had pleaded with Zack and Holt to allow her to talk to Scarlett before they arrested her, but they'd refused. At one point, Zack had even threatened to arrest her, too, if she didn't stop talking and stay out of their way.

But as she'd finally given up in defeat, Mrs. Wilcox had emerged from the powder room, where she'd gone to collect herself. While the police officers took Scarlett away in handcuffs, Kim asked Isabel's mother if she could ask her a few questions about Isabel. She saw a chance to delve a bit deeper into her theories about Scarlett's connection to Izzi—potentially even to gather information that could clear Scarlett of any involvement in Izzi's murder. She was glad Mrs. Wilcox had agreed.

"These are delicious, thank you," Kim said, even though she couldn't taste anything. The anguished look Scarlett had given her when she was being led away was seared in her memory. "What happened just now—I'm so sorry that she came here. To your home. Scarlett is . . . struggling."

She couldn't divulge any information about Scarlett's condition, but she also understood how painful the intrusion must have been for Izzi's parents. The best she could do was to try to learn more about the case to keep something like this from happening again.

For a long moment, Mrs. Wilcox was silent. "When Izzi was a little girl, she was afraid of monsters," she finally said. "We tried everything to calm her, but nothing worked. One night, I came in to kiss her good night . . . and she wasn't in her bed. We thought someone had taken her. We called the police.

"We searched everywhere until we finally found her, fast asleep with that doll in the cubby. The former owner of the house had built it to hide his coin collection, which was apparently quite valuable, and we thought Izzi might use it for a playroom, but she never showed any interest in it until that night.

"From then on, she would sometimes sleep in there if she was having nightmares. I think she felt . . . safe, there." She teared up again, dabbing at her eyes delicately with an embroidered handkerchief. "How do you think that girl knew about Izzi's cubby?"

"I . . . I don't know," Kim said. "I'm so sorry. I wish I had an explanation." As she forced the last of her cookie down, she felt the weight of Jen Wilcox's grief and bewilderment pressing in on her. What would this poor woman think if she knew the theory Kim was entertaining? That her daughter's soul might somehow be *inside* Scarlett? Was there any way to say something like that aloud without sounding completely insane? Without destroying a mother?

"I just . . . I've had this feeling I've never told anyone about," Jen said. "It's like . . . I can sense that she hasn't moved on. That she's waiting for something. Some kind of closure."

Kim's pulse quickened. Maybe Jen *would* be receptive to Kim's radical theories. And this matched her own evaluation of the Izzi alter: that she was restless, dissatisfied . . . *waiting*. "Can you tell me more about that?" she asked carefully.

Jen glanced up at her quickly, then away. "I don't want you to think I'm crazy," she said, with a heartbreaking little laugh. "But I've known she was lost to us. That she was dead. Ever since that first night when she didn't return my texts. I couldn't tell anyone . . . I mean, you're a psychiatrist, so I *really* shouldn't be telling you this."

"People think there's no room in psychiatry for the things we can't understand," Kim said. "When nothing could be further from the truth. Some of my colleagues don't want to admit it, but much of the way the human mind works—it's still a mystery to us. Science can go a long way in helping us diagnose and treat a variety of conditions and disorders. But there's this enormous, mysterious space where we're all just basically fumbling in the dark."

"*Fumbling in the dark*," Jen repeated doubtfully.

"I'm sorry, maybe that was a poor choice of words," Kim amended. "I like to think that when I use my intuition, I'm not so much relying on the mystical and unscientific, as opening myself up to the possibility that there are channels of knowledge outside the five senses, outside the current limits of medicine."

"You mean . . . like there could be spirits guiding you?" Jen asked, almost hopefully.

"Nothing as specific as that," Kim said carefully. "I don't believe in ghosts, if that's what you mean. But I do believe that the line between life and death is not as hard and fast as we like to tell ourselves. Just as science has discovered that there is a fertile space between the conscious mind and the unconscious, one that we have only begun to explore, I believe that there may be much more to learn about the place between life and death."

Jen's eyes were bright with emotion. "I think I agree with you," she said. "But half the time I think it's just—just a mother's hopeless yearning. I could never tell my husband any of this."

"If you like, I'd be happy to give you the name of an excellent therapist," Kim said gently, her heart aching for Jen. "Someone who could give you a safe place to explore thoughts like these, and to grieve."

"I—I think I would like that," Jen whispered.

Kim wrote down the names of two well-regarded therapists in town.

Jen took her hand. "Thank you," she said.

As Kim was leaving, she noticed an elaborately decorated journal lying on the counter. The colorful stickers were worn and peeling, the cover plastered with drawings. In the top right corner the name *Izzi* was spelled out in bubble letters that had been carefully outlined and shaded. Over the last *I* was a face with wide eyes and a tongue sticking out.

"Oh, that's Izzi's journal," Jen said. "I found it the other day when I was going through some of the things in her room."

"Do you mind if I take a quick look?" Kim asked, hope beginning to take root.

Jen understandably hesitated, then seemed to decide there was no point in preserving her daughter's privacy now. She gave a quick nod.

Kim picked it up and flipped through the pages. As she scanned the entries written in a careful, looping hand, an eerie sense of recognition came over her.

The handwriting was the same as Scarlett's from her intake paperwork at the hospital.

She dropped the journal, reeling. If she'd been looking for proof, here it was. Scarlett's handwriting that day was identical to Izzi's. And handwriting was difficult to fake, even for professional con artists. There'd be no way she could have so quickly and easily imitated Izzi's style that closely.

Plus, Scarlett knew about the secret cubby in Izzi's room.

And Scarlett had known that Izzi would be found in the bay . . . and the bloody water that poured out of her couldn't be explained away, as hard as Kim tried.

Scarlett had been telling the truth all along. Somehow, her body had become a sanctuary for the soul of Isabel Wilcox.

EIGHTEEN

Somewhere between walking out of the Wilcox house and getting into her car to drive away, Kim realized she needed more evidence to back up her insane theory, so she quickly hustled back up the front steps, knocked on the door, and asked Jen Wilcox if she could borrow Izzi's journal. Kim promised to return it quickly, and Jen reluctantly handed it over, silently hoping that it would be returned with some answers about her daughter's death.

Kim sped back to the hospital, snagged a parking spot near the side entrance, and took the stairs up, to avoid running into any of her coworkers. She was on a mission and was eager not to have to explain herself to anyone, least of all Kyle. After a quick stop in her office, Kim found who she was looking for in the fourth-floor break room.

"Hey, Nga," Kim said. "Any chance I can use your secret decoder ring? I have a handwriting sample I'd love for you to look at."

As the hospital's speech pathologist, Dr. Nga Nguyen was responsible for evaluating and treating a variety of communication disorders and delays, mostly vocal. But her interest spread to all forms of communication. Nga's fascination with handwriting analysis had left Kim bored to tears the one time they'd gone out for drinks. Suddenly, however, Kim found herself wanting to know more.

The petite doctor looked up, surprised to see Kim. "What the hell happened to you? Everybody's talking about it. Did one of your patients really try to kill you?"

Kim didn't have time. "Naw, that wasn't me. I think it was Dr. Griffin in Rehab. Can I see you in your office? This is kind of . . . personal."

Nga perked up. "Handwriting sample that's personal? Secret admirer, or stalker? Or both?" Then her eyes widened. "Is this about the affair you're having with Dr. Berman?"

This caught Kim off guard. Obviously they weren't being as sneaky as she thought. "Dr. Berman? Affair? No, again, wasn't me. Maybe that's Dr. Griffin, too."

"Dr. Timothy Griffin? So, Kyle and Tim are a thing?"

"I don't know; I don't judge. But I do need your help. Your office?"

Sixty seconds later, Dr. Nguyen was closing the door to her office as Kim produced Isabel's journal, as well as Scarlett's medical intake paperwork that the troubled teen had filled out while channeling Izzi.

As soon as Nga glanced at the writing, she peered up at Kim. "This was written by a woman."

Kim held her gaze. "Don't judge."

Nga swallowed her smile and began to examine the two samples, making some notes and using a magnifier to peer closely. Kim leaned over her shoulder, about ready to explode in anticipation.

Nga's eyes darted back and forth between the journal and the intake paperwork. She nodded. "The *D*. Both samples have this anger tick in the upper zone. And see here, her ovals are done clockwise, which is very unusual. The angles, the arcades, identical."

"So they're a match?"

Nga decided to hold Kim over a barrel for more information. "I don't know. Mind telling me what this is about?"

Kim definitely minded, and though she had anticipated the question, she wasn't prepared with an answer. "Oh, uh . . . just wanting to return this girl's journal."

"Lie."

"She's a friend."

"Lie." Nga held up the intake paperwork. "Unless you're treating your friend. Is this person competition? For Dr. Berman?"

"I told you, I'm not seeing Dr. Berman."

"Do I have to say it again?" Nga decided she did. "Lie." She herself was married to an accountant, and had offered to set Kim up with his brother.

"Okay, the truth, this journal could belong to a patient. She's a— waitress on the promenade," she said. "She works the night shift."

Nga shook her head, disappointed. "You're quoting 'The Ballad of Dorothy Parker.' That's a Prince song."

"Okay, can you just answer my question? Are these two items written by the same person?"

"Yes."

"So they *are* a match?"

"I'd say with ninety-nine percent certainty that the person who wrote in this journal is the same person who filled out this questionnaire."

So Isabel and Scarlett had produced identical handwriting . . . which meant that the alter truly *was* Isabel.

Scarlett hadn't lied.

Kim smiled. "I could kiss you, Nga."

Nga smiled back. "I wouldn't judge."

Kim kissed her quickly on the lips and moved toward the door. "Listen, thank you so much. I'd love to buy you a drink sometime to say thank you."

"Great. I'll invite my brother-in-law. He's a catch. And a better kisser than me."

———————

KIM WALKED INTO THE Jarvis police station with more confidence than she felt. Seated on the tall stool at the reception desk was a sixty-something woman with rhinestone-trimmed glasses and an elaborate bleached-blond updo.

"I need to see Scarlett Hascall," Kim said, flashing her most professional smile. She'd worn her only pair of high heels, along with a black pencil skirt, and, yes, her hospital name tag. She felt guilty using her title to try to curry cooperation, but not guilty enough to forgo using everything in her arsenal to try to help Scarlett.

"I'm sorry, dear," the receptionist said. "She's in holding."

Kim thought for a moment, buying time, trying to imagine how her father would handle the situation. Roger Patterson was known to be a gentle, easygoing man, and yet he nearly always got his way in departmental matters.

"Oh, that's right," Kim said, snapping her fingers and turning up the wattage of her smile. "Zack mentioned that. You know what, don't bother calling him, he's expecting me—I'll just show myself back."

She walked past the desk, feigning confidence, but half expecting the receptionist to catapult over the top and tackle her.

But no one followed her as she made her way through a maze of cubicles, reading name tags until she spotted Zack near the back of the large space, a coffee cup in his hand.

"Detective Trainor!" she called. "I need to speak to Scarlett."

"You can't be back here," Zack said, clearly not happy to see her.

"Please, just five minutes."

He scowled. "About what?"

"I . . . I don't . . ." She glanced down at the notebook in her hand—the one she'd borrowed from Jen Wilcox, filled with the thoughts and dreams of an adolescent Izzi. The one whose hand-writing, she thought, was a dead-on match for the girl they had ar-rested for murder.

If she didn't do something, Scarlett's case was going to move for-ward, taking her ever closer to being sentenced for a killing that Kim was certain the girl hadn't committed. Except . . . even Kim had to admit that the case against Scarlett was damning. There was no rational, scientific explanation for what was happening. Disso-ciative identity disorder—which already had plenty of detractors—had never, to Kim's knowledge, been associated with people who were *dead*. Never, in case history, had she come across a patient who had been proven to house the souls of the deceased. It was, frankly, impossible, according to the standard of proof that Kim held as a scientist.

But Kim's intuition was just as strong as her intellect. It had to be, to endure the things she'd endured—to survive the things that had happened to her. And as strong as faith—not traditional reli-gious faith, perhaps, but faith in the essential goodness of humans. And while there were certainly some people who were afflicted by various traumas or psychoses that caused the proper function of their conscience to deviate, Kim did not believe this was the case with Scarlett.

Either way, Kim *had* to talk to Scarlett, to, at the very least, settle the questions in her own mind.

"Let me guess," Zack said, clearly exasperated. "Doctor-patient privilege? Word of warning, Dr. Patterson, from here on out, I'd plan on doing Scarlett's psych sessions in state lockup."

"All I'm asking for is five measly minutes," Kim said through gritted teeth. She met his gaze, trying to tell him wordlessly how important this was to her, and for Scarlett.

The standoff lasted for another maddening moment. She took him in, noticing just how long his lashes were, and that he had brown eyes with flecks of gold around his irises. Finally, he softened. "Okay, fine." He led her back to a closed door, unlocked it, and stood aside for her to enter. "Five minutes."

The door closed firmly behind her. Scarlett was sitting at a table, looking frightened and alone, but when she spotted Kim, she brightened slightly. There were four chairs in the room in addition to the table, and nothing else—except for a large mirror that Kim knew was a one-way device that allowed investigators to watch. She had no doubt that Detective Trainor was watching her now.

She sat down in front of Scarlett and seized her hands. "We don't have much time, so listen carefully. You didn't do anything. Okay?"

"You don't know that. I don't even know. I had this dream . . . I saw her. I *killed* her." Scarlett's face was pale, her eyes bloodshot. Kim's heart contracted in her chest. She knew how devastating it was to think . . . to think yourself capable of something so terrible. She couldn't let Scarlett believe herself to be a murderer, not even for a second.

"I have a dream where a Japanese spider crab in ruby slippers teaches me how to juggle coconuts. Dreams don't mean *anything*. Listen, we're going to figure this out. I am going to do everything I can to help you."

Scarlett nodded, looking close to tears. "They keep asking me about the night she disappeared and—and why I went to Isabel's house, and I just can't remember anything. But no one believes me." The last words came out as more of a sob.

"Okay, take a deep breath." Scarlett complied, and her shaking slowed a bit. Kim nodded. "Good job. Okay. Scarlett, what do you remember from earlier?"

"I don't know. It's all kind of a blur."

"Do you remember coming to see me at my office? Do you re-member trying to hurt yourself?"

Scarlett refused to meet her eyes, scratching listlessly at the table with her fingernail.

"Hurting yourself isn't the answer," Kim forged on. "I know . . . I've been there. Please, Scarlett, look at me."

Bang. Bang. Someone was pounding on the one-way mirror. Sounds of yelling came from the hallway.

"What's happening?" Scarlett cried.

The door burst open, and Scarlett's father ran in. Zack followed behind, his hand on the other man's shoulder, trying to force him back. As Peter Hascall fought his way free, Zack glared at Kim.

"Time to go. *Now*. Both of you. Scarlett, you stay here," Zack commanded.

"Daddy?" Scarlett tried to get up, but Kim held her back with a hand on her arm.

"Get her out of here!" Hascall shouted, pointing angrily at Kim.

"I've got it, Mr. Hascall," Zack said wearily. "Dr. Patterson, I need you to step outside now."

"Get away from my daughter!" Hascall yelled as she went past him.

"I'm her doctor," she responded calmly.

"Not anymore, you ain't."

"She's an adult, so she can make—"

Hascall lunged at Kim, fist flying. Reacting quickly, Zack caught his arm mid-swing. He surely saved Kim from a black eye, if not a concussion. She looked to the detective, gratitude washing over her face.

Zack pulled Peter Hascall back as he continued to lash out at Kim.

"No, Dad," Scarlett cried. "Please."

Zack shoved Kim and Hascall into the hallway. "I'm calling a lawyer," Hascall said to no one in particular. "Right now!"

Zack turned his glare on Kim, before following Hascall toward the door, making sure the father didn't change his mind and return. After Hascall was safely outside, Zack turned on his heels and stalked wordlessly past Kim, disappearing into a back office.

Well, that had gone well. Kim's heart sank as Hascall trudged to the exit without looking back at her. She understood why Scarlett's father didn't trust her—she probably wouldn't, either, if she were in his shoes. After all, Scarlett's condition had seemed to become *worse*, not better, since Kim had started treating her.

With Scarlett in custody, Peter Hascall threatening legal action, and her own job in jeopardy, Kim had no idea what to do next. She walked back to the reception area and sank dispiritedly to a sofa facing an enormous bulletin board covered in missing-person flyers. As she tried to make sense of everything that had happened in the last few days, she idly scanned the images of the missing: the names, the dates they disappeared, the desperate pleas of their loved ones. They went back for years, some of them faded and creased, others—Isabel's among them—fresh and new.

Claudia Johnson. Julian Tate. Gloria Eng. Henry Beaumont.

She backtracked. *Julian . . . Henry.*

Kim leaped up from the sofa to take a closer look at the bulletin board. Henry Beaumont's faded flyer said the little boy disappeared when he was only five years old. The Henry alter had said he was five . . .

Kim grabbed the flyers off the board, pushpins flying and her heart pounding. Then she raced back the way she'd come. She saw Holt stepping out of his office, yawning, and headed straight for him.

"Chief! I need to speak with you!"

The receptionist was quicker to react this time, popping off her stool with alacrity and chasing after her. Zack must have forewarned her this time. "Miss, you can't be in here!"

"It's fine, Deb," Holt said mildly. "I'll handle this."

Reluctantly, Deb returned to her station, her eyes narrowed at Kim.

"Dr. Patterson, since you're here, you might as well come on in and join us," Holt said, and Kim followed him into his office, where Zack Trainor was occupying one of the chairs. She took the one as far away from him as possible. Just looking at him, knowing what he was putting Scarlett through, made her hot with anger.

"Chief, I'm sorry, but I don't know how to explain this without sounding like a crazy person," Kim said.

"I've already heard about your . . . dissociative what-was-it? Multiple personalities?"

"Like that movie *Fight Club*. With the guy," Zack said sarcastically. "But he's really the other guy."

"Listen to me!" Kim said, willing Zack to shut up for once. "Early on, it became very clear that Scarlett has at least three alternate identities. She may have more—"

"—and this is where you tell me she's actually innocent because one of her alters is the real killer." Zack turned his keen gaze on Kim, and for a moment, her anger subsided. Then all her fury and desperation came rushing back.

"No, that's not what I— I messed up. I misdiagnosed her. I don't believe she has DID now." She infused her statement with all the authority she could muster, even while confessing her error.

"Uh-oh," Zack said, leaning back with his hands behind his head. "Here we go."

"The names of Scarlett's alters that I know about are Isabel, Julian, and Henry. But . . . these personalities weren't created in Scarlett's mind. They are all real people."

"Come again?" Holt said curiously.

Kim lay three flyers on his desk, carefully lining them up. "Isabel," she said, tapping one with her fingertip. "Julian. Henry."

Holt and Zack exchanged a look.

"What exactly are you suggesting, Dr. Patterson?" Zack demanded.

"I'm not suggesting anything . . ." She pointed at the pictures, gulping down her doubts. "The *facts* are, Isabel, Julian, and Henry are all either missing or dead. And somehow, they're all . . . inside Scarlett Hascall."

NINETEEN

Kim took a sip of the stale coffee in her mug—really, at this point, more like tepid, congealing coffee grounds with milk—and pushed her notes away. She glanced at the clock: 3:02 a.m. She'd been at this for hours, ever since getting home from the station, and she was no closer to understanding what might be going on with Scarlett than when she'd started. But she couldn't stop, not until she'd figured out a way to free Scarlett from police custody and clear her from suspicion once and for all.

"Hey, Siri. Call Dad. Speakerphone."

Siri's muffled voice piped up from somewhere in the pile of paperwork, and after only a single ring, her father picked up.

"Honey," Roger Patterson's voice came on, sounding alert and awake. "It's three in the morning where you are."

"Yeah, what are you doing up at this hour?" Kim asked lamely, attempting to inject a note of humor into her voice and failing.

"Kim." The tone in his voice made her feel suddenly exhausted. "That last message of yours made me want to fly your mother up there to see you—see if she can help you make sense of things."

"Don't joke, Dad. Two psychiatrists in one family is two too many. Keep her away. Please." Her mother's interference was the last thing she needed right now.

"Okay, but . . . are you all right?" After she didn't respond for a moment, he added, "Kimberly?"

"Yeah. It's just . . . my new patient. She reminds me of . . . Joselyn." There was a weighted silence. "This case might be cutting too close to home."

"I'm sorry. I know that can be tough."

"Emotions are clouding my judgment. I'm sounding like a lunatic." She laughed a little, and then realized the deranged sound of her laugh wasn't helping her case.

"Well, Kimmy, your compassion is what makes you a great doctor. And, of course, you *are* a lunatic."

Kim couldn't help smiling at that. "You get my e-mail? Did you find anything? I figure since you've spent your life studying religions, you might have a take. What do you know about reincarnation?"

"Well, obviously you've gone down the Hindu route." Kim relaxed as her father's voice took on a professorial tone. If she kept him talking about academic subjects, she'd keep him away from asking more questions about how she was doing. "They're one of the largest groups that believe in reincarnation. But based on the notes you sent, I'd start investigating the Druze."

Kim grabbed her laptop and started typing in her browser's search field. "The Druze? What the hell is the Druze? Some crackpot cult?"

"Hey, it's got more than two million followers. It's a religion based on the teachings of Socrates, Aristotle, Plato . . ."

As her dad continued to describe the roots of this religion, Kim scrolled through the results on her screen, picked one, and started reading. "Wow. Casey Kasem was Druze? Shaggy from *Scooby-Doo*?" She kept scrolling. "Sorry, it's late, I'm punchy. But tell me, Dad, what's Shaggy's connection to my case?"

"Well, if you'd been listening to me instead of reading *Wikipedia* . . . The Druze believe that after you die, your soul moves on, not to an *after*life . . . but to *another* life. At death, the soul is instantly transferred to another body. Sounds like it lines up with your crazy theory."

"So theoretically, Isabel's soul could have transferred to Scarlett's body upon death, according to these people."

"That's the idea." She could hear her father padding around his office, probably picking up some book or another to check his facts.

"Do they believe that more than *one* soul can take up residence in a host body?" Kim asked.

"Not to my knowledge, but then, I can't say I'm an expert. I'll do some further reading . . ." Kim had to laugh at the eagerness in his voice. Any excuse for a new research project.

"Okay, then. How do the souls pick their hosts? I mean, why Scarlett?" Kim sat back in her chair, chewing on a thumbnail as she thought.

"Good question. Some of the prominent recorded cases involve coincidence of birth and death. In other words, the first soul's transference occurs exactly at the moment of the host's entry into this world. Perhaps something to look into?"

"Interesting," Kim said, clicking on a link about a three-year-old Syrian boy who found the man who had murdered him in a past life. "Thanks, Dad . . . so did you need anything else?" she asked distractedly.

"Uh, didn't *you* call *me*?"

Kim shuffled papers until she found the phone, kissed the air loudly, and hung up. Then she started banging away on the laptop, exploring the Druze, determined to find out everything she could about the single thread that seemed to lead anywhere close to Scarlett.

WHEN KIM'S PHONE RANG, she lifted her head groggily from her desk. She'd fallen asleep on her notes, her laptop pushed out of the way, its battery drained. Light poured through the windows, and for a moment, she panicked, wondering if she'd missed a shift. Then she remembered that she wasn't due in until the evening, which was the excuse she'd given herself for staying up most of the night doing research.

She grabbed the phone and managed a groggy "Hello."

"Kim." In that one short syllable, Kim recognized Kyle's voice—Kyle's *unhappy* voice.

"Well, hello, sunshine," she said, trying to stave off whatever he was about to tell her. She had a bad feeling that this time it wasn't going to be something she could solve by tackling him on her couch.

"You need to come in to the hospital. Now."

That didn't sound good. Kim looked at the clock—it was nine fifteen. Knowing Kyle's schedule, that meant he'd been there for only twenty minutes.

What could have happened in the first twenty minutes of the day?

"I'll be there in a half hour."

"I'd try to make it sooner if I was you. Graver is waiting. We'll meet in her office."

Kim's stomach dropped. "Miranda Graver?"

"You know any others?" Kyle said irritably, then hung up without another word.

As she brushed her teeth, splashed water on her face, and raced to put on a serviceable blouse and black pants, Kim tried to focus on reasons Graver would want to see her. The chief of staff was an imposing woman. She occasionally checked in on her doctors and oversaw diagnoses personally, as she had on the day that Scarlett had come in, usually terrifying the poor interns who stumbled into her path (hell, even the fully trained doctors were terrified of her). The rest of the time she could be seen striding through the halls, trailed by assistants and underlings, usually giving orders, as though on the way to fell an empire.

Was Kim about to be fired?

The thought was too awful to consider, and so Kim turned her mind back to Scarlett's case as she drove. After reading about the Druze last night, she'd looked up the missing persons who'd taken residence as Scarlett's alters and discovered something shocking: Henry Beaumont had disappeared from his home on precisely the same day that Scarlett had been born, just as Kim's dad had suggested. It all seemed to match up.

Maybe taking on that first soul when she was born had somehow made Scarlett's psyche more receptive, more open to taking on lost souls in the future. Or maybe, possibly, it was pure coincidence. But what if, as she had suggested to Jen Wilcox, Henry was neither alive nor fully gone, but existed in some nether realm in between? What if, as his own life ended, he slipped into another body—a host, a refuge where he could retreat from the terror of his death, where he could find shelter as he waited to move on?

Nothing that Kim had studied in medical school had prepared her for the possibility of reincarnation, and until recently, she'd rebelled against her father's wide-ranging and tolerant ideas about mysticism, inexplicable phenomena, and unusual cultural belief systems. It had been a mild rebellion, based on love and mutual respect, but Kim's attraction to the sciences had at least a little to do with growing up in a home where meditation was practiced with as much fervor as scholarship.

But things had changed, abruptly and profoundly. Kim had come face-to-face with an actual example of something that until now had been purely theoretical, even to her father.

At the hospital, she found her usual space taken by an Escalade with Oregon plates and had to park at the very end of the visitor lot. Almost jogging to make up the lost time, she was sweating and frazzled by the time she got to the top floor, where the administrative offices were located.

As if in reproach, Graver's secretary looked as though she'd stepped out of *Fortune* magazine. Dressed in an immaculate tailored jacket and a sophisticated silk blouse, her hair was swept back in a perfect, stylish cut. She gave Kim an icy appraisal before telling her to go on in, that she was expected.

Kim walked into Dr. Graver's office to find Kyle standing by the window, arms crossed, staring out over the view of the town below. Graver was typing, staring at her screen over her reading glasses, but as Kim entered, she removed the glasses and set them primly on the desk.

"Dr. Patterson," she said, in the impeccably enunciated voice that could strike terror into any resident's heart. "So good of you to join us. Please, have a seat."

Kim did as she was told, and Kyle sat next to her, avoiding her gaze.

"I'll come right to the point. Dr. Berman and I have been discussing your latest departures from policy. Please," she said, holding up a hand to stop Kim from responding. "Let me finish. This is only the last in a series of increasingly concerning violations of hospital code, a code that was constructed with enormous care by physicians who have a great deal more experience than you have. I am aware of your unorthodox approach to treatment, and you may be surprised to know that I admire you for being willing to push past accepted methods in the interest of your patients' care. *However*."

She leaned forward, emphasizing her words by stabbing at her desk blotter with a pale-polished fingernail. "Our duty to our patients is to balance their care with critical oversight. As far as I can tell, you have acted entirely on your own, and in defiance of your direct supervisor's orders. Time and again, you have taken actions that put at risk not only your patients but also the entire hospital. You have exposed us to possible legal action of a magnitude that could literally shut us down. In doing so, you have put hundreds of your colleagues' jobs at risk, with no apparent regard for their welfare, or the welfare of their families, or for the *other* patients who depend on them."

Kim longed to protest as Graver ratcheted up the stakes. Surely it was unfair to lay *all* of this on her; physicians made difficult judgments in hospitals everywhere, every day. But she knew saying anything to defend herself now would only make things worse. She stole a glance at Kyle, but he was staring fixedly ahead, his mouth set in a tight line. Clearly he wasn't going to have her back here.

She couldn't exactly blame him. If Graver found out about their relationship, his job would be in jeopardy, too. And though she knew well that it took two to tango, she had pretty much dragged him onto that particular dance floor.

"Am I fired?" she asked in a small voice when Graver's lecture finally ended.

The corner of Graver's mouth twitched. "You are on official performance review," she said crisply. "You can think of it as a form of probation. For the next three months, your work with your patients and your interactions with your colleagues will be closely monitored. You will have regular evaluations and status reports. At the end of this period, I will decide, with the board, whether you will be offered continued employment."

Kim opened her mouth to thank her, but Graver cut her off. "In addition, I want you to take the next two weeks off. When you return, the three of us will meet again to discuss a performance plan and develop concrete benchmarks. That will give me, Dr. Berman, and some of your other colleagues time to put together a strategy to save your career. Because let me be straight with you, Dr. Patterson—it's make-or-break time for you. If you fail here, I doubt there's any hospital in the country that's going to welcome you. So I want you to use these next two weeks to think very carefully about your priorities and how you might finally learn to work within a system designed to serve and heal."

It took a moment for that to sink in. "I see," Kim said, face aflame. She slowly stood up on shaking legs. "Thank you for your time."

Then she walked out before either Graver or Kyle could see her break.

Back in the parking lot, she'd almost made it to her car when she heard Kyle call her name. Turning, she saw him jogging toward her, his jacket flapping. For a moment, she thought he was going to apologize for leaving her hanging—maybe even offer to try to work with her, to help her prove to Graver that she was capable of doing the job.

But as he caught up with her, she saw the steely wall in his eyes, and she knew her hopes were in vain.

"If you're going to yell at me, maybe you could save it for another day," she said hollowly. "I think I've had just about all I can take for now."

"This won't take long," Kyle said. He was breathing slightly heavily, and his tie had flown up over his shoulder. He tugged it irritably into place. "I just got off the phone with the police, right before you came in. Dead souls. *Dead souls?* You actually said that the alters inside Scarlett are the 'dead souls' of three different people?"

Kim had never seen him so agitated. Kyle was normally imperturbable, almost to a fault. But now his face was mottled and red, his eyes distressed, his fists clenched. Almost involuntarily, Kim took a half step back. "I might not have used those exact words . . .

actually, I think I *did* use those exact words. And yes, there may even be *more* than three dead souls inside her."

"Why?" His voice sounded almost strangled. "Why would you say that out loud . . . especially to the police?"

Part of Kim wanted to apologize, to admit she'd screwed up, to backpedal, but doing so would only be an effort to placate Kyle. And she couldn't afford to put his interests ahead of Scarlett's. "Kyle, Scarlett is not bipolar. Now, given what I've seen, I don't even think she's DID. There's something . . ." She trailed off.

"Go ahead and say it—*supernatural*?" His lips curled sarcastically.

"Your word, not mine."

"Just because you can't explain something doesn't mean you have to leap to some 'supernatural' explanation."

"And just because you don't understand something doesn't mean it isn't real," Kim snapped, her anger overtaking her guilt and mortification. "When Louis Pasteur suggested that invisible things called germs caused disease, people thought he was deranged."

"That's hardly the same thing."

"Open your mind for a moment. *Please*. I have substantial evidence that the alter inside of Scarlett who identifies herself as Isabel Wilcox . . . truly *is* Isabel Wilcox."

Kyle shook his head in disgust. "I'm not even going to dignify that with a response."

"Wait." Kim resisted putting a hand on his arm to compel him to listen to her. "First of all, Scarlett didn't know Isabel and yet she has intimate knowledge about her. Her handwriting on the intake form is the same as the handwriting in Isabel's journal. She knew her secret hiding place as a child. And how do you explain the bloody water pouring out of Scarlett's mouth? Kyle, we're on the verge of an incredible breakthrough—"

"You're on the verge of getting *fired*! If the board of directors heard what you're saying—"

"Scarlett needs help. She was contemplating suicide. You *saw* her."

Kyle regarded her for a long moment before shaking his head. Some of the anger had drained from his expression; now he merely looked disappointed. "Look, I know it's not what you want to hear . . . but what if Scarlett's violent alter is pretending to be Isabel? Showing you only what he wants so he can hide something terrible? Or . . . what if your patient's just faking the whole thing? Scarlett Hascall could be a calculating, manipulative psychopath who stalked Isabel Wilcox and has done extensive research into Jarvis's missing persons in order to build these personas. I mean, I know it's far-fetched, but isn't it more likely than she's a vessel for lost souls?"

"That's not even—"

"*Stop*. Please, Kim." Kyle drew a deep breath and closed his eyes briefly before continuing. "In the past, I may have let my . . . feelings for you cloud my professional judgment. I've looked the other way too many times to count, telling myself that I was helping you. But I wasn't. Time and time again, you've managed to alienate people— our colleagues, your superiors. And now you've endangered the hospital.

"Kim, you're fucking brilliant. It's obvious. But you're also completely undisciplined. What may have impressed your professors when you were in school doesn't work anymore, because these are real people who come to us for help. Vulnerable people." Kyle shifted slightly as he delivered the last blow. "And it's not just them. This might sound selfish—maybe I *am* selfish—but I can't risk going down with you."

Kim blinked. It had been a hell of a speech—one that sounded like he'd rehearsed it. It mortified her to realize that he had clearly been thinking about breaking up with her for a while. Figuring out a way to distance himself from her fuckups and mistakes.

"I would never—" she began.

"Let me finish. I came to medicine because, yeah, I'm an idealist. I want, no, I *need* to help people. And I can't do that if I throw my principles away the first time a beautiful woman clouds my judgment. So—"

"So you're breaking up with me," Kim said tonelessly, her heart too numb to react.

"I . . ." For a long moment he just stared at her, his gaze searching her face. Then he said gently, "Yes. I am. Look, I'll do my best to control the damage around here, but I'm not sticking my neck out for you again. On the off chance—and I hate to say it, but I do think it's a pretty small chance—that you are able to be reinstated, we'll find a way to work together. I promise to remain professional. But, Kim, for me to make that work, there can't be any more . . . inappropriateness between us. No calls, no texts—"

"No nooky in the staff lounge," Kim said. The numbness was quickly sliding down into horrible acceptance . . . the same feeling she got every time she took a risk, hoping that finally she was ready for intimacy, for the sort of closeness that other people seemed to manage without effort—but then ended up alienating a lover or a friend.

It had been a long time since she'd let this happen. The move to Alaska, the thousands of miles between her and her past, the physical barriers of geography and climate—all of these had combined to trick her into thinking that *this* time it would all be different.

But she never should have tried. One of these days, she would finally have to accept that she was never going to be able to run from herself. "I get it. And I know you won't believe me, but I am sorry. For ever involving you. For . . . all of it."

All of it but Scarlett, she added in her own head, where her determination to help this girl was hers alone.

TWENTY

"Here you go, boss," Evelyn said, plopping a stack of folders on his desk that afternoon. She was wearing her signature scent, a heavy cloying perfume that went well with her bombshell-blond hair and shocking pink nails, but didn't exactly conform to dress code. Funny how neither Holt nor any of the other higher-ups at the station had ever called her on it.

Evelyn may have charmed half the station, and she was a damn fine officer to boot, but she was still several years Zack's junior, so she got stuck with the grunt work. Like digging up everything the station had on Scarlett Hascall, anything they might have missed before.

"I took the liberty of going through these," she said, plopping into her chair at the desk across from his.

"Naturally," Zack said drily. "Because that's exactly what 'get these to me as soon as possible, Evelyn' means."

"Fuck off, it only took me about five minutes. I'm a fast reader. And besides, they all say pretty much the same thing. Scary, creepy, messed-up girl with a tendency toward violence. But she's still just a little girl, and not all that strong. I could bench-press two of her. Do you really think it was her? Who killed Isabel, I mean?"

"I'm not saying it was definitely her. But I think we have to con-sider the possibility, yes. Hey, Evelyn . . ."

"Yeah?"

For a moment Zack deliberated about whether he should tell her all the details of what had happened at the Wilcoxes' house yesterday. It had been unnerving, to say the least. Seeing Scarlett Hascall with that ancient, ragged doll, in the cubbyhole that she couldn't possibly have known about, had disturbed him more than he'd let on.

Kim's theory that the girl was harboring the souls of dead peo-ple was as crazy as thinking Elvis was abducted by aliens.

But on the other hand, even if Scarlett had somehow managed to learn the most private details of Isabel Wilcox's life, Zack couldn't imagine that she was that good an actress. And no killer he'd ever encountered had gone to such elaborate lengths to throw off suspi-cion, especially when, if she'd simply done nothing at all, no clues would have ever pointed her way.

Still, the thought of explaining all this to Evelyn underscored yet again how insane the dead-soul theory was. Evelyn, a strong advocate of Occam's razor—the simplest answer is always the best—might not think Scarlett was capable of murder, but she would never let him live it down if Zack confessed that on some small level, Kim's theory was starting to resonate with him. Be-sides, CSI had combed through Scarlett's house for any trace ev-idence connecting her to Isabel, and they had confiscated her computer and some notebooks. If Scarlett was guilty, they'd know soon enough.

"Never mind," he said. "Thank you."

Evelyn got up and wandered off, probably in search of one of the younger officers to terrorize. Zack shoved the files into his back-pack. Tomorrow they'd have to let Scarlett go if they still didn't have enough evidence to officially charge her with Isabel's murder.

Maybe a change of scenery would be good—help him see an angle he might not have otherwise. Either way, if he sat in this station much longer, he was going to lose his mind.

———

ZACK WAS JUST PUTTING the finishing touches on a simmering pot of puttanesca sauce, watching the Mariners game he'd taped the night before, when his doorbell rang. He wiped his hands on a towel and turned down the sound, then went to the door to find Kim Patterson huddled on his porch, without a jacket, in the chilly rain.

"Hi," she said in a small voice, not meeting his eyes. Even if she hadn't been underdressed and freezing, her wet hair plastered to her neck, looking like a surprisingly attractive drowned rat, the way she uttered that single word made it clear that something was bothering the good doctor.

"You're not dressed for the weather," he said.

She shrugged. "I just spent eight years in Southern California. I'm not used to this."

"Is this some ploy to force me to let you in?"

"Um, if I say yes, will you let me in anyway?" Her nose twitched, and she brightened a bit. "What is that incredible smell?"

Zack rolled his eyes and stood aside to let her enter. She made a beeline for the kitchen like a hound tracking a scent, and appropriated a dish towel to dry her hair.

"Don't tell me you made this," she said. "I haven't eaten all day. Do you have a little Italian grandmother stashed somewhere around here?"

As if on cue, a young woman's voice called out from the other room, "Did you steal my razor again, Z, or have you switched to pink?"

Kim shot Zack an apologetic look, realizing immediately that he wasn't cooking for one. Before he could respond, Brielle wandered in. She was dressed in a paint-splattered old man's shirt with the cuffs rolled up, her hair piled on top of her head. Her expression of surprise quickly turned sly. "Wow, Zacky," she said, "you didn't tell me a *girl* was coming over!"

"My sister, Brielle," Zack said. "We're twins, believe it or not, despite her various deficiencies. Genetics—it's a crap shoot."

"I love you too, baby brother," Brielle said, extending her hand. "I'm three minutes older."

Kim shook hands, giving Brielle a shy once-over. Zack could guess what Kim was thinking: women were often intimidated by Brielle's casual beauty, something he was pretty sure his sister wasn't aware of—but about which he was in no rush to inform her. She was willowy and graceful, where he was muscular and forceful; she had wild dark ringlets down her back, where he kept his own hair cropped meticulously short. They shared the same wide, soft brown eyes, the sculpted chin, and cheekbones, but on her, they came together in effortless femininity.

"I'm Kim Patterson," Kim said at last. "Your, uh, brother is working on a case that involves a patient of mine."

"She's a headshrinker," Zack said, checking on the pasta. "Now, didn't you have somewhere to be?"

Brielle smiled, mischievously. "Oh, you want some privacy?"

"No, I didn't mean that, I just . . ." Zack stammered, causing Brielle's smile to grow wider, until Kim saved him.

"Do you live here, too?" Kim asked Brielle, looking around Zack's spacious living room. He'd knocked out a few walls when he bought the place, keeping the original pine trim and painting it warm shades of ochre and red.

"She has her own damn apartment in the back," Zack said. "Though you wouldn't know it since she spends all her time in here making a mess."

"I'm painting his study," Brielle said. "In exchange for his cooking me dinner all week. Want to see?"

"You were just leaving," Zack said menacingly.

Brielle sighed theatrically. "If you get bored, Kim, come on back, I'm in the guest room above the garage. I've got half a bottle of bourbon and I was going to watch *Dirty Dancing*."

"*Now.*"

Brielle slugged her brother, a blow that glanced off his bicep with no more impact than a gnat, and let herself out.

"She's trying to squeeze me out," Zack complained, picking up a hand-painted tray she'd given him for his last birthday and holding it as gingerly as if it was giving off deadly radiation. "Keeps leaving her shit everywhere."

"I take it you've never been married," Kim said.

"No, can't say I have." Zack felt his face grow warm. "So. What can I do for you? I guess you might as well join me, if you're hungry."

"Well, after that heartfelt invitation, how could I possibly say no?"

Zack dug his tongue in the side of his cheek before picking up a bottle of red wine. "Would you like to stay for dinner?"

Kim shook her head playfully. "No, I couldn't possibly." She started to walk toward the door before turning back immediately. "Well, if you insist."

Five minutes later, Kim was seated across from him in a borrowed, oversized, but dry, button-down with a glass of red wine in hand.

"I want you to help me research Scarlett's alters," Kim said. "I think they might hold the key to figuring out what happened to Isabel."

"That's a huge leap. And if I'm not mistaken, you're no longer treating her." Holt's friendship with Peter Hascall had come in handy—the man had confirmed that Kim was no longer Scarlett's doctor, meaning she no longer had any right whatsoever to interfere with the investigation.

"I mean, technically, no, but what I do on my own time is my business."

"Tell you what then, Nancy Drew, I made that from scratch," he said, pointing to the food on her plate, "so why don't you stop talking for a minute and try it."

Kim dug in and practically moaned with pleasure. Zack smiled in satisfaction. More than one woman had fallen for him thanks to his cooking. But he was well aware that Kim had a boyfriend already, a line that he'd never cross. Not to mention the fact that pursuing Kim would be thoroughly unprofessional.

She was cute, though. Even with the rogue piece of fusilli poking out of the corner of her mouth.

Talking around a mouthful, she asked, "How did you learn to do this?"

Zack shrugged. "My dad was a good cook, at least when he was sober. He taught himself—he'd buy cookbooks at secondhand stores, and he'd start with the first page and try every recipe until he got to the end." He smiled fondly. "Cooking and football—that's how we bonded. Until he died."

Kim's gaze turned sympathetic—a look he hadn't seen from her before. It changed her face, somehow. "It must have been awful for you and your sister—losing him."

"Yeah. Pretty much turned our world upside down." He twisted his wineglass by the stem, swirling the contents thoughtfully in order to avoid her gaze. "I don't want to give the wrong impression, though—Dad was a mess. He was in and out of trouble the whole time we were growing up. All minor stuff—check forgery, shoplifting, getting into bar fights—and he couldn't keep a job, so we were constantly leaving one cheap-ass apartment for another when he got us thrown out. Honestly, life got a lot more stable after he was gone."

"Doesn't take away from your loss."

Zack cleared his throat. "I had Holt—he and Dad had crossed paths more than a few times by then, and I guess Holt felt responsible. So he took in me and Brielle. It was easier with me than her, I think—he didn't have any idea how to handle a teenage girl."

"So you became a sort of surrogate parent for her."

She was watching him carefully, her eyes narrowed and unblinking. Zack resisted the urge to fidget under her scrutiny. "Watch it, Doc, I'm not one of your patients."

"Sorry, I'm just curious. I promise, no . . . head shrinking."

Zack took a sip and regarded her thoughtfully. "I saw a counselor back then, you know," he said. "Holt set it up. Guy he knew from the job. All he ever wanted to talk about was the trauma of Dad dying. And then I'd feel guilty if I had other things on my mind. Typical teen stuff, I guess, but I acted out a lot."

"So you were in trouble with the law," Kim said. "But Holt *was* the law."

"Yeah." Zack smiled at the memory. It wasn't something he talked about often—but it seemed natural somehow to confide in Kim. Which probably made her a very good psychiatrist. Definitely something to watch out for.

Still, he wasn't exactly confiding case details. "He deputized me at sixteen, after he caught me tagging the water tower, drunk on rotgut whiskey. That's what started to turn me around, you know, thinking I had a chance to be on the police force. I mean, Holt was totally acting outside his authority, and I'm sure none of it ever went on the official books. He'd just toss me a few bucks here and there, called it my training pay." He frowned, pouring them each more wine. "That was around the time people started disappearing in Jarvis, though, so Holt was pretty preoccupied."

"Yeah, what is it with this town, anyway?" Kim asked. "There has to be, what, twice the rate of disappearances of a normal town? Three times?"

"More than that. Town the size of ours, you'd expect to have maybe one unsolved every decade or two. And it's always the same thing—no trace of a struggle, no clues left behind, maybe a few false leads that turn out to be nothing—and in the end, no body is ever found, except for Isabel Wilcox. That's pretty damn unusual."

"How many have there been?"

"Around a dozen, give or take. And they're from every walk of life, which is also not so typical."

"Do you think one killer is responsible? Or several?"

Zack frowned. "A single killer . . . I don't personally see that. It's really hard to determine any kind of pattern. If it was one person, we'd see some sort of logical progression. There was a guy Holt had picked up a few times for break-ins, but then there was a house-wife with a couple of kids in middle school. Next was a five-year-old boy—"

"Henry Beaumont," Kim broke in.

"Yeah. His parents were heartbroken. Last time they saw him was when they tucked him in one night. Couldn't identify any signs of a break-in, but they were the kind of folks who moved here be-cause they wanted to feel safe at night—safe enough not to lock up the house."

Kim took a moment before introducing her theory again. "Lis-ten, have you had a chance to think about what I said earlier? The fact that Henry disappeared—potentially died—on the same day Scarlett was born?"

"I have, actually." Zack felt his guard going up, his voice going hard. "And the conclusion I came to is that all of that is in the public record. All Scarlett would have had to do was go down to the town clerk and she'd be able to find out all kinds of information. For in-stance, this Julian you think she's 'harboring'? His criminal record is an online search away. Easy for her to construct a 'personality' based on what she read."

"Okay—but how about the cubbyhole? How was Scarlett—who never even met Isabel as far as we know—supposed to know such an intimate detail of her life?"

Zack shrugged. That detail had confounded him, too, but he wasn't about to admit it. "Scarlett could be working with someone who knew Isabel well. They could be working as a team, and using her so-called DID as a distraction. I mean, she slept with Brad Chaplin—maybe she wanted more. A real relationship. Maybe Scarlett thought she was his girlfriend, or could be if Isabel was out of the way . . . or maybe he took advantage of her interest in him in other ways. I mean, I'll give you this—Scarlett is an intelligent girl. I do believe she's capable of a complex strategy."

He could see Kim growing irritated as he laid out his thoughts—and he couldn't help noticing that anger brought color to her cheeks, and made her lean in across the table. *Intense*—that was a word he'd use to describe Kim. He shook his head and forced himself to focus on the moment.

"She hasn't mentioned anyone in our sessions who would have had access to the kind of details of Isabel's life that she would have needed," Kim was saying.

Zack got up and began clearing the dishes to help distance himself from his wandering thoughts. "Well, there's Brad Chaplin, of course. And we know he and Scarlett have a connection."

"Oh, come on—you can't be serious!"

"Or maybe someone in Scarlett's life was close to Isabel—like Scarlett's sister. Or her father, even. Don't assume, just because he does a good job of acting concerned about her welfare, that he's looking out for her," Zack cautioned. "He could be covering up his own agenda."

"What kind of agenda?"

"I don't know," Zack admitted. "That's why it's called an investigation. But it wouldn't be the first time a parent sacrificed a child's welfare to cover up a crime. I arrested a guy a couple of years ago who raised hell about the band teacher's conduct at his son's middle school, when it turned out he himself had been molesting kids in the band on field trips. Pete Hascall hasn't exactly helped the investigation—he flies off the handle every time something comes to light on her case."

"Scarlett's father isn't a criminal," Kim insisted. "He's just a concerned parent—he's watching his daughter fall apart before his eyes and he can't do anything to stop it."

"Oh, so you're a psychic, in addition to being a shrink?" Zack scraped the dishes in the sink. "You know, I'm not exactly fresh out of the pumpkin patch here. I've testified on sex abuse cases where no one suspected the predator. Ministers, teachers . . . even psychiatrists. Parents can seem benevolent when they aren't. Isabel Wilcox wasn't a model citizen. There are plenty of reasons that Peter Hascall could have wanted her dead—and if he had a connection to her, that would explain why his daughter, who has plenty of challenges, might have locked in on her and become obsessed with her."

Kim glowered at him, but for once she didn't seem to have a comeback. "It's just one possibility," he said, softening. "Look, maybe it wasn't Scarlett. Maybe it's just being pinned on her by some third party. There's a reason we haven't charged her with the murder yet, you know. The evidence is still mostly circumstantial." He stopped, thinking. "A lot of people know Scarlett's unstable. She'd be an easy target if someone wanted to frame her for murder. A smart perp would know she'd have a hard time defending herself."

Kim chewed her lip and stared off into space, and for a moment Zack regretted drawing her into his thoughts on the subject. After all, she wasn't an investigator. She was a thorn in the side of the investigation. So far she'd done more obstructing than assisting.

Still . . . in her own way, she was just trying to help. Her professional insights into Scarlett's behavior, wild poltergeist theories not-withstanding, were certainly valuable. He had never encountered a person as unhinged as the troubled teen. And Kim clearly cared a great deal about this case. "Hey, I'll admit that Scarlett's situation . . . the things she's been able to tell us . . . are unusual," Zack conceded.

"Because she's harboring alters!" Kim burst out, clearly frustrated. She got up and carried the wineglasses into the kitchen. "I know it flies in the face of conventional thinking, but—"

"*Conventional thinking?* I think it also flies in the face of 'rationality'."

Kim implored. "Isn't your job to explore every possibility?"

"Within reason."

"This is within reason! Scarlett Hascall did not kill Isabel Wilcox!"

"Hey, hey, calm down," Zack said.

"Don't tell me to calm down!" she snapped. "My patient's life is on the line here. I'm just asking you to open your mind. Just a little! Just because someone is neuro-atypical doesn't mean they're capable of murder! It doesn't mean they shouldn't be taken seriously!"

"Are we still talking about Scarlett?" Zack countered. He wasn't sure what was more frustrating: being lectured as though he'd done something wrong—when he considered himself one of the most open-minded members of the department—or the fact that he couldn't find any evidence to prove to Kim once and for all that Scarlett was faking. "Or are we talking about you?"

Kim gaped at him for a moment, and Zack instantly regretted his words. He knew that his frustration with not being able to convince her about Scarlett didn't justify attacking Kim personally.

Kim, visibly collecting herself, strode up to him. "You've got a smudge," she said imperiously, tapping her cheek. "Also, I'm leaving."

She stalked out of the kitchen. Zack tried to check himself out in the reflection of the stainless-steel refrigerator, wondering if it was true or if she was just distracting him and making an easy exit. "Where?" he demanded, following her into the living room.

"Where what?" Kim whirled around, so that they were almost face-to-face, and Zack felt something ignite within him.

"Where do I have a smudge?" He struggled to keep his voice steady.

"It's just tomato sauce," she said grudgingly. Her expression was aloof, but still, she didn't move away.

"I didn't ask what." Zack put his hand on her wrist and pulled her even closer. "I asked where."

Kim gazed up at him unblinkingly, her lips parted in surprise, and possibly something else. Slowly, she raised her free hand and used her thumb to wipe a spot on his left cheekbone. "There," she whispered, letting her hand fall to his shoulder. Her fingertips curled around his neck.

Zack put a hand on the small of her back and pulled her against him. Now their faces were only inches apart. This close, he could make out a tiny, pale scar running through one of her eyebrows, not to mention the silver flecks that seemed to sparkle in her green eyes.

"I don't know who's crazier," he said. "You for all your crackpot theories . . . or me for listening."

He wasn't sure if he was in for a slap, an argument, or a kiss.

After a moment that seemed to last an eternity, she twisted out of his grasp. "Thanks for dinner," she muttered. "But don't for a minute think you can charm me out of my convictions. There's one person in this whole mess whose fate I take personally. And guess what—it's not yours."

Seconds later, his front door slammed.

TWENTY-ONE

The troubling discussion with Zack kept Kim stark awake—and for once, it wasn't Scarlett Hascall on her mind. The conversation with Zack, and his hand on her back before she'd fled his house, kept replaying in her mind over and over until finally Kim took two sleeping pills from her medicine cabinet, before slumping back down on the bed in defeat. The next time she opened her eyes, the sun was beginning to rise.

She got up, made coffee, and wondered what the hell she was supposed to do with herself. A two-week suspension meant more time off than she'd had in the entire time she'd been in Jarvis. This was the first day in months that she didn't have to go in to the hospital. Someone else was seeing her patients, making her rounds, and taking care of her paperwork.

One thing was certain—she needed to do *something* or her anxiety over Scarlett's welfare would overtake her. She took a good look around the apartment, realizing how little she had actually done to settle in and make it her home. It wasn't a bad place; its best feature was the view out onto the street that ran along the docks, a sliver of the ocean visible beyond the rooftops. She still had almost nine months left on her lease. If she got canned from the hospital, she could always wait tables, or learn to drive a snowplow, or . . . something. But she was going to do everything in her power to convince the hospital to keep her on—once she was off probation, that is.

Kim sighed and strode toward the wall of unopened boxes that she hadn't touched since she moved in. She pulled down the top box from the teetering stack along the wall, ripping open the flaps. Inside were books she'd lugged from one apartment to the next, the beloved science fiction and fantasy novels that had sustained her during her foster placements before she was finally taken in by the Pattersons. The old books were as good a place to start as any, and Kim lined them up in the shabby oak bookcase that had come with the apartment.

For the next six hours, she cleaned and organized, trying to make the apartment feel like it belonged to an adult rather than a lazy fraternity brother. When her stomach started growling, she made a trip to the store and stocked up on groceries for the first time in over a month. She was sitting at her dinette table, eating a turkey sandwich that she'd made herself, when a call came in from Zack.

For a moment, she just stared at the screen, tempted to let it go to voice mail. She wanted to believe she was angry with him for the *crackpot* comment. She'd had to defend her profession much too often to put up with casual dismissal, especially from a man who was openly interfering with her treatment of a patient.

But the truth was that she was mad at him for completely different reasons. Or maybe she was mad at herself for feeling drawn to the very person who was trying to charge Scarlett Hascall with murder. Either way, the last few seconds they'd been together the night before played on an endless, mortifying loop in her head.

She stabbed at the answer button. "Yeah, what?"

"I have some information I thought you'd want to hear right away," he said stiffly. "We just released Scarlett Hascall. We don't have enough to charge her. For now."

Kim exhaled in relief. "Thank God."

"In my profession, it's considered a good thing to keep an open mind," Zack said stonily. "If I find definitive evidence that someone else killed Isabel Wilcox, I'll be ready to admit I was wrong. But until then . . ."

"Whatever. You can save the speech for someone else. I get it. Nothing's going to make you consider that something could be true if it isn't part of your narrow worldview." Still, she felt her body sag with relief, even while her hand trembled as it held the phone. "But one of these days, something's going to happen that you won't be able to explain away even if you *investigate* it for the rest of your life. Not everything in this world is black and white . . . people's motives aren't always simple."

"You're seriously going to give me a lecture on the criminal mind?" Zack sounded both angry and amused. "That's just great, Kim. I've got a whole file full of cold cases. I guess I should have just asked you to take a look at them from the start."

Go to hell, Kim thought, but she hung up without saying the words out loud. Because as much as she hated to admit it, Zack was right about one thing—she didn't have any definitive proof of Scarlett's alters. The handwriting, the bloody water—all those things *could* have been faked, as much as Kim's instincts screamed otherwise.

Sighing in resignation, Kim realized that she had been moving toward this decision for days. There was one way she might be able to prove to even the staunchest skeptic that Scarlett's alters were real. But if the hospital board ever found out, Kim would never work as a doctor again.

TWENTY-TWO

Within twenty hours of Scarlett's release from custody, she was reclining on the couch in Kim's newly organized apartment. It felt a little like they were hiding out—Kim from her colleagues at the hospital, and Scarlett from her father, who had forbidden her from seeing Kim again. But when Kim had told Scarlett her plan, she'd instantly agreed it was worth the risk.

"I told Dad I was meeting a friend to see a matinee," she confided. "Never mind that I don't think I've been to a matinee since I was like ten years old. Or that I don't have any friends. But he just wants me to be normal so bad . . ."

"I can understand that, I think," Kim said. Her own parents had pushed her into extracurricular activities from the moment she'd been released into their care: ballet, music, soccer . . . playdates with every kid in a five-mile radius. They'd wanted so desperately to make her happy, to help her forget the horrors of her past, that they couldn't see that sometimes solitude—painfully lonely as it could be—was critical to her recovery.

"It's not like he really fell for it, though. He sent Heather to follow me. But I ditched her in the Starbucks. She's probably still standing outside the bathroom that I climbed out the back window of."

Kim nodded. "I'm sorry we're having to be a little deceitful." She corrected herself. "A lot deceitful. I wish it were different."

"So do I. But that's why we're here, right?"

Kim offered a warm smile and a nod.

Over the next half hour, Kim took Scarlett through the relaxation exercises, priming her to allow the alters to reveal themselves. When Scarlett had entered the semiconscious state where she was most suggestible, her breathing even and deep, her chest rising and falling slowly, Kim invited Henry to reveal himself.

"Don't be afraid," she said gently. "Nothing bad will happen if you come out. Can you open the door, Henry, and come into this safe room where we can talk?"

For several long moments, nothing happened. Kim continued speaking to the little boy, wondering if maybe he'd disappeared, if he'd vacated Scarlett and moved on. But just when she was about to give up, Scarlett's eyelids twitched rapidly and her lips formed a frightened O.

"Hello?" Kim said tentatively. "Henry?"

"What do you want?"

"Are you still in the spaceship, Henry?"

A tear rolled slowly down Scarlett's cheek as Henry spoke through her. "It's so dark. And cold. I want to come out *now*."

Kim's heart broke for the little boy, who'd been trapped all these years without understanding what had happened to him, or why his soul couldn't move on. What would it be like to be five forever, desperately missing your parents and never understanding that they hadn't abandoned you?

"I want to talk about when you went into the spaceship," she said, as calmly as she could. "It was a long time ago, wasn't it?"

Scarlett's face twisted in concentration. "I think so." She shifted on the couch, the cheap fabric of the cushions rustling.

"Do you remember your parents? Your mom and dad?"

The tears started again. "I just want my mom," she whispered.

Kim forced herself to press the issue, despite the fresh pain it seemed to be bringing to Scarlett's alter. "Can you tell me how you ended up in the spaceship? It's important, Henry. I want to help you get out of there, but I need to understand how it happened."

"I didn't do it," she said. "It was the old man."

"The old man," Kim repeated, her pulse quickening. "What old man? Do you know his name?" This could be it—the detail that finally got the police off Scarlett's back, and proved to Kim's colleagues that she wasn't going crazy.

"From the park," Henry continued as if he hadn't heard Kim. "When I was with my mom. I didn't like him, but my mom talked to him. My mom is nice to everyone."

"You and your mother met an old man in the park?" Nothing that Kim had read online about the case had mentioned such a suspect. Was it possible that Henry's mother knew the killer but never put two and two together? Could he have been a neighbor? A doctor, a grocery clerk, or someone else they saw in the course of daily life? "Did you see him more than once? Was he your mother's . . . friend?"

"I didn't like him," Scarlett murmured miserably. "But he took me. At first to his house."

"He lives in a house? Do you remember where it was?"

Scarlett scrunched her face, concentrating, but finally shook her head. Then she blurted out, "News birdie."

At first Kim had thought she misunderstood. "News . . . birdie?"

Scarlett nodded her head emphatically. "It had a news birdie."

"What's a news birdie, Henry?"

"On top. A news birdie. I saw it. When I got let out of the trunk."

Kim struggled to understand. "News birdie?" Again, Scarlett nodded, more frustrated now. "Can you tell me more about the old man?"

Scarlett shook her head. "I don't want to talk about him." She was starting to grow agitated, her breathing shallow and ragged, looking wildly around the room as if searching for an escape.

"It's all right," Kim said soothingly. "Let's talk about something else. I have an idea. Do you like to draw, Henry?"

Scarlett brightened a little, nodding.

"I was wondering if you might like to draw me a picture of the spaceship. Do you think you could do that?"

Scarlett looked at her shyly. "I like to draw dogs," she said.

Kim handed her a pen and her notebook, turning to a fresh page. "I know," she said, "why don't you draw your spaceship with a dog next to it?"

Scarlett gripped the pencil as a child would, in her fist, and bent her head over the notebook. The drawing that took shape was crude but identifiable: a balloon-figure dog next to a rounded cylinder with a pointed nose cone and some scratchy lines down the middle, like windows, or grooves in metal. Scarlett finished her drawing by scribbling a tiny 1998 on the body of the craft.

"That's very good, Henry. Now, can you tell me about when the bad man made you go into the spaceship?"

"N-no," Scarlett said, shaking her head insistently. "I don't want to."

"I'm sorry, Henry. I know this is hard to talk about, and that remembering makes you sad. But we need to make sure that the bad man doesn't hurt other little children. Don't you think that would be a good thing?"

Scarlett didn't say anything, but she put her fist to her mouth and chewed on the knuckles.

"Did the man push you, or hit you?" Kim said, as gently as she could. "Did he put something over your eyes so you couldn't see, or—"

"No!" Scarlett doubled over so her chest was on her knees, and she put her hands over her ears, trying to shut out Kim's words. "No. No. No. No! Stop it, stop it!"

Kim leaned forward in alarm. If the Henry alter didn't stop screaming, one of the neighbors was likely to call the police—which would definitely not help her case. "Okay," she said quickly, touching Scarlett's shoulder gently. "It's all right, Henry, we don't have to talk about it anymore. In fact, I think you've done enough hard work for today. I really like the drawing you made for me. Let's stop here and you can rest for a while."

Scarlett nodded, still snuffling, and allowed herself to be coaxed back upright.

"Good-bye, Henry. It was nice to see you today," Kim said. "Please do something for me—when you go back into the special room, will you please ask Izzi to come out? I promise I will keep watch and make sure you are safe there."

As soon as the words were out of her mouth, Kim regretted making promises that—despite all her best intentions—were beyond her control to keep. But before she could find the words to explain, Scarlett's face had gone slack. Henry was gone—and Kim hoped he found some peace in whichever recesses of Scarlett's mind he made his home.

A shift in Scarlett's breathing caught Kim's attention. Scarlett's brows knit together and her lips pursed, then her eyes opened and she scanned the room wildly.

"Izzi?" Kim said. "Is that you?"

Scarlett's gaze fell on her. "Oh," she said, in a tired voice. "You again."

"Yes, it's me, Dr. Patterson. Thank you for coming out to talk."

"Whatever."

"I'm here to help you, if I can."

"*Sure* you are." Scarlett's eyes narrowed and her mouth twisted in a sneer. "I've heard that before, a few too many times. So excuse me if I don't jump up and down with joy."

"Izzi," Kim said, choosing her words carefully. "I know that something terrible happened to you, and I think I would have a hard time trusting, too, if I were in your shoes. But I really am here to try to figure out what happened to you. Anything you tell me—anything at all—might help the police punish the person who hurt you."

"Go to hell."

Kim blinked, surprised by the bitterness in Scarlett's voice. She resisted pointing out the obvious—that no one could hurt Izzi anymore, since she was already dead—in fear of upsetting the alter further.

"Izzi . . ."

"Say I tell you who did it," Scarlett continued angrily. "What's to stop them from going after my family? Do you have any idea how much I've already put my parents through?"

Comprehension dawned, along with renewed sympathy for the girl who, despite all her poor choices, had not deserved a violent death. She had loved her family, and now they were all that she had left to care about. The tense set of Scarlett's jaw, the refusal to name names, was proof of how determined Izzi was to protect them.

"I . . . understand your concern," Kim tried. "I can promise you that the only people I will share our conversation with are those who can get justice for you."

"Like the *cops*?" Scarlett sneered. "Oh, because they've always had my back—is that it? Forget it, I'm not saying another word to you."

"Izzi, *please*—"

"Forget about it," Scarlett said, her expression already going slack. "Later, bitch." Seconds later, Scarlett's head dropped back against the couch, her eyes drifting closed.

Disappointment weighed down Kim's thoughts. She held little hope that further attempts would get anything more out of the Izzi alter, and she wasn't sure she could justify putting Scarlett through further hypnosis in an effort to try. As she tried to think about how to proceed, there was a knock at her door.

Damn. Kim willed the visitor away, but the knocking continued; if she had any hope of salvaging the session, she would need to send them away.

"Scarlett, do you hear me? It's time for you to come back now. Inhale again, and exhale on a count of ten," Kim said. "I'll be right back."

At her door, she squinted through the peephole and discovered that Kyle was standing outside, looking nervous.

"Shit," she muttered under her breath. She couldn't allow him to see Scarlett—but taking her out of her semihypnotized state now would risk creating additional trauma.

She'd just have to prevent him from entering. She opened the door a crack, and faked a sneeze. "Sorry," she said. "I think I'm coming down with something." Pretty weak, but the best thing she could come up with at the moment.

Kyle sighed. "I probably deserve that. Please, just give me five minutes. I'd like to explain. And apologize."

Not what she'd expected. "I'm sorry, Kyle, I just don't think now is the time to—"

"Oh, come on, Kim," he said, his eyes searching hers. "I've been thinking. We're both a little . . . uncompromising. It's one of the things I love about you. But it doesn't mean we can't both learn to bend—without breaking what we have."

Kim blinked. For Kyle, that counted as downright poetic—and reminded her of what had drawn her to him in the first place. Kyle was the first man she'd been with who treated her as a professional equal, who didn't seem intimidated by her abilities or by her outspokenness. But he had chosen the worst possible time to apologize. "I'm just confused right now," she hedged.

"Allow me to clarify," Kyle murmured, and before Kim could stop him, he spun her into the apartment and up against the wall, where he proceeded to pin her with her feet an inch above the floor, his strong hands holding her hips.

Kim pulled away, ever so gently. "I don't want to get you sick."

Kyle closed the distance again. "I don't mind." Even closer. "I've banked a bunch of sick days." Closer.

Under any other circumstances—before recent events had cast shadows over their relationship—Kim would have been thrilled to find herself there. Even now, she felt her body responding with delighted pleasure.

Until Scarlett coughed delicately from the couch.

Kyle dropped her like a hot potato. "What the hell—?"

He spun around to see Scarlett, who seemed to be fully out of her semiconscious state, sitting bolt upright and rubbing her eyes.

"You brought her here?" Kyle demanded incredulously. "Not even a day after she was locked up in a holding cell, and with you on probation?"

"This isn't what you think it is," Kim said, torn between going to Scarlett and monitoring her return to awareness, and keeping Kyle in the dark about what they'd been doing.

"Oh come on, Kim, don't patronize me. You're not going to convince me you two were playing Chinese checkers."

"I wouldn't even try," Kim snapped, feeling her face heat with anger. "But you—and Dr. Graver and the cops—didn't give me any other choice."

"That's—that's the height of arrogance," Kyle said. "You're doing what you always do—putting yourself above it all. Like the rules don't apply to you. No other *choice*? How about, you insist on choosing your own path, every single time? Forget it—I'm not rehashing this same argument again. You can take it up with the review board instead."

Kim gritted her teeth. "Would you just listen to me for a minute? One of the alters, Henry—"

Kyle shook his head in disgust. "Stop! This has nothing to do with one of Scarlett's alters, whether it's 'Henry' or 'Bob' or fucking 'Sybil.' It's not about DID. It's about you! It isn't a game, Kim. You've got to know that the hospital has a huge interest in this case. Our exposure is potentially enormous. And don't look at me like that. Yes, I care about our bottom line. It's part of my job as department head. Part of how I make sure my employees continue to get paid. Part of—"

"Stop it!" Kim yelled. "*Please.* I'm already on suspension. And your sanctimonious speeches are, frankly, a huge buzzkill."

"Oh, don't worry," Kyle spat back. "Consider the mood broken. My libido tends to retreat whenever I'm watching my career implode."

"*Look*," Kim tried. "I didn't want you to see this, obviously, because I knew you'd overreact. But I'm on performance review, and for the next two weeks what I do with my time is my business. I promised I wouldn't treat Scarlett anymore. But Jarvis Regional doesn't recognize hypnosis as treatment. So what I'm doing here can't violate the hospital rules."

"You can't seriously expect me to accept that bullshit excuse," Kyle sputtered. "You know that what you're doing is exactly the opposite of what Graver expects from an employee on probation, in danger of *losing her job*. You can't possibly expect me to keep this between us."

"That's exactly what I expect," Kim said. Then she softened her tone. "At least, it's what I hope. For Scarlett's sake."

Kyle paused at the front door. He looked like he was working up the last word.

In the end, though, he just shook his head and let himself out.

TWENTY-THREE

Zack was just getting back from lunch, chewing on a cinnamon-flavored toothpick from Stony's Bar-B-Q, when Holt motioned him into his office. Too late, he spotted Kim sitting in one of Holt's chairs.

"Oh no," he said, immediately backing away as Holt looked up.

"Ms. Patterson—oh, sorry, hon, *Dr.* Patterson—was just telling me about her session with Henry Beaumont this morning." Kim gave him a grateful look.

Great, Zack thought, so now she had Holt eating out of her hand. He paused, fingers drumming against the doorframe, contemplating how best to deal with this. "You *are* aware, Holt, that Henry Beaumont has been missing, most likely dead, for almost two decades," he said. "Right?"

"I brought out his alter," Kim said impatiently. "Don't play dumb. I've been telling you all along that he's taken up residence in Scarlett, so you know that's what Holt meant."

Zack refused to look at her, focusing on Holt instead. "So what you're really saying is that Kim came in here to tell you about her session with *Scarlett*," he clarified. "A potentially dangerous and almost certainly delusional suspect in our murder investigation."

"Would you just shut up for five minutes and let me tell you what happened this morning?" Kim said, raising her voice. Slightly embarrassed, she added, "Please." Zack tried not to enjoy the way her face looked when she was upset, the flush in her cheeks and the glint in her eye as she stared at him.

"We can spare five minutes," Holt said firmly. "Go ahead, dear."

"Okay, well, I was talking to Henry," Kim said, speaking quickly, as if trying to make the most of the time Holt had given her. "It wasn't the first time his alter made an appearance."

"You mean, through Scarlett," Holt clarified. "When you hypnotized her."

"Well . . . yes." Kim avoided looking at Zack, perhaps annoyed at his incredulous scowl. He tried to rein it in, if only for Holt's sake. "In the past, Henry told me he was in a spaceship, has been insisting on it, actually. I asked him all kinds of questions to see if I could get him to clarify, but he just said that it was dark and there wasn't much room to move around. It was cold. I was thinking maybe he was in a closet, or even something like a freezer, but we weren't getting any further, so I asked him to draw a picture." She reached into her handbag and brought out a folded sheet, smoothing it flat on the chief's desk. "Look, you can see that he's got the nose cone, I suppose you'd call it, and the cockpit here. I don't know what these squares are, but—"

"Nineteen ninety-eight," Holt interrupted.

Kim was relieved that Holt's voice sounded surprised, not derisive. And that surprise turned to recollection.

"I think I know what that is," Holt continued, sounding astonished. "I mean, I know he's only five—but damn, that's a pretty faithful rendition. That's the time capsule we buried in front of City Hall to celebrate Jarvis's centennial."

"When was that?" Kim asked.

"Just three months into the year . . . 1998. Right there." He tapped the scribbled 1998 on the drawing.

"Nineteen years ago," Kim exclaimed. "Exactly when Henry went missing."

"So the timing works," Holt said thoughtfully.

"That picture could be anything," Zack argued, taking it off the desk. It was just a stick figure, really, jammed into a rectangle with a triangle at one end. Any kindergartner could have drawn the same, asked to illustrate an astronaut blasting off to the moon. Was Holt really buying this?

"Still, it wouldn't hurt to follow up," Holt said.

"Follow up how? The only way to know if there's anything to this theory would be to dig the damn thing up." Surely Holt wouldn't take things that far, Zack reasoned.

"Yeah?" Holt said, giving him a placid grin. "Might go fetch a shovel, then."

"Very funny," Zack muttered. To Kim, he pointedly added, "Anything else before I walk you out?"

Kim held his gaze. "I get a police escort to the front door?"

He smiled, but he didn't mean it.

Zack only walked her as far as the reception desk. "Make sure she doesn't come back in," he told the receptionist. "No more hall passes for the good doctor today."

After he was sure Kim had left, he went back to Holt's office. "You can't be serious about digging that thing up," he said.

Holt pretended to look around in consternation. "Am I still the chief around here? Or did you guys stage a coup at lunch?"

"It just seems like a total waste of time. I mean, come on. You heard her. The doctor's crazier than her patient." Why was he the only one who could see that?

"What did I always tell you the key to effective policing is, son?" Holt said patiently.

"Keeping an open mind," Zack answered robotically, and sighed. "Speaking of which, there's an angle I want to run by you.

For the sake of argument, could you just for one minute assume Scarlett had something to do with Izzi's death, instead of pretending she's some kind of shaman or witch doctor, speaking for *lost souls*? Let's say, for the sake of argument, that she's the killer . . . and let's add the argument that someone helped her. Who else, besides Brad Chaplin, could that be? Who in her life is strong enough to help her hide the body—and is devoted enough to her to cover it up?"

Holt leaned back in his chair with his hands behind his head. "You want me to say Pete? Peter Hascall?"

"I know he's your friend. But he's got a boat. Isabel's body was found in the bay. Might have helped Scarlett hide the body to protect his daughter. It explains why he's been so volatile lately—I mean, beyond the fact that his daughter's been in all sorts of trouble."

Holt nodded reluctantly. "Yeah . . . I see where you're going. I just can't see Pete as an accessory to murder, though."

Zack looked away in frustration. What was that about keeping an open mind?

It wasn't hard for Holt to sense Zack's irritation. "What about George DeWitt?"

Zack reengaged. "The missing hunter?"

Holt nodded. "I've been thinking about how we found Isabel's body—you know, with the bear trap around her leg."

Zack's mind pondered the possibility. "It could just be coincidence, but maybe there's a connection there. You said you knew him, what do you think?"

"Now we might be getting somewhere. Did game and wildlife records come back with an ID on the bear trap, from the piece that washed up?"

Zack shook his head. "Still waiting."

"Let's stop waiting, son. No day like today." Holt picked up his phone and started dialing.

"And he's still MIA, right? Could be guilty," Zack said. "Then again, could be dead—like everyone else in this damn town."

"I'm on hold." Holt put the phone on speaker while he waited. "I guess while we're hovering at five thousand feet, we should consider a few more suspects, add a couple long shots to the board."

"Long shots?"

"Did you explore Scarlett's mother yet? Not sure you would remember her, she left town before your time. Been in Juneau for years. Daughter got a bit of her looks, and a lot of her crazy. Maybe we could see if she's left town recently—could be she's mixed up in this somehow."

"Okay. Well, I guess we just about tripled the suspect list."

Holt slapped him on the back. "Just keeping you busy, son."

TWENTY-FOUR

By nine thirty the next morning, a crowd had gathered on the lawn in front of City Hall, watching a trio of city building and grounds workers unearth the capsule. The day was overcast and humid, and it was hard, sweaty work; they'd made the initial dig with a backhoe but switched to shovels to avoid damaging the capsule.

A hushed murmur went through the crowd when the first shovel hit metal. There was a sense of anticipation, which, on another occasion, might have led to cheering—but word had spread quickly about the purpose of the dig. The police department hadn't made any sort of official announcement, but the news had leaked anyway, and in a town the size of Jarvis, the memory of a missing child was still fresh all these years later.

Kim had noticed Zack standing off to the side the minute she arrived. His face was tense behind his mirrored sunglasses, but he stood back behind the barriers erected by the grounds crew, his expression giving nothing away as the capsule was slowly unearthed. The metal no longer gleamed; dirt and roots clung to its sides. The crew ran ropes underneath the capsule so that it could be lifted out with as little disruption as possible.

It was a slow, laborious process, and Kim found herself distracted by Zack. She couldn't stop replaying images of their dinner, and the moment when it had seemed as though he wanted to kiss her. Maybe it was time to admit some things to herself. Kim wanted him. It would be silly to pretend otherwise. He was undeniably gorgeous, and, at the same time, he was a formidable opponent in what had become a high-stakes battle over Scarlett Hascall. She'd always liked a challenge—she couldn't deny that.

But there was something more to her feelings about him that went beyond just simple physical desire, or even the forbidden appeal of sleeping with the "enemy," so to speak. Kim recognized herself in Zack. They were both deeply committed to their work, both ready to put the needs of others—victims, in Zack's case, and the mentally ill in hers—ahead of their own. Then there was Zack's history of loss, his relationship with his sister and with his surrogate father. Kim couldn't help but be drawn to people whose journeys paralleled her own.

But with Zack, there was something more as well. And it both frustrated and fascinated Kim that she couldn't figure it out, catalog it, and put it away for later. That it kept coming up again and again, right when the moment was least convenient.

As the crew finally lifted the capsule from the hole and lowered it carefully onto the grass, Kim forced her attention away from Zack. The crowd pushed closer, talking in hushed tones. Kyle was there, along with a couple of members of the hospital review board. As far as Kim knew, they'd come out of genuine curiosity rather than any sort of official inquiry, since it seemed that half the town had shown up. The mayor was there, ordering her staff around as though she were about to kick off a parade; so far, they'd set up a cordoned-off area and succeeded in directing foot traffic to go around the lawn. There were a couple of people about Kim's age who were glued to their tablets. They might well have been reporters, probably from the chain of small papers that served this part of Alaska.

The crew worked at the seam of the capsule for a few moments before it became clear that it was jammed or corroded shut. One of the men went to his truck for tools, and the others rested with their arms on their shovels. The crowd seemed to collectively exhale, and some sat down on the lawn to wait out the delay. Zack turned and appeared to notice Kim on the edge of the crowd for the first time. He headed her way—just as Kyle came striding over.

She cringed as both men seemed to arrive at the exact same moment—then reminded herself that she hadn't done anything wrong.

"Hello, Dr. Patterson," Kyle said formally. "Detective," he added in a chilly tone, nodding at Zack.

"Doctor," Zack replied, equally tersely.

"Wow, this is just like the summer concerts in the park we used to have back in California," Kim said, falling back on sarcasm, one of her oldest defenses against social awkwardness. "Except the music sucks, and so does the food, and—oh, yeah, the weather does, too."

"I heard it was getting up to sixty-five today," Zack offered. He scanned the crowd while he spoke, his head moving fractionally, his eyes invisible behind his glasses. "Around here, that's bikini weather."

Kyle's eyes narrowed as he looked from Zack to Kim, and she wondered if he was picking up on the tension between them. "Looks like it might be a while. I guess I'd better get back to the hospital," he finally said. "Afternoon rounds."

"I think they've got it, actually," Zack pointed. The worker had returned with a long-handled wrench and his toolbox. He knelt over the seam of the capsule, and, with the help of his coworkers, pried at the opening with the wrench and a hammer. After a few moments there was a scrape of metal on metal and the two halves of the capsule creaked apart. The crowd found its energy again and everyone pressed closer.

Holt had been standing under a bank of trees with the mayor, but now he came forward, holding up his hand. "Hang on a sec," the chief said. "Let my guys in, please."

Zack went to join him, pulling on gloves, along with Officer Phil Taktuq. Zack had mentioned to Kim that Taktuq had worked on the Henry Beaumont disappearance case all those years before. Holt gave a slight nod, and the guy with the tools set down his wrench. He slid his fingers along the opening. "Ready?" he said, to no one in particular.

Then he pulled the hatch open.

A half-dozen boxes and padded envelopes fell out of the hatch onto the disturbed earth. Zack picked up one of the packages from the ground. "Nothing but papers," he said, examining the label. "This one's marked 'Mrs. Piercy's Third-Grade Class.'"

The mayor walked over to join them. "They had the kids write essays," she said. "Every class from third through sixth grade."

The crew carefully pulled the sides farther apart. The smaller segment rolled onto its back, like a bowl; the other stayed on its side. The sun went behind a cloud, and Kim felt a chill move through her. She pulled her sleeves down over her hands, squinting and leaning forward in spite of herself.

Zack knelt on the ground and peered inside the dark interior of the capsule. The mayor crouched next to him, unmindful of her skirt and heels. Kim felt as though everything paused for a moment.

Then the mayor gasped. "There's a skeleton in there. It's—it's so small."

"Henry," Kim said, mostly to herself. Her mind was racing. Part of her still hadn't believed he'd be in there, she realized. But he was. This was real, all of it. Henry—Isabel—all of Scarlett's alters.

Kyle pressed forward with the rest of the crowd, trying to get a glimpse of the body, Tigger pajamas still wrapped around the corpse.

Kim, however, just watched from where she stood, rooted to the spot. She could imagine the condition of the body. She'd seen many bodies in various states of decomposition, so she knew it wouldn't be much more than a collection of bones by this point. But that wasn't what was bothering her. Her mind was reeling about her theory, and what it meant.

Henry Beaumont had died on the day Scarlett was born—a cruel, violent death. Somehow, his young soul had slipped into another body, unable or unwilling to pass through to whatever lay on the other side of life.

Was his restless soul seeking comfort? Revenge? Or just understanding of what had happened?

Kim was now certain that Scarlett's alter was Henry Beaumont, the real Henry. There was no other explanation for how the girl could have secret knowledge of something that had happened the day she was born. But the only hope of learning the truth, learning what exactly happened to Henry and why he ended up in that capsule, did not lie here, on this verdant lawn on a beautiful late summer day, in this sad gathering of citizens confronting the evil that had stolen one of their children.

Kim turned and began threading her way back through the crowd toward her car. Behind her, she heard Kyle's voice.

"Kim, wait!"

But for once, Kim didn't care about what Kyle had to say to her, or even about keeping her job at the hospital. There was only one person she wanted to talk to: Henry Beaumont.

TWENTY-FIVE

"I still don't think this is a good idea," Scarlett said nervously. She had been chewing two pieces of gum furiously ever since Kim picked her up, a block away from her house. The girl now tossed the mangled wad into a trash can outside the police station's front doors.

After leaving the town square that morning, Kim had texted Zack that she urgently needed to talk to him. After she typed her request, there had been a long silence on Zack's end, so long that Kim had been close to giving up. But finally, he texted back:

I'll give you one hour.

"I mean, you saw what he thinks of me," Scarlett continued. "What if he decides to arrest me all over again? If Dad takes any more time off work, I'm worried he's going to get fired."

"It's going to be fine," Kim said, with more conviction than she felt. She'd actually been surprised that he'd agreed to talk to them. Maybe Zack was desperate enough to give her a chance. The community would be clamoring for justice, now that after almost two decades it was clear that an innocent young boy had been brutally murdered. And what other leads could he possibly have? She forced herself to ignore the accompanying resentment that he hadn't listened to her until now, that it had taken her possibly throwing away her career to treat the frightened girl he had wanted to arrest, not to mention the gruesome discovery of Henry's remains, to convince him.

Kim took a deep breath and opened the door, letting Scarlett go ahead of her. The receptionist smiled wryly and invited them to go on through—Kim was back in good graces here, she supposed. Kim and Scarlett made their way to Zack's desk. He stood waiting for them, and he gave them a terse nod. "Dr. Patterson," he said stiffly.

"Call me Kim." He shot her a look, and she pretended to reconsider. "Actually, I prefer Dr. Patterson. But can I call you Zack?"

The detective just stared, but Kim could tell he was holding back a grin. Then again, maybe not. "Ms. Hascall. I've secured a room for us. Right this way, please."

He led them back to the interview room, where he'd set cans of soda in front of two chairs, one a folding plastic chair, one a bit more comfortable. Kim chose the plastic, leaving the cushioned seat for Scarlett. After she and Scarlett were settled, Zack closed and locked the door behind them and pulled down the shade on the window.

Kim glanced up at the camera in the corner of the room. She turned to Zack. "Are we live?"

Zack shook his head. "No camera. No tape. Just the three of us." Off Kim's reticent look, he offered, "Would you like me to turn the lens away?"

Kim shook her head, reassured.

"And just so you know," he said, "nearly everyone's already gone for the day anyway, so we can be sure we won't be disturbed."

In the silence that followed, Scarlett kept her chin down, staring at the scarred oak table where generations of suspects had carved all manner of graffiti.

After several moments passed, Zack cleared his throat. "I'm not sure exactly how this is done. Do I need to drag a couch in here or something?"

"No, this is fine," Kim reassured him. "I mean, the lighting is a bit industrial . . . and I wouldn't call the atmosphere particularly calming, but if you're ready, I can lead Scarlett through the relaxation exercises and we can see if we can summon her alters."

"All right, have at it," Zack said.

Kim could tell he was at the limits of both his credulity and his patience. "I just want to say thank you for giving this a chance," she said. "I know it's not . . . something you've run across before."

Zack leaned back in his chair and thrummed his fingers on the table. "You can say that again. And I'll be honest, I'm not expecting a whole lot. But Ms. Hascall, your . . . prediction turned out to be correct, and because of your help we've been able to find a boy whose disappearance has haunted this town for almost twenty years. I don't need to point out the obvious—if you hadn't been a newborn at the time, the fact that you knew about the body would make you a suspect. I'm mindful of the possibility that Henry's killer could have shared that location with you, so don't make the mistake of thinking you're in the clear."

"Wow," Kim replied. "You really know how to give a pep talk. Have you thought about coaching peewee baseball?"

Zack let out a frustrated breath. "I was about to add that Henry Beaumont's family will finally be able to give him a proper burial. So, you've bought yourself a chance to show me what you've got."

Scarlett peeped up at Zack from under her long fringe of lashes, her pretty eyes momentarily visible from under the curtain of hair behind which she so often hid. "Thank you," she said in a small voice.

"Dr. Patterson has advocated tirelessly for you, so if you want to thank anyone, it should be her. If she's right, and your, uh, alters can help us solve other cases, then I'm willing to suspend my disbelief." The tone in his voice said anything but. Kim had to keep herself from rolling her eyes. "But I have to warn you," Zack continued, "if you turn out to be faking, or trying to get attention, I'll come down on you with the full force of the law."

"She *knows* that," Kim said, exasperated. "And the more stress you put on her, the harder it's going to be to make this work. Hypnosis requires a relaxed patient—remember?"

"Okay, fine. I'll be quiet. Do your thing."

Kim nodded and turned toward Scarlett, but before she could start, Zack interrupted again. "So, if Henry's home, you can just ask him who the killer is?"

Kim shook her head. "It doesn't work like that."

"Convenient." If Zack was trying to hide the sarcasm in his voice, he wasn't doing a good job of it.

Kim turned back toward him, knowing that the sooner she could satisfy his question, the sooner they could get to work. "The personalities we're dealing with have experienced intense trauma. Usually, when we're dealing with patients with *actual* dissociative identity disorder, the reason the condition manifests itself in the first place is that the psyche is dissociating from harrowing memories. They might not even know who did this to them. Now, can I begin?"

"Sure thing, Doc."

"Thank you, Detective."

Zack shifted in his seat. "Do you use a metronome? Or a crystal ball on a chain or something?" Kim shot him a look, but he quickly added, "That was me lightening the mood. Helping everybody to relax."

Kim nodded. "Appreciated."

After a full ten seconds, once Kim had already turned back to Scarlett, Zack added, "That's what I'm here for."

It took a little longer than usual to guide Scarlett into a relaxed state, given the stark, overly bright setting and the remaining tension in the room. Kim knew that Scarlett found Zack's presence deeply unsettling, and patiently repeated the exercises over and over until Scarlett's breathing finally evened out and slowed, and Kim sensed that she was ready.

"Are you in the room, Scarlett? The room with the doors?"

The girl had curled up in the chair, an enormous old upholstered desk chair that looked like it had been dragged in from some higher-up's office, her arms wrapped protectively around herself. She nodded, her eyes closed.

"All right. Behind one of the doors, is Henry waiting?"

Kim held her breath as she waited for Scarlett to answer. She'd half hoped that the discovery of his body might have given Henry the permission he needed to leave, to let his soul finally rest. But after a moment, Scarlett nodded. So it was as Kim suspected—the little boy wasn't done with Scarlett yet. And presumably he wouldn't be until his murder was solved.

"Can you please invite him to come out and talk to me?"

A few minutes passed and then Scarlett's face changed. Her mouth pursed into an O, and her eyes fluttered open, as she looked uncertainly around the room.

"Is that you, Henry?" Kim asked gently.

"Yes." Scarlett's voice, small and quiet, was no longer as frightened as it had been before. "It's nice here. I like the light."

"You're out of the scary spaceship now, isn't that right?"

She nodded. "It was so cold . . ."

Kim made her voice as steady and soothing as possible, hoping she'd get more information today than she had during the last conversation with this alter—otherwise, this second chance Zack was giving her wasn't going to do any good. "Henry, I'm going to ask you some questions about the day you got put in the spaceship. And after that, you will be all done and you can go rest. Does that sound like a good idea?"

"So sleepy," Scarlett said.

"I know, sweetheart, and you're almost finished here. There's just one thing left to do. Whoever put you in the spaceship was very, very bad. You know that, right?"

Tears puddled in Scarlett's eyes and spilled over, coursing down her cheeks. What was remarkable to Kim was that even though it was Scarlett's body in the chair across from her, Henry's alter took over her so completely—his expressions, the childlike way his mouth wobbled—that it was easy to forget that he was inhabiting the body of a nineteen-year-old girl. There were moments when she was completely convinced that a child sat across from her.

"Very bad," Scarlett agreed, snuffling.

"And I know this is hard to talk about, and it makes us all sad, but that bad person needs to be punished. We need to make sure that what happened to you doesn't happen to another little child. Doesn't that sound important?"

"Yes," Scarlett mumbled. "I hate him. He is *very* bad."

Him. He. Kim's pulse quickened—progress, at last. Henry wasn't shying away from the subject, at least. Now they just needed some description, something they could pursue as a lead. She glanced at Zack, who gave her the smallest nod of encouragement.

"What can you tell me about the bad man?" she asked, willing herself to take things slow, not to let her urgency frighten Henry.

"Old," Scarlett said. "Mean. Smells bad. Put me in a car. . . a big car."

Zack made a note on his legal pad and turned his gaze back to Scarlett.

"Did you ride in the car, Henry?" Maybe there was some detail here that could identify the killer, some distinctive feature of the vehicle that Zack could trace in a police database.

"Yes," he said. "It bumped a lot."

Kim bit back her frustration. "Do you remember anything else about the car? Like what color it was?"

Scarlett frowned and shook her head.

"Okay." Time to take a different tack. "Do you know where the bad man lived?"

"No. Just the car. And the spaceship. And the game." More tears welled and spilled down Scarlett's cheeks. "He made me play a very bad game. It hurt."

Kim's heart broke for the little boy, for the things he'd been made to endure. The terror and pain he'd felt. "Can you tell me anything else about what he looked like? Take your time, Henry. There's no rush. Just think, and let us know if there's anything else you remember."

Scarlett was quiet for a few minutes. Then she poked a finger at her top lip, pushing it up. "His teeth. They were big and ugly. And one went this way." She twisted her finger halfway around."

Zack broke in. "What color was his hair?"

Scarlett wouldn't look at Zack. Instead, she whispered to Kim, "Is he mean?"

"Detective Trainor? No—no, he's a good guy," she said reassuringly, glaring at Zack to be quiet. "He's here to help. It's okay to talk to him."

But Scarlett turned and buried her face in the chair's upholstery. Her shoulders shook as she cried.

"Henry. Henry, it's all right. Henry . . ." Kim got out of her chair and went around the table, and crouched down next to Scarlett, touching her shoulder. "Honey, it's going to be okay."

"I didn't like the stomping," she whispered.

"The stomping? What stomping?"

"When he walked. His foot went stomp."

Kim thought for a moment. "Do you mean he had a limp?"

"It was too loud. It went *stomp!*" Scarlett made a fist and hit her other arm with it, then dragged her fist along her forearm. Henry was too young to know the word *limp*, perhaps, but he could be describing a leg dragging along the floor.

Kim exchanged a glance with Zack, who frowned and made another note.

She patted Scarlett's shoulder again. "Okay, honey, you've done really well today. Is there anything else you remember?"

But Scarlett just continued to sob, her shoulders shaking more and more. Kim realized this was about as far as she was going to get, at least for this session.

"It's okay, Henry. You've done a great job here. And now it's our turn. It's Zack's job to find the bad guy and make sure he never hurts anyone else ever again, and Zack and his friends are going to work very hard to take care of that, so you don't have to worry about the bad man anymore. Do you understand?"

After a long moment, Scarlett nodded. Then, as if as an afterthought, she turned to Zack. "Does your police car have red and blue lights?"

Zack nodded. "Yes, it does. And a siren." When Scarlett smiled meekly, he smiled back. He caught himself, realizing that he believed . . . for a split second.

Kim saw it, too. She turned back to Scarlett. "So you and I are going to say good-bye now, and you're going to leave this—this place where you've been staying, and go home." Kim was completely out of her element, talking about an afterlife of which she had no firm concept. All she knew was that the soul of a dead child had taken up occupancy in a living young woman, and for both their sakes, it was time to move on. "Do you . . . do you know where home is, Henry?"

"Yes," Scarlett said, and wiped her tears away with a fist, sitting up straighter. "The silver place. It's nice."

Kim kept her tone even. "Okay, that's good. Very good. Are you ready to go to the silver place?"

Scarlett nodded, a tiny smile playing at the corners of her mouth.

"You've done so well, Henry." Kim took her hands and squeezed them gently before releasing them. "Good-bye."

Scarlett's eyes closed and she slumped back in the chair. After a second, her face went slack, and she was instantly recognizable as herself again. She stirred and rubbed her eyes, slowly sitting up, blinking and looking around the room. Her gaze fell on Kim crouching next to her.

"How was it?" she asked anxiously. "Did you learn anything? Did I do okay?"

"Better than okay," Zack said, letting out a low whistle. "I'm pretty sure Henry just identified his killer. The limp? And the tooth? I think I know who he's talking about."

"That's— Who?" Kim breathed.

But Zack was already out of his chair, his hand on the doorknob. "Sorry, active investigation—can't tell you more yet. But thanks, Scarlett. And, Kim. This has been a big help. I'll, uh, buy you a beer sometime."

Then he was gone. Kim and Scarlett looked at each other, and Scarlett burst into unexpected laughter. "A beer? He wants to buy you a *beer*?"

"And all I had to do to earn it was for you to be falsely arrested, hassled, and possessed by restless spirits," Kim said, feeling a small laugh of her own bubble up inside her. It felt good to release the tension—it had been so long since she'd had anything to laugh about. "Listen, I know that had to be tough on you. What do you say to getting out of here? Can I take you to dinner?"

Scarlett's smile faded. "Thanks, Kim, but I'm really tired. If you could take me home, I just want to see my dad. And my sister. And then I want to crawl into bed."

"Of course," Kim said. As they left the stark, cold interview room, her heart ached for Scarlett for the thousandth time. Until all the alters found what they were looking for and moved on, Scarlett's life would never be her own.

***

"WHY ME?"

Kim had already pulled up to Scarlett's house. She had said good night. She had even offered to walk the girl to the door, risking a run-in with the girl's father. But Scarlett sat, legs pulled up to her chest, barely breathing.

Of course, Kim didn't have the answer to Scarlett's question, not that she hadn't struggled to answer it already. It dogged her from the moment she gave voice to her theory that Scarlett had . . . absorbed these lost souls.

"The time capsule . . . it was buried on the same day I was born?"

Kim nodded. "Yes."

"And the little boy, he died inside? On that same day?"

Kim nodded again. "It looks that way."

"That must have been horrible. To die alone like that. In the dark."

Kim reached over and touched Scarlett's hand. "You shouldn't think about this."

"I was dead once."

At first, Kim thought maybe she misheard Scarlett; the girl was whispering so softly that it sounded as if she hadn't meant anyone to hear her confession.

"What do you mean, Scarlett?"

The girl shrugged. "I've heard my dad tell the story before.

About the day I was born. He was in the delivery room, and I guess there were some complications . . . my heart stopped. When I came out, I was . . . dead."

"You were stillborn?"

Scarlett nodded. "I was dead. The, um . . . doctors and nurses, I guess they gave me CPR, compressions, broke my rib cage. When my dad tells the story, he always cries, talking about seeing his tiny baby on that big steel table, not moving. Not crying. He says they worked on me for close to three minutes before I started breathing again."

Kim teared up just hearing the story secondhand. She could only imagine what it was like to be there. The desperation.

And that's when it hit her. What if Scarlett had died at the exact same time that Henry died? Maybe in that traumatic moment, in the chaos of Henry's fear, he lost his way to the afterlife, and in his panic, found haven inside an empty vessel—inside Scarlett's empty vessel, which was, for a moment, soulless.

Or maybe Kim just needed more sleep.

But deep in her gut, something about her theory rang true. She reached out and took Scarlett's hand. "Whatever the reason, we'll find a way to fix this. Together."

TWENTY-SIX

I t took Zack until the following afternoon to get the necessary warrants, but at a little after two o'clock he texted Kim to say they'd picked up a suspect and would be interviewing him immediately.

Kim had called him the night before, begging for more information about the man Henry had been describing. "I promise not to say a word to anyone," she insisted, "but I can help you."

Kim's pulse quickened with excitement when Zack immediately agreed. "That's a great idea." He hesitated for a beat before adding, "I'm honestly not sure why we don't *always* invite civilians to help interrogate possible child murderers."

Despite her frustration, Kim smiled. He got her. But she continued to plead her case. "I've had experience working with sociopaths. It's possible that, if you let me watch your interrogation, I might be able to help you learn something he wouldn't ordinarily disclose."

Zack refused adamantly, but Kim patiently described some of the other cases she'd seen during her internships and in San Diego, working to convince him that she had the skills to discern the truth even when faced with the most gifted liar. With a sigh, Zack

relented and told her about the man he'd encountered at the basement porn production studio.

"Sullivan had the same tooth," he said. "The same limp. And
while we don't have any proof of his involvement with the studio—
these kids were smart enough to run the business all in cash—it's
very possible he was there for underage material, which seemed to
be a specialty of the place."

He explained that he had pulled Albert Sullivan's record and
discovered complaints going back as far as the seventies. Peeping,
following children home, lurking outside of schools—and a notable
incident where a complaint from a young mother had resulted in
his arrest. But there had been insufficient evidence, and in the end
no charges had ever stuck.

"The age could be right, too," Zack continued. "Twenty years
ago, he would have been in his late fifties—and that definitely would
have seemed old to a five-year-old. Plus, he already had the limp by
then, we confirmed that this morning—it all checks out."

In the end, Kim had convinced Zack to let her be present at the
interrogation by reminding him that he'd never have gotten this far
without her help, and swearing that she wouldn't divulge anything
she learned or interfere with his investigation in any way. After he
reluctantly agreed, Zack told Kim a few details from the police investigation that the public wasn't privy to, like the fact that the little boy was wearing Winnie-the-Pooh Tigger pajamas when he was
abducted, and the fact that he had been taken from his bed in the
middle of the night.

At 8:58 a.m., Kim breezed past the front desk at the police station
—at this point, she recognized nearly everyone in the place—and
headed for the interview room where yesterday Henry had finally left Scarlett for good. That morning Scarlett had called Kim
to tell her that she could actually *feel* his absence in her body and
her mind. Kim felt a new confidence bubbling up; if she could help

Scarlett to get her other alters to tell *their* stories, perhaps she could actually cure the girl for good. It might not be easy, but for the first time, it seemed possible.

Zack had left the shade up on the one-way mirrored glass of the interview room window, and she peered through at an old, shabbily dressed man sitting in the same chair Scarlett had occupied yesterday. His chin was held high, and he was looking around defiantly. Even with his mouth closed, his snaggletooth protruded slightly from his withered lips. The bald patch on top of his head gave way to gray, ratty snarls that hung limply around his face.

Kim knocked, and Zack got up and let her in, never taking his eyes off his suspect. Even though he was handcuffed, Sullivan's eyes were bright and alert, as though he was looking for an opportunity to bolt.

"Albert, this is the expert I was telling you about."

"You didn't tell me she was such a looker." He grinned at her, showing his yellowed, twisted teeth.

"Dr. Patterson is a psychiatrist," Zack said coolly. "Your little games won't have any effect on her, so you might as well drop it."

Sullivan licked his lips and made wet smacking sounds. Kim had faced men like him during her training, but she still chose a chair on the other side of the table, next to Zack.

Before Zack sat down, he clarified, "If at any time, you'd like Dr. Patterson to leave the room, just say the word."

Sullivan still hadn't taken his eyes off Kim. "What if I want *you* to leave the room? So I can be in here alone with her?"

Zack responded flatly, "And here I was questioning my boss as to why we picked you up. I tried to tell him you weren't as creepy as people claimed."

Sullivan's eyes shifted toward the detective while his head remained motionless. Kim's pulse picked up again. She knew that her best course was to say as little as possible, to give nothing away that could provoke him. But, clearly, Zack had a different agenda.

"To fill you in, I've been through Mr. Sullivan's alibi for March 1998," Zack said, tapping the pad of paper in front of him, which held a few scribbled notes. "Says he can't remember anything. County records show he was employed by the building and grounds department at the time."

"Hard work, that was," Sullivan said. "Kept my head down and did my job. Didn't have time to go chatting up anyone like you're accusin' me."

"No one is impressed by your act, Albert," Zack said calmly. "Don't forget I've got your record right here in front of me. We received complaints of lewd behavior—peeping and inappropriate interest in children in the public parks."

"That's a lie," Sullivan snarled. "Can't very well work in a park without talking to a kid now and then. That's all it was." He then turned back toward Kim, biting his lip before smiling. "Besides, *this* one's my type."

"Maybe if you shaved off twenty years. And she were a boy."

Sullivan shook his head toward Kim, putting on his best innocent face. "Can you believe this? Is this any way for a police officer to act?"

Kim didn't say anything, worried that if she got involved, Zack might pull her out of the room himself—so she was surprised when Zack nodded, welcoming her to respond.

"You are attracted to children, Albert," Kim said, keeping her tone clinical and detached. "You find them sexually arousing."

Sullivan shrugged, irritation flashing across his features. "Only the ones who go around showing off."

"Showing off," Kim said. "That is an interesting choice of words. How do children show off to you?"

"You know," Sullivan said. He grimaced, his twisted tooth pressing into his bottom lip, and glared at the table. "The way they . . . *you* know."

"Actually, I don't. Albert, my interest here is purely professional. I'm not here to judge you," Kim lied. "There is a huge range of human sexuality that includes many things that our society considers . . . aberrant. In other cultures, these same practices may and often are considered within the range of 'normal.'" She made air quotes with her fingers, willing him to focus on her words, not the emotion behind them, knowing she could never completely hide her revulsion at the thought of what he had done.

She had his attention. His eyes glittered in their wrinkled, spotted nest of flesh.

Under the table, she felt Zack's foot touch hers—it was clearly a sign to continue. She realized that at this moment, he was the bad cop and she was the good cop. Encouraged, she drove the spike a little deeper. "Sexual mores are an artificial construction. What that means is that what one society might consider healthy and natural, another might consider deviant. Neither is 'right' nor 'wrong,' because it's all viewed, in scientific and anthropological circles, as dependent on context. Do you understand what I'm telling you?"

"Hell yes, I do," Sullivan said. "Means people shouldn't judge what they don't understand. People are sheep, that's what I think."

"Sheep?" Kim took a chance and looked over at Zack, who was busy writing notes.

"Look at you," Sullivan said. "Society tells you that you have to act all stuck-up and snooty, just because you're a damn doctor. But I bet your panties are soaking wet for the detective under those polyester pants. I bet you wish you could climb right on his lap, don't you?"

Kim felt the blood rush to her face in anger and embarrassment. But she wouldn't let Sullivan get to her. She'd trained for this; had spent many hours with patients with psychoses just as troubling as Sullivan's. She'd worked at professional detachment harder than anyone she knew—but then, she had more to detach from than most.

She wasn't about to let him win.

"My sexual tastes are not the issue here, but I'll tell you what, Albert—if you tell me what you like, if you tell us *all* about it, and answer all the detective's questions, I'll tell you mine."

Sullivan laughed, leaning back in his chair. His eyes were bright with delight. "Heh, so that's how it's going to be, eh? Okay, you're on. I do like 'em young. I like how soft their skin is. I like it when they smell good and clean, like baby powder. I mean, who wouldn't?"

Kim kept her body rigid and her expression neutral. "Go on."

And he did, Zack scribbling furiously, as Kim prodded Sullivan to describe in more and more detail the twisted fantasies and perversions he'd been harboring. It was clear a part of him wanted to talk about this, relished confiding in them. Girls, boys, he liked both—the younger the better. He described acts he fantasized about in such detail that she had to swallow down her nausea, and even Zack looked like he was having difficulty keeping his emotions in check—but the one thing Sullivan did not do was admit having ever acted on these fantasies.

And when Zack took over, supplementing Kim's guidance with questions about specific dates and times, Sullivan clammed up entirely. "Uh-uh, buddy boy," he said, smirking. "Ain't no law against thinking all these things. But I never have done more than think. Not once in my seventy-six years."

"But you knew Henry Beaumont," Zack prodded.

"Yeah, I remember him. Used to pull this little wagon to the park with his mom. Liked to fill it up with sand. But that's all I know. I never touched him, never went to his house, never grabbed him out of his bed."

He turned to Kim, winking slyly. "Your turn, Doc. I told you mine. You promised, now you got to tell me yours."

Zack gave her a look of frustration, but Kim felt triumphant, having caught Sullivan's mention of Henry being taken from his bed. As far as Kim was concerned, Sullivan had as good as admitted that she'd killed Henry. She hoped that Zack would be able to use the recording they were making to prosecute, though she suspected she'd need more than that. But it would at least be enough for them to get a search warrant for his house, wouldn't it? And she knew that offenders like Albert Sullivan liked to keep trophies of their crimes, to help them relive the transgressions in their imaginations.

"Okay," she said, standing. "It's a little sick, though. What I'm into? What gets me really, really hot? What I'm imagining right now, in fact?" She closed her eyes and pantomimed a little shudder of excitement. Then she opened them and stared directly into his face. Zack reached out and turned off the recording device, giving her an inscrutable look. "Tying you up to a pole, Albert. Naked as the day you were born. I'm picturing a flock of hungry buzzards coming down and taking one look at you—all that old, sagging flesh—and starting to attack. First they'd go for your little pecker. One snap of those powerful beaks—sliced clean through. Next would be your eyes. Stabbing through the membranes, right into your brain. But not enough to kill you. No, you'd die while they sliced open your stomach and dragged your entrails out on the ground. You'd be screaming for your life, even as it drained from your fouled, ruined body."

She smiled at him. "*That's* what turns me on, Albert. Like I said . . . it's all context."

Then she walked out of the room, shaking all over, wondering what the review board would make of her now.

TWENTY-SEVEN

Back at her apartment, Kim uncorked a good bottle of red wine. Good, that was, in the sense that it cost more than ten dollars and had an appealing label, which was pretty much the extent of Kim's knowledge and resources.

As she showered and changed into a pair of old, faded jeans and a simple scoop-necked top, she couldn't help hoping that Zack felt equally celebratory. The quick conversation she'd had with him an hour ago, when he'd called her to tell her that they needed more to charge Sullivan, had only slightly dampened her spirits. Zack relayed that he and Holt were hopeful that this new information, coupled with a follow-up investigation of the many complaints against Sullivan, would give them enough to make a real case against him. They'd continue holding him until the full forty-eight hours were up, in hopes they'd have the proof they needed by then. Kim felt sure they'd find what they needed—after all, this was definitely their man. They'd solved the case—and all because of Scarlett.

What's more, Zack had finally confirmed that Scarlett was off their radar. At least for now, he said he no longer suspected that Scarlett had been working with Henry's killer, nor did he suspect her, at this point, for Izzi's murder. She'd even admitted that Scarlett didn't seem to be faking her condition, although he wouldn't go so far as to accept the dead-soul theory. Still, it felt like progress, finally.

Not to mention that now that she had a better grasp of what Scarlett's alters needed to move on, Kim hoped the girl might eventually be rid of all the restless souls she harbored.

And once *that* happened—once Kim's treatment of Scarlett was proved to be effective in helping the girl deal with the alters—she might not just get her job and her professional standing back, but maybe she could convince the hospital to devote resources to alternative therapeutic techniques, like the hypnosis that had been so effective in treating Scarlett. Lawsuits involving hypnotherapy were usually brought against hucksters preying on the weak, or psychiatrists who didn't understand how to perform the technique.

It was the most hopeful Kim had felt since her suspension, and she felt like celebrating. Since she and Zack had come through the last of the investigation together, it was only natural to invite him to join her. It wasn't hard to find his cell number on her phone's call history; after all, he was the only one she'd called for two days.

He picked up, after one ring, with a curt, "Trainor."

"Hey. It's me. Your new partner." Even the long pause he responded with couldn't dampen her mood. "Listen, I was thinking, maybe we could meet over at the gun range; I could show you my new gat."

"*Gat*? Have you been watching 'twenties gangster movies?" Zack asked.

"They don't use that term anymore? How about beanshooter? Pocket rocket? Fire stick?"

"I'm a little busy right now. What can I do for you, Dr. Patterson?"

"If you'd rather not meet me at the gun range to see my Glock, I was hoping you'd let me repay you for making me dinner the other night."

There was another long pause on the other end. She decided to let it ride. Finally, he responded, "I guess I gotta eat."

Not quite the answer she was looking for, but she took it.

SHE'D TAKEN A LITTLE extra care getting dressed, feeling embarrassed as she checked herself in the mirror. After all, this wasn't a date. Though when the doorbell rang, her heart pounded with a sense of anticipation that was hardly professional.

"Don't be an idiot, Patterson," Kim muttered to herself. Then she opened the door and tried not to stare at the six feet two inches of perfection on her stoop.

"Hi," Zack said, handing over a bottle of wine that she suspected was far superior to the one she'd picked out.

"Come on in," she said a little breathlessly. "Welcome to my, uh, place."

He walked into her living room and looked around, taking in the rental furniture, the moving boxes doubling as end tables and a TV stand, the bare walls with no ornamentation except a hand-woven prayer mat that had been a "new job" gift from her parents. On the small dinette table were a pair of place mats so new they were still creased from the wrapper, the plain white plates that came with the place, and the only glassware Kim owned: two drinking glasses and two wineglasses.

Zack walked straight into her kitchen and started opening cabinets. "This is a crime," he said, staring at the paltry contents.

"Come on, it's not that bad," Kim said. She was standing two feet away from him, a bunch of green onions in her hands. Earlier, in the grocery store, she had thought they might be nice in a salad. Now, with the ingredients laid out on the counter, she wasn't so sure.

"Do you have cumin?"

"That's a spice, right?" Before he was able to respond, she followed up, "A joke. I know what cumin is. Although I couldn't tell you what it tastes like. I'm more of a salt and pepper girl. Garlic powder when I'm feeling really crazy." He stared at her, a smile threatening to break out on his lips. "I have allspice. I think that has cumin in it. At least I'm guessing it does from its name. If it doesn't, it's false advertising."

He poked around in her practically empty cabinets for another moment, and then gave her an incredulous look, as though she'd been storing cat carcasses up there. "Get out of my way, or we'll starve to death before you get anything on the table."

For the next half hour Kim watched in wonderment as he grabbed things from her cabinets and fridge. He sliced, sautéed, sprinkled, chopped, and finally slid a pan into the oven. "Ten minutes should do it," he said.

"Okay . . . should I open the wine?"

He picked up the bottle she'd purchased and gave it a suspicious look. "Is this the wine you cook with?"

She gave a sheepish grin. "Yeah . . . I mean, you think I'd drink that stuff?"

He backpedaled. "I'm sure it's great, but maybe we open the Pinot instead?" Then he twisted up the cork with the ease of a professional and poured them each a glass.

Conversation was so stilted and awkward during much of the cooking, she was half expecting him to bring up the weather. But when Zack took the pan from the oven and slid the contents onto plates mounded with pasta, Kim stopped worrying about what to talk about and focused on eating.

"This is amazing," she said with her mouth full. "I take back every bad thing I ever said about you."

Zack was picking at his food, regarding her with an inscrutable expression. When she'd eaten the last bite on her plate, he set down his own fork. "Kim, I'm not really sure why you invited me here."

"I felt like celebrating. I mean, who else would I call but my partner?"

"I don't know, maybe . . . Dr. Berman." The name hung in the air. Then he said, "Kyle." As if she wouldn't know who Dr. Berman was.

Kim stared at Zack for a long moment. "I'm pretty sure Dr. Berman wouldn't have taken my call. We're not exactly . . . seeing each other at the moment." If Zack was relieved to hear this new detail, he wasn't letting on. "But maybe you already knew that, I mean, with you being a detective and all."

Zack turned his attention to his half-eaten meal. "I can't say I'm sorry to hear that." She held back a smile. "But I have an early morning."

"But—but we just ate. I haven't even given you the tour of the apartment yet."

He looked around the living room. The door to the bedroom was open, the brightly colored quilt visible on the bed. "No offense, but I think I should probably stay here in the East Wing. I'll get the tour next time."

As he pushed his plate away, she leaned forward. "Thank you for coming. I just wanted to . . . talk." The electric current she felt whenever she was with him was back in full force—and they weren't even locked in violent disagreement. "I've really wanted to thank you for letting me help with Albert. And for giving Scarlett a chance . . . for suspending your doubts long enough to see for yourself what it's like for her."

Zack lifted one eyebrow. "If this is some misbegotten effort on your part to apologize for being such a pain in the ass, you can really let it drop."

"No, it's not that." She picked up her napkin and started tearing little pieces off it. "I mean, yeah, sorry. Sort of. But I kept you from putting an innocent girl in jail, at least for now, and helped you solve a cold case, so shouldn't you be thanking me?"

He pushed back his chair. "Right. You're right. Because I couldn't have done it without you."

Kim stood, too. "I didn't say that."

"You kinda just did, Dr. Patterson."

"You can call me Kim."

"I was given implicit instructions, by you, to call you Dr. Patterson."

"Well, now I'm giving you instructions to call me Kim. And why are you always mad at me?"

"Is that a serious question?"

"Um, I think so." She pushed her hair out of her eyes. "I mean, usually people don't just— Well, okay, *some* people seem to take an instant dislike to me, but I was actually trying . . . trying . . ."

"To be my friend?" Zack's tone was gentle. He reached out and pushed the same lock of hair behind her ear. It fell forward again. "You're an unusual woman, Kim. Do you hear that a lot?"

"Mmm. No. Maybe." She could feel her cheeks flaming. "I've been told that I'm not a 'people pleaser.'"

"I find that hard to believe." Zack's voice, already in the low registers, thundered lower.

"And I don't have a lot of friends."

"Harder still."

"No, I mean, like—you know—I have the basics down. And I'm really, really good at first impressions . . . if I want to be. It's the second impressions. And third. And all the ones after those, that are the bitch."

"Could it be because every time someone suggests you turn right, you go left? Or because every time you see an off-limits sign you have to drive right over it—then back up and do it again?"

Kim stared at him, at a loss for how to convince him that this time she *wasn't* trying to be contrary—she just sincerely wanted to thank him for being on her side. How had this all gotten so complicated? She thought of and abandoned a half-dozen retorts.

"Are we talking about our jobs here?" she finally settled on. "Because I've always done only what I thought was best for my patient."

"And I've done only what I thought was in the interest of justice. The difference is that everything I do is in my job description. From what I can tell, you do your best to ignore the rules. Now, you want to do that to your own career, that's your business. But you'll forgive me if I get a little uncomfortable when you come in my patch and stir things up."

Before she could respond, he picked up her hand and pressed her knuckles to his lips. The gesture was almost chaste—but it made Kim feel like she was melting on the inside. "I get it—you care deeply for your patients. Maybe too deeply, if you ask me. There's a place for professional distance. But it's one of the things I like about you, too. Your . . . fearlessness."

"You think I'm fearless?"

"I do. As well as stubborn, willful, and infuriating." He brushed her knuckles against his cheek, which was both soft and stubbly, the line of his jaw hard. "You've done your best to provoke, annoy, and confound me ever since the moment we met."

"I have not! Not on purpose, anyway." Kim couldn't help but be amused at how much of her behavior Zack thought was motivated by him.

"You know what I think? I think you're scared."

"I'm not," Kim said, instantly on the defensive. For as much time as she spent analyzing the people around her, it made her intensely uncomfortable when the roles were reversed. "Not of you, anyway."

"Yeah? Prove it." Then he kissed her.

As kisses went, it was relatively brief—just the softest brush of his lips on hers—but it was also very, very deliberate. He kissed her with his eyes open, and then he watched her react. Or, not react—because she was completely frozen.

Until he did it again.

For a moment, his lips—warm, soft, so inviting—lingered against hers, but then he put his heart into the kiss, moving his hands down her back to pull her closer against him. It was every bit as hot and delicious as Kim had imagined it would be.

After that, things moved in the proper direction with very little hesitation. When Zack picked Kim up and took her to her room as though she was no heavier than a bag of groceries, she made one last effort to do the right thing. "I'm not very good at relationships," she gasped, as his lips grazed her collarbone.

"I've noticed. Let's see if you're good at anything else."

TWENTY-EIGHT

An hour later, when things finally seemed to have come to a stop, or at least a rest, Zack lay panting on the edge of Kim's bed while she went in search of snacks.

Now that she was out of the room, no longer distracting him from his better judgment, a nagging sense of misgiving reared its ugly head. Kim was, despite all his efforts to prevent it, a part of an active case. Sure, he was starting to believe she was right about Scarlett's multiple personalities, or alters, or whatever they were called—especially since they had a solid lead in Albert Sullivan—but he wouldn't be ready to rule out any suspect entirely until they had Izzi's killer behind bars.

Zack hadn't expected this evening to turn out the way it had, though he had certainly entertained the idea. Hoped, even, if he was being honest. If Holt found out . . . but he would *never* let Holt find out. Zack was good at keeping his private life private—at least at work. Brielle was another matter. He'd bet fifty bucks that she'd taken note of his departure from the house earlier . . . and his twin sister was awfully resourceful when it came to keeping tabs on his social life.

Zack got out of bed, shaking his head. He'd have to be careful:

Holt wasn't just *his* surrogate father, he was Brielle's, too. Brielle wouldn't understand this tryst. Or rather—she'd probably understand all too well . . . and the last thing he needed was his sister teasing him mercilessly, or worse, running to Dad.

He was on his way to Kim's bathroom when he accidentally bumped into a stack of papers sitting on top of her dresser. Several folders slid off the edge, their contents spilling out onto the floor.

Zack got down on his knees and gathered them up. They looked like financial records, something he had no desire to pry into.

But one stapled sheaf of papers caught his eye. Along the top, they read Massachusetts Department of Children and Family Services. Underneath: Foster Placement Report.

He flipped through the pages, unable to help himself. The date on it was August 2004. A photograph of a much younger Kim, with freckles and bangs cut straight, glared into the camera.

Then his gaze fell on the name.

Joselyn Miller.

What? Zack quickly put all the papers back in the stack, his mind filled with questions. He went to the bathroom to wash up. By the time Kim returned to bed with a tray of saltines and peanut butter and two cans of orange soda, he'd managed to compose himself.

"That looks terrible," he said. "You should really think about using natural peanut butter."

She smiled. "Natural peanut butter tastes like ass left in a hot car for two weeks. Besides, the chemicals in Skippy are what make it taste good. And—I'm having a craving," Kim said, setting the tray down and snuggling up next to him, her body warm and soft and perfectly molded to his own. She smeared peanut butter on a cracker and held it up to his lips. He took a bite, and found that it tasted just right, artificial coloring, preservatives, and all.

Kim slid down until her head was resting on his lap, the sheet he'd pulled up over himself doing little to disguise his resurging interest. He stroked her hair, wondering about the mystery of the report but knowing that he wouldn't bring it up.

Zack knew that he had issues trusting people, probably because of the way his dad hadn't always been there for him. There was a reason he could count on two fingers the people he'd let get close. So it wasn't surprising that a part of him wanted to leave right now, convinced that Kim was lying to him, that she'd never reveal who she really was. That she was untrustworthy, like his father. That things would almost certainly end badly.

But the bigger part of him had no intention of getting out of this bed tonight. They hadn't discussed it, but he figured they both knew he was staying over.

He picked up her hand and licked the peanut butter from her middle finger, eliciting a sigh of pleasure. Kim Patterson was probably trouble—but for the moment, she was all his.

ZACK WAS AT HIS desk the next morning by eight, after an early debriefing session spent with Kim, revisiting some of the pleasures of the night before, as well as discovering new ones. He'd successfully put all thoughts of the foster care report out of his head while they shared a shower and a pot of coffee, and when he kissed her at the door, it felt dangerously natural.

Now, he was staring at the old materials from the Henry Beaumont case, as well as Albert Sullivan's file. Holt's notes were typically terse; the chief wasn't much for the written word. Sullivan had been arrested twice for public indecency; both times, he'd been caught urinating in public on the way home from one of Jarvis's seediest bars. More potentially relevant was an incident in which a young mother complained that Albert had been lurking at the playground in the town park, that he'd exposed himself to her and her children; Sullivan claimed that his pants had merely slipped down because he'd forgotten his belt.

He'd have to see if Holt could remember anything else when he came in. Zack glanced at the clock—it was still likely to be at least an hour until the chief arrived.

Idly, he checked his favorite news site and scrolled through his Facebook feed, rolling his eyes to see that his sister had posted a terribly unflattering sixth-grade picture of him with the caption "Jarvis's Finest??" It had already racked up more than thirty likes.

Zack poked at the keyboard, a thought forming in his mind, a thought very unlike him. Zack prided himself in keeping a certain distance between his career and the women he dated. Better, he felt, for all concerned, particularly given the sensitive nature of his job. But Kim was already inextricably linked to his current investigations, whether he liked it or not. And the photograph on that foster report kept coming back to him. Was it really Kim? And if she'd really been in the foster system, why hadn't she mentioned it when he told her about Holt taking him and his sister in?

Zack knew that he and Brielle had been lucky. His experience had been completely atypical, as far as foster care was concerned. Although Holt had been a touch awkward with them initially, he had always at the very least treated them like a beloved niece and nephew.

Maybe Kim's experience had been much worse.

Zack gave in and googled her name.

Turned out there were quite a few Kim Pattersons out there. Columbia, South Carolina. Englishtown, New Jersey. Sarasota, Florida. He scrolled through at least a dozen more before refining his search. *Dr. Kimberly Patterson* yielded more information, and after ten minutes, he'd been able to trace her past, from her most recent biography on the hospital website, back through medical school at UCSF, college at Stanford, and an all-girls high school in Massachusetts. Both her hospital bio and an alumni newsletter listed her place of birth as Acton, Massachusetts. Though he searched, records indicating the reason she had left her internship at a hospital in San Diego were murky at best.

Zack thought for a moment before entering those details into a database not readily available to the public. It was against department regulations to use it for personal use, but in a way, this was relevant to his ongoing investigation of Scarlett. After all, if he couldn't trust Kim, could he trust her assessment of Scarlett's mental health?

After five minutes of searching, he was convinced that Kim had lied. There were no Kim Pattersons born in Acton in 1987 . . . or in the five years before or after.

Zack stared at the screen, a chill settling into his veins.

When he and Brielle were growing up, after losing their mother at such a young age, Zack had been desperate for the support of the adults in his life. He'd do practically anything to earn their respect and love. When his first-grade teacher told him he could have an important job someday if he worked hard in school, he practiced the alphabet until his fingers ached. And when his T-ball coach told him that jogging around the field would make him tall and strong, Zack ran until his sides ached and he couldn't catch his breath.

But there was one adult in his life who broke his trust over and over: his father. Errol Trainor was a drinker and a brawler, and his wife's death only increased his need for alcohol. He lost job after job and came home later and later each night. His paychecks seemed to evaporate before the bills were paid. Neighbors took to checking in on Zack and Brielle; if it hadn't been for the kindness of their community, he and his sister would have starved.

For every lie Errol told, for every promise he broke, Zack would come up with an excuse, even if he never shared them with anyone, not even Brielle. *Dad lost that job only because he got sick*, he told himself. *It's my fault he ran over my bike, because I left it in the drive-way. He missed my baseball game because he had to work late.*

When he started getting into trouble himself, it was all too easy to make the same kind of excuses for his own behavior. *I only stole the candy bar because they charge too much at that store. It's Mr. Friedrich's fault I ran into his mailbox, because he didn't trim his trees. I'll help Brielle study for her math test after one more game of Tetris.*

All of that changed the day Holt picked him up for loitering outside the pool hall downtown, trying to get older guys to buy him beer. "You're gonna turn out just like your dad," he'd said. Zack, blinded by fury, had struck out, not caring that it was the chief of police he was hitting. But Holt had blocked the punch as easily as if he was swatting a fly, and twisted Zack's wrist behind his back in a hold that brought him to his knees.

"You may think you're hurting now," Holt said calmly, tightening his grip. "But it's nothing compared to the pain of looking back on your life and realizing you wasted it. Next time I catch you screwing up, I'm going after you with everything I've got. But if you promise me today to make a real effort to change"—he'd released Zack's arm and allowed him to get up, tears of pain stinging his eyes—"if you decide to make a change in your life, I'll help."

The best thing Zack ever did was to take that deal. Within a year, his father was dead, having wandered drunk into the path of an oncoming truck. But by then Zack was already working for Holt, and he had a goal for his life: to become a cop.

He wasn't about to sacrifice the ideals he'd worked so hard to uphold. He stared at the database, trying to imagine any possible justification for Kim lying about her background in the hospital's biography, but he came up short.

The medical school degree seemed real, at least, so she wasn't practicing medicine without a license. Nothing she had said or done in regards to Scarlett Hascall called her integrity into question . . . her common sense perhaps, but she did genuinely want to help the girl.

After a long moment, he typed the name Joselyn Miller into another classified database.

Half an hour later, he logged himself out of the various databases and search engines, cleaning up the trail he'd left. He'd found more than he ever imagined . . . more than anyone could have imagined. It all made sense. And he sympathized with Kim, he really did. But that didn't change the fact that he'd never be able to trust her again—especially not about Scarlett's diagnosis.

"Zack?" Phil Taktuq was standing in front of his desk, and from his expression it was apparent he'd been standing there for a while.

"Hey, Phil, what can I do for you?" Zack said, attempting to keep his voice neutral.

"Two things. First—you know the phone we found on the Wilcox girl? Looks like there may be some DNA we can lift off it. The forensics lab found a little bit of hair, wedged in. Not a match for Isabel, we already know that much. We're running some tests, should have more information in the next few days. Maybe we'll get a match. My money's on Sullivan."

Zack shook his head. "He's into little boys."

Phil shrugged. "Maybe he's into the occasional sorority girl as well. That basement Blockbuster you found him visiting? Maybe he was picking up some college porn, too, for a double feature? Just because I like redheads, doesn't mean I can't appreciate a sexy brunette from time to time."

Zack frowned disapprovingly. Not a good comparison.

Phil smiled. "Anyway, we'll hear if they extract some DNA off the phone soon."

Zack nodded. "That's great news." Phil was right. If there was a match in the system to Albert Sullivan, they'd be set—case closed. He tried not to get too excited. "You said two things. What else?"

"Tech managed to crack Scarlett Hascall's password. They downloaded her hard drive and mirrored it on the system. Thought you'd want to know right away. Here's the temporary password—use it to log in and they said it'll basically be like you're on her computer."

"Thanks," Zack said, accepting the Post-it note. He waited until Phil ambled off in the direction of the coffee machine, staring at the scrap of paper.

He'd actually forgotten that they'd confiscated Scarlett's computer, in the chaos of the last few days' developments in the case.

He tapped the password into the departmental server.

Instantly the background changed to a scene of the coast at sunset, a lone fishing boat silhouetted against the orange-streaked sky. Several browser windows were open: a WebMD article about an antianxiety medication; the Jarvis High football schedule—which made sense, if she wanted to watch her sister cheer; and Facebook. He clicked over to Facebook and started scrolling through the posts.

It took Zack a moment to figure out what was off. The profile picture, a girl with her lips pursed in a trout pucker, enormous sunglasses, and a flat-rim ball cap, wasn't Scarlett at all.

It was Isabel Wilcox.

Facebook was open to Izzi's profile.

Which meant that Scarlett had logged in as her.

Zack had seen the profile before, after her parents gave permission for the police to search her social media. It hadn't yielded anything useful then, and the more recent posts were all reactions to the discovery of her body. Expressions of grief and sadness, shared memories, "We miss you" and "Keeping the faith" and "Gone too soon." There were pictures of her as a little girl, selfies with friends ranging back to her middle school days, poems and inspirational quotes and prayers.

None of which was unexpected . . . except that Scarlett had no business logging into it. He scrolled even further back, to the weeks leading up to her disappearance. He'd been over all of it before, but he was struck again by how Izzi seemed more like an ordinary young woman than a calculating criminal. She had a sentimental, introspective bent, posting thoughtful musings that sometimes bordered on the poetic.

Accompanying an old picture of her playing in a sprinkler with a cousin her age, she wrote, "We never thought summer would end / I always thought we'd be forever friends / But life brings pain that we never intend." Another old photo of a young Izzi sitting cross-legged on the floor and clutching a doll, peeping out of a dark closet into a bright, sunny room strewn with toys—her bedroom, with the same white-painted bed frame and dresser visible in the background that Zack had seen when he visited the house. "Bad dreams chased me all around / But there was a special place I found / Away from scary sights and sounds." She wasn't a gifted poet, but neither did she seem like a conniving career criminal.

Something about the photo caught his eye—something was off. He stared at the image, trying to discern what it was. Eventually he figured it out: the closet was in the wrong place.

No, wait—it wasn't the closet; it was only a small space carved out of the wall. The cubbyhole that he'd seen just the other day when they discovered Scarlett hiding behind the wall. The cubbyhole that Isabel had used as a safe space when she was having nightmares.

The hairs stood up along Zack's arms. Kim had used that cubbyhole as proof that Scarlett wasn't faking—saying there was no way that Scarlett could have known about it.

But now, here was possible proof that she *did* know about it. She could have studied Izzi's life, broken into her social media, deliberately adopted details that would make Scarlett's dead-soul infestation more credible. Perhaps she'd learned about the cubbyhole and used that knowledge to carry out a cruel ruse, causing Izzi's parents even more pain, just to deflect suspicion from herself.

On the other hand, if Kim's theory was correct and Scarlett had these restless souls inside her, Scarlett must have been even more desperate to understand her alters' history than the police or Kim were, which would be good reason for her to conduct the searches.

But increasingly, Zack felt that he was having to work harder and harder to sustain his belief in her. Especially when there was another, far more likely explanation: Scarlett had been doing research to help her construct her alibi, her whole concocted story about the alters.

And there was still the disturbing fact that she had never produced a satisfactory alibi for the possible nights Isabel disappeared. Combined with her connection to Brad, things definitely slanted against her again. Now, if the DNA from the phone was a match for Scarlett . . .

Zack checked the browser history and somehow wasn't surprised to discover that Scarlett had made dozens of recent searches into active cases. Isabel Wilcox, Brad Chaplin, Henry Beaumont. There was his own name—"Zack Trainor Jarvis Police"—and Chief Holt Plunkett. The chill that had come over him was hardening into anger.

"How's it coming?"

Zack was so absorbed in his work that he hadn't noticed Holt come up behind him. He tilted the screen toward Holt.

"Check this out. Last week, Scarlett started logging into Facebook."

"Her and about twenty million other teenagers."

"But how many of them have been logging into Isabel Wilcox's account? Using Isabel's password?" He scrolled down to the post with the picture of the cubbyhole. "Look familiar? She *knew*, Holt. Scarlett knew about the secret hiding spot in Izzi's room. She could have used it to shore up her whole alternate personality fairy tale. I think she might have played us."

Holt leaned down to peer at the screen more closely.

"She's been logging in as Izzi for days," Zack continued. "Look, Scarlett is obsessed with this girl. Killing Izzi might have been a crime of passion for her."

"Interesting." Holt scratched his temple. "What about Henry? What about her fingering Sully?"

"I don't know. That asshole killed that little boy. That much I know. How Scarlett fits into it . . . I'm still working that part out."

"Well, keep at it, boy genius—see what else you can dig up."

"You heard about the hair? On Izzi's phone?"

"What?" Holt turned around, face creasing in amazement.

"They found DNA evidence, a hair, wedged into Isabel Wilcox's phone case. Fingerprints would have been long gone after Izzi was submerged in the water for so long—but the hair, we can get something off, maybe."

Holt appeared pensive. "This could finally crack the case wide open, son."

"Yeah, well. Let's just hope the hair has a match in our system." After Holt headed back to his office, Zack poked around for a while without discovering anything new, and finally ended the connection. He stared at his shut-down computer for a long moment.

Twenty-four hours ago, Zack had been working hard to keep his faith in Scarlett, and Kim. But his trust in Kim had shattered when he learned that she wasn't exactly who she'd said she was. And now, that erosion of trust was spreading to encompass Scarlett, too.

One thing was certain, at least: he and Kim were finished.

Zack was not a man who made the same mistake twice.

TWENTY-NINE

Kim didn't sleep well. The twists and turns of Scarlett's case were challenging enough, and it had been extremely difficult to stay detached and professional during the interview with the Henry alter, hearing about the horrors he'd endured.

Then, there was Kim's frustration that Kyle hadn't fought to get her back to work yet, considering the revelations about Scarlett's condition. She felt she deserved a ticker-tape parade, not the radio silence that was still in effect. The fact that she was still on suspension triggered feelings of shame and self-criticism that had plagued her childhood and teenage years. The fact that she'd been involved with her boss now seemed like more than a simple error in judgment. And the long, empty day with nothing to do but mull it over and over and over certainly hadn't helped matters.

Plus, there was what had happened with Zack. After spending what she considered to have been a pretty spectacular night together, he hadn't called or even texted. Another woman—someone without Kim's history—might be able to let that go, and not look for reasons to take it personally. Instead, Kim found herself wondering what she did wrong. Had she been too aggressive? Was he frustrated that she wouldn't let him see her naked in the light? Maybe he, in fact, knew the troubling reason *why*.

Falling into bed with Zack had felt suspiciously like the first giddy foray into falling for him, which was something she hoped to prevent. After the Kyle breakup, she knew she needed to do some work on herself first: she had too many skeletons in the closet, too many barriers, too many scars.

She was tempted to call her parents, or maybe just get on a plane and go home to Massachusetts for a few days, but after her humbling exit from her last job, she couldn't bear to tell them the truth about her suspension.

The residency in San Diego had come to an abrupt end—a firing disguised by the lawsuit-leery HR department as a mutual agreement—when Kim had taken a patient off a course of medication that was causing a host of dangerous side effects. Unlike the hospital, which encouraged the distribution of pills like they were Tic Tacs after a garlicky dinner—all to up their bottom line—Kim felt that, often, overmedication concealed the symptoms without actually improving the health of the sufferer. Kim was fearful that her patient was showing suicidal ideation, and chose *not* to follow her supervisor's recommendation. She took her patient off the pills, and he *did* improve, but not before his condition became temporarily worse.

She'd known it was a risk—just as she knew it was a risk to pursue treatment of Scarlett Hascall.

She finally fell into a deep and dreamless sleep in the early hours of the morning. Waking when the sun was already high in the sky, she felt groggy and disoriented. She made coffee and sat down with her notes on Scarlett's treatment, more to distract herself than anything, and then she went online to see if there were any new developments in the various missing-persons and murder cases.

There was a heartbreaking photo of Henry Beaumont's parents

kneeling at his graveside during his re-internment service, but no comment from the authorities concerning arrests in his case. Which meant they still didn't have enough on Sullivan to press charges or release an official statement. *Damn.* And there was nothing at all new in Isabel's case. A small item in the local online paper mentioned that George DeWitt, a local hunter, had been missing for nearly three weeks. The article quoted his wife as saying, "He gets a wild hair now and then, but he's never been gone this long before." When asked why she didn't report him missing for over two days, she responded, "I wasn't missing him until then."

Kim clicked over to the site that friends of the Wilcox family had set up initially to communicate news of the search, and later to support her parents and to share memories of Izzi. The latest posts by her friends featured photos from Izzi's senior trip to Seattle, laughing teenage girls linking arms and making faces, standing in front of the Space Needle. They looked so innocent, girls on the brink of womanhood, with their whole futures in front of them.

Something had made Isabel turn away from the safety and security of her family, her friends, her seemingly happy childhood. Kim wondered if there was an untreated mood disorder in Isabel's past, perhaps a struggle with untreated attention deficit that had led to frustration and poor performance in school. None of these things necessarily made a person more prone to self-destructive life choices, but the co-occurrence was high enough that Kim wished she could have talked to the girl when she was alive. Perhaps if Izzi had tried to get real help earlier, she wouldn't have been attracted to the criminal types she associated with at the end. Perhaps, if she could gain Izzi's trust now, through Scarlett, Kim could discover who had killed her—and, in turn, help her to *move on*, for both her sake and Scarlett's.

But maybe there was still a way. If she could "talk" to the Isabel alter through Scarlett, focusing on her past this time rather than the murder itself, maybe she could dig up something that the police could use. Maybe her mistake had been to focus solely on her death. Instead, she needed to ask Izzi about her life before, any secrets she may have had that could shed light on the case.

Energized at the prospect of this new approach, Kim quickly showered and dressed. She would head over to the police station and talk to Zack first: if she could get him to share some key information from the case, she'd have a jumping-off point for a session with Isabel. And if she was able to glean any information about how he was feeling about their night together, well, that would only be a side benefit.

As Kim drove to the station, she felt a measure of relief. There was a time long ago when, overwhelmed by the various problems she both encountered, and *created*, in her life, she would end up cycling through a manic episode—acting out, self-sabotage, even resorting to hurting herself, which she hadn't done since she was a teenager. This time, she'd managed to stay the course and interrupt the stressors near the start, in time to chart a better path. Her treatments with Scarlett had worked. She was hopeful that this progress would translate into forgiveness at the hospital. If she could prove to the review board that her treatments with Scarlett had not only set her on a path to be cured but also that the police department apprehended a *killer* because of Kim's efforts. . . . If only they could arrest Albert Sullivan already.

Most important, if she could get Zack a solve on the Isabel Wilcox case, maybe another one of Scarlett's alters would leave the poor teenager alone. A girl could hope.

When she arrived at the station, she gave the receptionist a cheery wave, along with a box of cherry Danish for the officers, and strolled back to Zack's cubicle. He was turned away from her, but she enjoyed the view of his broad shoulders and strong neck, which, if she wasn't mistaken, bore a few scratches for which she was responsible.

"Hey there," she ventured. Zack spun around in his chair.

He did not look happy to see her. He looked like hell, in fact, his face drawn and exhausted.

"Um . . . is this a bad time?" Kim said.

Zack ran his hand over his face and sighed. "What are you doing here?"

Kim tried to respond, but suddenly the confidence she'd felt in the car drained out of her. It looked like she had her answer about Zack: he looked plagued with regrets, and bent on shutting her out—of course he was, he was a by-the-book kind of guy, and she was a player in a case that mattered to him. "I . . . I think I'll just go."

"No, wait. Kim."

Slowly, she turned. Zack stood and stepped closer, regarding her with what looked like pity. *What the hell was going on?*

"About the other night . . ." she ventured.

"I'd rather not talk about that right now. I appreciate you stopping by . . ."

Kim forced a smile. "Yeah, I could tell by the warm welcome." He didn't answer. "You *do* know that I'm a psychiatrist, which gives me mad skills reading body language and voice cues. Call me crazy, but you're either *not really* appreciative that I stopped by, or you just got a phone call that your dog died."

"I don't have a dog."

He stepped closer to her, so that prying ears couldn't hear. "I think we need to formally agree that your involvement in my case—in *any* of my cases—is over."

"What happened?" Kim asked, her voice quavering.

He stared at her for a moment, then walked into the interrogation room. While he didn't ask her to follow, the request was implied.

After he closed the door, he seemed to relent a little, dropping the rigid pose. "Oh hell, Kim, I wasn't even going to say anything. But I saw something in your apartment."

Kim had no idea where he was going with this. She decided to deflect. "It's a back massager. I know what it looks like, but . . ."

He didn't smile. "It wasn't on purpose, it fell off the dresser. A file from the Massachusetts Department of Children and Family, with your picture . . . and a different name."

Kim was still. She couldn't move. Not by choice.

"After I saw it, I did a little looking—and I'm sorry about that, I shouldn't have pried—but I think it's pretty clear you've got some . . . issues. For one thing, you weren't born in Acton like you've claimed."

Kim felt woozy. "I . . . was. But it's complicated."

Zack held up a hand. When he spoke, his voice was quiet. "I'm sure it is. And I'm not asking you to explain yourself. But I can't— I don't need that kind of . . . complication in my life. I've got a zero tolerance policy for dishonesty."

A tear spilled over Kim's cheek, to her horror. She brushed it angrily away. "I never lied to you."

Zack shrugged. He seemed almost sad. "I won't say anything to anyone else, if that's what you're worried about."

"I'm not—but look, you've got to trust me. At least where Scarlett is concerned."

"I don't think that's going to happen."

"Just because there are things in my past that you don't understand, that you *can't* understand—please don't give up on Scarlett. None of this is her fault. Please, Zack." Kim hated how quickly she'd lost control of this situation. But she couldn't let her problematic past color Zack's view of Scarlett—not when he and his team had so much power over the girl's future.

He shook his head slowly. "What you're asking . . . I made a mistake the other night. I should have known better. I do my job to the best of my ability, every day, and in order to do that I need to follow my instincts. Not get distracted."

"Is that what the other night was? Just a distraction? That's what I am? A distraction?"

"*Kim.*" He took a step closer, so they were only inches apart. "You're not listening to me. I didn't want to discuss this with you, but you aren't giving me a choice. I can't let you anywhere near this case because you're not credible. I know about your past, okay? I have access to records that the public doesn't."

Kim felt the color drain from her face.

"I know that when you were six, carjackers murdered your parents right in front of you; I know you escaped by hiding in the backseat. I know you saw the entire thing."

"You don't know anything." She wasn't able to control the tears now.

"And I know that the experience supposedly caused a . . . split in your psyche."

"*Supposedly?*"

He took a deep breath. "I read the psychiatrist's case notes, Kim, the ones that were included in your DCF file."

No. Kim felt an absurd urge to put her hands over her ears to keep him from saying the rest. How could she have been so stupid? He was a cop. An investigator. Following the trail to the truth was what he did, who he was. Getting involved with him was asking for trouble.

She took a deep breath. "Those records . . ."

"They're sealed. I know. I had no right to read them. What I did was wrong, Kim, and I apologize. It's just that—what we did, the feelings I had for you . . ." He seemed to be battling with himself, searching for the right words. "I had to know the truth," he finally said. "To protect myself."

"To protect yourself from what?" Kim cried, knowing she shouldn't say another word. That she should turn around and go, instead of trying to convince Zack that she'd done nothing wrong. But his words had sent her back in time, to a memory her own psyche had tried to help her never to revisit again.

Those moments in the car—less than a minute, start to finish— would eventually transform her life forever. Her father whispering for Joselyn to "stay down" as two men approached their car in the dark. The driver's door opening, her dad saying, "Hey—" That was as far as he'd gotten before the man punched him in the throat. Her mother screaming. They'd killed her first; the other man had simply reached through her open window and shot her in the face. Through her right eye. The bullet exited the side of her head, the slug coming to a stop inside the foam of the seat next to her bowed head. Her father had fought back, but only for a second, perhaps because he realized that his struggle might reveal his daughter in the backseat. He took two shots to the back of the head. And Kim, terrified, could only cower on the floor of the car.

The two men had pulled her parents' bodies from the car and tossed them to the street like bags of trash. All she remembered of the men were the ski masks they wore, their angry eyes. Their silence as they drove faster and faster through the light midmorning traffic. She learned later that they'd sped south on 495, and for reasons that were never known, pulled off near Milford and dumped the car in a parking lot of a vacant auto parts store. Kim had stayed in the car for hours before a man out walking his dog heard her crying through the open windows.

"If you read my files," she said shakily, trying to regain her composure, "you know that four years after they were killed I had a . . . a breakdown. But I received excellent treatment and I'm completely—"

"You suffered a psychotic split, Kim," Zack interrupted. "It was right there in the files. The person you were, 'Joselyn,' disappeared forever. Kim is an alternate personality."

"My name is Kimberly Patterson."

"You've suffered from dissociative identity disorder all along."

"It's not . . . it's not like that." Kim heard a rushing in her ears, an overwhelming urge to run, to close her eyes, to hide. "I healed. I learned. I studied everything that has ever been written about DID, damn it. I'm . . ."

Normal. The word mocked her from a host of memories—all the taunts she'd suffered as a child, all the pained rejections when she tried to tell the truth later. The boyfriend who called her a freak when he learned the truth. The supposed best friend who shared Kim's deepest secret with other girls behind her back. Always, always, reminding Kim that she would never be like everyone else.

Despite the loving parents who adopted her, the caring professionals, the hundreds of hours of therapy; despite becoming an expert in the field herself, a champion for the neuro-atypical, there was a part of Kim that longed to be *normal.*

Zack was shaking his head. "Who is Joselyn Miller?"

"She's gone."

"Does she come back? Will I meet her one day?"

"She's gone."

"Gone! Your fucking name is Joselyn Miller!"

"I don't know who that is. I've always been Kim Patterson," Kim insisted.

"And I've always been James Bond."

"I didn't know you were so . . . cruel."

There was a long moment as Zack just stared at Kim . . . at Joselyn . . . at whoever the fuck he thought she was.

Finally, Kim shrugged. She had been to this dance before. "Listen, I don't expect you to understand."

"Kim, it doesn't matter that you've learned to manage your

condition," Zack was saying, as if he could read her thoughts. "It doesn't matter that I . . . care for you. Given what I found out, I can't let you anywhere near this case. Your point of view is just too compromised."

"Please . . . please just listen to me."

"What about these, Kim?" Zack said gently, touching her arm, sliding her sleeve up to reveal the very faint scars underneath. The ones he'd no doubt seen the other night, even in the dark.

"I haven't . . . cut . . . since I was a teenager." She wanted to defend herself against the conclusions Zack had drawn, but it was all happening too fast, and she'd come here expecting something very different. She wasn't prepared, and now that the lid had been opened on the past, painful memories were slamming her faster than she could cope.

"I was wondering why you wouldn't undress in front of me in the light. Why you insisted we stay under the covers in the morning. There are other scars. No?"

She stared him down, defiantly. *Yes, of course, yes.*

"Look," Zack said softly. "I deplore what happened to you. I've devoted my life to protecting people from horrors like what you and your family went through. But I can't change who I am. If things were different . . . if your past wasn't all twisted up in this case, if you'd been honest from the start—"

"If I'd been honest, there *wouldn't* have been a start!"

He continued on over her. "—and I didn't have all these unsolved murders on my hands—" He cleared his throat. "I think you're special, Kim, and the other night was . . . but we can't do this. *I* can't do this."

Kim backed away from him, bumping into the next desk. She couldn't get away fast enough. But she had a feeling that no matter how fast she ran, the past would never loosen its grip.

He stopped her by putting his hand on her arm, compelling her to look at him. "You've got to let this go. You're in way over your head here. I've found evidence that Scarlett has been lying all along. You're just too close to see it."

Kim tried to absorb what Zack was telling her, but it was all wrong. She didn't care how much "evidence" accumulated that seemed to implicate her, Scarlett wasn't a killer. She was just desperate for some relief from the pressure of harboring so many alters. Kim knew firsthand how overwhelming it could be when one's identity slowly splintered, how terrifying the loss of control. And Scarlett had the added burden that no one believed her. At least in Kim's case, she'd had the support of her counselors, her case manager, and her foster parents. She'd never had to fight just to be believed.

Scarlett had no one in her corner. Even her father didn't know what to believe.

And that meant that Kim couldn't give up on her. Especially now.

"Let it go," she echoed, knowing that she couldn't do it.

Zack nodded firmly and gave her arm a little pat. "That's right. It's time to let us do our jobs. You need to step back, get a little rest. Focus on yourself for a while, Kim." His expression softened as he took in her wild expression. "You need some help. And I'm only saying that because I care about you."

Kim looked at the window of the interrogation room, knowing what lay on the other side: officers pretending not to watch them, the bulletin board with the missing-persons posters, the file cabinets filled with case notes for all the terrible things that had happened in this town.

How had she ever believed that she could escape her past, even in a place as remote as Jarvis, Alaska? How did she ever think she could make a difference?

It all came down to Scarlett. Kim couldn't save Henry or Isabel

or any of the other murdered souls, but she could, just maybe, help
one girl who had no one else to turn to. Because she knew what it
was like to carry trauma around inside her. So she wouldn't give
up. Even if that meant walking out of here and losing Zack forever.
Even if it meant losing her job and her future. Hell, she'd basically
lost it all already. What difference would it make?

"I'm sure you're right," she said tonelessly, and turned away
from him.

"Kim . . ."

She kept walking, through the onslaught of glances from his
colleagues, out the door and through the parking lot. She got back
into her car and turned the key in the ignition. The ancient Civic
rumbled to life, and she backed out of the parking space, only to see
Zack standing in the doors of the station, watching her.

She held it together for almost five minutes, long enough to
take the road out of town as far as the turnoff for an abandoned
fisherman's shack she'd stumbled upon while hiking one day.
Nothing remained but the stone foundation, with an incredible
view of the steely blue sea below. Kim parked and got out of the
car, grateful no one else had chosen today to visit her favorite
hideaway.

She took a seat on the crumbling hearth that was all that remained of the original chimney, and let the salty air blow her hair
gently around her shoulders. She closed her eyes and focused on
the rest of her senses, trying desperately to stay in the moment. The
cries of the sea birds, the sounds of traffic up on the road, the scent
of wildflowers and the ocean and sun-warmed earth . . . all of these
had the potential to heal.

But today they weren't enough. Zack had learned her most
distressing truth. She believed him when he said that he wouldn't
tell anyone else, but it was too late to protect her psyche from the
memories he had stirred up. This was why she didn't tell anyone

the truth. It wasn't to protect them, it was to protect her*self*—she couldn't handle it—the chance that she might remember.

Memories of that day confused her senses, overwhelming her. The smell of the dirty carpet and the rubber mats as she pressed herself into the floor of the station wagon. The sound of her mother's screams, of her father gasping for breath after being struck in the throat. The odor of her own urine when she wet herself. The feel of the car bumping and jostling underneath her painfully as the attackers sped away.

Kim's psyche had worked so hard to distance itself from that day. She'd turned herself into someone new . . . someone strong, someone capable, someone who helped others. But now she felt no different from the helpless, hurting little girl she'd been that day.

Zack had tried to do the honorable thing. He had no way of understanding the damage he inflicted by following that thread back to its origin.

No one understood. No one but Kim . . . and maybe Scarlett.

THIRTY

Kim spent the next couple of days in a haze of anxiety, trying to stave off the despair that memories of the past could trigger. She knew she should reach out; she could seek out a psychiatrist who wasn't affiliated with the hospital, or at the very least make a call to her parents, or her old therapist from college, or even high school. Instead, she went on long, punishing runs, and spent her evenings on the couch, losing herself in hours of mindless television. When she slept, she woke up feeling more tired than the night before, as if all she did in her dreams was keep running, hurtling toward a solution that didn't exist.

She thought about texting Scarlett, but given her own fragility, as well as a reluctance to do anything to jeopardize Scarlett being cleared of suspicion, she held off. Several times a day, she found herself coasting by the Hascalls' house, hoping to catch a glimpse of Scarlett and assure herself everything was okay. Most times, it seemed like no one was home, but once she caught sight of what she was fairly sure was Scarlett in an upstairs window.

Two days later, a text came through early in the morning, while she was drinking her fourth cup of coffee. She was surprised to see that it was from Kyle.

Please come see me at my office at your earliest convenience.

She did her best to ignore the trepidation that seized her, and responded that she'd come immediately. After dressing in a conservative skirt and blouse, and doing her best to obscure the dark smudges under her eyes, she drove to the hospital, where she found Kyle sitting at his desk in his office, staring at his computer screen. When he saw her, his expression cycled through a host of emotions.

"I'll make this quick, Kim. Dr. Graver spoke to me late yesterday and let me know that the board is leaning toward terminating you. They'll be meeting next Monday, and it's almost certain that the decision will be unanimous. I'm sorry."

Kim watched his lips moving and tried to make sense of what he was saying. She'd suspected that whatever he wanted to discuss with her wouldn't be good, but she hadn't been ready to believe she was being fired. Instead, she'd spent the last few days trying to talk herself into making a fresh start. She'd even dared to hope that returning to work might help her work past the shock of Zack finding out the truth about her past.

And now, despite her most ardent hopes, it was all being ripped away from her.

She forced a brave smile. "And here I thought you called me in because you wanted to have a go at a little breakup sex."

Kyle knew what she was doing. She was trying not to cry. "Look, I shouldn't have said anything. I could get in a lot of trouble over this. But I . . . felt like I owed you at least a little notice." Kyle sighed deeply, and she could see the purple circles under his eyes. He'd been losing sleep, too. "I tried to fight for you. I know you may not believe me . . . but despite how things ended between us . . . I *did* try."

"I do believe you," Kim managed to get out, her voice dry and brittle. "And I know I've hardly made things easy on you."

"Hardly."

"Will I get a chance to plead my case. To the board?"

"Dr. Graver—oh, hell, you know what she's like. She gets her mind made up about something and—and then no one wants to end up on her bad side, so they just all go along with her."

"But I thought . . . I mean, we were making progress. With Scarlett. The Henry Beaumont case—it proved that she really is harboring alters. I know it's not an official diagnosis—not yet, anyway, but—"

"That's the thing," Kyle cut in. Kim froze, already anticipating his next words. "The police contacted me this morning. About Scarlett."

Kim was silent, trying to process this new information. She tried to keep her voice optimistic. It didn't work. "What did they want?"

"They wouldn't give me any specifics, but your friend, Detective Trainor, strongly hinted that they have new evidence implicating her. He was requesting her records. Of course, I turned him down, Kim, but he's just going to come back with a warrant. It sounds serious."

Kim ignored Kyle's frosty tone when he mentioned Zack's name. "What was the evidence?"

Kyle regarded her over his glasses, clearly conflicted. "Listen . . . the only reason he told me anything was to try to convince me to release the records, because he was frustrated about the delay getting a warrant would cause. And I shouldn't be telling you, either, except I feel like it's the only way to get you to finally drop this whole thing with Scarlett."

"Just tell me—please."

"Scarlett's DNA matches a hair strand they found on Isabel's phone, which they found with the body. They believe it might have ripped off in a struggle. They're likely going to arrest Scarlett later today."

"But—" Kim's mind reeled. How was that possible? That would mean that Scarlett would have had to have been with Isabel shortly before her death. "It had to have been planted there."

Kyle rolled his eyes. "Please," he said thinly. "Tell me you don't seriously still believe in her innocence, after everything. Not after what I just told you."

"I just want to—"

"You're incapable of being wrong! Even when the evidence clearly points to the contrary. And this is exactly why you're in the situation you're in, Kim. You hold to these preposterous beliefs, like your insistence on the DID diagnosis, and then when another answer seems more likely, you just dig in deeper and come up with this nonsense about harboring dead souls."

"But I don't—"

"None of which is the least bit appropriate for a clinician, *obviously*."

"Kyle, don't do this. Just listen to me, please."

He held up a hand to stop her. "No . . . if I were you, I'd go home right now and start looking for a new job. Leave Jarvis behind, and find a new place to make a fresh start. That's the smart move here."

Kim simply nodded. They both knew there would be no new job, at least not in her profession. And this new evidence against Scarlett . . . it was impossible to comprehend. She needed time to digest it. She had to talk to Scarlett. She turned and left the room, not bothering to say good-bye to Kyle.

As she walked to her car, she felt strangely numb. She barely registered the faces of her coworkers, their embarrassment and discomfort as they greeted her. They likely all knew her fate already, thanks to the hospital grapevine.

She knew she should feel something: mortification, shame, even anger. But the only thoughts in her head were of Scarlett . . . and of her own past. The memories of what had happened to her so many years ago now seemed to be propelling her to finish what the un-known killer had put into motion . . . to protect Scarlett and get justice for Izzi. Identifying Henry's killer, with Scarlett's help, now felt like a mission that she had been chosen specifically to carry out; wasn't it possible that she was meant to do more? Had the past somehow prepared her, shaped her into the person who could pro-tect the innocent victims of a phenomenon *she* was uniquely quali-fied to understand?

As she pulled out of the parking lot, she knew what she had to do. She turned the car in the direction of the Hascalls' house.

KIM ARRIVED IN LESS than ten minutes and parked across the street, under the branches of a tall red cedar, wondering how she might convince Scarlett to do what needed to be done.

While she was trying to formulate a plan, Heather and Peter Hascall came out of the house. Heather was swinging her backpack and laughing at something her dad said. Peter opened the car door for his daughter before going around to the driver's side. Heather looked far more relaxed than she had the first time Kim laid eyes on her. She wondered if it was because Scarlett had become calmer with one less alter to manage.

It was a critical time for Scarlett. If she was arrested on the basis of the DNA evidence, Kim had a feeling her condition would worsen, leaving her psyche ever more open to the most damaging of her alters. They'd made so much progress already in their sessions to-gether; Kim couldn't let that be undone. There was no telling what an alter like Julian might do to a weakened host. No, there was only one way to help Scarlett, and any of her alters, now—Kim had to some-how solve the case herself, to keep Scarlett from being prosecuted.

Once Peter Hascall had driven away, Kim got out of the car. She approached the house and rang the doorbell. Scarlett answered, still in flannel pajama pants and an old sweatshirt, with her hair in a ponytail and big fuzzy slippers on her feet.

"Hi." Kim tried to smile. "Something has happened, Scarlett, and I just thought it would be better if I told you in person."

"Told me what?"

"It's not good news, Scarlett. The police have matched your DNA to Isabel's crime scene somehow. We need to leave, now, before they have a chance to arrest you and charge you with murder. We need to go somewhere where no one can find you."

"What, you mean—run away?" Scarlett's face, freshly scrubbed and without makeup, looked even younger than her nineteen years.

"Don't think of it as running away," Kim said, feeling a brilliant clarity for the first time in days. She was doing the right thing, beyond a doubt. "We need to convince people that you're telling the truth, and that's going to be a lot harder once you're in custody, without access to a psychiatrist who understands your condition. We both have a lot riding on the outcome of the Isabel Wilcox case. For me, it's just a job, but for you . . . well, I want the rest of the world to know that you're not a criminal—that you're a smart, capable person with a . . . highly unusual but manageable psychiatric condition."

Scarlett grimaced. "I'm not sure I like the way that sounds," she said.

"I don't blame you. I wouldn't, either. If I could wave a magic wand and banish your alters, I would," Kim said. "But if I've learned one thing since deciding to study psychiatry, it's that there is no such thing as 'normal.' Everyone is different and unique, and it's our challenges that shape us as much as anything."

"You sound a lot like my last shrink," Scarlett said with a strained smile. "She used to say that being ordinary has its challenges, too."

Kim laughed, despite herself. "It doesn't really have much of a ring to it, as far as slogans go—but I think I could get behind it."

Scarlett looked past her, out into the neighborhood, the tidy tree-lined streets. "Still . . . things were just starting to return to normal again around here. Heather and me, we're getting along, and Dad seems happier than he's been in ages. I haven't *switched* in days. I haven't lost time. I just wish—"

Her voice cracked, and along with it, Kim's heart. "I know," she murmured. "I know." Kim took a step toward her. "I'm just worried that it's the calm before the storm."

Scarlett sighed. "I had a feeling this was too good to last. So what's your big plan? Are we heading for Mexico?" She tried to laugh, but it came out as a strangled sob.

"Listen . . . Do you trust me, Scarlett?" Kim looked at her steadily, trying to reassure the girl with her gaze.

"Yes."

"I mean . . . I'm asking a lot of you here. There are plenty of people who would tell you that I'm . . . unstable myself. That I can't provide you the guidance you deserve."

"I don't care about them," Scarlett said simply. "You've never lied to me, have you?"

"Never."

"And you've always believed me, right?"

"Yes."

Scarlett shrugged, getting control of her emotions. "That's good enough for me. Can I just leave my dad a note and grab a few things?"

"Sure," Kim said. "Just make it quick, okay?" Every moment they delayed the plan, Kim could feel her anxiousness returning. It was much better to stay in motion—to keep things charging ahead— now that Kim had finally figured out the correct path.

She waited downstairs, pacing back and forth across the kitchen floor, while Scarlett went to get her backpack and a change of clothes. It was only a few minutes until Scarlett was ready, but to

Kim, who'd spent the time peering out the window, anticipating the lights of a squad car at any moment, it felt like hours. Kim tried not to rush Scarlett as she watched her set a piece of paper on the counter and tenderly position her dad's favorite coffee mug, which read "You Can't Scare Me, I Have Daughters," on top to anchor it. Kim quickly scanned the short note, making sure it didn't hold anything that could be used against the girl later:

> Dear Dad and Sis,
>
> I love you guys more than anything in this whole world. I promise I'll do my best to stay safe and get home as soon as I can.

Her signature was surrounded by tiny hearts, and Kim was struck again by how Scarlett was truly in the balance between childhood and adulthood; that the things that happened to her now could well set the tone for the rest of her life.

"I won't let you down," Kim promised softly, as she led the way to her old car. She'd defend Scarlett with her very life, if it came to that.

THIRTY-ONE

Kim had driven past the old motel earlier in the summer when she'd gone for a drive, hoping to get to know the area around Jarvis. This was before she'd fully absorbed how cut off the town was from civilization. There was only one road that ran to the larger Alaskan cities and, eventually, beyond the state's border. Other than that, there were a handful of dirt roads that led to hunting camps and ghost towns to the north and east.

Along the edge of one such dead-end road was the Golden Motel, a long, narrow building featuring four guest rooms and what had once been an office. Some of the windows were broken now; the drapes in the remaining ones were pulled tight. The office had been ransacked, the parking lot littered with beer cans and food wrappers and used condoms. The road had deteriorated until it was nothing but a pair of deep ruts, and the only people who ventured there were snowmobilers in the winter, and teenagers looking for a place to party in the summer.

Whoever had once imagined that people might pay to enjoy a night in the beautiful Alaskan wilderness, nestled in the Sitka pines a mile above town on a road that was virtually impassable after the first snowfall, had had their dream dashed. But now, it might be Kim and Scarlett's best hope for escaping the authorities. The Golden Motel was the only place she could think of to hide.

By noon, Kim and Scarlett were winded and sweating from removing the fallen, dead tree branches that blocked the road. They'd stopped again to allow a flock of wild turkeys to cross in front of them. The Civic had threatened to spin out in the mud on its balding tires, but Kim goosed the gas while Scarlett pushed, and they managed the treacherous ascent to the motel. Scarlett got out and swung open the wood gate that was the last obstacle before the building, closing it after Kim drove past. She parked around the back, making sure the car wasn't visible from the road, and she and Scarlett unpacked the trunkful of groceries and supplies.

They set up camp in the least trashed of the guest rooms, forgoing the moldering mattresses and instead laying their sleeping bags out on scarred wooden floors.

Kim's anxiety was somewhat lessened by the remote setting—it was unlikely that the police would think to check up here, since Kim had no real connection to the place, nor did Scarlett. But even though she logically knew they were safe for at least the present, she still found herself unable to relax entirely, so as a distraction she sorted through their grocery bags and set about preparing a lunch of fruit and cold cuts. When it was ready, she grabbed them each a bottle of water and they sat down at the splintered picnic table outside the main office.

After a long moment, Scarlett finally broke the silence. "I like what you've done with the place."

Kim nodded appreciatively, not smiling. "Thank you. I had all the fixtures flown in from Paris."

"Impressive."

Kim turned to Scarlett and took her in. "I'm sorry we're having to keep you out here. Hopefully it won't be too long."

"I really appreciate what you're doing," Scarlett said. "I've put

Dad through enough. If I can just keep out of the way until they figure out who really killed Isabel—"

"I think we're going to have to do a little more than just wait," Kim said. "I think we may just have to figure this out ourselves." While she was determined to see this plan through, a part of her still cringed hearing the words come out of her mouth—even now she realized how desperate a plan of action this was. But what else could be done? By bringing Scarlett here, Kim had already set things in motion. Now she had to see it through.

Scarlett looked doubtful. "But how? I mean, if Chief Plunkett and Detective Trainor can't find the killer, what chance do we have?"

"But that's just it," Kim said eagerly. "They've got their hands full trying to make their case against Albert Sullivan. They know he killed Henry all those years ago, and he's been in and out of trouble ever since. They ought to look at him for Izzi's murder, too, but now that they have evidence pointing to you, what's their incentive to follow up with him?"

"You really think Albert killed Izzi, too?"

"I think it's as good a place to start as any. I mean, it's true that violent pedophiles rarely pursue adults. But Izzi was young, and Albert has lived in this town for a long time. What if Albert molested her in the past, when she was a child? It would certainly explain some of her behavior. Maybe she tried to tell her parents, or another adult, and they didn't believe her . . . even more reason for her to turn away from her family and toward someone like Brad Chaplin."

"Why wouldn't she just go to the police?"

"If she'd trusted people in the past, and been burned, she might be more likely to take things into her own hands," Kim said, choosing not to think about how easily her words could be applied to their current situation.

"I guess," Scarlett said doubtfully.

"Or maybe . . . from what I could get out of Detective Trainor, it sounds like Isabel was mixed up in some bad stuff. She could have unearthed something about Albert, been threatening him, or even blackmailing him for money. Albert could have snapped and killed her on the spot. Then he disposed of the body in the lake, weighing her down so she hopefully wouldn't be found."

"I guess that makes sense," Scarlett said. "But how are we ever going to convince him to confess?"

"It's past time for convincing," Kim said. She was tired from the exertions of getting to the motel, and her mind was buzzing with the need for resolution—it was time to force things into their proper places. "I'm tired of being nice about this. I'm tired of relying on Chief Plunkett and Zack."

"Zack?" Scarlett's eyebrow raised. "Detective Trainor is Zack now?"

Kim held her gaze. "Oh . . . is his first name not Zack?"

"No, it is."

Kim nodded.

Scarlett let it drop. She clearly knew there were more important things right now than calling her doctor out for possibly sleeping with one of the most attractive men in Jarvis. "Okay, so you don't want to rely on Chief Plunkett or Zack. What are we going to do?"

"*You're* going to stay here. *I'm* going to get my gun. And I'm going to have a . . . friendly conversation with Albert Sullivan."

Scarlett looked horrified. "You can't be serious."

"I'm just going to threaten him," Kim said, though her mind was shifting with all the various possibilities. She had to admit it would be satisfying to put the muzzle to Albert's forehead and pull the trigger, to put an end to at least one evil in the world. "Just enough to get his confession."

"Do you even know where to get a gun?"

Kim nodded impatiently. "You know the pawn shop behind the

Hidey-Ho? One of my patients told me about it—his cousin owns it. They sell guns under the table."

Scarlett took a sip of her water, her expression clouding with concern.

"Don't worry, Scarlett, I'll be careful. I just have to make Albert *think* I'd kill him. Once he confesses, everything else will fall into place and you'll be in the clear—they'll know you've been telling the truth all along."

Scarlett frowned. "I don't know. It seems dangerous. And there's a lot that could go wrong."

Kim felt a rush of annoyance toward Scarlett, and then quickly tamped it down. Scarlett was young. She didn't realize how important it was that they figure this out. The idea of a lifetime in jail probably just didn't feel real to her. Sure, what she was doing right now had its risks. But what mattered most was Scarlett's freedom and safety. Kim had never taken seriously the idea of having her own children . . . but she thought that this is what it must feel like. She might not be Scarlett's mother, but she felt like a mama bear.

Kim picked up their paper plates and stuffed them in the trash bag she'd brought, deliberately changing the subject. "I bought you some magazines," she said, "and you can use a flashlight as long as you're careful. No light at the windows. I'll be back sometime tonight."

"Wait—you're going to go see Albert today?"

"Just as soon as I get the gun. The sooner the better."

"Then I'm coming with you," Scarlett demanded.

"That's adorable. Really. But no. It's too dangerous. Look, this is a one-woman job, okay? It'll be over before you know it." She smiled, feeling her anger and anxiety settle into a steely confidence. "Trust me . . . tomorrow we'll take the confession to the police. Albert's too old and slow to make a run for it—even if he tries, he won't get far. Trust me. We are going to fix this. I promise."

"All right," Scarlett said doubtfully. "If you really think this is the best thing to do."

Kim knew Scarlett still had doubts, and realized that she hadn't thought through every piece of this plan as much as she might like. A million things could go wrong, not to mention the possibility of Scarlett *switching* while Kim was gone, but she was safer out here, far from the triggers that would normally affect her . . . arguments, fights, stress. Anyway, they didn't have time for caution. And it was much better to do *something* than to simply wait, like sitting ducks, for the police to come for Scarlett.

If only she'd done something herself, all those years ago. If she'd screamed . . . if she'd distracted the carjackers long enough for her parents to make their escape . . . if she'd launched herself at her father's killer before he could aim his gun.

When she was six, she hadn't been able to stop the evil that had come roaring into her life and taken everything she cared about.

She wasn't going to make that same mistake again.

THIRTY-TWO

From the outside, it didn't look like the home of a dangerous man. Kim was looking down on Albert Sullivan's house from the hillside above, having parked her car at the end of the street and hiked up through the woods above the neighborhood, using the thick pines for cover.

The house was shabby, and the lawn was overgrown, but wildflowers bloomed at the edges and an untended lilac hedge scented the air, the peacefulness of the scent in stark opposition to Kim's rapid heartbeat. On the rooftop, a rooster weathervane creaked as the wind gently directed its rusted beak. The drapes were closed tightly over all the windows, but the back sliding door was open a few inches to let in the breeze. Kim could see nothing inside, though she thought she noticed a flash of movement—maybe someone passing by the door in the interior of the house, maybe nothing.

The afternoon was warm and she was sweating slightly from exertion, but Kim felt ready—more determined than ever to see this through. A part of her knew there was a danger of her thoughts becoming slightly manic and disordered if she didn't work to resolve the issues brought up over the last few days—but there simply wasn't time for her to deal with that now. Once Albert Sullivan was locked up, once Scarlett could return safely home to her family, she would focus on herself.

At least the visit to the pawnshop had gone as well as she could have hoped. The young man behind the counter seemed to accept her claim that "with all these dead bodies washing up, I just need something to protect myself with." He had suggested a Ruger 9mm that was small enough to sit comfortably in her hand and took up very little room in her purse. She didn't ask who the gun used to belong to—and he didn't volunteer the information. Kim had always been a staunch advocate for stronger gun laws, especially considering the elevated risk of violence to social workers, but in that moment she was happy for the "don't ask, don't tell" lenience of the Alaskan firearms market.

"You know how to use this thing?" he'd asked, eyeing her skeptically, but a stack of extra twenties encouraged him to keep his thoughts to himself, and he threw in a box of cartridges for free, even showing her how to load them. Kim had shot a gun once at a bachelorette party for her college friend Kathy Fabian—a party that she left early after feeling the kick of the gun in her hand, her mind flashing to the thought of the bullet piercing her mother's brain as she still screamed. While she had only fired the gun once that night, she had relived the moment so many times in her memory that she felt sure she'd be able to handle the handgun.

Now she took the little gun from her back pocket and crept down the slope. As she drew nearer to the sliding door, she could make out a table and chairs beyond, and hear the sound of the television. She checked the neighboring houses, but there were no signs that anyone was home. Soon, children would be returning from school and parents from their jobs, but Kim hoped to be long gone by then. Her phone was in her other pocket, Zack's number queued up and ready to go, just in case anything went wrong. She worried that he might screen her call, maybe not even listen to a message, if she had time to leave one.

A sudden creaking sound from above caught her attention, and she looked up to the roof, relieved to see that it was the corroded rooster weathervane responding to the breeze. The rooster turned slowly and the metal directionals spun.

North. East. West. South.

N-E-W-S.

The rooster preened above it.

Kim audibly gasped as she made the connection to Henry's confounding declaration. *On top, it had a news birdie.*

It was too late to turn back. When Kim reached the house, she flattened herself against the siding, trying to ignore the pounding of her heart, and listened. The television was blaring one of those courtroom shows, and the plaintiff seemed to be accusing the defendant of pouring paint on his brand-new living room floor. The defendant hotly protested that he owed him money.

Slowly, slowly, Kim turned her body until she could peek inside. The house was dim; the smell of burnt toast and mold wafted from inside. As her eyes adjusted to the gloom, she could make out the top of a greasy, balding head above the easy chair facing the television.

Kim took a deep breath and then launched herself through the door, running through the kitchen and into the living room. She stood between the television and the easy chair, and found herself face-to-face with Albert Sullivan.

He was asleep. As she watched, his face contracted with a snorting cough, and then he settled back down and snored quietly. Kim felt herself deflate, some of her nervousness draining away. She took a moment to look around the room and assess her options. Next to Albert on a side table was a nearly empty glass of iced tea, the ice cubes still melting on the bottom; so he hadn't been out for long. A stack of newspapers was held in place by an ugly figurine of a dog wearing a tweed hat and smoking a pipe. A magazine rested faceup on Albert's thighs, threatening to slide down onto the floor.

Kim squinted at the image, then suppressed a gasp of horror. The little boy pictured in a variety of poses on the glossy pages couldn't have been older than nine.

Her fury renewed, she lifted the gun so that it was pointed straight at Albert's face, and kicked him in the shin.

He came awake with a yowl of pain, looking wildly around the room, then focused on her. He reached down and massaged his shin as his expression changed from one of surprise to crafty contempt.

"What you got there, miss, a li'l old peashooter?" Kim suspected he made himself sound more backwater and old-fashioned so people would underestimate him. Well, she wouldn't make that mistake.

"You know damn well this gun could kill you, Albert," Kim said. "Do you know who I am?"

"Sure I do. You're that headshrinker bitch. Thought you could shrink *my* head, didn't you, down at the police station." He laughed, and the sound startled Kim for a moment, but she managed to keep the gun steady. "But I'm too smart for that."

"You killed Henry Beaumont nineteen years ago. And you killed Isabel Wilcox, too."

"Blah, blah, blah," Albert wheezed. "I ain't listening. I know why you *really* came over. You want to get fucked."

Despite his smile, she could see the fear in his eyes. "You killed Isabel Wilcox, didn't you, Albert?"

His smile grew wider. "That's a good one. You wanna hear another good one? What's the difference between love, true love, and showing off?" He waited for her to guess, but she just kept the gun directed at his face. "Spitting, swallowing, and gargling." He chortled and then added, "You wanna show off for me, sweetheart?"

It was amazing how good he was at winding people up—he knew just what to say to upset Kim. With effort, she kept her face neutral. "You need to confess, Albert, or else I'm going to give you a little taste of what you've done to all your victims."

"How's that? Don't tell me you think you're actually going to *fire* that thing?" His laughter collapsed into another coughing fit. He pulled a filthy handkerchief from his pocket and spit into it. Kim's stomach turned with revulsion.

She pointed the gun at the mirror hanging over the dingy fireplace mantel and pulled the trigger. The explosion was near deafening, and the glass broke into a million tiny splinters that clattered to the floor.

Albert only laughed harder, pointing at the broken mirror as though it was the funniest thing he'd ever seen. "My poor mirror," he said, wiping his eyes. "What'd it ever do to you, huh?"

Frustration combined with adrenaline, making Kim's head pound. This wasn't how she'd envisioned this going. Albert was supposed to have realized he was outmatched. He was supposed to be afraid of her.

But maybe, when he'd given in to his own amoral urgings, when he'd committed acts so vile that his very humanity was no longer intact, he'd stopped being afraid. Maybe he felt he'd made a bargain with the devil, anticipating his own ignominious end all these years as he spiraled down to join the lowest dregs of humanity, as trade for the heinous things he'd done.

Could she kill him, if he refused to confess? Give him what he deserved after the terrible things he'd done all these years? No. Even in this heightened state Kim could never go that far. But, maybe she could hurt him badly enough to force him to talk to her. To make him confess.

Kim thought of Scarlett, imprisoned, forced into a state psych ward or worse, unable to go to school or get a job or do any of the ordinary things young women did. If Scarlett were convicted of murder, she would never have an opportunity to receive treatment, to learn to live with her alters and lead a good life.

Yes. Kim could do this. To help Scarlett, she would do whatever she had to. She slipped her hand into her pocket to press Record on her phone.

Albert grinned. "Don't tell me, you got a *real* gun in there?"

"Men like you can't satisfy a real woman, so you turn to children," she said thoughtfully. It wasn't true, of course—plenty of pedophiles were married or in seemingly typical relationships—but she was trying to provoke him. "When did you stop being able to perform with women, Albert? Sexually, I mean."

Albert's mouth snapped shut and he glared at her. "Don't you dare try to psychoanalyze me. I ain't never been the problem. Women are. They let themselves go. Quit giving a crap what they look like."

"We all age," Kim said conversationally. "*Normal* people continue to enjoy healthy sexual relationships well into their seventies and even eighties. But there's definitely a problem with *you*—when did you stop being able to satisfy a woman?"

"Shut up," Albert said. His fingers twitched spasmodically. "Just shut the hell up."

"You wouldn't be the only one," Kim said, feigning boredom. "Most times we can treat dysfunction with drugs and therapy. But some men—the ones who prey on children, for instance—it's like their whole manhood has drained right out of them. They might as well be eunuchs, since they can only get it up with children."

"That's not true!"

"Ha," Kim said contemptuously, pointing the gun at his groin. He was rapidly losing his composure. If Kim had to guess, she'd say his mind was battling between protecting his fragile identity—everything that "being a man" meant to him, including power and dominance and control—and admitting that underneath it all he was merely a bully, a predator, a coward, and weak. If she could just push a little bit harder . . . "In fact, I wonder if that's why you ended up killing Henry. Because you couldn't manage to *get it up*."

"You *bitch*!" Albert said, lunging for the gun, and managing almost to reach it before Kim stepped out of the way. "I got rid of that little bastard because he wouldn't shut up. Kept crying and whining, even after I gave him candy. He was gonna say something. He was gonna rat me out. So I put him in a place where no one would find him. Well . . . not for a hundred years, anyway." Albert chuckled wickedly. "You should have heard him pounding from the inside of that capsule. Lasted a good half hour . . . before the oxygen ran out."

Bingo. Kim gripped the gun more tightly, knowing that she'd just recorded a confession that could be used to put Albert away. But she was going to need more in order to save Scarlett. "And what did Isabel do to you? Laugh at you? Reject you? Did you offer her money, was that it? Did it finally sink into your pathetic twisted mind that you can't even *pay* for sex anymore?"

"I don't need to pay!" Albert hollered, his face purpled with rage. "And I didn't touch that girl!"

This time when he lunged for her, Kim was ready. She was poised between the recliner and the wall, and her plan was to dodge behind the sofa. Albert would never be able to pose a threat to her once she had a large, heavy object between them—he was too old and too weak.

But as her foot came down behind her, it struck an object she hadn't noticed before: a soda can that had rolled there during the scuffle. It crumpled beneath her shoe, but on the slick surface of the wood floor, it slid easily, her leg going out underneath her.

She was able to right herself by grabbing the back of the sofa—but not before Albert, seeing his opportunity, came at her with all of his strength. His shoulder butted her in the chest and she fell to the floor, on her back with him on top of her. He pounded her face with his fist, once, twice, and though the blows weren't hard enough to do any lasting damage, she made the critical mistake of putting up her hands to defend herself. The gun loosened in her grip. Albert's eyes lit up and he snatched the gun.

Before she had time to react, he had rolled off her and aimed, his finger steady on the trigger. Clearly he was no stranger to firearms. He crouched in a ready position, aiming at her heart, while she struggled to sit up.

"Don't move," he snarled. "Not one more inch, or I'll blast you through and through."

"No," she tried to scream, but it came out as a breathless whimper. So this was how it was going to end. Kim would die here, and nothing would have changed, nothing would be gained from her death—and Scarlett would be left with no one to believe her.

Suddenly, Albert tilted sideways and tumbled onto the floor, hitting his head on the coffee table as he went down, the gun flying out of his hand and skittering away. There had been a flash of movement, a collision of shapes at the periphery of Kim's vision. Her brain tried to catch up to what had just happened.

Someone crouched down next to her. "Oh my God, are you all right?"

Scarlett.

Scarlett was pulling her up, her face a map of fear and worry. The front door stood open, sunshine pouring into the dim interior of the house. The tacky dog figurine had been shattered over Albert's head—no great loss.

"How . . ." Kim managed to get out.

"It wasn't that hard, you left the car door open when you got out to swing open the gate at the hotel. I climbed in the back. You never knew I was there." Kim stared her down. However grateful she was, she was also annoyed. Scarlett shrugged. "I'm a teenager. We're good at sneaking around."

Kim felt a wave of dizziness pass through her as she managed to pull herself up to her knees, then awkwardly crawl up onto the couch. On the other side of the coffee table, Albert lay crumpled facedown, motionless.

"Kim, what the hell were you thinking?" Scarlett sounded furious. "He almost killed you."

"I had to . . . try to get him to confess."

"By almost getting yourself killed?" Scarlett shook her head in disbelief. "You tell *me* to take care of myself, and then you do this crazy shit?"

Far in the distance, Kim heard sirens. "You called the cops?" she asked incredulously.

Scarlett rolled her eyes. "Of course I did. What was I going to do, let you kill him and go to jail for murder?"

"But I was never going to *kill* him." Slowly, Kim absorbed the full import of what Scarlett was saying—she'd jeopardized her own safety to ensure Kim's. Been willing to face the police and the accusations against her, just to make sure Kim was okay. "Listen, Scarlett, I recorded everything. Albert confessed to—"

Suddenly Scarlett yelped. Albert rolled over and shot out his arm, grabbing her ankle and pulling it savagely. Scarlett lost her balance and fell practically on top of him. Albert moved much faster than Kim would have thought him capable, looping his arm around her neck in a stranglehold and jamming the gun up under her chin.

"So you came to save the day," he said, and all traces of weakness were gone from his voice. "You think you got the stones for it, girlie?"

Scarlett whimpered in pain and fear, her head forced back against his shoulder. How many other young people had he threatened, just like that? How many had he killed?

"Don't do it," Kim pleaded, afraid to move, worried any sudden motion would unsettle him and make him shoot. "Let her go, Albert. We'll leave—"

"Don't see how that does me any good," Albert said, almost conversationally. The sirens were closer, from the sound of it, only one or two streets away. "If they got that conversation you recorded, why, I'm cooked. Won't matter what I do to you two, I still end up in jail for the rest of my life. Only way I don't kill the both of you . . ."

"What?" Kim demanded frantically. He had shoved the gun up into the soft underside of Scarlett's chin so hard that she was making soft choking sounds. One reflexive squeeze of his trigger finger and she would die. "Tell me what you need us to do, Albert!"

"Gimme that phone," he said. "If there's no recording, there's nothing for me to confess to. I'll tell them you broke in here talking crazy. I have a right to defend myself in my own home. They'll see what you did to me. They'll see you for what you are, a couple a lyin' whores."

The recording was the only proof Kim had. Without it, it would be his word against hers. And given the things she'd done recently, the mistakes she'd made, the people she'd angered and betrayed, who would believe her?

But if she didn't do as he asked, Scarlett could die.

She tossed the phone on the floor between them.

Albert stared at it for a moment. Then he pointed the gun at it—and fired.

But at the last possible second, Scarlett twisted in his grip, breaking free and staggering backward. The shot went wide, clanging off the metal coffee table leg and lodging in the sofa. The phone lay, unharmed, exactly where she'd tossed it. Kim lunged for it.

Albert fired again.

THIRTY-THREE

Zack peeled into Albert Sullivan's driveway with a screech of tires and leaped out of the car without bothering to close the door. He ran toward the house, ready to shoot out the lock if he had to, but the door was standing wide open. Just as he crossed the threshold a shot rang out.

He hit the floor, rolling, and came up in a shooter's stance, trying to make sense of the scene. Scarlett Hascall was cowering against the wall next to the kitchen. Sullivan was lying on the floor, moaning. And Kim was standing over him, one foot smashing his hand into the carpet.

"Are you hit?" Zack yelled, alternating between pointing his gun at Albert and at Scarlett. There were dark stains on Albert's clothes, but they didn't appear to be blood. Scarlett looked more agitated than harmed, but a thin trickle of blood was running down the side of Kim's face.

"We're fine," Kim said, though she sounded anything but. She appeared to be putting all her weight on the old man's hand. He'd be lucky if she hadn't broken his fingers. "But Albert Sullivan confessed to killing Henry. I recorded it all. It's on my phone. He tried to shoot it twice, to destroy the evidence. Luckily he shoots like he probably fucks."

She pointed at the floor, and Zack took his eyes off the scene just long enough to see that an iPhone lay on the carpet barely out of Albert's reach.

"What happened to your head?" he demanded, ignoring the phone for the moment.

"Oh," Kim said. She touched her cheek, and her fingers came away bloody. She shrugged. "He shot at me, grazed my forehead." She looked at her fingers again and realized that there was actually quite a bit of blood. "At least I think it just grazed me." She turned her head toward Zack. "Is it bad?"

Zack stepped forward and dug his knee into Albert's back, taking Kim's face into his strong left hand, as his right one kept his gun trained on the back of Albert's neck. He studied her forehead. "I think you're going to live." Kim nodded, obviously relieved. "It might even improve those looks."

Kim smiled, her body coming down from the high of the pandemonium. "I hear guys like a girl with scars."

Zack shrugged. "If they're earned."

Zack's demeanor shifted as a second cruiser arrived, its sirens blaring, and its tires squealing to an abrupt halt. Two other officers burst through the door. Now there were three of them with their guns drawn on an old man and two unarmed women. After a moment, the officers relaxed and holstered their guns.

Zack felt a little ridiculous. "Cuff this guy," he ordered the others. "And please search Ms. Hascall. Make sure she doesn't have a weapon of any kind."

He turned to Kim, who already had her hands in the air. She must have thought he was going to search her, too. Instead, he pulled her into his arms and hugged her hard.

"Don't ever do anything like this again," he ordered.

But Kim's focus wasn't on the welcomed hug but rather on Scarlett. She had noticed that Scarlett didn't seem to register her name when Zack referred to her as "Ms. Hascall." Her eyes looked distant.

After the female officer frisked a confused-looking Scarlett, Kim approached the teenager, pulling her gently aside. She could tell by looking into Scarlett's eyes that she had switched—certainly caused by the traumatic incident.

Kim whispered, "Izzy?"

Scarlett's eyes darted up, making immediate eye contact with Kim. It was most definitely Isabel Wilcox who stood before her.

Scarlett glanced up at Kim's forehead, seeing the blood. The girl made an effort to comfort Kim. "That's going to be fine. The face has a lot of capillaries, like a spiderweb of blood vessels just under the skin. A paramedic told me that once. That's why we blush, when the blood rushes to the surface."

Kim stayed cool, knowing that Isabel was there to help Scarlett deal with the distressing experience of having a gun to her head. She quickly and calmly helped Scarlett transition back, without Zack or the other officers even aware that the switch had happened. It was better that way, for all involved.

IT TOOK A WHILE to sort out what had happened. Everyone was talking at once, until Evelyn told Albert that if he didn't shut his mouth, she was going to stuff his underwear in it. After that, he sat glumly on his sofa, muttering from time to time.

"Please take good care of that phone," were the first words out of Kim's mouth after Albert was cuffed. "It is my professional opinion that this man cannot be rehabilitated."

The CSI folks were on their way—their van was seeing more action this week than they ordinarily did all summer—and Holt was driving in from Two Pines Lake, where he'd been fishing with an old buddy. The paramedics would be there in moments. Zack needed to make some quick decisions.

"Bag that," he said, pointing at Kim's phone with his shoe. "Get Fogliano over at the station to process it—all we need is for one of you guys to accidentally erase that recording. Scarlett, Kim, I want you both checked out. You'll ride to the hospital with the paramedics."

"I'm fine," Scarlett said. "I'm not hurt."

"Kim may have been injured more seriously than she thought, as I'm very sure she is aware. She needs to be checked out. And I'd rather have you both looked over, if you don't mind. You've been through something pretty traumatic here."

Zack had a long night ahead of him. Phil would ride along to the hospital, and he'd already said he didn't mind taking the overnight shift outside Sullivan's room. Sullivan was only slightly banged-up—none of the shots fired hit him, but he was sporting a nasty lump on the top of his head—so he had to be checked out. The police would post a guard until he'd been treated and medically cleared. Zack wouldn't be able to listen to the recording until the phone had been logged into evidence and examined by their tech specialist. Holt would need to be present, too.

It was true that he was concerned about Kim's injury, but mostly he just wanted her in one place until he was ready to talk to her.

It was going to take him a little while to figure out the right words. And he didn't want to screw this up.

IT WAS NEARLY SIX o'clock in the morning when Zack finally left the station. He'd stuck around the scene until the investigators were nearly finished. They'd had a hell of a time finding the stray bullet, which had lodged in a couch cushion so filthy that the entry hole was nearly invisible among the stains. Zack had personally logged eight boxes of evidence, mostly old magazines, DVDs, and photos that Albert Sullivan had purchased through the mail over the years. There was enough in those boxes alone to keep him in prison for the rest of his life. But when Officer Jennifer Fogliano finally finished with the phone, having made backups of everything on it, and they listened to the recording Kim had made, he felt certain that Albert Sullivan would be convicted of murder, too.

Getting into his car outside the station as dawn broke, he decided to leave a message for the Jarvis Hospital's chief of staff. To his surprise, Dr. Graver herself picked up, explaining that she liked to get in early so she could catch up on her work before things got too busy. Zack gave Dr. Graver a brief summary of the confrontation and Sullivan's confession, emphasizing Kim's role in helping to solve Henry Beaumont's murder and de-emphasizing the risks she'd taken in the process. Graver knew that he was making a case for Kim, without saying it directly.

Having already heard that they'd treated Sullivan downstairs in the ER, Dr. Graver predicted that he'd be released into police custody after morning rounds, having suffered nothing more serious than a bump on the head. Zack thanked her and asked that Kim not be released until the afternoon.

"She's slept through the night with no issues," Dr. Graver said. "She had no sign of concussion. She should be able to rest at home."

"We need to get her statement," Zack said. "I'd like to get that out of the way before she leaves the hospital. That way we don't need to call her back in while she's, ah, recuperating."

There was a longish silence before Dr. Graver said, "All right. I suppose that makes sense. But, Detective, I wonder if you could convince your officers to . . . treat her gently. She's been through a lot."

"I think I can make that promise," Zack said.

Once he got home, he practically fell facedown on his bed. But when his alarm went off a few hours later, he forced himself to get up and stood with his face in the shower, keeping the water cold enough to leave him gasping. He needed to be in top form for what he was about to do.

THIRTY-FOUR

Despite the fact that Kim had been there fewer than twelve hours, and had suffered only a cut requiring a mere four stitches, there were already three enormous bouquets of flowers in her hospital room when Zack arrived to see her. She caught him noticing and shrugged, appearing embarrassed. "My parents; my former boss; and, uh, a secret admirer," she said sheepishly. When he nodded, she added quickly, smirking, "It's not actually a secret admirer, it's my father and he's been pulling the same joke since I got stood up at my high school prom and he sent me flowers to make me feel better and I saw his name on the return receipt and . . . I'm telling you too much, aren't I?"

That earned a smile from Zack. The nurse who was going through Kim's release paperwork smiled at Zack. "Maybe you could help her get those home?" Zack couldn't help but think there was something conspiratorial about the woman's glance back at Kim.

"Oh," he said. "I, um—"

"I'll call a cab," Kim said quickly. "It's no problem."

"I'll take you home. I'm happy to. In my car. My work car, which I drove here." He was babbling—and the nurse winked at him.

"Take the ride, honey," she advised Kim. "Maybe he'll let you play with the lights." As she exited the room, she added over her shoulder, "Or maybe something else."

When they were finally alone, Zack and Kim both spoke at once.

"I just want to say—"

"You didn't have to—"

Neither of them laughed. "We seem to do that a lot," Zack mused.

"What—interrupt each other?"

"Well, I was going to say we were on the same wavelength." Zack smiled weakly. "But I guess that hasn't really been true. Look, Kim, I owe you an apology. Ever since we met, you've been trying to convince me to give Scarlett a chance. And I never really did, not until you had to go and practically get yourself killed to make me believe you."

"Well, to be fair, this isn't something you see every day. The, um, alters and everything."

"Thank God for that," Zack said with feeling. "The field of forensics isn't really equipped for it."

"But the other things you said . . . about me." Kim hesitated. "The things you read in my files."

"I just want to reiterate again that my conduct was wholly inappropriate," Zack said quickly. He hoped this apology didn't sound rehearsed. "I had no right, legal or ethical, to look up that information. And I also had no right to draw any conclusions about . . . about decisions you made or, uh, consequences of the, of . . ."

"I know it must have been hard to read that about me," Kim said, coming to his rescue. "And I'm not mad, exactly, that you looked me up. I mean, I Google-stalked you, too, for what it's worth. And I found some things that were pretty shocking. Like that pink tie you wore to your senior prom. I can't imagine that night ended well for you. Probably wasted a hotel room as a result."

"They wouldn't give me back my deposit, either."

"Well, did you see yourself?" She enjoyed seeing him smile at her. Her voice turned serious again. "Zack, just so you know, I probably would have done the same thing. I don't think I'd be able to resist the temptation if I had access to those resources."

"Thanks, Kim. But I think I'm apologizing for a little more than . . . spying on you. What I'm trying to say is that I haven't walked in your shoes. I've never been through what you endured. So I had no place judging how you reacted. I'd like—I'd like to ask you for another chance. I mean, if you ever feel like talking about it. Or not."

Kim didn't answer for a moment, then said slowly, "I don't know if I can tell you how much that means to me. To be treated like a . . . for want of a better word, a *sane* person, someone capable of making my own decisions about my life—it means the world to me. It's why I went into psychiatry, in part—to advocate for people that the rest of the world considers crazy. To make the world see that just because someone's mind operates a little differently from the norm, it doesn't mean they aren't capable of living full, rich lives."

"Well, you're definitely a little different, Dr. Kimberly Patterson," Zack blurted. "But I wouldn't *want* it any different."

Kim grinned. "So, am I under arrest or anything?"

"Nah. At least not for this. Although . . . I will be keeping tabs on you."

Kim liked where this was going. "So, does that mean you won't be frisking me?" She sold it with a faint hint of disappointment in her voice.

"Even if I wanted to, I wouldn't be within my rights."

"What if I grant you the right?"

Zack peered back toward the hospital room door, which was still open. He decided to abandon their verbal foreplay in favor of getting back to business. "Holt didn't even want to talk about the gun. He said in light of everything, he felt you were acting in self-defense." He returned her smile. "Though, you know, you could have helped your case by screaming in fear a little more on the recording."

Kim laughed. "Not really my style."

"No, I guess not. Well, maybe next time try not breaking into a criminal's home in the first place?" Zack offered her his hand. On the bed was a plastic bag full of the clothes she'd worn when she arrived. Someone—probably the officer who'd relieved Evelyn this morning—had brought her a Jarvis PD sweatshirt and a pair of sweats. On her feet were hospital socks.

She took his hand and allowed him to help her up. When he reached for the bag, she shook her head. "I don't ever want to see those again."

Zack understood. He lobbed the bag of clothes into the trash can.

"Not so fast, Kim." The day nurse was pushing a wheelchair into the room. "You know the rules. No one gets out on foot. Hey, Detective." She winked at him.

"Thanks for the lift," Kim said, a little hoarsely. After a second she hugged the nurse. It kind of looked like they were both about to cry. Kim pulled away and looked down at the wheelchair. "You're really going to make me ride in that thing?"

"Yes, I am. Make yourself useful, Detective—go pull the car around."

———

AFTER ZACK HAD GOTTEN Kim and all of her flowers up to her apartment, then stood around awkwardly for a few minutes while she swore she didn't need him to run any errands or bring her anything, he beat a retreat back to the station. The receptionist looked up when he walked in and said, "Chief wants to see you ASAP."

Holt motioned him into his office excitedly. "Phil and I took another run over there to Sullivan's place," he said. "That county crew did a half-ass job. Must not have checked the baseboards. Loose one in the closet came off in Phil's hand—and look what was behind the paneling."

He handed Zack a grainy photograph. At first Zack couldn't tell what he was looking at—it seemed to be a collage of gold and red and black, against a royal blue backdrop. After a moment the various shapes came into focus.

"Holy shit," he breathed, "Is that—"

"Isabel Wilcox dead on a tarp," Holt said, tapping a stubby forefinger on the photograph. "Head's still attached, barely, in this one, but see here."

He handed Zack another photo, in which there were no masses of blond hair, and all that was left—

Zack handed the photos back. "Okay," he said shakily. Ordinarily he was pretty good at this sort of thing, but connecting these images with the body that had washed up in the bay was a little more than he could handle on four hours' sleep. "Sullivan took these photos?"

"Yeah. Another thing? I took a look at that Cutlass of his. There's blood in the trunk. Not much—he cleaned it pretty good—but I was able to get a sample. Sent it in, and the lab's rushing it."

"Wait a minute," Zack said. "Where would he have killed her? And how'd he get a full-grown woman into that trunk? She had to weigh a hundred ten, hundred twenty. He's an old man with a limp. Doesn't that seem unlikely to you?"

Holt shrugged. "From what I heard, he put up quite a fight with your girl."

Zack instinctively responded, "She's not my—"

But Holt cut him off. "I don't know how he did it. Winch, maybe? Could have done that just about anywhere, then just drove out to the bluffs and dumped her. That old boy's obviously in better shape than he looks. We'll get it out of him, don't worry." Holt squared up the photos by tapping them on his desk. "That's two cases, all wrapped up like Christmas morning. Maybe you can finally take a weekend off and take your sister fishing like you've been threatening to all these years."

This was an old joke between them; Brielle would no sooner fish than she would stab herself in the eye with a rusty knife. But Holt had a point: Zack had let his work-life balance get a little, well, out of balance.

"Or maybe I could help her finish painting my home office," he said. "If I leave it up to her, it'll never get done."

"Now you're talkin'." Holt leaned back in his chair, his hands behind his head. "Listen, though, I need you to do one thing before you start filling up your dance card. I got a tip on George DeWitt."

"The hunter?"

"Yep. He wasn't hunting blacktail deer, like he told his wife. Guy called in anonymously to say he'd been with DeWitt up in Harrick County, and they were after black bear. And it ain't bear season until late October, not to mention the fact they were on private land."

"You're saying they were poaching," Zack clarified.

"That I am. Anyway, this guy said the owner of the land came up on 'em and they had words. Got a little heated. That night he and DeWitt were out drinking at some bar up there, and after a while, DeWitt went out for a smoke. Never came back. The caller said he didn't say anything until now on account of they weren't supposed to be there in the first place, but when he heard DeWitt was reported missing, well, his conscience got to him."

"Just not enough to offer up his name," Zack said drily.

"Yeah, well, you know what I always tell you about human nature," Holt said.

"'A weak man is his own worst enemy.'"

"'Atta boy. Anyway, he did give me the name of the bar, and I need you to run up there and see what you can find."

Zack suppressed a groan. "Why me? Isn't Evelyn working this one?"

"She was, until she sprained her ankle this morning running along the docks. She's not up for any long drives right now."

"Great." Zack started shuffling papers on the desk, trying to get them in order. "I'm guessing you want that done sooner than later."

"Doesn't have to be today," Holt said. "Get a good night's sleep, and then head up there tomorrow, okay? Don't need you falling asleep at the wheel."

"Sure thing," Zack said. "I'll just catch up on things around here this afternoon. Been letting things pile up a little."

Both men stood. Holt offered Zack his hand, and when they shook, the older man held on for a moment. "Been a rough few weeks around here," he said gruffly. "Glad to have you be my right-hand man."

"Thanks," Zack said, a lump forming in his throat. "It's my honor, sir."

ZACK HAD WOLFED DOWN leftovers with Brielle and filled her in on his day, then waited impatiently until she finally left so he could call Kim without his sister eavesdropping.

She picked up on the first ring, and Zack quickly explained about Holt finding evidence in Albert's house that he had killed Isabel. While it wasn't standard procedure to update non-police personnel in this kind of situation, he felt he owed it to Kim after all she'd done to close this case, and without his support for most of it.

"I can't tell you the specifics," he said, "at least not now. But I can tell you that Holt's sent the blood sample down to Anchorage for analysis, and if it bears out, it's going to be an open-and-shut case."

"That's . . . that's wonderful news," Kim said.

"Listen, I've got to run up north tomorrow on something un-related. Might have to stay a few nights, depending on the roads. But I was wondering, any chance you might want to have dinner later in the week?" Zack was surprised at the sudden spike of ner-vousness he felt—he hadn't been anything less than confident with a woman in a long time.

There was the briefest pause before Kim answered, "Yeah, I could probably squeeze that in." He couldn't see her smiling. "Espe-cially if you're cooking."

"Oh. Good. Great." Zack cleared his throat, searching for some-thing to say that wasn't inane or embarrassing, and coming up empty. "Okay . . . well, I guess I'll talk to you soon, then."

After an awkward good-bye, Zack hung up and rolled his eyes. He felt about the same as he had when he invited Callie Whittaker to his middle school dance. Only Callie had turned him down, so he guessed this was progress at least.

Of course, later Callie became a minister, moved to Nevada, and adopted seven children. So maybe they hadn't been a match made in heaven.

As for Kim . . . Zack was way too exhausted to try to figure out whether seeing her was a smart move. What he probably needed more than anything was just a good night's rest.

Some things would probably look very different in the morning.

He was pretty sure Kim wasn't one of them.

THIRTY-FIVE

"**Y**ou can go in now," Dr. Graver's receptionist said, nodding crisply at Kim. Kim wondered if the chief of staff had hired the woman for her poker face, which was utterly imperturbable.

Surely every member of the Jarvis Regional staff, from physicians to janitors to the man who restocked the vending machine, knew all about Kim's breathtaking fall from grace. She'd certainly received a number of curious glances on the elevator ride up. She imagined that one or two of the hospital workers assumed she was admitting herself.

As far as she knew, the board had met yesterday as scheduled. But she hadn't received a call afterward.

Rather than sit around wondering and waiting how they had decided her fate, she'd spent the last day and a half in a furious fit of cleaning and organizing. She'd finished unpacking her apartment, hung some photos on the walls (including her party selfie with Dave Grohl), and stocked her refrigerator and pantry (purchasing cumin to place alongside the allspice). If she lost the job at the hospital and had to start hunting for some other form of employment, at least she would have a reasonably comfortable place to come home to, and it wouldn't be as easy to procrastinate with her job search.

Rather than face everything head-on at once—like the tenuous nature of her relationships with her former colleagues, and Zack, and even Scarlett—she was trying to shape her own fate in a round-about way. On a subconscious level, she had accepted that Jarvis had become her home: prior defeats, like the one in San Diego, had spurred her to make sweeping and ill-considered changes, throwing everything on a moving truck and heading home. This time, she was taking her time, letting the dust settle. She hadn't even called her parents.

Maybe this was a good thing. A healthy thing.

That was the attitude she tried to keep in mind as she walked into Dr. Graver's office.

"Good morning, Dr. Patterson, have a seat," Graver said with a very uncharacteristic smile. "I'd offer you some coffee, but I seem to have drunk it all." She tutted, shaking her head. "And it's not even nine thirty. So much for practicing moderation today."

Kim laughed—she couldn't help it. Graver raised one silvery eyebrow. "Something amusing, Kim?"

"No, it's just—everyone's so intimidated by you. *I'm* intimidated by you. I guess it's just . . . reassuring, to see that you have flaws, too."

"My dear." Graver looked at her with amusement. "I am constructed of flaws glued together by sheer Irish stubbornness. The only thing that saves me is my . . . plucky determination. A trait that I've noticed we have in common."

Kim shrugged. "Most people just call me a stubborn bitch."

Graver nodded. "They say the same about me. Just not to my face." She glanced down at Kim's medical intake chart. "How's the head?"

"Just a scratch. I'm actually more concerned about my job."

"Then I'll get right to the point—we aren't firing you. We want you to come back. We—or rather, I—wish to convey my regret that I came down on you so hard, especially considering that your methods, although forbidden, turned out to be a success. Of course, I wish to stress that you're expected to follow hospital policy in the future, and the legal department's preparing a mountain of paperwork for you to sign to that effect."

"Oh," Kim said, trying to let the news sink in. This was better than she'd dared to expect—reinstatement *and* acknowledgment, even if it was unofficial, that her actions had led to a positive outcome in Scarlett's case. "Wow. That's . . . thank you, really."

"So you'll return?"

"Are you kidding? I can start right now." Something dawned on her. "Oh . . . uh, just wondering, is Dr. Berman okay with this?"

"Dr. Berman made a point of enumerating all of your successes since you joined the staff," Graver said drily. "It became truly monotonous after a while, to tell the truth. But he got the message across—he believes you to be an incredible asset to the department."

"Oh." Kim felt energized with relief. "Wow, that's great, then."

"Go see HR on your way out, and they'll work out scheduling your return and so forth. But, Kim, while I've got you in my clutches . . . I have to say I'm quite curious as to the outcome of this whole mess in the papers. Anything you can tell me, confidentially of course, that isn't being reported?" When Kim hesitated, she added, "My interest isn't the least bit professional. I just want the juicy insider information so I can feel superior to everyone else around here."

"Oh, well, in that case," Kim said, grinning, "we nailed that bastard, Albert Sullivan." She explained about the "materials removed from the home" and gave Graver a spirited account of the scuffle that ended with Albert trying to kill her. She even showed her the little patch of scalp where they'd shaved a strip to accommodate her stitches, which she'd covered by parting her hair on the other side and letting it sweep over her forehead.

"So that explains why you actually styled your hair for a change," Graver said. "And here I thought you were trying to impress me. Looking good, Patterson. Now get lost, I've got interns to terrify."

THIRTY-SIX

The human resources department suggested Kim come in on the following Monday, which coincided conveniently with the start of the month, which in turn made some detail of accounting easier. The result of her reinstatement schedule was that she had several days before she officially reported back to work—after the punishing hours she was used to, Kim felt like she was drowning in all the free time.

Two mornings later, she'd finished every chore she could think of around the apartment. Her books were alphabetized, she'd purchased new towels and sheets, and she even invested in a houseplant—not a plastic one, but an actual living houseplant—never mind the fact that it was a cactus so that when she'd forget to water it, which would inevitably happen, it would take an extra month or two to die. She even finally called her parents to let them know that everything was fine. She'd gone for a run that would leave her sore the next morning, and visited her elderly neighbor for a spirited match of Hearts.

Kim was waiting for the coffee to finish brewing and her whole-wheat bread to pop out of the toaster when her phone rang. It was Kyle, her phone displaying the goofy photo she'd snapped of him before things between them had become strained. In it, he was peeping through the hole in a hospital cafeteria bagel and grinning, looking happier and more relaxed than he'd been in quite a while.

He was probably calling in his capacity as her supervisor, to formally welcome her back onto the staff. While Kim was surprised and grateful that he'd stuck up for her in the review board meeting, she felt a little hesitant about seeing him anytime soon. She doubted whether she could wholly trust him again. She let the call go to voice mail.

The rest of the morning stretched out in front of her, without an obligation in sight. Kim felt a bit at a loss on how to fill the time. She couldn't very well water the cactus yet. Maybe she'd put on her sneakers and go for a jog down to the water and along the trail that led up to the cliffs. Maybe she'd Facebook-stalk some of the guys she liked in high school.

Or maybe she'd just curl up in the corner of the couch and watch a scary movie on cable. 1977's *Satan's Cheerleaders* was about to start—its commercial promised that is was: "Funnier than *The Omen* . . . Scarier than *Silent Movie*." *Sold.*

She fixed herself a cup of coffee, heavy on the cream, and drank it with her toast at the kitchen table, alternating between watching the movie and enjoying the activity on the street below. A mom was getting her kids into the minivan on the way to school. A guy headed to work on his bicycle, his tie flapping behind him. The postman was getting an early start, stuffing flyers into the apartment complex mailbox. Ordinary people going about their ordinary lives.

There was going to be a memorial service for Henry Beaumont on Saturday. A tree was going to be planted in the hole where the capsule had been, with a plaque bearing his name. His parents and the mayor were going to speak. They'd reported these details on the Anchorage syndicate, the on-air reporter looking suitably grave, saying that Sullivan's arrest "closed the book on a sad chapter in

Jarvis." The news reporter had speculated about some of the other missing people in Jarvis throughout the years, whether Sullivan may have been responsible for their deaths, too. It was possible they would never know for sure.

Maybe Kim would attend the service. But probably, she wouldn't. She hadn't been a part of the community two decades ago when Henry disappeared, wouldn't know what to say to the grieving parents. They'd almost be old enough to be grandparents now—Henry would have been about Kim's age if he'd lived. Kim wondered if they'd gone on to have other children, if they'd stayed married, if a day ever passed that they didn't think about Henry. If they really did feel better now, knowing what had happened to him.

Kim contemplated if it would have been different for her if her parents had simply disappeared, rather than being killed right in front of her. The trauma was the source of her initial dissociation with reality and her adoption of an alternate identity. Psychological repression erased not just the horrible memories of that night but all the memories of her childhood. As she had explained to Scarlett in one of their first sessions, her brain just *blew a fuse* to protect itself. She wondered what it would have been like to, instead, spend all these years wondering whether her mother and father were alive or dead. Agonizing over their loss without ever knowing for sure if she'd see them again.

Kim had let her coffee go cold. She got up, dumped out the rest, and poured herself a fresh cup. While she was stirring in the cream, she called Scarlett.

"Hey," she said. "You busy?"

HALF AN HOUR LATER, Kim drove to the Hascalls' house, and she and Scarlett went for a walk on the dirt path that led from the cul-de-sac up the slope to a ridge from which they could see the entire town laid out below. Scarlett took a couple of protein bars from her day pack and offered one to Kim. They ate in silence, enjoying the sunshine.

Since she had last seen Scarlett, Kim knew that Scarlett had twice been to see Kyle for psychiatric sessions. Until Kim was officially "on the clock," Kyle wanted to help her avoid breaking any more rules than she normally would, and he felt that being a stopgap with Scarlett's therapy was the least he could do to help.

"You have to agree, there are a few things that just don't add up," Kim finally said. Kim's doubts had been nagging her for the last few days, as she watched the coverage of the case on television, and corresponded with Scarlett online, who was anxiously hoping, upon Albert Sullivan's arrest, that the Izzi alter would disappear, too, just as Henry had. Here, with Scarlett, was the first time Kim allowed herself to voice these doubts out loud.

"Cops sure seem to think it's all neat and tidy." Scarlett's expression was hard to read.

"Well," Kim said, making a face, "they've been known to be wrong before. I mean—how did your DNA end up connected to Isabel? How could a strand of your hair *possibly* have ended up in that phone case?"

"A mistake." Scarlett shrugged. "Down at the lab. With the DNA sample."

"Yeah, okay, let's say you're right. A simple mix-up. I guess it's bound to happen now and again, even with something this important. But what about Albert?" Kim pushed. This had been bothering her, and it felt good to finally get it out. "The way he denied knowing anything about Isabel? Didn't you feel like Albert's whole energy was different around that?"

"Mmm," Scarlett said, folding up the wrappers and stuffing them back in her pack. "I don't know. I mean, he's a criminal. He lies; it's what he does. He could easily have killed her and a half-dozen other people, like they've been saying on the news."

"Yes, but then why would he confess to killing Henry but not the others? Why even admit he was attracted to children at all, instead of just denying the whole thing?"

"Kim, you were pointing a gun at him. I was there. You shot out a *mirror*. He just didn't want you to kill him! He confessed to save his own life."

"I don't know. It still doesn't add up for me. I feel like . . ." Kim paused, knowing that what she was about to say would be taking the top off a hornet's nest that had just barely, finally settled down. "I feel like we should say something."

"*Say* something? To who?"

Kim took a breath. "I feel like we should talk to Chief Plunkett."

Scarlett's face fell and she slowly shook her head. Kim could read the weariness and reluctance in her expression. She felt terrible for dragging the girl through more ugliness, but she was convinced it would be better to dig down to the truth than to lay the case to rest now.

After all, Scarlett's alters apparently wouldn't move on until they had seen justice done. And while Albert deserved the harshest punishment a jury could give him for what he'd done to Henry, Kim wasn't convinced that Izzi had been his victim. If the incriminating photos were real, and Albert Sullivan killed Isabel Wilcox, why hadn't she . . . moved on?

"We can drive over to the station now," Kim said. "I'll be right there. I'll do the talking. You'll be safe."

"Dad won't like it," Scarlett said, but Kim could see that she'd already resigned herself to the task. "Could we at least talk to Detective Trainor instead?"

"Seriously?" Kim asked, surprised. "Holt's always been more open-minded about your condition than Zack. Zack's the one who pushed for your arrest, was convinced you were involved in Izzi's murder. Why would you want to talk to him instead?"

Scarlett shrugged. "He's nice, most of the time. Besides, he's into you. So that might come in handy." Scarlett smiled. "I mean, come on, you call him Zack."

Kim blushed, wondering if Scarlett was trying to do a little matchmaking. "I'm not sure what that has to do with anything . . . and, besides, he had to go out of town. He's chasing down some lead in the missing-hunter case. Anyway, it might be better for us to talk to Chief Plunkett . . ." She quickly corrected herself to make a point. "Holt."

"You feel like . . . Holt . . . might be more receptive?"

Kim considered. "Put it this way—I don't think he'll be any *less* receptive."

"I just don't know."

"I do," Kim said. "Did you kill Isabel Wilcox?"

"You know I didn't."

"I know you didn't. But neither did Albert Sullivan. Which means that there's still a very bad person out there."

Scarlett sat still, going over all this in her head. But Kim went in for the kill. "Look, I've thought about it a lot these past few days . . . what if your alters have been just wanting justice all along? What if—I mean, Henry kept talking about how cold he was, how dark it was. Now finally his parents are going to be able to lay him to rest. Maybe that's what he needed all along. And I saw Izzi after we took down Albert. You tell me, Scarlett, is she gone? Is Izzi gone?"

Scarlett shook her head silently.

"You know I'm right. I mean, presumably Izzi wants the same thing as Henry did—to see the person who killed her locked up, so he can't hurt anyone else—so she feels like she was avenged. And yet, even though Sullivan is behind bars, she's still there, waiting for something more. If the wrong person is blamed for her murder, and then the case is closed, she'll never be able to rest." And, she didn't add, she might continue to plague Scarlett indefinitely.

But it seemed like Scarlett didn't need her to draw that connection for the truth to sink in. After a few more moments of thought, she stood and shouldered her pack. "Okay then," Scarlett said. "Let's go."

———

THEY WAITED AT THE front desk while the receptionist went to find Holt. The station was a hive of activity. Some of the officers were working at their computers, while others crowded around the open-case bulletin boards; Phil Taktuq was alone, sitting calmly at his desk. He gave them a long, pointed look as they walked in, as if he knew why they were there. Kim looked away, pretending to be interested in a phone conversation that Evelyn was having. "I told you I can't comment," she kept repeating in exasperation, presumably to a pushy reporter.

The receptionist came back and said that the chief could give them a few minutes in his office. Kim and Scarlett made their way back, and Holt stood up behind his desk and gave them a tired smile that quickly faded from his face.

"Might as well shut the door, girls. Kind of a crazy day out there."

He offered them chairs and took a seat with his meaty forearms resting on the desk. "I don't want this going anywhere before we take it public," he said. "Gonna have a press conference this afternoon. But I feel like you two deserve to know. Albert Sullivan killed himself in the holding cell overnight."

"*What?*"

"I take the blame—he just used the usual crap sheets on the bed. He hung himself." Holt shrugged. "Wouldn't have thought the old bastard had it in him. Anyway, that's pretty much the end of the road for the Beaumont and Wilcox investigations. We're shutting 'em down. I'm just disappointed that we haven't been able to link that degenerate to any of the other disappearances first." Holt looked beaten, like he had let the community down by not stopping Sullivan sooner. After a long moment of reflection, he shrugged. "I guess Albert gave himself the easy way out."

"Chief Plunkett," Kim said. "Sir. We wanted to talk to you. We're concerned about the inconsistencies in Isabel's murder." She laid out the issues they'd discussed earlier—Albert's stark denial of ever having met Isabel. How Scarlett still felt that the Isabel alter was inside her, waiting for something more.

"Now hold on a minute," Holt said. "You two, I know you've both been through a lot. We owe you a debt of gratitude and probably an apology for not giving your story more of a chance the first time you brought it to us. But what you're talking about, honey, is evidence that pointed to *Scarlett*. I'm sure you can agree there isn't much sense to opening up that whole can of worms now."

"But I never knew Isabel," Scarlett protested. "I don't think I ever even met her. There's just no way that my hair could have gotten on her phone. What if—"

"Listen, dear, let me tell you something I've learned in forty years of being a cop," Holt said kindly, folding his hands on the desk. "Sometimes, you get to the end of the road and you still don't have all the loose ends tied up. Our evidence room is full of cases like that, all the odds and ends that didn't perfectly fit. Who can say why? Life is messy. Crooks don't generally help clear things up much. So you do the best you can. And the best we can do here is to give the families the chance to bury their children and finally sleep at night knowing the monster who took them will be punished."

"I guess," Scarlett said reluctantly.

Kim started to speak, but Holt pushed back his chair, signaling the end of the conversation. "Okay, ladies, I sure appreciate you stopping by, but I need to run home and change into something presentable before the news conference. You see all the news vans in town? They'll all be up here soon, taking up every damn space in the parking lot, acting like they own the place." He shook his head in disgust. "They're like a swarm of piranhas. Only way to control 'em is to feed 'em a little bit of what they came lookin' for."

He offered Kim his hand, nearly crushing hers when he shook it.

Back in Kim's car, Scarlett slumped dejectedly against the door. "Well, that didn't go anywhere," she said.

"I'm sorry," Kim said, regretting that she'd ever brought it up.

"It's okay. I mean, once I started thinking about what you said, it kind of bothered me, too. Kim . . ."

She paused, clearly unsure of what she was about to say.

"It's okay," Kim reassured her. "You can tell me anything."

"About Isabel . . . her alter, I mean. I don't even know how to explain it, because I sort of go blank when they take over, but I can sort of feel her underneath my thoughts, waiting." Scarlett was silent for a long moment. "She's not happy."

"You think she's waiting for us to solve the case, like with Henry? That she doesn't feel the right person has been arrested yet?"

"I don't know. Maybe?" Scarlett shoved her hand through her hair in frustration. "I mean, whenever I sense her presence, I feel all these emotions sort of flash by. It scares me, because I know it's only a matter of time before she comes out again. She's afraid, and sad, and desperate. I feel like she's trying to . . . not get out exactly, but *see* out, to understand what happened to her, if that makes sense."

"Can you tell me a little more about—about what that feels like? For you?"

Scarlett squeezed her thighs. "I mean, it's nothing new. I never talk about it, because it makes me sound, you know, crazy, but ever since I can remember, sometimes these weird thoughts flash through my mind that aren't connected to whatever I'm doing right then. It's *them*, I think . . . just, like, waiting. And usually I don't even notice, but whenever they get upset or whatever, sometimes it sort of . . ." She shrugged, unable to find the right words.

Kim came to her rescue. "I think what you're saying is that when an alter experiences a powerful emotion, it can spill over into your own thoughts."

Scarlett took a deep breath. "Sometimes, I feel this . . . uncontrollable urge to run. As fast as I can. But I just can't run away from myself. You know?"

Kim reached over and grabbed the girl's hand. "I *do* know." She squeezed it. "I know."

Scarlett twisted a lock of hair around her finger, unable to meet Kim's eyes.

Kim ached for her. She'd spent most of her own life plagued by memories and thoughts that she couldn't share with anyone—that she couldn't run away from—so it was devastating to know that Scarlett felt the same way.

"I believe we can compel the alters to leave," Kim said carefully, "but the only way to convince them is to resolve whatever issues are keeping them from moving on. In your case, it seems like what they're waiting for is justice."

"But how can we possibly give them that?" Scarlett said. "If Albert Sullivan didn't kill Izzi, how are we going to possibly find who did?"

Kim responded resolutely. "We've already succeeded with Henry. And we're going to find out the truth about Izzi, too. Come on, let's go talk to the chief again. We've got to try, before he makes an announcement that the case is closed."

"You want to talk to him *now*? Before the press conference?"

"Why not?" Kim asked, pointing across the parking lot, where the chief was just walking over to his car. "There he goes. He said he was going home. Maybe we can talk to him there. He might be more open to . . . alternate theories."

"You were going to say 'crazy' theories."

"Fine. Crazy theories. He might be more open away from the pressure of the station, and all the press."

"What about Detective Trainor?" Scarlett asked. "Maybe *he* could get the chief to change his mind."

It wasn't a bad idea. Kim dialed Zack's cell phone but only reached his voice mail.

"Hi, it's me," she said. "Uh, Kim. Kim Patterson. Zack, I really need to talk to you as soon as possible about the Wilcox case. This might be a bad idea, but we're going to find Chief Plunkett . . . maybe at his house . . . try to convince him to keep the case open. I don't think Albert Sullivan killed Izzi. I know that sounds crazy, but I just want to be sure we aren't making a mistake. Especially now that he's dead. Anyway. We don't have much time. Zack, if you could just talk to him. . . . Call me?"

The chief's SUV was turning out of the parking lot. Kim started her car and followed. He kept up an even speed through town—there was light traffic this time of day—then continued along the coast road that rose above the water, edged by the jagged bluffs. They were a couple of miles out of town when the chief turned onto a private road marked only by a leaning mailbox.

Kim took the turn, taking it slow as her old car bumped and jounced over the rutted dirt road. If the chief noticed her car behind his, he didn't slow for her to catch up, and soon he'd disappeared into the trees. A few moments later, Kim came around a sloping bend to find Holt's SUV parked in front of a lovely cabin anchored with tubs of flowers and an enormous stone chimney. A cat snoozed on a porch swing, barely blinking when they pulled up and parked next to the SUV. Scarlett got out of the car, but Kim stayed put while she dug for her phone. She tried Zack once more, but again, only got voice mail.

As she hung up and got out of the car, Kim saw that Scarlett was standing a few feet from the porch steps, looking up at the cabin's upstairs windows. Her face bore a strange expression—her features were twisted in fear, but her eyes were hollow and empty.

"Scarlett?" Kim asked gently, approaching slowly and touching her elbow. "Are you all right?"

"H-h—" Scarlett began to tremble violently as she stammered. *He brought me here.*

"He—who? Who brought you here?"

But try as she might to get Scarlett to look at her, the girl's gaze remained unfocused, tilting up at the house. Her breath was coming fast and shallow, perspiration shining along her brow. "*Help me,*" she whispered.

In a voice that was not Scarlett's.

"Isabel?" Kim asked, fear snaking into her heart. She took Scarlett's hand and squeezed it, trying to force the girl to turn and look her way. She peered up into the windows, trying to see if there was an intruder or something else frightening inside, or if she was caught in the grip of memories. "Is that you?"

"He chased me," Scarlett gasped, trying to back away, stumbling on the smooth stones lining the walkway. "I fell. I got caught in the trap. My leg. It snapped on my leg. There was a man—a man tried to help me."

Kim held her arm so she wouldn't fall. They were several yards from the car, close enough to bolt if the threat was real—as long as she could keep Scarlett focused. "Who tried to help you? What man?" Kim asked.

"He took us both. He pushed me onto—onto—oh God," Scarlett sobbed. "I fell. So much blood."

Scarlett reached up and grabbed her head, half expecting not to find it there. Her fingers scrambled along her neck, as if trying to protect it.

"Calm down, it's okay now. Who? Who pushed you, Isabel? Who hurt you?" Scarlett was quickly falling apart. She gripped Kim's arm tightly, her whole body beginning to tremble.

"He's supposed to help people. But he didn't." Scarlett's entire body shook. "He's the one who took me. He locked me in the basement. But I escaped. I ran. Through the woods. And then . . ." She suddenly gasped and seized her leg, as if she were experiencing the pain of the bear trap once again. Scarlett was in the midst of a full-blown hyperventilating fit now. "The man, the hunter, he tried to help me. But then . . . he pushed me forward, my head in the trap . . . and . . ."

Suddenly, Scarlett's head twisted in an unnatural way, again, as if reliving the horrific event. Kim cradled Scarlett in her arms, supporting the weight of her head as Scarlett choked out a few more words. "He . . . killed . . . me . . . he . . . did . . ." Her eyes were bulging, looking up at Holt's house.

"Wait a minute—are you saying the *chief* brought you here?" Kim must have misunderstood, or perhaps the Izzi alter was confused, making a mistake. "Isabel, please, it's important."

Scarlett's mouth moved as though she were trying to form words, but all that came out now was a breathless wail.

"Well, look at that," came a hard, bemused voice above them. Kim looked up to see Chief Plunkett leaning over the porch rail, a can of root beer in his hand. "Seems I've got visitors."

THIRTY-SEVEN

"**C**hief," Kim said shakily.

"Is there something I can do for you girls?" he said lazily, as if he didn't notice that Scarlett was melting down.

"It was you in the woods," Scarlett cried. "You chased me. You pushed me down. You—"

"Well now, Scarlett, I haven't the foggiest notion what you're talking about," Holt said, taking a pull of his root beer and wiping his mouth on his sleeve. "Look, I know you've got a few bats in the belfry, but it seems like you're confused about who Isabel Wilcox really was. Let me tell you, that young lady was no Girl Scout. Town might even be better off now that she's gone—you ever think about that?"

"What are you trying to say?" Kim demanded, her blood running cold. His eyes were cruel, his laugh bitter. This was not the affable, genial chief of police she'd talked to in the past.

"What? You think Isabel was some kinda honor roll student? You think she and Brad Chaplin would go out for milk shakes and volunteer down at the food bank?" He shook his head. "The two of them spread their drug filth all over town. Can't begin to guess how many lives they ruined, how many families they tore apart. And don't even get me started about that little porn ring they set up. If you had seen what I saw on some of those tapes . . ."

Kim shook her head. "I *still* wouldn't have killed her. She didn't deserve to die, not like that."

Holt took several steps down the stairs, a smile washing over his face. "Wait. Did I say I killed her? I don't think I said anything about killing her. You know, one of the first things you learn in the academy is *not* to jump to conclusions."

Kim thought about running, but Scarlett was still in her arms, paralyzed with fear.

"Personally, I'm happy that Little Miss Troublemaker is dead, but I know *your* kind. Oh, hell, I knew you were a bleeding heart do-gooder the moment I met you," Holt sneered. "It's folks like you who let evil take hold. And fester. And then guys like *me* have to do the dirty work, trying to keep the rest of you safe. You're like sheep, you can't see the true threat even when it's staring you dead in the face. Tell me this: Did you know that Isabel Wilcox got all chummy with perfectly respectable girls over at the community college . . . just so she could get them hooked on the drugs that Brad supplied her with?"

As Holt advanced another step down the stairs, Scarlett grew more agitated, pulling at Kim's arm and whimpering.

"Just a little free taste, to get them nice and mellow before she started telling them how pretty they were, how they could make *a lot* of money if they'd pose for just a few tasteful pictures. Next thing they knew, those girls were strung out in a basement shooting filthy movies."

"It wasn't like that," Scarlett protested, her voice chattering miserably. "It wasn't ever supposed to go that far. It was supposed to be just the pictures and a chat room, and then it turned into streaming online . . . it just got out of hand."

"Try telling that to those girls' parents," Holt thundered, crushing the empty soda can in his fist as though it were as fragile as an eggshell. Any pretense of jocularity was gone as he continued down the porch steps, his footfalls heavy on the wooden planks. "Try telling that to the girls I put on buses headed for home, so far gone they can't sit up straight, begging me for a hit."

"I wanted to stop," Scarlett pleaded, starting to cry. "I wanted to shut it down, but Brad said—"

Holt bellowed out a laugh. "Brad, huh? You want me to believe it was all his fault? Doesn't work that way. I know trash when I see it. Isabel Wilcox was exactly the kind of trash I've worked so hard to clean up in this town. But don't you worry, girls. Brad's time is going to come soon. He's on my to-do list."

"You *did* kill her," Kim said, frozen in shock and horror.

Holt's demeanor shifted again, standing in mock defense. "Again, did I say I killed her?"

Holt offered up a paternal smile. "Hey, you know what? I'd like you to meet someone." He walked down the rest of the steps. Scarlett recoiled as he approached, but Holt turned and passed them by, moving toward the side of the house. After removing a padlock, he opened a heavy basement door and motioned for Kim and Scarlett to follow. "Come on, I think you're both going to get a kick out of this."

Kim nodded and stood, but handed her keys to Scarlett. "Wait for me in the car."

Holt chuckled. "Yeah, that's not going to happen. I'm going to need you two to stay together." He motioned again to the basement stairs. "Don't make me beg now."

Kim helped Scarlett stand. They walked slowly toward the basement door, and as they reached the thick concrete walls that led to the storm cellar, they heard a low, barely perceptible howl—if the sound was human, it certainly didn't sound like it. As they drew closer, the sound of wailing grew louder. Holt made sure to confiscate Kim's car keys from Scarlett as she stepped into the basement. As they descended the stairs into the dark underbelly of the cabin, Kim surreptitiously reached for her phone in her bag, fumbling with the device and sliding it into her pocket.

When they reached the floor of the dank room, Holt turned on a light, revealing the source of the muffled cries. Kim and Scarlett both gasped involuntarily.

Naked, spread-eagle on a bed of concrete blocks, lay a bloody and beaten man, his arms and legs stretched tightly over the cement bed.

"George DeWitt. You may have seen his missing-person poster hanging up in the station. You'll have to trust me that it's him. I know it's hard to tell, but believe me when I say that that really is old George."

Scarlett was shaking, her voice high and fearful. "He was there. He helped me."

"And he's going to help *me*, too." Holt walked toward George, who continued to produce a sickening, low wail through the blood-soaked gag meant to keep him quiet.

Kim put her hand into her pocket, cautiously gripping her phone. Fumbling to turn it on with the touch ID.

"You know why I've kept old Georgie alive for this long?" The chief waited for Kim or Scarlett to respond, but neither bit. "Insurance."

Kim hoped that the phone was now on—she nimbly moved her finger toward the bottom of the screen, hoping it found the familiar phone app, and then pressed so hard she worried the phone's screen might crack. She was calling Zack, but she kept her eyes locked on Holt . . . if she could keep him talking, it might keep him from killing. "Insurance? Insurance for what?"

Holt shrugged. "Insurance in case *this* happened. In case someone decided to point the finger at me. When you're in my line of work, it's important to take out an insurance policy for . . . unforeseen emergencies. And you and your patient here . . . who woulda seen this coming, huh?"

Slowly, Holt pulled one of the large cinder blocks out from George's makeshift bed. With the support gone under the hunter's head, it lowered back gently into a hole. He was too exhausted to raise it back up.

Kim's stomach sank, realizing what Holt was planning. She tried to stall. She tried to give him a reason *not* to follow through. She also knew that, by now, the phone in her pocket had either been answered by Zack, or it was recording on his voice mail. "So this man killed Isabel Wilcox. We'll turn him in. He'll be punished."

"Let's stop playing games, Dr. Patterson. You know, and I know—even Sibyl here knows—that George DeWitt didn't kill Isabel Wilcox."

Scarlett nodded furiously. "You did."

"I did. You're damn right, I fucking did. I did this town a *favor*," Holt said, lifting the concrete block off the floor. "I made sure she'd never hurt anyone again." He then hoisted the concrete block onto his shoulder. "This one here, he made the mistake of hunting on my land. And poking his nose in where it shouldn't have been."

All the pieces fell into place in Kim's mind. Holt was behind *everything*. She guessed that he had faked the DNA results connecting Scarlett to Isabel's phone. Hell, he probably processed the evidence himself. More "insurance" for him. If Kim hadn't pushed for further inquiry, he might have just left it at that. But when Albert's arrest gave him an even more convenient suspect, he'd been only too happy to shift the blame.

And with Albert Sullivan dead—

"You killed Sullivan," she said, the truth dawning on her. "He didn't hang himself, did he?"

"Now, *that* man was the worst kind of scum," Holt spat. "Pedophile, remorseless murderer. He didn't deserve to live. I guess I should thank you for that," he said to Scarlett, who was cowering by Kim's feet. "But you ought to be thanking me for getting rid of him. This town is safer without him in it."

Kim wondered, if Holt was willing to take justice into his own hands by killing those he saw as a scourge, how far would he go to keep his secret safe? That question was answered almost immediately as Holt Plunkett raised the cinder block over his head and slammed it down on the face of George DeWitt. The block hardly slowed as it severed the hunter's neck before splattering the contents of his skull onto the floor. His skull shattered, gray matter and pieces of flesh shot out as the concrete block dug into the floor.

Scarlett screamed as Kim pulled out her phone, seeing that she had indeed successfully dialed Zack. Whether Zack was on the line right now, or if her call had gone to voice mail again, it didn't matter . . . as she pulled Scarlett away, she yelled into the phone. "It was Holt, he killed—"

But before she could finish, the chief bounded toward her and grabbed the phone from her hand. He threw it hard against the wall, and Kim helplessly watched as it exploded into as many shards as George DeWitt's skull.

Holt maneuvered himself between Kim and the stairwell leading to freedom. He folded his arms over his chest and smirked at Kim, as if daring her to try to get past him. He outweighed her by at least eighty pounds and had already proven how fast and strong he was—going through him wasn't an option.

"Now, I don't expect any thanks. But I can't very well let you go around telling people, now can I? If I'm not here, who's going to watch out for the good people of Jarvis?"

Kim backed away slowly. Holt stalked after her, offering Scarlett a clear path to the steps leading outside. She pleaded, "Chief Plunkett, you don't have to do this."

"You know, that's what they all say. When they realize that it's over."

"Holt, please . . ."

"That's better. Establish a rapport with your abductor. That way he'll be more reluctant to harm you."

She continued to back away, but slipped on the floor, falling in a puddle. She didn't look down; she knew what the slippery liquid was. Instead, she remained focused on Holt. "I know, Holt, I know what happened to your wife. I read about it in your file."

"Nice. Appeal to your captor's emotions. If you allow them to put themselves in your shoes, you stand a better chance of escape."

"That's not what I'm doing." Kim backed farther away as Holt continued to move toward her.

Holt smiled, curious. "No? What do you think you're doing then?"

Kim smiled back. "Giving Scarlett a head start." Holt cocked his head as Kim screamed, "Run!" Hearing the violent command, Scarlett stood and scrambled up the stairs.

Kim urged her on. Holt reached for his gun, but realized that he was no longer wearing it, having been in the middle of changing his clothes in preparation for the press conference. But the moment of hesitation allowed Kim to sprint past him, and she followed the girl up the stairs. Kim knew there were plenty of weapons in the house, probably some right there in the basement. There wasn't much time; she needed to get Scarlett deep into the woods, where they had a chance of hiding from him.

Kim pushed Scarlett up the final step, forcing her out into the yard. She nearly yanked Scarlett's arm out of the socket as she pulled the girl, who seemed to be in a daze, toward the trees. "Isabel," she cried desperately. "Please. Run!"

Kim dragged Scarlett through Holt's yard toward the dense evergreen forest, past neat flower beds and hydrangea hedges, an old barrel spilling over with ivy. The home was so inviting, so lovingly tended; such a stark contrast to the disturbed, violent man who lived there.

As Kim hurried Scarlett along, she looked back toward the house: Holt had just reemerged from his basement, and sure enough, he was carrying what looked like a hunting rifle in addition to a police-issued handgun, which he stuffed into his front waistband. He called toward the girls while loading his rifle, "Where do you think you two are going? I got your keys. And I need you here. How else am I going to blame Scarlett for killing old Georgie boy?" Holt pushed the bolt handle forward to lock it down, raised the gun, and aimed.

As Kim and Scarlett reached the tree line and leaped into the woods, the shot rang through the air.

THIRTY-EIGHT

The sound of the bullet was a loud, angry crack as it passed by Kim's head. If she had jumped a fraction of an inch to the left, she'd have never heard it coming.

They ran hard, branches snapping against their arms and faces, their feet breaking through an underlay of fallen leaves and twigs. Within moments, Kim was out of breath, but she pushed herself harder, keeping up with Scarlett. A branch scraped her face and she tasted blood; her ankle twisted painfully on an exposed root.

She didn't dare turn around to see if Holt was gaining on them. Kim had been following the slope upward, knowing that if they could just reach the ridge, they would have more options: circling back around the rock slope on the other side toward the northeastern end of town, or heading farther into the cover of the woods.

"Wait," Scarlett gasped, pausing in a small sunlit clearing, bent over with her hands on her knees, gasping for breath. Kim, too, needed to let her heart slow for a moment. She realized that she had a gash above one eye, blood smeared across her forehead. Or maybe her stitches had torn back open.

Kim held on to a tree trunk while she mopped up her face and attempted to dislodge a stone from her shoe.

A few yards away, Scarlett was turning around, looking confused and disoriented. She started shaking her head, panicked. "We ran past this. We were here."

Kim shook her head, moving closer to calm the girl. "No, we've been running toward the ridge. It's okay."

Scarlett's head was shaking, almost uncontrollably. "No! I've been here!"

Kim remembered that she wasn't speaking to Scarlett; she was with Izzi. Maybe Izzi *had* been here.

Scarlett pulled away from Kim and sprinted toward a huge cedar, her fingers moving toward a section where the bark had been recently torn away—dislodged by Isabel's careening head. The bark was stained red where the blood had cascaded out of Izzi's forehead.

Scarlett started shaking uncontrollably as she sidestepped the tree and moved several yards past it. Her terrified gaze refocused on the ground.

Kim stepped behind her, peering past Scarlett to figure out what was spooking her.

It took Kim a moment to understand why the leaves and branches in the small clearing looked so peculiar. It was their color. A sickening circle of deep red.

Scarlett dropped to her knees and clutched her head, as if trying to keep it from falling off. She started to hyperventilate. Kim dropped down next to her and held on to her tightly.

"It's okay, Izzi, it's okay—breathe. Please, just breathe."

But over Scarlett's sobs, in the distance, Kim heard the sound of crackling brush and snapping twigs. *Holt*. How had he found them so quickly? How had he caught up? She froze, Scarlett looking at her in silent terror.

"Girls!" came the chief's voice, barely sounding winded.

Kim hastily covered Scarlett's mouth with her hand and stared into her eyes. Willing her to be quiet. Scarlett struggled to take control over her faculties.

Again, the sound of Holt's singsong voice rang out, this time closer. "Oh, girls."

Kim held Scarlett's face in her hands while looking deep into Izzi's frightened, dazed eyes. She whispered, "Isabel. Please. You've got to let Scarlett come back now. Isabel, go back into the room, please, and let Scarlett come back. Scarlett—think about Heather. Think about your dad. We've got to keep you safe for them. Help me!"

She felt Scarlett's muscles suddenly tense for the briefest second. And then, her eyes came into focus.

"How did we . . . what's—"

Scarlett whipped her head around and took in the scene; the woods, her doctor's bloody face, her own scratched hands. Kim again established eye contact, whispering, "Shhh. He's close. We have to run. Do you understand?"

Scarlett nodded once and took off running, grabbing Kim's hand. She was back. Somehow Kim had managed to convince Isabel to let Scarlett take over—or maybe Izzi had been so frightened that she'd retreated back inside Scarlett's psyche. Either way, Scarlett had returned with a vengeance. She ran hard, holding on to Kim's hand tightly.

Holt's voice cut through the woods. "Where do you think you're going?" Somehow, he sounded even closer than before they had started running.

As they weaved between trees, Kim realized that she had lost all sense of direction. They might be running right back toward Holt. Stumbling along blindly, Kim looked frantically around for somewhere to hide. Up ahead stood a pair of ancient pines whose trunks had fused and, over the course of time, formed a sort of hollow. Kim shoved Scarlett into the space, watching as the girl wedged herself tightly so that she was completely hidden by the lowest branches and the trunks. Kim darted past her another dozen yards to a tall hemlock with a thick trunk and evenly spaced branches descending almost to the ground. She grabbed a sturdy branch and swung herself up, barely noticing as she scraped her skin on the rough bark, and grappled her way up the interior of the tree until she was almost twenty feet high, hidden by neighboring trees, as well as the branches below her.

Her breath was coming hard and fast, but she forced herself to stay calm. She was crouched painfully next to the trunk in order to stay both balanced and out of view, her arm hooked into another branch for support. She was slowly, carefully adjusting her body on the branch when she heard the chief's voice again.

"I know you're nearby," he said. "I've hunted these woods since I was eight years old. Want to know your mistake?"

His words seemed to echo in the silent woods, answered only by the chattering of a chipmunk somewhere in a neighboring tree.

"You girls circled back on yourselves," he said. "Common problem up here. You think you're following the land, but it's full of these tricky hollows and turns. Only real way to stay on track is to use the sun to keep true. Too bad you all didn't have a compass."

He chuckled to himself. While he talked, Kim could hear his voice moving slowly as he searched, but she couldn't tell if he was getting closer to her hiding spot—or to Scarlett's.

She didn't know if he was telling the truth, or lying in an attempt to force them to give up and show themselves. But they had another problem now; they were separated. One of them might be able to escape if the other kept Holt occupied. Kim could yell, and force Holt to come after her, drawing him closer and closer until she'd put enough distance between him and Scarlett that the teen could make a dash for it. Surely he'd take the quarry up in the tree, the one with nowhere to run, over the one who was moving.

But she also knew that Scarlett wouldn't leave her behind.

She had to do something, though, other than simply wait to be sacrificed.

"I've suspected it was you since the start," she yelled out, a lie calculated to anger him. His calm was his greatest asset, but if she could chip away at it, he might start making mistakes.

She watched him turn, testing the wind, trying to calculate the source of her voice. She knew that Holt wouldn't be able to pinpoint which tree she was in right away, and she held on to the faint hope that Scarlett would see her opportunity and escape.

"That's a load of bull," Holt said. "You may have a fancy medical degree, but you don't know the first thing about me."

"You'd be surprised," she called. "You're a classic narcissist. Utterly transparent, if one knows what to look for."

Holt whipped around, but he miscalculated, and as he crept forward, he put distance between himself and Kim. However, now he was getting dangerously close to Scarlett's hiding place.

"You crave power," Kim shouted, willing him to turn around. His head came up and he seemed to sniff the air. "But like all bullies, you only prey on the weak. Old men. Defenseless women. If you ever confronted someone who could fight back, you'd probably retreat like a scared little girl."

"God damn it," Holt muttered, cradling his rifle. "You got it all wrong."

She'd angered him—it was working. She'd challenged his core identity, and he'd taken the bait.

"You want to know why I do what I do?" he demanded, as he advanced through the tall brush. He was growing careless, not bothering with stealth. If they were lucky, maybe she'd make other mistakes as well—something that might allow them to escape. Kim forced herself to breathe evenly as she listened, watching and waiting for any opportunity. "Twenty-five years ago, when I was just a new recruit to the force, my wife met me at the door one day with a big smile and told me we were gonna have a baby. I was so damn excited, I told her to put on her best dress and I'd take her out, even though we didn't have two nickels between us back then."

Kim spotted him approaching through the leafy branches, losing sight of him only to see glimpses of his dress shirt as he drew nearer.

"Went down to Stuart's—little place on the west side of town, it's not there anymore—bought Betty a Shirley Temple and had myself a beer. Bought a round for the house, too, because I was itching to share our fortune. Only Betty asked me not to tell anyone yet, because it was so early—and this—this—*son* of a gun took issue with me, thought I was just showing off. He wasn't local; I knew that much, and I just ignored him. My mistake. You don't give a worthless cuss like that what he wants, it just lights him up. But what he wanted was a fight."

Holt had warmed to the story, as though he'd been dying to tell it for years. "Now I've gone over what happened next about a million times. Could it have gone another way? I don't know. But that bastard pulled out a .38 when it became clear he was on the losing end of the fight. I didn't see it coming and neither did anyone else in the place. I tried to take it from him, but it went off and—and it hit Betty. She died in my arms.

"Then that drifter saw what he'd done and decided to go for broke. Put one in my chest. Came damn near close to killing me. Time I got out of the hospital, Betty'd already been buried and he was long gone."

Holt was facing away from her now, and Kim cast around carefully for something she might use against him—some way of distracting him, or taking him down—but came up short. He continued his tale as she inched her way farther out onto the branch, hoping to find something, anything.

"I took my grief and I stuffed it away. Signed up for the service and did a couple tours in Iraq. Saw things and did things I never would have done before I lost Betty and our baby. . . . Didn't care if I came back or not. Didn't care if I died there. But that wasn't God's will for me, I guess, because I found myself back in Jarvis. On the force.

"One day, about ten years after Betty died, I stopped in to get coffee at the filling station out by the middle school late in my shift. That same drifter—he didn't have the sense to steer clear of my town—he was there. I saw him stealing a Hostess pie, but I didn't say anything. I waited twenty minutes and then I drove real slow and found him about a mile down the road. Offered him a lift. Didn't recognize me, either, even after I drove him out to the old slaughterhouse. I worked there when I was just a kid; I knew how to get in by the old loading doors. Sat him down on that dusty old killing floor and told him how it was going to be. How he was going to have to come up with a good reason why I ought to set him free. How he was going to beg for his life the way I begged God to let Betty live."

Kim wondered what Scarlett was thinking, listening to this tale. What was it like to hear about the evolution of the killer who was responsible for at least one of her alters' deaths? The thought of Izzi lurking beneath the surface, trying to break free . . .

"And the crazy thing was, I never did plan to kill him. I was going to deliver him up for the justice system to deal with, just as soon as I had the satisfaction of hearing him admit it all. See, I still believed in people back then, at least a little. But when he opened his mouth and all manner of hate came spewing out—vile things, about Betty and her honor and—well, there's no sense telling any of that. Because next thing I knew he was dead. I'd taken my hand to the back of his head and smashed it down on that cold floor, over and over until there wasn't anything left but mess."

A branch snapped almost directly underneath Kim's tree, drawing her attention back to her dangerous position, and away from Holt's horrifying tale. Grief had broken him; the war had twisted what was left. Then pure chance had delivered him an opportunity to begin his killing spree, and Holt—in his fury and his madness—had mistaken that opportunity for God's will.

Another twig snapped, and Kim held her breath. She hadn't heard a single sound from Scarlett's hiding place. She prayed the girl could stay still and silent long enough to give her a fighting chance. This man she'd once seen as so kindly, as Zack's beloved mentor and friend, wouldn't hesitate to kill her or Scarlett.

The thought of Zack tugged at Kim. Zack would never know what had happened to her, would keep coming to work each day right down the hall from Holt, the man he loved like a father. He would accept the version of events that Holt gave him. He would believe that he'd been wrong about Kim, about Scarlett, about everything.

Her despair caught the spark of her bitter anger and coalesced into something else, something sharp and dangerous. Yes, she had almost no chance of surviving. But no—she wasn't going to go down without a fight.

"Who else, Holt?" she yelled, knowing he was almost directly underneath her. *Run*, she telegraphed to Scarlett with all her might. Maybe, just maybe, Scarlett's mind—already having proved itself open and receptive enough to host the alters—might be able to pick up on her message intuitively. *Run as fast and far as you can.*

"*Who else?*" he repeated in his booming voice. "Well, that would take me a while, Doc. See, once I decided to take care of my town, all kinds of troublemakers seemed to pop up. Oh, not all at once. Sometimes years would go by and I'd think I'd finally cleaned up the place. But evil has a way of coming back. It's just the nature of the human race. Some folks are made to do wrong—and some folks are made to stop 'em.

"Way I see it, it's like a garden. You do your best, amend the soil and mulch and fertilize, make sure there's water and sun to suit your plants. But you do all that and you're gonna attract the *weeds*, too. Weeds thrive on the same things as any other plant, see, just like human trash thrives on the same things as good folks. A town like ours, it's beautiful, prosperous, growing. You think it gets that way by accident? Let me tell you something . . . in order to keep a well-maintained lawn, you gotta pull out a few weeds. And that's what Albert Sullivan was. He was the worst kind of weed, preying on the innocent, on the young."

A flash of movement caught Kim's eye, and she glimpsed Holt's silver hair below her, his bulky frame moving gracefully between saplings.

But he was turning *away* from her. He'd pivoted slightly, maybe alerted by a sound from Scarlett, maybe by an animal or bird. If Kim didn't do something, he was going to walk directly into Scarlett's hiding spot. Kim realized then that she'd made a terrible miscalculation. He knew she wasn't going anywhere, that he could kill Scarlett first and come back to finish her off. She looked frantically around for something to use to draw him back. But there was nothing, not even a dead branch. She had nothing with her; Holt had even destroyed her phone, the only thing she could think to throw at him.

With no other ideas, she slipped off one of her shoes, a plain canvas sneaker with a rubber sole. She whistled sharply, and when he turned back toward her, she shouted, "Over here!"

His head tilted up, searching the trees. He knew she was nearby, and she had only seconds to act. It was a long shot—all she could hope to do was strike him with the shoe and confuse him long enough to get out of the tree and run—and pray that Scarlett was running, too.

Holt disappeared under the shady canopy of a young hemlock

for a moment, and Kim cocked her arm. When he reappeared, not five feet from the base of the tree, in a shrubby open space, she threw.

The shoe hit him on the side of the head, glancing off his ear. He cursed and put his hand to his face, but didn't falter. She'd barely slowed him, and he was coming straight for her. And now, even if she could somehow get by him, she had only one shoe.

"Scarlett, you've got to run!" she screamed. "Now!"

Holt reached her tree and ducked under the lowest branches. He peered up along the trunk, and their eyes met. He was sweating, and a lump was already forming on his scalp above his ear, but there was a calm, crafty smile on his face.

"Well, look at you," he said.

Then he aimed his rifle directly at her.

"I do like a fair fight," he said conversationally. "Well, somewhat fair, anyway. By the time someone crosses me, I figure they've already stacked their own deck. But I never take anyone down without giving them a shot. Guy who killed my wife—all he had to do was repent. Isabel, well, I let her run just like I let you run. Not really my fault she stumbled on that trap. Though I would have got her in the end.

"Now you two, if you would have gone right along the ridge, you might have made it to Ted Willoughby's cabin. Maybe he would have been home, maybe not, but at least you had a chance. It's only sporting, way I see it."

He put a hand on the low branch, testing its strength. "But unfortunately for you, you turned left. And now, I'm afraid to say, it's time to finish this up."

THIRTY-NINE

It had taken Zack less than five minutes with the bartender from the Outpost Grill in the tiny town of Seward to realize it was a dead end, but he let the man rattle on with his theories about the missing hunter for a good half hour, and left him a twenty for his club soda, to boot. The idea of getting straight back in his car exhausted him. At least the drive had been a beautiful one, up into the dense forests of northern Ukiuk County, the little crossroads so remote that there was no cell service, as quaint and unspoiled as a scene from a classic film.

The Outpost Grill was one of only two businesses in town, the other being a combination gas station/general store, tucked in among a couple dozen shacks and cabins. The bartender figured that George DeWitt might have met up with the Senator, an enormous brown bear that'd allegedly terrorized the northern part of the county for several years. The Senator had gotten its nickname because its muzzle supposedly had gone gray in a fashion that called to mind former Alaskan Republican Senator Frank Murkowski's distinguished silver hair. The bear was rumored to be nearly ten feet tall and more than nine hundred pounds, and had supposedly killed a prize hound and treed a hunter a few years back, clawing through nearly half the trunk before getting bored and wandering away.

Zack figured that every time that story was told, the bear got bigger and meaner. If he really had killed the hunter, the remains of the body would probably have turned up by now. He questioned the bartender about DeWitt's buddy, the man who'd called in the tip, but drew a blank there, too.

"Honestly," the bartender said, scratching his head, "I don't recall anyone of that description in the last month. Mostly we get the regular folks, and outsiders stand out enough to get remarked on. And greenhorns and city folk take a lot of ribbing. I feel like if your man was in here, I'd remember."

Zack thanked him for his time and got back in his cruiser, giving the place one final appreciative glance before starting the trip home. The mountain air was cool and crisp, scented with smoke and lilac; nearby was a lake whose water, he'd wager, was as clear as glass. Maybe he'd bring Kim up here camping, he thought, but he shut down that line of reasoning before he could get a mile ahead of himself.

Instead, Zack forced his attention back to the case. He checked cell service as he drove, planning to let Holt know that the trip hadn't panned out. He thought he might check in on the hunter's wife when he got back to Jarvis, see if she'd thought of anything else unusual that her husband had said or done in the days leading up to his disappearance. Maybe go see the buddy in person, see if his story held up under questioning, if they could somehow track down his location.

It wasn't until he was half an hour away from Jarvis that the bars on his phone popped back up—along with two missed messages.

Both from Kim.

Zack tapped the play button. His phone was dash-mounted and Bluetooth enabled, so her voice filled the car a moment later.

"Hi, it's me," she said, then got all flustered and added, "Uh, Kim. Kim Patterson."

He was grinning—couldn't help it—when her tone caught his attention. "Zack, I really need to talk to you as soon as possible about the Wilcox case." Her tone was urgent. Kim said that she and Scarlett were going to go find Holt, maybe at his house.

"I don't think Albert Sullivan killed Izzi. I know that sounds crazy, but I just want to be sure we aren't making a mistake. Especially now that he's dead. Anyway. We don't have much time. Zack, if you could just talk to him. . . . Call me?"

What?

Sullivan had been alive just that morning, when Zack had swung by work to pick up his case notes. The duty officer reported that when a female deputy had slid his breakfast tray into the cell, Sullivan had grabbed her hand and licked it before she could pull it back out.

The second message, however, was even more disturbing. There was a split second of what sounded a lot like screaming, then Kim's voice shouting something about Holt—and then the call was abruptly cut off.

Zack tapped the flashers on and pushed the pedal down, taking the winding road at a dangerous speed, his heart racing. He dialed Kim and got her voice mail—then dialed her twice more just to make sure.

He knew that Kim probably feared what would happen to Scarlett if the case was closed. Zack still wasn't fully convinced that Scarlett was harboring souls, no matter how vehemently Kim suggested it—and while he no longer thought Scarlett was a murderer, he was 100 percent ready to believe that Scarlett might lose it if she felt that Isabel's killer was going to go free. Maybe she'd turned on Kim, attacked her like she'd attacked Darren and Brad.

Zack called in to the station, and found that the chief had headed home to change. Although he had yet to return, the sidewalk in front of the station was packed with reporters waiting. Next, Zack dialed Holt. But there was no answer.

Holt's place was up in the woods above town. He'd built it about ten years ago, after Zack and Brielle went off to college and he didn't need the house in town with its extra bedrooms and swing set in the backyard. Nowadays, Zack and Brielle were frequent visitors, stopping by regularly for chops on the grill and beer after a long week at work. Although it had been more than a month since their last house call.

The recorded scream echoed in his ears as he reached the turnoff for Holt's place and took the ascent much faster than even his heavy cruiser was equipped to go, feeling clods of dirt smash against the undercarriage and hoping he hadn't broken an axle. Rounding the turn to the house, he saw Kim's little beater parked next to Holt's SUV. The front door of the cabin was open, interior light on, and a quick inspection confirmed that no one was inside.

He had just called into the station for backup when he heard the gunshot.

ZACK RAN.

The sound had come from straight up the ridge. Zack had walked these woods many times with Holt and knew the area well. But there was nothing in that direction for miles, other than the thinning trees higher up the mountain, the snow line that receded in summer but never disappeared. There were other houses in either direction, mostly seasonal and hunting cabins, but they were much farther away than the shot had sounded.

If Scarlett had somehow gotten a gun . . .

If she was in the grip of delusion, angry about Sullivan . . .

Suddenly, a figure came crashing through the trees toward him.

Zack reached for his holster just as Scarlett came into view. Her hair was wild and studded with leaves and she had scratches on her face and hands, but she wasn't holding a weapon.

"Oh God!" she screamed, and then ran straight into him, nearly knocking him down. "Detective Trainor, please, you have to help, he's going to kill her!"

He held her arms and tried to force her to be still. There was blood on her face, and he prayed it wasn't Kim's. "Who, Scarlett? Who's killing who?"

She desperately tried to wrench herself free of his grasp. "He's going to kill Kim!"

That got his attention. He loosened his grip fractionally, and she grabbed his arm and tried to pull him back toward the woods.

"Who?"

"Chief Plunkett's going to kill Kim! He killed Albert, and Isabel, and—and I don't know who else!"

Clearly, Scarlett was delusional. Zack shook his head as Scarlett pleaded with him to move faster, spewing more nonsense about Holt threatening Kim. "He said he had to pull the weeds."

But then, something Holt used to say echoed around Zack's head as they ran. *Someone's got to pull the weeds, son.* He said it every time they picked up a drunk driver, or took an unregistered gun off the streets or settled a domestic abuse complaint by locking up a guy who needed more than an anger management class at the county extension. Said it often enough that Zack used to tease him about it, even getting him a bottle of weed killer as a gag Christmas gift one year. Holt had chuckled and put it, red bow and all, up on a shelf in his office.

But Holt never took it further than that. Because that would be crazy. Right?

The hairs stood up along Zack's arms. "Take me to her," he yelled, releasing Scarlett, and she bolted back into the woods.

Zack followed easily. He could have gone faster, but the girl was winded. There were cuts and welts on her arms and legs, as if she hadn't watched or cared where she was going.

As if she had been running for her life.

A cold terror built inside Zack, but he couldn't bear to face it head-on. Instead, he focused on the ground in front of him, on Scarlett, on searching every possible hiding place for threats.

"There!" Scarlett gasped, as they reached a small clearing. Chief Plunkett stood at the base of a huge old evergreen, peering up into the branches. In his hand was his gun.

"Holt?" Zack called, the cold fear now spreading through every inch of his body.

Holt glanced over, and Zack watched his face pale as he took in the sight of his adoptive son.

"Your timing's not great, Zack," he said. "Don't suppose I can get you to take Scarlett back to the cabin while I finish something up?"

"What are you *doing*?" Zack demanded, just as he heard a cry from up in the tree. He craned his neck, stepping back so he could peer all the way up. The tree had to be several hundred feet tall, and it took him a moment to understand that the large nest up in the upper reaches wasn't a nest at all.

It was a person.

"Zack!" the voice screamed. It was Kim, much higher than the tree could be expected to support her weight, clinging to the narrow crown as it swayed and dipped. There was no way that the spindly trunk would hold much longer. A crack signaled that the branch she was clutching onto had given out, and he watched in horror as her feet scrambled for purchase. One of them, inexplicably, was bare.

"Hang on!" he yelled.

Scarlett started to scramble to the tree, clearly preparing to catch Kim if she fell, despite the fact that they might both be killed if she did.

Holt aimed his gun at Scarlett. "Back away," he said. She skidded to a stop in the brush. "Zack, throw me your piece."

Zack shook his head, in disbelief. "What are you doing?"

Holt mirrored him, shaking his head in agitated frustration. "Son, I'm sorry we've got to do it this way. Hell, I'm sorry you ever had to see this."

"Holt, what's going on?" But before the chief could answer, Zack called up to Kim, "Hold on, I'll get you down. You're not going to fall."

Holt raised his rifle, and although he didn't point it at Zack, the intention was implied. "It wouldn't be all that bad if she did. Save me some difficult work."

"Sir, please put down the gun."

Holt chuckled. "You took the words right out of my mouth. See, Zack, you and me . . . we're gonna need to have a long conversation. Take some time and talk this out. But first . . . you're gonna need to trust me."

"Put down the gun."

It wasn't helping that Scarlett kneeled nearby whispering quietly, "Shoot him shoot him shoot him."

When Zack refused to drop his pistol, Holt's voice grew more serious. "You're threatening a superior officer, son. I need you to follow my orders and drop that gun. Or I'll be forced to drop you. Way it's got to be."

Holt doubled down by pointing his gun at Scarlett. He spoke very slowly and unambiguously. "Zack, if you don't throw me your revolver, I will kill Scarlett here and now."

Zack was reeling. Paralyzed in place as he tried to understand what was happening. How the man who had raised him, set him on the right path, taken him in when no one else would—how *that man* could possibly be threatening to shoot him.

Then somehow, his brain turned off, and his police instincts kicked in. He let it happen—let his emotions sink down below until all that remained was the job. "Lie down," Zack ordered Scarlett, who immediately sunk down, pressing her body into the leaves. Not seeing any other choice, he lowered his service weapon, and, after a moment's hesitation, he clicked on the safety and tossed it toward Holt.

The gun landed at Holt's feet. The chief picked it up and then threw his own rifle to the ground. He clicked the safety off and pointed Zack's weapon up at Kim. Zack looked on in horror, knowing Holt was seconds from pulling the trigger. Holt was an ace shot—a little rusty these days, but he still scored above nearly everyone in the department at the range.

If he shot Kim, there was no way she'd survive. If the bullet didn't kill her, the fall would.

Zack ran at Holt. His only hope now was to knock the gun from his hand. He'd make himself an easy target, but at least it would give Kim a moment to shimmy back down and escape, if they were lucky.

"No!" Kim screamed as Holt swung his gun around at Zack. "Chief Plunkett, wait! Zack, please, *stop*!"

There was another cracking sound as one of the branches splintered from the trunk and came crashing down just as Holt fired the gun. The bullet gave Kim a haircut as she slipped two feet down the tree—a broken branch pierced her foot but kept her from falling. Holt, hearing Zack sprinting at him, swung his gun back toward the officer. Zack skidded to a stop ten feet from Holt, frozen. If Kim didn't come down lower in the tree, she'd fall anyway.

"Holt," he said carefully, "look, I'm not moving any closer. Please, just let Kim come down. We'll talk. Like you said. I know you don't want to do this."

Holt chuckled sadly. "I don't, son. You're right. But over the years I've had to do any number of things I didn't want to do. Don't see why today should be any different. I don't want to hurt you—you've got to know that."

"I do, I—"

"Chief Plunkett," Kim said, her voice calm and clear. All eyes followed it up into the tree, where she'd managed to climb down just far enough to rest on a larger branch, buying herself a little time. "Listen to me. I understand what you've done. I even sympathize with it. I think anyone would. No one can fault you for punishing your wife's killer—"

"Wasn't just my wife," Holt muttered. "My baby. *Our* baby."

"I know that. I doubt there's a jury in the world that would convict you for what you had to do. But, after that, you took it too far . . . trying to right wrongs for the whole town . . ."

"Had to," Holt said. "No choice."

"I can understand why you felt that way. I talked to Albert myself—I think I saw what you see, the evil that can rest inside someone, poisoning them until redemption simply isn't possible anymore. I respect what you do, going up against that day after day after day. I'm not sure I could do it. You have a noble purpose."

Her voice was strong, soothing and sympathetic. Zack found himself calmed merely by its tone. Scarlett, too, was listening raptly. But would it be enough? He inched a step closer.

"I even understand why you'd hurt me. I've—I've made a lot of mistakes. I've upset the balance you've worked so hard to maintain. I was only trying to help, but sometimes—most of the time—I rush into things without thinking clearly. So . . . I understand if you feel like you need me gone. I understand if you feel you need to sacrifice me. But what about Zack? He hasn't done anything wrong."

"No, Kim," Zack yelled, seeing what she was doing. She was going to offer herself in exchange for him and Scarlett. "Don't say that."

Holt pointed the gun Zack's way again, emotions warring on his face.

"He's *innocent*," Kim continued. "All he's ever done is try to be the best cop he could. And you know why, Holt—you know he's always wanted to make you proud. He only ever wanted to follow the example you set for him."

"I know that," Holt said, voice anguished. "But I didn't ever mean for him to end up like me. He's better than that."

"He *is* better. You're right."

Zack held his breath, afraid Kim's words would anger Holt enough to make him shoot her.

"You only kill people who've done wrong, Holt. *I* understand that. What has Zack ever done? Nothing but try to help people. His father. His sister. You. The people of this town. Wasn't that the whole point, anyway? Who's going to clean up Jarvis if you and he are *both* gone?"

"I—I don't—"

Holt wavered, his face a tormented mask as he tried to process Kim's words. Zack realized she'd set up an impossible problem for the chief. Holt couldn't kill Zack without sacrificing the principles that she'd worked so hard to uphold all these years.

He lowered the gun slightly, only to raise it again at Kim. "You should never have come here," he said. "It all worked fine until you got here."

"You know that's not true," Kim said. "Scarlett's innocent. All the alters who found sanctuary inside her, they only wanted justice. And not just victims like Henry. Isabel Wilcox made a lot of mistakes, sure. She hurt people. She deserved to be punished. But losing her life? You went too far. And that man inside, the hunter, George DeWitt? Was that justice? What had he done wrong? What great crime had he committed? Hunting without a license? Witnessing a murder? When does it stop?"

Holt's hand began to shake. His eyes clouded with doubt.

"You did good at first," Kim said gently. "I'm not going to deny that. But it got away from you. And it has to end."

"It got away from me," Holt echoed. He looked up at her one last time, and nodded.

Then he placed the gun into his own mouth and pulled the trigger.

FORTY

Sirens could be heard down the mountain as what seemed like every member of the police and fire departments answered the call Zack had put out when he arrived on scene.

Holt had crumpled to the ground, and now he lay glassy-eyed as though he was staring at the sky. Kim had still been up in the tree when he fired, but she made it down the rest of the way in seconds, falling to her knees from the lowest branch.

Zack was holding Scarlett, shielding her from having to see the grisly scene. But when Kim met his eyes, she saw that he was in shock as well.

She would have to take charge.

This, she could do. For two people she cared about. For two people who had already lost so much. Gently, she took Scarlett's hand and tugged her away from Zack. Scarlett moaned softly and didn't protest. Zack stood straight and tall and gazed at the man who had given him his first job, raised him like a son—who had taught him what it meant to be a man.

Kim desperately wanted to go to him. But she couldn't abandon Scarlett yet. Zack took his radio from his belt and gave directions from the house. Kim was pretty sure he was supposed to say something about Holt having shot himself . . . but he just returned the radio to his belt and continued to stare at the dead chief.

The first of the responding officers came running up the hill. "Oh sweet Mary May." Phil Taktuq gasped when he came to a screeching halt a few feet from Holt. "What on earth—"

"It's, um, complicated," Kim said, trying to keep her voice down. She beckoned the officer closer. There was so much to explain.

But Zack came out of his daze as though a switch had been turned on. "Chief Plunkett took his own life," he told the officer. "There were no other shooters. We need this whole area processed for evidence. Holt Plunkett should be treated as a suspect in the murders of Albert Sullivan, Isabel Wilcox, and George DeWitt. Probably more."

For a moment, Phil gaped at the scene—Holt lying unmoving, his blood seeping into the earth; Kim with her arms protectively encircling Scarlett; Zack standing ramrod straight and utterly alone.

Paramedics came rushing into the clearing. Two of them dropped to the ground on either side of Holt's lifeless body. As Scarlett sagged in Kim's arms, the third paramedic caught her, and gently lowered her to the ground, talking to her in a soft, low voice.

More officers arrived, and still the sirens sounded in the distance. There were gasps and shocked curses as each newcomer took in the scene.

"Zack," Kim whispered, and she lifted a hand to comfort him, to offer him some small measure of solace.

But Zack didn't appear to have heard her. He turned and walked into the woods, alone.

MANY HOURS LATER, LONG after the paramedics had taken Holt's body and a colonel from the state troopers' office had dealt with the swarm of media, Zack agreed to let Kim drive him home.

The colonel took over the conference room and spent most of the evening on the phone with county law enforcement. The Ukiuk County chief would arrive in the morning; everyone agreed it would be best to wait and let him take statements from Zack, Kim, and Scarlett.

Peter Hascall arrived looking white as a sheet, and it wasn't until he'd swept Scarlett into his arms did he exhale the breath he appeared to have been holding since he got the call to come to the station. Scarlett burst into tears, but they were the kind of tears that Kim figured had a fair amount of healing in them. Kim promised to call the next day.

The colonel offered to deliver the news of Holt's death to Brielle, but Zack said he figured maybe he ought to do that himself. On the way to his house, his eyes fluttered closed and Kim wondered if he'd fallen asleep.

Then he spoke without opening his eyes.

"Can you stay, just for a while?"

That she could do.

She stood off to the side while Zack, looking completely exhausted, gently broke the news to Brielle. He didn't tell her everything. He probably needed to wait until the inquiry had made everything official.

All he told Brielle was that Holt Plunkett, her surrogate father, had killed himself. Brielle dissolved into tears. Kim felt awkward, watching the two of them hug, until Zack looked up and held out his hand. She stepped forward and took it, and the siblings scooted over on the couch and made room for her, and then they all just held on to one another and didn't speak.

At some point, Kim woke up to find that Brielle had left and gone back to her own apartment, and Zack had gone to bed. Someone had draped a blanket over her and given the fire a final stir, so that the embers glowed a deep orange.

Kim snuggled deeper under the blanket, closed her eyes, and went back to sleep.

———

THE NEXT TIME SHE woke up, it was because someone was holding a mug of steaming coffee under her nose.

"Mmm," Kim murmured, stretching and opening her eyes, only to remember where she was and why.

She sat up in the tangle of blankets. Zack had changed into flannel sweats and a faded University of Portland T-shirt. He gave her a tired smile that didn't match his eyes, and sat down next to her.

For a while, they sipped their coffee in silence.

"I keep going over it and over it—and trying to figure out a way that could have played out where he'd still be alive," Zack finally said. "But Holt could never have lived with himself, once he realized that he'd violated his own code."

"I'm sorry. I know that what I said—it was . . ."

"If you hadn't led him to realize that, we'd all be dead right now. I'm so . . . so . . ."

Kim put her hand on his. "He was a father to you," Kim said gently. "What happened, it's never going to feel . . . right. It'll get easier, but that feeling will never go away completely."

Zack would have a great deal of grief to process—much of it complicated. At some point, Zack was going to have to reconcile his good memories with the dark side of the man who'd meant so much to him. Eventually, he might be able to cherish the part of Holt that had been idealistic and loving and brave.

For now, though, her profession offered no hard and fast rules. No right way or wrong way to help the adjustment. But she was determined to help him get through it.

"I can recommend someone good," she said gently. "If you need to talk."

His eyes dropped. "I like talking to you."

"And I, you. But you should have someone, more . . . neutral."

Slowly, Zack nodded. "Guess that's probably a good idea. For me and Brielle both. I imagine I'll be taking some time off. County chief won't give me a choice, probably."

"Time off is a good idea."

"What about you?"

Kim thought about it, letting the steam rising from her coffee warm her face. What about her? She was newly reemployed, and work would probably do her good. She ought to call her parents and let them know what happened before they saw it on the news.

"Taking things slow might be a good idea for me, too," she said.

"I've got some juice in the fridge," Zack said. "Brielle will probably be over here any minute wanting pancakes. You're welcome to stay."

Kim was tempted. She loved this house, with its wood and cedar and wool and leather, its scents of woodsmoke and baking bread and Zack's aftershave. She wanted to know every book on the bookshelves, every photo in the frames arranged on the sideboard.

But Zack and Brielle needed to be with each other right now.

"Thanks," she said, untangling herself from the blanket and setting down her mug. "But I'd better get home."

Zack walked her to the front door, and to Kim's surprise, drew her in for a hug as they said their good-byes. For a long moment, she let him hold her, feeling strangely safe despite all the horrible events of the past twenty-four hours.

Then she slipped away, hoping that Zack had absorbed some of that safety, too. Hoping that he and his sister would find some peace.

FORTY-ONE

Zack stood in the front row of the mourners on a rainy Saturday morning, as Holt Plunkett was laid to rest in the plot next to the grave of his wife and unborn child. Next to him, Brielle shivered in her black dress and high heels. As the pastor led the mourners in prayer, Zack took off his suit jacket and slipped it over his sister's shoulders.

Holt had taught him to be a gentleman, among many other things.

Last Thursday, it seemed like the entire town had turned out for Isabel Wilcox's funeral. Dozens of her relatives, from as far away as Florida, had attended, and Zack could hear her mother sobbing all the way from where he stood up on a hill overlooking the service.

Today, the crowd was much smaller. The shocking rumors about all the people Holt Plunkett had killed had started circulating immediately after Holt's death, even though the department was trying to keep the investigation secure while it began opening old cases and procuring help from county and state agencies. It could easily turn into Alaska's biggest serial murder case of the century.

Zack knew that if he turned around, he would see friends, neighbors, his old teachers and coaches. He'd spotted more than one old girlfriend and his current barber in the parking lot, as well as members of Brielle's book club and her entire recreational soft-ball team. The town was there for them, even as they faced the reality that their chief of police was not who they'd believed him to be.

Zack knew that the next day, and the day after that, and next month and next year, he would always have a home in Jarvis. Eventually, the wounds that felt devastating now would begin to heal. He would be strong for Brielle, and he would do his best to serve Jarvis even as he was excused from working on its biggest case. There would still be crimes to investigate, citizens to serve, traffic stops and barroom fights and the insidious drug trade to stem. And he didn't want to be anywhere else or do anything else for a living.

The thing he couldn't figure out, as the uniformed cemetery workers began slowly lowering the casket into the deep hole in the ground, was how was he supposed to get through the next moment, the next hour, the reception in the church basement where he'd once attended Cub Scout meetings?

How was he supposed to get through tonight, knowing that the character of his adoptive father was being forged into the town's memory as a villain, not the hero Zack had always believed Holt to be?

Something brushed against his hand, and he looked down to see a slim, pale wrist in a gray silk cuff, familiar bitten fingernails. He took Kim's hand gratefully, and as the pastor intoned the final prayer, he felt the smallest spark of warmth.

FORTY-TWO

One month later

"How'd you score this place all to yourself?" Scarlett asked, looking around Kim's new office. The packing boxes full of her books, the overflowing trash can, the chair Kim had stolen in a midnight raid on Orthopedics—all of them were gone. In their place was a small but attractive bookshelf lined with framed photographs of family and friends, a beautiful ficus tree, and her diploma, which she'd finally hung.

"Dr. Sing has a thing about our working conditions meeting ADA standards," Kim said. The new department head, who had been hired after Kyle accepted a position in Iowa City, insisted Kim be upgraded from the supply closet, in which her former workplace had been housed, to a legitimate office. "So—how've you been?"

This was their first official meeting since Dr. Graver finally gave Kim the thumbs-up to schedule a single follow-up session with Scarlett. After that, it was agreed that they would sever their doctor-patient relationship, and Scarlett would be referred to a psychiatrist who was not on the staff at Jarvis Regional. Even this compromise was highly unusual, but Graver had agreed to make a one-time exception to hospital policy in the interest of giving the patient some much-needed closure.

Kim had broken with her own long-standing act-first-apologize-later approach by asking Dr. Graver for permission to keep in touch with Scarlett outside of treatment, and they had all agreed that contact initiated by Scarlett was permissible as long as Kim reported anything of clinical concern to Scarlett's new psychotherapist. It was a little awkward, but Kim knew it was also the correct way to handle the situation. Besides, Scarlett had a supportive community to fall back on now.

"Great!" Scarlett looked, for the first time since Kim had met her, like an ordinary teen. Peter Hascall had taken his daughters to Anchorage for a long weekend after the standoff with Holt. They'd gone to museums and shows and done some shopping, and Scarlett had gotten a haircut and highlights and a tiny tattoo of a willow ptarmigan—the Alaska state bird—on her shoulder. Today she was dressed in leggings and fashionable boots. Her eyes sparkled as she told Kim all about her plans to enroll at the community college in the fall, and possibly look into transferring to a four-year university the following year. "But I'll be here for at least a year," she added quickly. "So I can, you know, be there for Heather."

Kim was delighted to hear her enthusiasm for the future. Peter Hascall had called her to report that Scarlett was reconnecting with friends her own age, and there had been visits from a trio of girls who never stopped talking and ate everything in the fridge like a swarm of locusts, as well as a young man who'd been Scarlett's lab partner during her junior year.

"I guess I'm done testifying," Scarlett said, turning serious. "Detective Skorczewski says I'm no longer a person of interest in anything."

Kim smiled. "That sounds like good news."

"Yeah, but know what's even better? I haven't had a blackout since that day. I ask Heather all the time. She says I've been totally normal."

Kim studied her carefully. "So you think the alters are gone?"

"Not completely, no. I mean I can still *feel* some of them, deep inside me, but it's like they're asleep or something—you know what I mean?"

Kim nodded, though she could never really understand how it must feel to be Scarlett, harboring the souls of the dead. She had been planning to ask Scarlett if she wanted to undergo hypnosis one final time, to do an inventory of any remaining alters and make sure that Isabel had moved on, now that justice was being done. After all, Julian, the most aggressive of her original alters, was presumably still in there—buried underneath the control that Scarlett had learned, true, but not gone.

But Scarlett seemed so relieved and happy that Kim changed her mind. There was a lot to be said for serenity, and Kim didn't want to do anything to ruin this new happiness. There was a part of Kim, though, that was starting to question her own past. For the first time ever, she had decided that she might undergo hypnosis—perhaps to unlock some of her own repressed memories—perhaps to learn more about Joselyn, and maybe even the identity of her birth parents' killers.

But that was for another day.

"So," she said. "Tell me about this guy who's been hanging around your house."

FORTY-FIVE MINUTES LATER, KIM walked Scarlett to the elevator. As they waited for it to arrive, Scarlett gave Kim an impulsive hug. "Thanks," she whispered. "For everything."

As she pulled away, the doors of the elevator opened and Zack stepped out. "Just the two women I wanted to see," he said. "Scarlett, if you can give me a few minutes, I need to get your signature on a few things. The new chief's wrapping up his report and I said I'd stop by and take care of it."

His eyes met Kim's, and she saw right through the ruse. He didn't even try to hide it: he'd volunteered to take care of Scarlett's signature on the report as an excuse to come see her.

"Why don't you two use my office," she said.

She hadn't seen Zack since the funeral, unless seeing his face on the news and in the papers nearly every day counted; the media had kept up its frenzied interest in what they were calling Jarvis's "decades-long murder spree." But they'd spoken on the phone a few times. Things were hard, Zack had confessed. He wasn't getting a lot of sleep. He'd lost more than just Holt—he'd lost his entire connection to his childhood, all the ideals that Holt had shaped with such care.

"Thanks for listening, and for putting up with me," he'd said during their most recent marathon phone conversation. "I know I'm not much fun right now. But . . . that headshrinker you sent me to says I'm processing everything all right, so. Uh, don't give up on me."

"Never," Kim had reassured him.

While she couldn't see Zack, she could feel him smiling on the other end of the line when he added, "I'm surprised you recommended such a cute therapist for me. Dr. Behrenfeld is really something."

"Um . . . Dr. *Randy* Behrenfeld is a man. So unless he's helped you find some new hidden side of you, I'll assume you're just saying that to make me jealous. Unsuccessfully, I might add."

"Randy could be a woman's name, too."

"Mmmm." Kim didn't mention that she had purposely given him the name of a seventy-four-year-old male psychiatrist.

Now, she waited out in the hall while Zack got the requested signatures. When Scarlett came out, she practically bounded down the hall, on her way to meet her friends at the frozen yogurt shop.

Zack followed a second later, the file tucked under his sleeve. "So . . . you're doing well?" he asked formally.

Kim grinned. "Better than ever, actually. I've kept a houseplant alive for almost a month, which is a record for me. They've got Cool Ranch Doritos in the vending machine now. And I beat my neighbor fair and square at gin rummy the other night. Of course, she fell asleep at the table during our game . . . twice."

"Nice," Zack chuckled. Then he started to say something, and stopped himself.

After an awkward pause, Kim spoke. "How about you? Everything good?"

"Yeah. Really good. For the most part. Brielle seems to like Dr. Behrenfeld, too."

Kim nodded; Brielle had actually called to say the same thing the week before.

"And, uh, the group I've been going to has been . . . good."

"I'm glad. Really."

Zack cleared his throat. "So listen, I was wondering . . . if you have time, maybe we could get together one of these days. For dinner or something."

Kim smiled at him. "I'd like that."

"Yeah?" He looked adorably uncertain for someone usually so confident.

"Yes."

Zack gave her one of his megawatt grins. "Okay, then, I'll call you," he said, and turned to go. When he reached the elevator he turned back before he stepped through the open doors.

Kim returned to her office with a smile on her face. Scarlett was doing well, and Zack had promised to call. The cafeteria was serving pasta alfredo for dinner, one of their least terrible offerings, and she had an interesting case to pursue, a woman who claimed to hear messages from the president whenever she brushed her teeth.

For the first time in her life, Kim's future felt wonderfully ordinary. Not in the way she might once have dreamed about long ago, but . . . *perfect* for her.

Dr. Sing emerged from the secure doors at the end of the hall, consulting his watch. "Just about ready for group?" he asked. "Everyone's on their way to the room."

For the next hour, Kim led a group doing trauma work, using mindfulness practices to refocus their experiences of their past triggers. Two women and one man in the group were under special observation for self-harm risk. All of them would see her privately as well, but there were often things that came out in a controlled group setting that proved beneficial.

"Ready," she said with a smile. "I just need to grab my notes."

Dr. Sing gave Kim a thumbs-up and headed to his office.

Kim stood in the empty hall for a moment, inhaling the familiar chemical scent of the place, and taking in the bland institutional artwork. From somewhere nearby, the night janitor's polka music played on his radio.

Just for today, Kim was exactly where she needed to be.

ACKNOWLEDGMENTS

My sincere gratitude to the incredible team at Alloy Entertainment for their continuing love and support of *Incarnate*. Lanie Davis, you were the best editor that a first-time writer could hope for—full of encouragement and imaginative ideas—thank you for helping to bring this "MS" to life (and thank you for not making fun of me when you realized that I that no idea that "MS" stood for "manuscript"). I am also vastly appreciative of Annie Stone for her enthusiasm and insight.

I had originally envisioned *Incarnate* as a television series, and had many champions while developing it. I owe a huge debt of gratitude to Alloy's artistic architect, Les Morgenstein, and to the first person I pitched my story to, Cheryl Dolins, who was even more passionate about it than I was. A heartfelt thanks to Gina Girolamo, Amanda Bowman, and Maggie Cahill, all of whom were instrumental in *Incarnate*'s development. My journey on the television side also included many words of creative wisdom from the incredible teams at the WB and the CW, including Clancy Collins, Jennifer Robinson, Jennifer Vasquez, Michael Zeeck, Thom Sherman, Joanna Klein, Michael Roberts, Gaye Hirsch, and Mark Pedowitz. I would also like to thank some of the talented television writers who have been helping me ready *Incarnate* for the screen: David Wilcox,

Jeff Vlaming, Bianca Sams, Austin Badgett, and the inspirational Tripp Reed.

I can't thank Emily Bestler enough for this opportunity. Also, I owe a debt of gratitude to Lara Jones at Emily Bestler Books for all her support.

Personally, thank you to my mother, Pat, for encouraging me to follow my dreams, and for always loving me, even when I fell short while reaching for them. Thank you to John and Nora, for allowing me to "borrow" Kim's name . . . she was an incredible soul and will always be missed. To my boys, Asher and Xander, you two are the reason I love my life. And to Leila: when your father called "no backsies" at our wedding, he had no idea how raw a deal he got— "you own my heart and mind, I truly adore you."

Finally, a word of love to my father, who was one of the first people to read this book, but unfortunately will not see its publication. Thank you for showing me how to be a good man. I love you, Dad.

ABOUT THE AUTHOR

Josh Stolberg, who lives in Los Angeles with his wife and two kids, is the screenwriter of such films as *Sorority Row*, *Saw: Legacy*, *Good Luck Chuck*, and *Piranha 3D*. He's the director of such indie movies as *Conception*, *Kids in America*, and *Crawlspace*. In his spare time, Josh enjoys photography, much of which can be seen at his website, JoshStolberg.com. He can regularly be found on Twitter and Instagram at @JoshStolberg.